Sprenger and Soekka worried about few things growing up in their village of ancient fighters; train hard and they could be the best, be confident but not arrogant with their abilities, and fight for their home, even if it costs their lives. But as the boys rise to the top of their class, their lives become muddled with secrets of their families long dead.

Stories begin to become histories and the boys learn of monstrous animals that once resided in their forest and the fighters that tamed them. One secret after another leads the boys to the greatest discoveries of their lives, and the greatest deceptions of their village. With the ghosts of their parents haunting their every thought and the guidance of the most feared fighter in their village, Soekka and Sprenger must decide who to trust and who to betray. Quickly, the boys learn that secrets are sometimes kept for a very good reason...

This book contains references to violence and gore that may not be appropriate for younger readers.

Contents

Prologue 6

Chapter 1 15

Chapter 2 26

Chapter 3 34

Chapter 4 44

Chapter 5 56

Chapter 6 60

Chapter 7 69

Chapter 8 77

Chapter 9 93

Chapter 10 110

Chapter 11 120

Chapter 12 134

Chapter 13 142

Chapter 14 149

Chapter 15 161

Chapter 16 168

Chapter 17 178

Chapter 18 189

Chapter 19 196

Chapter 20 204

Chapter 21 216

Chapter 22 229

Chapter 23 238
Chapter 24 261
Chapter 25 269
Chapter 26 283
Chapter 27 296
Chapter 28 300
Chapter 29 309
Chapter 30 316
Chapter 31 329
Chapter 32 337
Chapter 33 345
Chapter 34 355
Chapter 35 367
Chapter 36 380
Chapter 37 386
Chapter 38 402
Chapter 39 419
Chapter 40 434
Chapter 41 441
Chapter 42 449
Chapter 43 463
Chapter 44 472
Chapter 45 480
Chapter 46 488

Chapter 47 498
Chapter 48 510
Chapter 49 523

Prologue

Karla sighed as she turned away from the root-framed mirror in the main room of her house. The last few days had been some of the worst of her life, and now she was beginning to see it in her reflection. Her black hair had grey streaks forming through it, and the wrinkles on her face were becoming more pronounced. Grieving had certainly taken its toll on her in every way it could.

She buttoned up her tan vest and secured a blade in her sleeve; she rarely brought her chained blades around the village with her if she could help it. She slowly turned around when she felt a soft tugging on her pant leg. Soekka looked up at her with his large, beautiful brown eyes, one hand clinging to a small blanket and the other to her pant leg. *He looks so much like his father,* she realized with both admiration and sadness.

She smiled at him, then knelt to the ground to be at his level. "Hello, my dear," she said softly, trying to keep the grief out of her voice as much as possible. "Are you ready to go to the market with me?"

He just stared at her with his brown eyes and then held his arms out to her. She smiled even more, then picked him up and held him on her hip. This was a scenario that Karla never thought she nor anyone else would see her in; holding a child on her hip. It was not the sort of retirement that was expected for a general of the Great War.

Soekka just let his tiny arms hang limply and laid his head on Karla's shoulder. He was a wonderful child; he never cried nor screamed, but just wanted to be close to Karla whenever possible. Karla was very hesitant at first to even accept her nephew's son, but it didn't take long for her to fall absolutely in love with him. She had seen him several times before, when visiting her nephew and his wife, but she never paid much attention to him then. Now, two years of his life had passed, and Karla was the only other member of his family still alive, and he was all that was left of hers.

"Come," she whispered in his ear, "let's go find some nice apples for breakfast."

She walked over to the table and snatched up her purse of coins, but as she put it in one of her vest pockets, someone started to knock softly on the door.

Who in the world would be bothering me at home? Karla had thought that everyone would leave her to grieve for a few more days before interrupting her peace, though she did worry that she would be questioned in the current investigations. She trusted Jacob to defend her until a certain point, but she knew that, eventually, scythe would be knocking on her door with inquiries.

She headed up the hallway and past the kitchen to her front door, and began to open it, but stopped when she saw who it was.

"Good morning, Lady Karla," Sasha said with a kind smile. "I hope I'm not interrupting anything." Karla remained silent, not sure she trusted herself to speak or to open the door completely. She just stared in disbelief at Sasha's presence. She was a beautiful woman with wonderful features, but her thick brown hair stole most of the attention. It practically stood on end at its roots, but the weight of its length pulled it down somewhat. It appeared to have an almost unnatural volume and body to it, but her family has always had it, and they all wear it equally well. She held it back with a thick leather headband that had the symbol of Durado branded onto its center. Soekka rolled his head on Karla's shoulder to see who was talking. Sasha gave him a kind smile as well. "Hello,

Soekka." Karla turned her shoulder away so that she was between the two of them. Sasha gave an understanding nod.

Karla readied the blade in her sleeve behind the door, just in case she would need it. "What do you want?" Karla finally asked.

Sasha put her hands behind her back. "I was hoping I could speak with you."

"I think it may still be too early for that," Karla said sternly.

Sasha nodded. "I do understand, and I grant you my apologies, but I'm afraid that I may not have much longer to wait."

Karla was about to say something, but then she noticed something move behind Sasha. A small head peered around Sasha's leg. Karla hadn't noticed him standing there before; she hadn't taken her eyes off Sasha's since her arrival.

Sasha gently urged the small boy forward. He was certainly her son. He already had a head of short, spiky brown hair that matched his family's. The small boy was sucking on his fingers, curiously staring up at Karla.

"Say hello, Sprenger," Sasha insisted, but the boy just started giggling instead.

Sprenger, Karla thought as she watched him, *what a strange name.*

"I know that you are angry," Sasha said softly. Karla looked up from the small giggling child and back into Sasha's eyes. "I know that you might even hate me, but I ask that you indulge me this conversation."

Karla just stood there silently for a time. She was mad, but she certainly didn't hate Sasha. In fact, she had no personal qualms with her at all. Karla knew that she did what she had to do as a scythe, and Karla also knew that it was her nephew whom her anger should be directed. Still, this woman was partially responsible for her family's death, and that pain was fighting with the logic of the situation.

Finally, Karla stepped aside and silently ushered Sasha in. All of them headed to the kitchen where Karla placed Soekka on the floor by the table and offered a chair to Sasha. She thanked her with a smile and then led Sprenger to where Soekka was standing; the boy still had his fingers in his mouth and giggled again when Soekka looked at him.

The two boys just stared at each other curiously, until Soekka went over and grabbed his little wooden ball from the corner of the kitchen and then came back and handed it to Sprenger. Sprenger giggled again and then sat down on the floor and waited for Soekka to do the same. When he did, Sprenger rolled him the ball, which caused Soekka to giggle as well.

Karla watched them with a warm smile as the two rolled the ball back and forth to each other. She had not heard Soekka giggle in the few days that she'd had him, and the sound almost made her want to cry with joy.

Remembering her place, Karla wiped the emotions from her face and turned her attention to Sasha, who was waiting patiently in the seat across from her. "So what is this about?" Karla asked.

"Before I tell you what I came here for," Sasha said, "I must beg your forgiveness and tell you how truly sorry I am for your loss."

Karla could see the genuine compassion in her eyes, and Karla knew that no matter how much she tried, she would not be able to hate this woman. Karla looked back at Soekka as she spoke. "My nephew shocked us all when he betrayed our village. Demaedura saw the darkness in him and fed it until it grew out of control." She sighed. "You do not need my forgiveness, child, you did nothing wrong." She turned back to Sasha. "I would not be a dura-scythe if I was mad at you for protecting our village. If anything, I should be apologizing to you." That seemed to confuse Sasha. "I knew my nephew's lust for power, ever since he was young," Karla clarified. "I should have done something about it myself long ago."

Sasha looked down at her hands in her lap. "Our families have always been rivals, but I still considered Sortan my friend, and same with Sullia. I foolishly thought that our families' blood-quarrel would end with Sortan and I, but I was wrong. He had refused to let his hate go in the end. None of us expected them to do what they did, and now I must grieve for my friends in private, knowing that they will be buried without the honor that they deserve."

Karla felt the same. She was to watch the burial in the forest with Soekka tomorrow, but there would be no honor given, no headstone made, and no friends invited. It was the worst death a scythe could have; being buried with not even the gratitude of their village.

"If you would like," Karla said almost hesitantly, "you may join me for their burial tomorrow."

Sasha seemed to be at a loss of words for a moment, but then gave Karla a thankful smile. "I would very much like that. Thank you." The burial of an honorless scythe was not celebrated. It was a shallow grave beneath an unmarked tree. The family was brought along to say their goodbyes out of respect but others were seldom told of it. It was meant to show that they are being forgotten from the village and stripped from people's memories.

Karla nodded and straightened her posture again. "Now, back to the original reason for your visit."

"Yes," Sasha said, looking over at Sprenger and Soekka, who were still happily playing on the floor. "I'm sorry to say that the damage from Demaedura's coup may not yet be finished in our village."

"What do you mean?"

"Because of the damage that Sortan and his wife caused, the Council of Elders has begun to worry about Feral Beasts and their Nymphigori breaking the fragile peace treaty between the Great Villages. They worry what would happen if another of us went rogue." Karla had worried about that. "Now, to make things worse, I've even heard that Juriah destroyed a small village in his pursuit of Demaedura."

"What?" Karla whispered.

"It was a village of no more than thirty people, but apparently Demaedura has hidden there before. In his search for him, Juriah practically leveled the place. Now, the Greddo village is threatening us since the village was near their border."

"Then it should be Juriah that answers to them," Karla said sternly.

Sasha shook her head. "The council sees it as proof that Nymphigori are the cause of warfare." Her voice suddenly turned somber. "They are asking for the destruction of all Feral Beasts and their Nymphigori." Karla's mouth dropped slightly. "They are saying that any village that does not comply will be marked as the enemy of the newly peaceful nations."

"But," Karla began, not entirely sure what to say to that, "that's madness. The majority of you have done nothing wrong." Karla stopped. She was beginning to feel great pain for Sasha as she realized that this woman just told her that she was about to die. "I'm sure Jacob will not allow this to happen," Karla tried assuring her.

Sasha forced a smile through her fear. “He will have no choice. It will either be my and Kirra’s deaths or the return of war to this village.” She shook her head. “I will gladly die before I allow this village to return to war.”

“Oh child,” Karla whispered. “I’m so sorry. This is my family’s fault.”

“No,” Sasha protested softly, yet sternly. She reached out and placed her hand on Karla’s. “This was Demaedura’s fault and the fault of those of us that were close enough to him to see his malice. Your family is not to blame.”

Karla smiled weakly at her, and then realized something. “What of Juriah? He will be forced to die as well?”

Sasha pulled her hand back and placed it in her lap once again. “I’m sure they realize that Juriah will fight them until his last breath, even if it means war. Jacob and I are working to convince them to take Juriah's Feral Beast and leave it at that.”

“But do you think he will agree to even that?” Karla asked skeptically.

Sasha half-chuckled. “No.” She shook her head. “No, Juriah would never allow someone to hurt Konn, especially the Council of Elders that he hates so much.”

“So then we are doomed,” Karla realized.

“Not necessarily,” Sasha said confidently. Karla should have realized that she had a plan. “There are three fully grown Pantrores in our village. I will arrange it so that Konn and Juriah are both left alive. The council does not know our numbers, and I will tell them that the two Pantrores are the only two, that they are mine and Juriah's Feral Beasts. They will not know any different.”

"That seems risky," Karla admitted, "but crafty. I'm sorry that such a fate will become of such a gifted scythe as yourself."

"I will die as a gifted scythe should," Sasha said confidently, "protecting my village."

Karla admired her bravery. "So, I must ask," she said. "Why are you telling me all this? I imagine that this should be kept as much a secret as possible."

Sasha looked down at her hands in her lap. "Because I must call upon you for a favor that you do not owe me in the least. In fact, you should not do it if there is any reason in it all." She looked back over at Sprenger and Soekka, who still continued to entertain themselves with the lone wooden ball. "Do you know why our families hated each other, Lady Karla?"

The question caught Karla off guard. Their families had been rivals for generations, but Karla never paid it much attention, and Sasha seemed the same. Sortan on the other hand, was just like his father –Karla's brother-; Every move that Jacob made was the wrong one, and every decision could have been made better if it was one of their family that was Scythrith. It was a pointless blood feud that Karla had to admit was mainly fueled by her father's side.

"It was something about my grandfather and your great grandfather competing to become Scythrith long ago," Karla answered. "My father always told the story but I never paid it much attention."

"Which is why I'm asking this favor of *you*," Sasha said. "You are not a hateful person. You know the pointlessness of quarrelling families." She shook her head. "Our village is becoming divided, Karla. The coup only made things worse. Scythe don't trust one another anymore, and I fear that if war does start again, Durado will not be strong enough to survive. Our families have been fighting with one another for generations and me battling with Sortan and his wife only made people more divided."

"You can't blame yourself for our families' feud," Karla protested.

Sasha straightened sternly. "I don't blame myself for it starting, but I do blame myself for allowing it to continue. My time in this village is running short, but I will not leave my son in the hate that his ancestors created. I want him to show this village that love and comradery are what makes a scythe-village strong." She looked back at Sprenger and Soekka. "Look at them," she said with a smile. "Look how little they know about their families' problems. I don't want my son to grow up with hate in his heart, and I don't want Soekka too either."

"Nor do I," Karla agreed.

"Then I ask you this," Sasha whispered, still watching Sprenger. "Will you raise him for me?" Karla almost flinched with surprise, and just looked at Sasha wide-eyed and silent. Sasha turned back to look at her. "Will you raise the child of your family's rival? Will you show this village that hate can be overcome, and that strength can be found in love?"

Karla remained silent, not entirely sure what to do. "Sasha," Karla sputtered.

"I don't want Sprenger knowing anything about his family," Sasha continued. "I want him to learn from you how to be a strong scythe, while you do the same with Soekka. Together, those two will prove that blood-ties mean nothing." Her eyes were dead serious.

Karla was in shock. She didn't know what to say. She looked from Sasha to Sprenger then back. *What do I do?*

Chapter 1

Welcome to Durado

Since a time before any alive could remember, the Greater Land was divided into five kingdoms: the sea-viewing cliffs of the Northern Kingdom, the treacherous rocky mountains of the Western Kingdom, the ocean of tall grass in the Eastern Kingdom, the towering ancient trees of the Southern Kingdom, and murky swamps of the Central Kingdom.

Hidden amongst these various elements, were people that did not answer to the kings and queens of the ruling kingdoms. Embedded within the corners of the map, with strictly-guarded borders of their own, were villages; but not just any villages that could be found speckled throughout the kingdoms. These were scythe-villages.

Originally built to protect the boarders of kings from mythical dangers that were rumored to lurk in the wilds, scythe-villages were found in the most remote and secluded places of the Greater Land. Though rarely seen by outsiders, scythe-villages were spectacles of extraordinary proportions with their towering white walls and homes built directly into the elements of nature. It was not just the rich beauty or these villages' ability to merge with their surroundings that made them marvelous, however; it was the villagers themselves that made scythe-villages extraordinary.

Like all villages, scythe-villages had bakers and butchers and tailors and keeps, but the one thing that made them unique, that set them apart from any other kind of village, were the scythe. Trained from their adolescence in intricate fighting techniques, stealth, and honor-bound loyalty to their villages, scythe were the apex of fighters in all the world. They were the result of the finest warriors, finest teachings, and finest skills of ancient times. Though few outside of their villages ever saw scythe, their skills as silent killers were known to all. Like the blades they kept concealed in their sleeves, scythe preferred to remain hidden from the world and only revealed themselves when necessary.

Where there were once five, there were now four Great Villages that each held sway in the four-winds. There were many smaller scythe-villages spread across the land as well, but they lacked the size and majesty of the Great Villages. More importantly, they lacked a Scythrith to lead them.

Still, no matter the size, scythe villages were renowned for the secrecy of their existence, walls that were constantly guarded with deadly force, and the loyalty of their people that were descendants of the original warriors that founded them. Few dared to visit a scythe-village without just cause, and few left a scythe-village without strong reason. Only traders ever visited the villages from outside, eager to sell goods at high prices to the rich and prospering that could rarely be found elsewhere in the world. Other visitors were often driven by the need to recruit scythe to their cause. Those wishing to hire scythe would seek the borders of a village's territory and wait for lurking scythe to bring them to the village. Hired for protection, bounties, and even the occasional war effort, scythe-villages had wealth to spare.

To the rest of the world, scythe seemed like cold-blooded killers, showing little or no emotion in anything they did. It was no secret, however, that scythe were trained to keep their emotions hidden, lest they give away a weakness that could be advantageous to an opponent in combat. This was especially important when scythe fought one another. All scythe were trained well enough to know how to use someone's emotions to their advantage, but emotions were a difficult thing to contain, especially in the heat of a fight. A scythe's ability to contain them under any circumstance was a strong indication of their skills, and quite often, their rank.

In the southern reaches of the Greater Land, an ancient green forest dominated the landscape. Warm air from the deserts in the east met the moisture from clouds trapped by the mountains in the west and south, which created the perfect conditions for trees to engulf the landscape. The warm, damp climate allowed its plants to grow without restraint. The trees bore deep green leaves spanning wider than dining platters, stemming from branches that loomed higher above the ground than many birds would fly. The heavy barked arms of these giants could be as wide as a road, and the trunks wider than a house. Their thick roots twisted in and out of the soil, entangled around one another, making the forest floor a mossy labyrinth. Hardy thorn bushes with intimidating spikes adorning their thin branches filled many of the sparse patches of open soil. Anywhere light was able to break through the uncountable layers of leaves, lush grasses and vines burst out of the ground to claim the sun's energy.

To adorn the endless branches, were a variety of birds, squirrels, snakes, and insects. Agile deer constantly roamed over the roots as though they were simply bridges made to take them from one feeding area to the next. Beneath them, large forest boars burrowed and rooted for anything to eat. They grunted and snorted as they used their tough snouts and thick tusks to examine the soft ground and churn the soil.

Long ago, it was said this forest also once held beasts of such intimidating size that they were outgrown by only the ancient trees themselves. They slowly roamed their natural empires like gods surveying their creations. However, as time went on, and the influence of man came to the world, these beasts were gradually lost from existence and even from story. Now, only a few clung to the old devotions of spirits and the life they granted to the inhabitants of their forest. Many believed that these spirits still existed somewhere in forest, hiding in secret for a time that they could roam freely once more.

The scythe-village hidden deep within the massive trees of the Ancient Forest was one of the four Great Villages: Durado. Like all of the Great Villages of scythe, Durado was surrounded by a tall, smooth, white wall that had only one gate at its front. A small road in the trees lead up to the gate, but only after miles of treacherous navigation through the forest. A few secret paths existed through the forest's intricate maze of roots, which were only used by traders and rarely found by those that had not used them before. The paths themselves were hardly a concern to the scythe of Durado, however. Using their arboreal home to their advantage, scythe were more often found navigating high above the forest floor in the vast canopy of the ancient trees.

Behind the tall wall, the streets of Durado bustled with strong and happy people that had little care of the world beyond their borders. There was no rest to the happy gossip and fraternizing around the streets as people went about their days, knowing with confidence that they were protected by hundreds of the finest fighters in the world. The villagers simply bustled with life.

Much like the residents, the buildings and structures within Durado also brimmed with life. Their homes were the result of their ancestors masterfully merging with their forest home. Ancient roots that were larger than hills rolled and entwined amongst each other, creating row upon row of grass and bark-covered tentacles. Within these giant roots, however, homes had been carved out. Hollow branches spewed smoke from the fireplaces within, men and women walked along pathways carved into the woody sidings, and families lived and loved beneath the thick bark and wooden walls of their roothomes. Some roots were large enough to hold several homes and shops each, while others were smaller and more private. No matter the size, each forest home would blossom and grow leaves with the seasons, seeming to thrive with their residence dwelling within them.

At the very center of the village was the most prominent of Durado's structures. This looming building was no mere root, but the source of all the surrounding roothomes of the village. Towering the mossy homes around it, stood the remnant trunk of a massive tree. Though all that remained of this tree was the skeleton of its monstrous trunk, the specimen to whom it once belonged would have dwarfed even the giants that surrounded the village. From this giant trunk, the roots that made Durado's roothomes were born. Adorned with windows, balconies and woody chimneys, the trunk now was hollow and held Durado's grandest structure, the Rithhold. As the name suggested, this is where the Scythrith of Durado resided. Much like the trunk that made the Rithhold was the heart of the roothomes, the Scythrith was the heart of the people. The greatest scythe of the village, the Scythrith was chosen by the people to protect the people.

The combative culture of scythe was not born out of desire of war, but out of desire for justice. The scythe of this village were all sworn to use their deadly training to protect the life of not only the villagers, but of the village itself. The trees provided them with life and home, and the scythe repaid this life by swearing theirs in service of its protection. To that end, Durado trained as many of its residents as it could to take up blades and call themselves scythe.

In the back of the pristine village, was a large flat area set aside specifically for the training of these scythe. Here, experienced scythe could practice with one another and keep their skills honed, while young ones practiced in organized classes to someday join the ranks of elite fighters. All children of the village went through basic training from the time they were old enough to run, and eventually graduated near their thirteenth year to either continue as scythe, or to take up another profession. It was the end of the year, and all the age groups were eagerly finishing their fighting routines to show that they were ready to move up to the next class or to finally graduate.

Master Cerri stood in front of the oldest of the classes and gazed upon them with pride. He had never had such a talented group of students in all his years of teaching. He stood straight-backed with his hands clasped behind him. His grey hair was slicked back, and his thin mustache was neatly combed around the corners of his mouth. It took all his effort to keep a straight face while watching his class perform their final graduation routine. Most everyone in the class had it perfected. There would be very few who did not go on to join a squad, and luckily, the one's that would not likely join a squad were standing towards the back, where the onlookers would not see them.

All around them, the younger classes were busy learning the basics to what these fifteen students had already mastered under the careful watch of their teachers. Most of the other classes left much to be desired, but so did all at young ages. Fortunately for them, Durado had the finest teachers in the world to drive them towards perfection. Master Cerri would be sad to see his class graduate, but also very excited. Today they would prove themselves to Lord Scythrith and would become pentin, scythe-in-training. Master Cerri only hoped he would live long enough to see what great masters this class would produce. *Especially those two,* he thought looking at the two boys at the front of the class.

Sprenger and Soekka were without a doubt the best students Master Cerri had ever had as a Teaching-master. He even wondered if it was because of them that the entire class excelled. *It only takes a few to set the standard,* he reminded himself. Master Cerri loved watching the boys compete with one another. After all, nothing sparked motivation like competition.

Soekka was usually the first to perfect something; his talent came so naturally, but Sprenger never lagged behind for long. Sprenger's skill came from pure willpower and never allowing himself to stop until he had proved he was Soekka's equal. He demonstrated endurance that Soekka could rarely match.

The two boys had done amazing things in their efforts to keep pace with the other, and in so doing, pulled their classmates along to try and keep up. Master Cerri had seen it before in previous generations, but never like this. Usually rivalries were fueled by hate or some other petty emotion, but Sprenger and Soekka were different. They were best friends, siblings of the same home, never apart, never one without the other, never a competition that didn't end in a smile.

Master Cerri watched them as they entered the final motions of their routine. They had demonstrated skill after skill the whole day, working to prove to their Scythrith that they were ready to graduate.

Sprenger, with his short spiky hair, was clearly growing bored with the routine he had done dozens of times, and Soekka with his ear-length black hair was showing nothing but focus at the task at hand. Their form was flawless as they punched, kicked, and balanced in various ways.

The class, in perfect unison, slapped their palms to the ground and bowed their heads in total silence, signaling the end of the routine. *Perfect,* Cerri thought contently to himself.

Master Cerri looked over his shoulder to the old man with the white pointed beard at the end of his chin, wearing a loose black cloak with intricate white designs along its hems. "Well, Lord Jacob?" Cerri asked confidently. "Did I not tell you?"

Scythrith Jacob walked up and stood next to the teaching-master, a proud smile on his face. "You were right my old friend, they are an amazing lot. You have done well, as usual."

Master Cerri could see that Jacob was staring at Sprenger and Soekka more so than the others. He knew he would. "They're everything we had hoped they would be," Cerri said softly. Jacob nodded slightly.

Having waited the appropriate amount of time, the class gradually started rising to their feet. As Soekka began to rise, Sprenger gave him a playful push, knocking him off balance. Sprenger chuckled to himself until Soekka attempted to push him back and the two became locked in a playful tussle.

"Sprenger! Soekka! Knock it off!" Cerri shouted aggressively. The two boys immediately separated and stood straight-backed like the rest of the class. Cerri gave a sigh. They may be his best students, but they were also his biggest troublemakers. Cerri would not miss the headaches those boys caused.

Jacob chuckled softly. "Boys will be boys."

Cerri began rubbing his temples with his forefingers. "Indeed," he grumbled. He returned his attention to his class and cleared his throat. "I expect to see great things from all of you as you move on to be taught by the other masters of our village. It has been my pleasure and honor to be your teacher for the last few years." Cerri leaned forward slightly into a shallow bow. The class responded in kind with bows of their own. Cerri straightened again. "Good luck to you all. You're dismissed for the last time as my students." Proud parents began to clap from different places all around the training grounds, eager to hear Cerri approve of their children. The group of young students immediately became a buzz of excited conversation among themselves, congratulating one another and giving audible sighs of relief that it was over. Sprenger and Soekka, unconcerned with passing, resumed their tussle.

Cerri and Jacob stood proudly watching the class for a short while before Cerri said in a low voice, "Do you think Kanto is ready for those two?"

Jacob gave an unsure grunt. "I think he's been waiting for this day for quite long enough. He has had plenty of time to prepare."

"If you don't mind my asking," Cerri said, "who will be the third member of their squad?"

"I like your suggestion about Tenni. She has a lot of strength and potential, not to mention she won't allow herself to be discouraged by the boys."

Cerri smirked to himself. *I doubt Sprenger and Soekka will be happy about that.* His smirk got larger the more he thought about it.

Cerri noticed Sprenger look over from the conversation he was having with Soekka and gave a big grin as he locked eyes with Jacob. He and Soekka ran up to them excitedly. "Hey, Old Man!" Sprenger shouted excitedly. "What did you think?" He skidded to a stop right in front of Scythrith Jacob with Soekka close behind. "Pretty impressive, huh?"

Cerri gave Sprenger a sharp smack on the top of his head, which Soekka snorted a laugh at. "What have I told you about calling Lord Scythrith that?" Cerri said sharply. Sprenger ducked away as if he was going to get hit again, rubbing the top of his spikey-haired head with both hands. "And don't get overconfident," Ceri warned sternly. "You still have a long way to go before you do anything that I consider impressive."

It wasn't necessarily true. Sprenger and Soekka had both done things that were very impressive, but it was important to make sure they didn't become arrogant with their abilities. *There are already enough scythe like that,* Cerri thought grouchily.

Jacob gave a deep chuckle and smiled down at Sprenger and Soekka. "Yes, my boy, you did wonderfully. You all did."

One of Jacob's four guards came up behind him and whispered something in his ear. Jacob nodded his understanding. Then Jacob turned to Master Cerri and said, "You may tell your class that I will assign them to their new masters and squads in two days' time." He looked down at Sprenger and Soekka. "Enjoy your break, boys, because after this point, your training intensifies."

"Good," Sprenger said smoothly. "We were getting bored." Jacob chuckled robustly again.

Cerri sighed. *Sprenger and his mouth.* Soekka at least had the decency to be silent.

"So, Old Man," Sprenger continued eagerly, “have you decided who my master is going to be yet?” Cerri resisted the urge to hit him again.

“Not yet, Sprenger,” Jacob lied with a light chuckle, “but you boys will both know soon enough.”

Chapter 2

Classmates

In the middle of their class' training grounds, Sprenger and Soekka rejoined their classmates by sitting on top of a pile of large wooden targets that were used for blade-throwing, around which their classmates quickly congregated. They were all excitedly buzzing about whether or not they wanted to continue their training, and who would be on squads together.

Sprenger wasn't really listening to them, even after he and Soekka sat on top of the targets in the center of the group. He watched as Jacob strode away with his bodyguards until they disappeared behind a mossy roothome. Sprenger had wanted to speak with him more, but Jacob had to go do something, as was common after he showed up. Jacob's visits were rare, and usually were around times of record setting in events like blade throwing, uprights, or sprints. Everyone pushed themselves exceptionally hard when he was there, which is why Sprenger figured he showed up on those important days.

Today, Scythrith Jacob had graced them with his rare presence because it was graduation day. Master Cerri's class demonstrated their most complicated routines for Jacob to show that they were ready to start training under a batennin, or master-scythe.

However, it was only Sprenger and Soekka that ever approached him to talk. They had done it for as long as Sprenger could remember, all the way back to when they were toddlers. Jacob was the Scythrith, the leader of Durado, so people tended to give him great respect but at the same time felt inadequate to approach him. It was something Sprenger never understood. He was an incredibly kind and patient man and even had a good sense of humor, but most didn't realize this about him. Sprenger and Soekka were lucky enough to get to know him when they were young because Jacob was a personal friend of their caretaker, Granny Karla. They weren't intimidated by him, but only because they knew him before they really understood his importance in the village.

"What master do you hope to get, Sprenger?" Sprenger turned his attention to the girl who asked him the question.

"What?" he asked, having not been listening to them this whole time.

She gave him an annoyingly amused smile. "What master do you hope to get, silly?" She giggled with her friend. Sprenger didn't understand why that was funny, but he rarely did.

"Oh, I dunno. I don't particularly care. As long as the Old Man doesn't stick me with a bad or mean one."

"Well we all know you'll do great no matter who you get," she smiled again.

Sprenger gave a fake smiled back. "Thanks."

Sprenger turned and looked at Soekka, who was sitting next to him with an amused look. The two boys often found themselves surrounded by their classmates, no matter where they chose to rest. They were the center of attention most times, usually from the girls of the class, but where the girls go, the boys of the class often follow. Sprenger and Soekka weren't particularly fond of the attention, but they didn't mind it either. It was something that had happened since they began training in Cerri's class five years ago. Being at the top of their class, Sprenger and Soekka received a lot of praise, but they were taught by Granny Karla to always remain humble, which they did for the most part.

Sometimes, however, the attention was more than they could handle, especially when it seemed to turn into some sort of competition amongst the girls when it came to favoritism. A few fights had even broken out that Sprenger still didn't understand the cause of. Every once in a while, a boy would also try to get in good favor with them by complementing them excessively or following them around, but Sprenger and Soekka's lack of response usually led them to give up eventually. The boys were kind, but they had little interest in spending much time with others, and they preferred each other's company above anyone else's.

Even still, here they sat, surrounded by their classmates, many of whom were still trying to pull them into conversations that Sprenger and Soekka found pointless.

"Are you guys upset that you won't get to train together anymore?" A different girl asked Soekka.

Soekka shrugged. "Yah, but you never know what Lord Scythrith will do." He gestured to Sprenger. "I know he's been bugging him to put us on the same squad, but we'll just have to see."

"You guys can't be on the same squad," a short boy named Nellan protested. "The two best have to be separated to make the squads equal."

"Yah," Sprenger interjected, "but Granny Karla told us that siblings are often put on the same squad because they look out for each other and already train together. It would make no sense to separate two people that work well together when the goal is to have a successful squad."

There was a bit of an awkward pause. It seemed people didn't know what to say to that, especially since they all knew that Sprenger and Soekka weren't technically siblings. Sprenger could tell that they were deciding whether or not to say so.

Sprenger and Soekka were raised together since they were babies; both orphaned by their parents. Though they knew they came from different parents, Sprenger and Soekka were as brother-like as any pair of siblings could get. The boys often had to be reminded of the fact that they weren't technically related because to them, their bond was their relation. They were raised believing they were brothers, and even after Granny Karla explained their pasts in vague terms, they couldn't really break the habit of being siblings.

"I agree," someone behind them said.

Sprenger turned around and attempted to hold back a grin when he saw who it was.

"I think they should be together," Korran continued. "Sprenger's right, Durado needs the best squads it can get, and they already work better together than anyone else here." She came up and stood next to the pile of targets that Sprenger and Soekka were sitting on. She had dark brown hair that she held back with a headband and slightly tanned skin that everyone in her family shared. In Sprenger's opinion, she was one of the few girls of their class worth talking to. Walking with her was Tenni, who had dirty blond hair that was pulled back into a loose braid with the exception of her bangs.

The two girls were almost opposites when it came to personalities. Korran was exceptionally nice, even when Sprenger knew it to not be genuine, while Tenni was very blunt and had a short temper. Sprenger didn't really like being around Tenni. She could be a very mean girl, and had no problem starting fights with the boys. Neither Sprenger nor Soekka had ever had the displeasure of upsetting her that far, but they had seen her make her mark on a few of the boys in class during sparring practice.

The two girls spent all their time together, appearing to avoid the other annoying girls in their class. They did all training and preparing with one another and were about as inseparable as Sprenger and Soekka. The four of them had an unspoken understanding of one another's determination and skill that no one else in the class seemed to really understand. *Except Cayman,* Sprenger reminded himself, *but he was a little too determined.*

Korran gave the boys a kind smile, and Sprenger hoped it didn't cause him to blush.

Tenni came up and crossed her arms. "You should also consider, Nellan," she said to the short boy who was talking, "the fact that if we had to have even squads like you say, then *you* would also have to be on their squad to even out their talents with your lack of talent."

Everyone started laughing as Nellan turned red.

"Be nice," Korran whispered to Tenni. "You know he's not continuing his training."

"For a good reason," Tenni grumbled to herself, yet audibly enough for others to hear. She seemed to notice how red Nellan was getting and softened her tone. "Sorry, Nellan, I was only joking."

"It's okay," he replied, still clearly embarrassed. "I wouldn't be a very good scythe and we all know it. I'm better off practicing my cooking."

"Well," Sprenger said, "if you become as good as your dad then you can bet I'll be a regular at the Steaming Pot for meals."

Everyone started talking excitedly about how they would do the same, and Nellan began smiling as he became the center of everyone's conversations about his parents' foodhouse.

Sprenger, Soekka, Korran, and Tenni turned to each other, seeing the opportunity to pull into their own conversation without everyone else.

"I am really curious what the squads will look like, though," Tenni admitted. "But I don't really think you could go wrong with our class."

"I agree," Soekka said. "We're way better off than the class before us. All those that are continuing with their training in our class are all decently skilled. It will be interesting to see the squads, but I don't see how any of them could be bad."

Sprenger apparently was just staring at Korran, and when she looked over at him, he realized he had to say something otherwise he would just appear creepy. "So," he said quickly, "is there a master that you hope you can train under?"

Korran nodded. "My mother is close friends with Master Kobei, so I believe she wants him to be my teacher."

"Isn't he the big one that always looks like he's just accomplished some great task?" Soekka asked.

Everyone giggled. It was true. Master Kobei was known to be a very proud man and would often be seen standing around with his chest pushed out and an odd smile on his face. The posture, for any other man, might appear that he was trying to appear larger than he was, but that would be a bit moot in Kobei's case. The man was a good deal taller than most everyone and was as heavily muscled as a bull.

"Yep," Korran laughed, "that's him. My mom says that he actually is a really good scythe, he just has a 'different personality'."

"What about you Tenni?" Sprenger asked.

She shrugged. "I honestly don't know many master-scythe and my parents certainly don't either. So I'll just see who I get when the time comes."

Sprenger nodded. Tenni lived in the Manor, which was the largest home in Durado. The couple that lived there owned the only herds of deer, forest hogs, plus forest fowl, such as pheasant and cock. As scythe no longer hunted much in their forest, the family was the sole providers of all meat in Durado. Jacob once joked with the boys that the animals didn't really look like their wild brethren after generations of domestication. He said that, much like Jacob's generation, they had gotten slow and laughably fat. They kept their animals in large glades just on the edge of the Ancient Forest, that were fenced by both roots of the nearby trees, and fences that were built by the manor family's ancestors long ago. Such an inconvenient distance did not matter to the couple, as they had plenty of workers to watch out for their herds so they rarely left their large home. They even hired some of the village's scythe to guard their livestock, since they were outside the walls, and the family feared theft from desperate travelers as well as the occasional pack of wolves that would come down from the mountains.

Sprenger never asked, but he assumed that Tenni's family was one of a few that lived and worked in the Manor full-time either cooking or cleaning.

"You guys don't seem too worried about who you'll get as a teacher," Tenni said.

Sprenger and Soekka smirked at each other.

"That's because Granny Karla has very poor opinions of most scythe," Soekka explained. "She was pretty highly ranked when she was a scythe, so we think it's just her nature to criticize the scythe around her. So, we really don't know who is a good master, because Granny Karla only points out all their flaws."

"We stopped asking a while ago," Sprenger mumbled.

The girls smiled at them. “She sounds like quite the woman,” Korran teased.

“She certainly is one tough old crone,” Sprenger smiled back.

“I think you two are incredibly lucky to be raised by a woman like that,” Tenni said, much to Sprenger’s surprise. “I’ve heard about what she’s done in her youth,” Tenni explained. “She was the only woman of her rank and more respected than most of the men. It’s a shame she’s retired now. I’d love to have a teacher like that.” Soekka and Sprenger exchanged a look and Tenni put her hands on her hips angrily. “You mean to tell me that you two don’t know anything about your caretaker?”

Soekka shrugged. “We know that she was highly ranked and know that she probably was as strict of a commander as she is a parent.” Sprenger giggled at that. “We never asked more than that.”

“Just another rare gift wasted on you two,” Tenni said with a fake smile.

Sprenger rolled his eyes. *I pity whoever will be on a squad with you, Tenni.*

Chapter 3

The Legendary Adimortis

Footsteps echoed down the steep stairway, resonating in the stone room below. The walls dripped and shimmered with water that leaked from cracks. The floor was littered with rubble from the decaying ceiling. Large stones covered the floor where parts of the walls had collapsed and piles of dirt filled the space they left behind. A few torches were lit on the walls, casting flickers of lazy light and shadows.

Four cloaked men stood silently in the center of the room as the fifth man descended the stairs.

The first cloaked man had his long yellow hair tied into a ponytail, hanging loosely down his back. He had a comely face, but an arrogant smirk was commonly on his lips. He was known as Peatra the Treacherous to some, though he hated that name and few were brave enough to say it in his presence. He hailed from the northern most village, Shreelo, where his crimes and talents were still whispered in hushed rumors amongst the villagers.

The second cloaked man was rather pale and his sickly-ill appearance gave him an eerie aura of death while still in life. He was shorter than the rest and had thin black hair, but his appearance was only a distraction from his hidden skills. On his left hand, a metallic glove glimmered in the torchlight; sharp blades adorned each finger like unkempt nails. Less obvious, was the deadly poison that coated each blade of this unique gauntlet. His work with poisons and venoms had earned him the name Hexis of the Toad. Though few knew of his origin, he was originally the first member of the elite group that was now being gathered in such drab conditions.

The third cloaked man was taller than the first two and had dark black skin that seemed charred in the dim lighting of their hideout. The reflection of the flames danced on his bald head and in the whites of his eyes. Though he lacked a proper title that most others had, he was content to simply remain Ajax. Unlike the first two men, Ajax was not from one of the Great Villages. His people were nomadic and prided themselves on being the original peoples of this land, before it was discovered by an ancient king long ago. Where his people once wondered throughout the land, now they stayed hidden in the east, preferring not to interact with the rest of the world. Ajax was one of the very few that had chosen a life outside of his people's traditions, and for that, he was certain he could never return to them.

Behind all of them stood the final member of the impatiently waiting group. Towering a whole head and a half over the others, the fourth man was exceptionally adorned with limbs of unmatched size and strength. Though his cloak covered him well, the thick double-muscling that covered his body could be seen climbing his bull neck and into his broad jaw. His eyes seemed small compared to the rest of him, and he had a simple head of brown hair that sat atop his robust square head. His own size was complimented by a massive sword hung across his back. Nearly as long as a normal man is tall, and half as wide. A ridiculous instrument for any other person. For this giant, it was no heavier than a broadsword. Like his partner, Ajax, this man came from a people hidden away from the rest of the world. Like him, his people carried a trait that exaggerated their muscles in unimaginable ways. For years, the giant had protected his people by serving the man the group had assembled to meet. Through this time, his hulking physique and unimaginable strength led him to be known as Grogin the Unstoppable. Though none of these elite fighters would admit such a thing, Grogin was commonly considered the most dangerous of them. Luckily for them, he was particularly mellow and soft-spoken in nature.

The four men waited in the dark at the bottom of the small staircase for their approaching comrade to join them. Finally, the fifth man, garbed in the same black cloak as worn by the others, emerged from the stairwell. A shimmering chain draped across his body in several clanking loops. Hanging from the end of the chain in his left hand was a rather crude end-piece; four blades protruding from a center sphere. The man gently swung the sphere back and forth at his side. As he approached, the torchlight revealed a fresh scar running from his left temple to under his chin.

"About time you got here, Phenex," the yellow-haired Peatra complained. "Where's Horkk?"

Phenex approached the group and said, "he fell in battle." The group exchanged looks, silently having a frustrated conversation.

Peatra broke the silence once more. "I like the gift that the battle left on your face, Phenex." The smirk on his face remained, even after Phenex gave him a look of warning.

"Was it Juriah?" asked Ajax in his deep, smooth voice. Phenex nodded, and a flicker of frustration ran across Ajax's face, along with others of the group. "With all the trouble he gives us, there will be none of us left by the time Lord Demaedura's plans are executed." His deep voice boomed in the empty room. "Why doesn't Demaedura just end him and be done with it?"

"It's not that simple, Ajax," Phenex replied in his harsh emotionless tone.

"Sure it is," Peatra shrugged haughtily. "Instead of avoiding Juriah, let's just kill him together. I doubt that even a Hessiet can handle all of us." He crossed his arms seeming very pleased with himself. "Juriah clearly saw the weak member of the Adimortis and took his chance. Hopefully your next partner will live longer, Phenex."

"I see your mouth remains loosely hinged, Peatra," Phenex growled at the yellow-haired man. "Show respect for your fallen comrade, or the next insult will be your last." He fingered the chain above the end-peace of his bladed-flail as he spoke.

There was slight hesitation as Peatra considered his next words carefully, while still trying to appear unintimidated. "I merely pointed out that the scythe that died *is* dead," Peatra defended arrogantly. "There is no insult in that."

Phenex glared at him fiercely, but continued his explanation. "As for Juriah, we will deal with him as we always have. Lord Demaedura does not want him killed yet. Keep to your assignments, and continue to avoid Juriah whenever possible. Even together, the Reaper of Durado would not fall easily."

"He can be killed, like every other man," the pale man, Hexis, challenged. An eerie touch to his voice made it distinct from all the others. "I look forward to ripping his eyes from their sockets just for the trouble he's caused us." The bladed fingers of his glove began to click excitedly.

"You are so creepy," Peatra sighed, shaking his head. "Of all the great scythe that Lord Demaedura recruits, I had to be partnered with *you*."

"Enough of this chatter," growled Ajax. "Why are we here, Phenex? It was not easy getting this close to Durado without being noticed, and now I'm getting tired of waiting. Many of us have matters to attend to in distant places."

"I know as much, or as little, as all of you," Phenex admitted. He paused and skimmed the room thoroughly before continuing. "We must prepare for Lord Demaedura's arrival. Start moving this rubble out of the way. We need to alternate watches outside, as well. There still may be dura-scythe patrolling this far inland. We must make sure our presence goes unnoticed and that Lord Demaedura was not followed when he arrives."

"Then I'll take first watch," Peatra said as he smoothly walked past Phenex. "I'm not cut out for manual labor anyways." With that he headed for the stairwell that Phenex had just emerged from.

Phenex watched him over his shoulder as Peatra ascended the steps. Irritation was clear in his eyes, but he said nothing before he looked back at the rest of them. Silently, they separated to each ends of the room, pushing and rolling rocks out of the way. The rubble was accumulated into waist-high piles neatly around the room. Wood was placed sparingly between the crevasses in the rocks, and covered with oil, before being set ablaze. The room glowed brighter and became filled with the sounds of hissing oil and wood.

"There," announced Ajax satisfied. "Much more suited for Demaedura and his lavish tastes." The rest nodded in agreement. "I suppose you expect us to just wait now?" he said, looking over at Phenex, who just stood there silently. Ajax gave a heavy sigh and began flipping a small blade between his dark knuckles.

After a moment of silence, the giant announced, "I will go switch watches with Peatra if there is nothing else to be done." His voice was deep and harsh sounding, but little more than a grumble.

"What makes you think we want his big mouth in here?" hissed Hexis. The monstrous man didn't reply, but instead began his somber walk to the exit, bowing his heavy head to avoid it hitting the top of the stairwell. When his footsteps could no longer be heard in the hallway, Hexis glared up the steps, clearly not approving of being ignored. "Not much of a talker, Grogin," he stated bitterly. "I think he should be partnered with Peatra. They would balance each other out." His nose puffed as he chuckled softly at his own joke.

As time passed, each of the men waited quietly and many took the chance to care for their individual weaponry. Upon his return, Peatra found it amusing to break the silence by harassing his comrades until he received a death threat or threatening gesture from them. He eventually pushed Phenex to the point that the scythe attempted to hit Peatra with his flail, but Peatra readily avoided it. The end-piece smashed into the stone wall with such force that pebbles began falling from the ceiling. Phenex gave the chain another swing, and it wrapped back around his body like a constricting snake at his command. He snatched the chain above the end-piece as it made its final loop and held it at his side, ready should Peatra decide to test his patience again. Peatra hotly moved to the other side of the room, making no attempt to hold back his laugh.

Peatra's laugh suddenly stopped, and nothing but the snap of the burning oil was heard. The smell of burnt, rotting berries filled the room. The stale stench overwhelmed all other senses and announced the presence of the man they had been waiting for. All the robed men stood and faced the man that was emerging from the stairwell. As he descended the final steps, even the flames of the torches around him seemed to cower to his presence. He seemed younger and more modestly built than the other men in the room, but all came to stand before him nonetheless. In silence, the group dropped to a knee, and supported themselves on one clenched fist as they bowed their heads. A blond boy, no older than mid-teens stood behind him, staring curiously at the intimidating group kneeling before them.

The new figure stood with a sly grin on his pale and slender face, his features exaggerated by the dim lighting. His sleek black hair curtained his forehead and his sharp cheeks, while reflecting the dancing firelight. His eyes were shadowed under his brow, making his gaze impossible to follow. He wore a dark green robe and tunic that clung tightly to his body, accompanied by a slim leather strap around his waist that held the sword across his lower back. The pommel at the end of his weapon was decorated with gold flames that erupted out to form the handhold.

No one spoke as the group waited silently for the new arrival to speak or move. Eventually, the hulking man joined them from outside, awkwardly forcing himself out of the undersized stairwell. Once in the room again, he towered over both the new arrival and his young ward, but still he gave them a wide berth before dropping to knee at the man's left side.

In his low, rumbling voice, Grogin said, "There were no dura-scythe following you, Lord Demaedura."

Demaedura paid him no attention, as if he was already aware of the information he was just given. He continued smirking down at the five men in front of him, letting the intimidating silence build to demonstrate his authority.

“Six of you I sent out," Demaedura finally said, "yet five of you remain before me." His voice was smooth and content, yet had a chilling effect.

“Horkk has fallen in battle," Phenex said, raising his gaze to Demaedura’s. "He fought intensely, but to no more avail than myself." He traced the scar on the side of his face with his finger. “It seemed our presence in Cortiana did not go unnoticed by some.”

The room started to pulse with Demaedura’s chuckling. “Juriah,” he said under his breath, as if he had to force the name from deep in his throat. Phenex nodded to confirm. "No matter, I have someone else who has shown great skill. He simply needs to be persuaded to join us. When we finish here, you will go and win him over, Phenex." He walked past the four of them, with the young student trailing closely behind like a pet. The group rose to their feet and turned to face him.

"It has been a long time since you have called us together like this,” Ajax said to Demaedura. “It must be important to require all of us so close to Durado.” His tone remained polite, but there was still something accusing about it.

Demaedura didn't turn around, but remained staring into the stone room in front of him until finally he said, "You remember our old friend Tranis?” He said to no one in particular. “He has information that we need." He looked over his shoulder at them. "Information that will help narrow your searches and help you with your assignments."

Ajax seemed unsatisfied by this response to his query. "Tranis is an idiot," he protested flatly. "An idiot well-guarded in Durado’s prison. I hope we are not here on his word. Spies often say whatever they need to in order to get what they want. *He* is not worth invading Durado for.”

Demaedura turned his head to face the empty room again. "Your arguments are understood, but misplaced, my nomadic friend. We will not initially invade the village. I have arranged for Tranis to come to us. You are here to simply ensure he escapes the borders safely. My informant in Durado has put a plan in place that will occur shortly, and I expect you to be ready for him when it happens."

The five men exchanged subtle looks behind Demaedura's back.

Peatra crossed his arms defiantly. "Five Adimortis to escort one pisson spy? Surely he's not that valuable."

"Right now," Demaedura said coolly, unswayed by the protests of his servants, "Tranis is the most valuable person in the world. He is the final key to unravelling the years of riddles we have uncovered."

Seeming to realize that he was not going to reveal more than that, Ajax and Peatra remained silent.

"What will we do should he fail to escape?" Phenex asked. "Juriah will soon return to the village, and we-"

"Should Tranis fail," Demaedura interrupted, "we will need to retrieve him ourselves. I need Tranis's information and I will not allow Durado to keep me from what I need. You are the legendary Adimortis of the scythe world. I expect a simple prison break to be within your abilities. Cut down any dura-scythe in your way."

"But Juriah-"

"I will deal with Juriah!" Demaedura snapped, bringing quick silence to Phenex's concerns. Phenex bowed his head obediently and Demaedura's student smirked to himself. "Do not crumple with fear like a dog to the whip, Phenex." Demaedura warned darkly over his shoulder. "We will wait three days until Tranis arrives, and retrieve him ourselves if he does not. Am I understood on what needs to be done?"

All the men reluctantly agreed.

Chapter 4

The new squads

Lady Karla gracefully made her way to the training grounds. She walked with her hands in the sleeves of her grey cloak; the same grey cloak she wore everywhere. She had spent her entire life constantly adorned with fighting apparel, but now that she was retired, she much preferred her loose-fitting casual wear. She thought about dressing up for the occasion today, but after she had finished with the boys' breakfast and cleaning up, she didn't have much time to put into thinking up an outfit. She made sure her grey hair was well kept in a bun and called that good enough. *After all,* she thought, *no one particularly cares what I look like at my age.*

She nodded politely as she passed people, and they gave her a small bow of respect in return. They all knew exactly where she was headed; there was no one in the village that didn't know what today was. Many were probably headed to the same place themselves.

She had wanted to leave earlier but Sprenger and Soekka were not moving particularly fast this morning. Karla had to literally pull Sprenger away from the rolls to get him to go clean up. Then cleaning up with those two boys this morning, as it often did, turned into a whipping fight with the cleaning rags. She had to personally wipe down their faces herself, like she would when they were toddlers, and finally send them on their way.

Karla sighed to herself. *It's a good thing they're good-looking boys, because their smell is anything but charming.*

As she approached the training grounds, she could see the huge mass of people crowded around trying to get a look and hopefully hear what Jacob was saying.

Good, it hasn't started yet.

She made her way through the crowd of onlookers that happily cleared a way for her. She gave people a friendly nod and smile as they stepped aside for her with a small bow. Eventually, she made it to the front of the crowd and found Master Cerri sitting in the only row of chairs that were reserved for the ranking members of the village. He was wearing his finest white outfit, which he only wore for special occasions. His shoulder-length grey hair was combed back and his thin mustache was slicked down around the corners of his mouth. He looked very handsome. Next to him were the village elders, Jaydon and Bakkon, who were wearing their freshly cleaned silk tunics. They, too, were looking very handsome this morning, and Karla began wishing she had taken more time to get ready.

Cerri smiled at her as she sat in the open chair next to him. "I thought you might miss it," he teased.

"Not for the world," she smiled back. "Though I thought the boys might miss it at the rate they were going."

"They were a bit late," Cerri admitted, "but there's little I can do about it now."

"You're talking as if you're saying goodbye." Karla noticed he was staring at Sprenger and Soekka, who were standing in line with the rest of their class in the center of the training grounds. All of the students were wearing nice clothing that was well-tucked in and presentable. Sprenger and Soekka were no exception, and each boy was looking very good in their dresswear. Soekka had his black hair very nicely combed, but poor Sprenger could never do a thing with his brown hair. It would always return to its spiky origin no matter the amount of time or water spent on it. A small proud smile touched the corner of Karla's mouth as she admired her boys in their line of well-groomed classmates. They, however, were the only ones whispering and giggling with one another when they should have been trying to appear disciplined.

"A teacher never says goodbye," Cerri said proudly, "but I will admit I am nervous handing them off. It's difficult for me to trust their precious fates to someone else after carefully guiding them for the last few years." He turned his complete attention back to her. "Even if that someone is Kanto."

"Then don't trust Kanto with their fates," Karla said softly. Cerri gave her a curious look. "Trust the boys with their own fate. You have taught them well, and I think they have learned enough from you to make the correct choices."

Cerri looked back at the boys. "I certainly hope so. Too much rides on them for it to be wasted now."

Karla looked across the crowd as Jacob stepped forward from the large group of scythe that had gathered to see the ceremony. The scythe all dressed the same, wearing tan vests over light green silk shirts and light leather pants. The outfits helped them hide amongst the trees, but Karla was glad to be rid of the attire.

The stern and stoic-faced batennin stood at the front of the crowd, and rank decreased farther back into the crowd. Karla noticed eager young pentin at the rear, trying to see over the lines in front of them. Many, having just been where the students are now a year ago.

Jacob was wearing his cloak of a Scythrith, black silk embroidered with spiraling white designs and the symbol of Durado on its back. Everyone fell silent as he walked out into the center of the training grounds and stood in front of the ten anxious students, who straightened up if they hadn't already.

Jacob gave them all a reassuring smile and nod, then turned and spread his arms out wide to the crowd, "Welcome," Jacob called out over the large crowd of gathered scythe and villagers with a booming voice. "Welcome my friends and comrades. It is that time once again when we gather to admire the next generation of scythe. Once again, we see the fruits of our village's training, and the hope that it brings us. The students that stand here with me, as you well know, will no longer be students after today. They will be scythe. And with that commitment, they deserve our respect and thanks." He lowered his arms and looked around the crowd. "There is great potential in this group, and it has made my decision on how to split them up very difficult, but I feel that I have chosen the best squads that will work together and the best masters to teach them. I want you to take heed of these faces, for these are those that choose to take up arms to defend Durado. They are the faces of tomorrow's legends, and the hope that this village has for the future."

Jacob turned to the ten kids behind him and looked at them with a stern expression. "Students," he called so all others could still hear him, "you are about to commit to your lives as scythe. Do not take this commitment lightly. The lives of your squadmates, comrades, and fellow villagers, depend on your commitment to your training. With the title of scythe comes the dedication and resolve to fight any enemy without retreat. That is the scythe way. Should you run from your duty, your life will then be forfeit." He paused to let his words sink in. "Now," he continued, a bit brighter, "if still wish to take this step, I will assign you to your new teachers and squadleaders. When I call your name, you will come up and stand next to me. Your new master will then join you and you will stand aside to allow the next squad to be formed. Is that understood?"

"Yes, Lord Scythrith!" the line called out together.

Jacob nodded to them. "Then let us begin."

"Here we go," Cerri mumbled out the corner of his mouth.

"Naibi, daughter of Lailla." The black haired girl on the end came up and stood next to Jacob. "Warren, son of Warrok." The slender light haired boy in the center came forward. From what the boys told Karla, he was the weakest of the continuing students. "And Pillas, son of Porten." The larger and more muscular of the boys stepped forward. "I have chosen Master Tarak to train you from this point on." The crowd watched with interest as Tarak joined them. He was a young, clean-shaven, bald-headed man, but Karla still thought he had an attractive face. Though he was a young master, there were already stories of his victories on missions. Karla knew him to be a very polite and kind scythe from their brief history on the battlefront many years ago. She noticed Cerri nodding his agreement as he examined the new squad. The group moved aside and stood silently with Master Tarak standing behind them with an expressionless face. The students in the new squad were trying desperately to keep their excitement contained as they eagerly nodded and smirked to one another.

"Next," Jacob announced. "Caymen, son of Caddmon." A boy with shoulder-length black hair and a serious expression stepped forward. Karla knew of Caymen well, as he was a constant rival for the boys and they would talk about how he could never take a joke. That didn't surprise Karla, knowing the boy's father. “Rejeno, son of Raken.” The handsome blond boy with freckles joined them. Soekka once told Karla that Sprenger didn’t like him because he was always talking to Korran, which Karla didn’t entirely doubt, but Sprenger wasn’t the type to really dislike anyone. “And Korran, daughter of Meila.” Karla smirked as Korran came forward. She could see why Sprenger liked her; she was a very pretty girl. “I have chosen Master Kobei to train you from this point on.” Kobei came out onto the grounds, strutting the whole way. He was a big man with strong limbs and a confident face. Karla didn’t care for that man much and could see some of the scythe rolling their eyes behind him as well. No one could deny his skill, but no scythe should carry themselves with such confidence. *Humility shows more character*, Karla thought sternly. Cerri nodded again, approvingly.

As that group moved to the other side of Jacob, all that was left was Sprenger, Soekka, and Tenni, who Karla couldn’t tell was upset or not. Whatever she may be feeling, she certainly did not look excited. Sprenger and Soekka, on the other hand, did a very poor job of keeping their grins in check. Then Karla noticed another boy with very messy brown hair and dirty clothes standing off to the side.

Karla leaned in close to Cerri. “Who’s that boy there?” She whispered.

“His name is Gerret,” Cerri whispered back, “a bit of an oddball. His parents train the hounds, and they asked to continue his training personally, so he will not be joining a squad.”

Ah, there’s always one in every class. Karla understood when scythe wanted to teach their own children, but most did so in addition to having them train under a master. Having your child learn from only you, and with no squad, rarely turns out successful scythe or sociable individuals.

Gradually, Karla noticed the whispers all around her. It was obvious who the last squad was, and apparently a few people recognized the situation. One whispering junettin caught Karla's eyes as he murmured to his squadmate, but fell silent when he noticed Karla looking at him.

"That leaves our final team," Jacob announced. He turned to them, "Tenni, Soekka, Sprenger," he said gently to them. "Please come join me, you three." They did so, and Jacob turned back to the crowd and raised his voice again. "To train them I have chosen Master Kanto." An average-looking young man stepped out of the group of batennin and walked out to join them. He had short brown hair and a sturdy expression that showed no hint of emotion: the mark of a master-scythe. The crowd nodded, but Karla could still hear some people whispering curiously.

Well done Jacob, Karla smirked to herself, *you pulled it off without having to bring up their parentage. Hopefully the three of them did not find that too suspicious.*

Sprenger, Soekka, and Tenni all smirked at the crowd along with the two other new squads.

"People of Durado," Jacob concluded, "I give you our newest pentin!" The crowd erupted in applause. "May luck be on their side in their future endeavors, and may their training serve a great purpose in the name of our village."

Karla and Cerri stood and began clapping. When the boys looked over at her with their big smiles, Karla almost began crying.

-<>-

Sprenger beamed as he looked around the crowd of clapping people. He smiled especially big when he saw Granny Karla off to the side by Master Cerri. They were both giving him and Soekka proud looks, something that gave Sprenger a feeling unlike any other.

After a while the crowd quieted and began to break up. Granny Karla gave them a small wave, and also departed along with Master Cerri. Jacob turned around, clasped his hands behind his back and gave them all a serious look.

"There you have it," he said in a soft but conclusive tone. "These will be your new squads for as long as you are in training, and likely longer than that. Learn from one another, keep each other safe, and above all else, listen to your masters." He scanned each of their faces with his kind old eyes to make sure they were listening to his words. "Remember that they were once like you. They went through the same training and the same discipline that they will soon be asking of you." He made sure to look each of them individually in the eye for a short time. "If you accomplish what they ask, then you too may someday have students of your own." He nodded to them with a smirk. "Good luck. I now leave you to your new masters." With that, he rejoined his accompanying guards, and they all headed off down the street. Each master called for their squads to join them and the students separated into their new groups.

Sprenger, Soekka, and Tenni all turned around and looked up at Master Kanto, who stared sternly back down at them. There was an awkward pause of silence in their group, especially since Sprenger could hear Master Kobei next to them beginning to describe himself to his new students.

Shouldn't somebody say something? He thought apprehensively. Sprenger decided he would be the one to break the tension. "My name is Sprenger," he said,

"I held the record for longest uprights in our class and set a new one for the village." Sprenger wasn't trying to brag so much as just give a topic of discussion, but noticed Tenni still rolled her eyes.

"So it's you then?" Kanto said curiously.

"It's.. me.. what?" Sprenger asked confused.

"There is always someone in every group that has to be the first one to talk." Kanto said flatly. "I guess that's you. Typically," he continued in a stern tone, "when there is a difference of rank, those of a lower rank wait until one of a higher rank speaks. It shows respect." Sprenger shied away, a bit embarrassed. "And trust me," Kanto continued, "we will break that record of yours in the very near future."

Sprenger noticed Tenni attempting to hold back a smirk. Soekka too.

"In fact," Kanto said, looking to Tenni and Soekka, "I'd say Sprenger's record should be our new minimum time for upright drills starting first thing." That wiped the smirks off their faces.

Kanto turned his stare to Tenni. "Tennirria, correct? So what do you find yourself gifted at?"

Tenni seemed caught off guard for a moment. "I prefer Tenni, please, sir." He nodded his understanding. Tenni thought for a moment before answering him. "Though I don't excel in routines or kicking, I am a fair sparrer. Master Cerri said my hand-to-hand was one of the best in the class."

"I see," Kanto said curiously, but unimpressed. "So we have the 'hitter'," he nodded to Tenni, "the 'talker'," nodding to Sprenger. "So that leaves," he turned to Soekka, "the 'listener'."

They all looked at each other, not really able to object to their new labels. *He's pretty much right, actually,* Sprenger realized.

"If you are wondering," Kanto explained, "*that* is why Lord Scythrith put you together," he said with conviction. "You are all each other's balances. If you lot learn to use one another's skills to accompany your own, then you will be a stronger team than any. I will teach you how to do this. I will teach you to use your teammates' strengths to your advantage and vise versa. Even the greatest scythe in the world can be brought down by a well-coordinated team, but it will not be easy, and it will take time. If you commit to me and my teachings, I will give you the strength to become the scythe you wish to be." He raised his voice. "Do I have your commitment?"

"Yes, Master Kanto!" they said together, drawing the attention of the other squads, who then turned back to their own, much more casual, conversations.

Kanto nodded to them. "Then come with me," he said, turning on his heels and walking away.

The three students looked at one another, confused. Sprenger looked over to the other two squads, who had each sat down to get to know their masters in greater detail and clearly not going anywhere. Master Kobei was still in the middle of a story of himself, and Master Tarak was having each of his students describe themselves to him individually.

Hesitantly, Sprenger, Soekka, and Tenni followed Kanto deeper into the training grounds until he found an empty sparring circle.

"You three have confidence," Kanto finally said to them as he stood in the center of the dirt circle. "While that is important for a scythe, it can also be dangerous. I have reviewed each of your records from Master Cerri and you all excelled in his class." They all exchanged subtly proud looks with one another. "Those days are over," Kanto said sternly, causing each of them to be taken aback. "You were the best of your class, but this is no longer a class. As scythe, you have barely begun to learn." His stern eyes swept over each of them. "It is just as important to understand what you know as it is to understand what you don't know." Kanto put his hands behind his back and widened his stance. "Your first task as my students," he said stoically, "is to strike me." They all looked at him and one another incredulously. "You just swore your commitment," he reminded them. "I have given you an order. Strike." Still the students hesitated.

"But," Tenni started.

"I assure you," Kanto said, "if you make contact, it will be my own fault, and not yours. Do not hold back. Begin." He waited in the center of the circle as the students exchanged one last look.

Sprenger shrugged, then ran at Master Kanto, swinging his fist, but Kanto stepped aside and tripped Sprenger. As Sprenger fell into the dirt, Soekka came flying to the ground next to him. When Sprenger pushed himself up, Tenni swung so hard at Kanto that she lost her footing when she missed and nearly came toppling on top of Sprenger.

"That was half-hearted and pathetic," Master Kanto said down to them, hands still behind he back. "I said to not hold anything back."

"Fine," Sprenger said quickly as he shot to his feet. He jumped at Kanto again and punched repeatedly. Kanto avoided most of them, but then he blocked so fast that Sprenger had no time to respond before he was flung to the ground.

Soekka came kicking at Kanto, who used a single hand to knock them away, then slid away as Tenni tried yet again to hit him with impressive force.

The two tried to combine attacks, but nothing made it through before Kanto swung his leg and knocked them both to the ground next to Sprenger.

"You all have skill," Kanto said without emotion as he looked down on them, "but you are no longer the best. I can teach you to work together. I can teach you to defend yourselves from dangerous attackers and how to engage skilled enemies." He raised a finger to them. "But first, you need to accept that you have a lot to learn. Humility will keep you alive on missions, and over-confidence will get you and your team killed." He put his hand behind his back once more. Any questions?" All three students shook their heads as they stood up. "Good," Kanto said with a nod. "Now, go home and prepare to begin again at sunrise." He turned around and began walking away.

They all exchanged befuddled looks. "Wait, what?" Soekka said confused. "That's it?"

Kanto stopped and looked over his shoulder at them. "Go home. Have holders sewn into sleeves for blades, prepare training clothing, and enjoy the rest of the day." He started walking away again. "It will be one of your last of leisure," he called back to them.

The three of them stood there dumbfounded, having expected to start training immediately or at least talk about what to expect in training. Now they weren't sure what to do.

"Well," Sprenger said, "he seems..."

"Strict," Tenni finished.

They all exchanged an apprehensive look.

Chapter 5

Breakout

A man with mangy long hair, thin clothing, and poor hygiene sat in the darkness on his hard cot. He was not a frail man though; years of isolation leaves prisoners little to do but strengthen themselves in their cells. In fact, Tranis was stronger now than he was when he entered the prison eleven years ago. It was difficult to stay sane while in the small cell day after day, but in addition to strengthening their bodies, the guards allowed them a deck of cards or tiles to entertain themselves with every once in a while. Nobody benefited from a prisoner going mad, so all was done to keep them sane, but little was done for comfort.

Unlike the entirety of Durado, the prison was the single building that was not carved from an ancient root. Instead of hardened wooden walls that curved around the frame of the room, these walls were flat, straight stone. Durado residents did not like buildings of stone, as they were cold and lifeless. They much preferred their living roothomes with leaves and branches that would grow outside their carved windows. This building was meant to take that joy away from those that lived here. They were not even permitted the feel of sunlight.

There was only faint torchlight in the hallway outside his cell to help illuminate his tiny cage. The light was pathetic and was hardly worth burning the oil for, but still, Tranis would rather have that than sit in complete darkness.

The jail was not a crowded place; Tranis's only neighbor was three cells down and kept to himself (not that they were allowed to talk anyway). Tranis and his old partner, Cellic, used to be next to one another before Cellic was moved because the two of them were caught talking too often. His move couldn't have happened at a worse time either. They were close to their plans coming to light, and this was the time that they should have been collaborating the most, not least.

Tranis stood and walked up to the bars and looked up and down the hallway. No one was there. He sighed and began pacing his cell again. It was difficult for him to tell what time of the day it was. He normally used the guards' patrol to keep track but he lost count of them today, his mind racing with excitement and nervousness of what was to come.

He's coming before sunrise, Tranis kept reminding himself. *I'll be out of the village by morning, but I won't be able to get Cellic anymore.* He hated leaving his partner behind, especially after everything that they had been through together, but he didn't know where they had moved him and this had to be done quickly and precisely. He hoped Cellic would understand his abandonment.

When I get out, I will do whatever it takes for you to be free, too, Cellic, Tranis promised himself.

Tranis spun around as he heard the door open down the hallway. *He's here.*

There were quiet steps approaching, then a hooded and cloaked man peered around the corner of Tranis's cell. "Are you ready?" he whispered.

"Yes," Tranis whispered back. He had no idea who the man was, nor had he ever seen his face. *For good reason*, Tranis supposed. H*e's a traitor, after all. I didn't trust anyone either when I spied for Demaedura.* He just randomly appeared one day, asking questions. When Tranis realized why he wanted the information, he began bargaining. For months they had been in contact, and now their planning was about to be tested.

"Do you remember where you are going to meet him?" The cloaked scythe asked.

"Yes."

The man knelt and slid a small brass key across the floor to Tranis. "You have twenty minutes to leave the prison without interference from guards, so long as you use the route that we discussed. Leaving the village will be up to you. Be patient about it, but keep in mind that they will begin hunting you the moment they find your cell empty."

"I understand." Tranis knelt and picked the key off the floor. He admired it for a moment, as if it was an item of far greater value. *This is quite literally the key to my freedom.* When he looked back up, the man was gone.

Tranis wasted no time unlocking his door and heading down the route he had repeated to himself a hundred times in the darkness. Sneaking around was something Tranis was very good at. Leaving the village should not be a problem if he had thought it through correctly, which he was confident he had.

He and Cellic had snuck in and out of many villages together and were never once captured. It was ironic that the only village that was able to catch and imprison him was his own. Now that time was at an end. He had asked a demon for help and was granted freedom. Tranis hoped his answered plea was not at a greater cost than what he was trading for it.

Hastily and silently, Tranis darted down one stone hallway, then another. His path was leading him to the back of the prison, away from the other cells, where others might see him and start a ruckus. Before his next turn, Tranis slowly peered around the corner, nervous he would encounter his first flaw of the plan. To his disbelief, the door at the end had no guard.

He did it, Tranis thought, impressed. He headed for the door as quickly as he could. He didn't know how someone was able to influence the happenings of the village like Demaedura was, but he knew better than to question it for too long.

The door made a spine-curling creek when he opened it, so Tranis clenched his teeth and flung himself in before closing it loudly. Someone was sure to have heard that, though it was impossible to know if they found it suspicious or not.

Rather than wait and find out, he spun on his heels for the thing he was looking for. He didn't even glance at the piles of supplies that filled the room before his eyes were drawn to the very thing he needed. Like beacon of hope, the small window was glowing with the earliest light of the rising sun outside.

He held his breath as he ran over to it and peered through the ground-level glass. This was only the first step to his escape. For the first time in eleven years, he was about to set foot in the village once again, and if he did not do it perfectly, he would be dead before the sun had completely risen above the trees.

Chapter 6

Early Problems

Sprenger pulled his covers over his head to muffle Granny Karla pestering him to get up. He got momentary comfort when she left to go see Soekka's progress but now she was back and Sprenger groaned with distain.

She didn't say anything to him this time, but he was suddenly exposed to the cool morning air as she ripped his covers off his bed. He now laid in nothing but his silk bottoms on his bed, with no covers to hide under, and not even a pillow, as he managed to push it to the floor in the middle of the night.

"Now," she snapped. "Wash, eat, go." She was a woman who truly had a way with words.

Sprenger groaned again as she left the room, still carrying his covers. He pushed himself up and rubbed his eyes. When he looked out his window he groaned even louder. It was barely past dark outside; the sun had only just begun to rise. Sprenger reluctantly stood and headed for the washroom, which Soekka was just leaving. They exchanged tired looks as they passed each other in the hall.

Sprenger splashed water on his face and chest, and used the rag to dry himself quickly. He hated washing early in the morning because the cold water only made him miss his warm bed even more.

After dressing, Sprenger joined Soekka downstairs at the table where Granny Karla had rolls and some ham ready for them. Sprenger eagerly dug in and was soon grappling with Soekka for the last roll, which Granny Karla took and ate to end the squabble.

"Now be off," she said. "Kanto wanted you to meet him at sunrise, so you have little time left. And trust me," she warned, "you don't want to be late with him."

"Great," Sprenger mumbled, "sounds like we really got the fun master."

Soekka grumbled his agreement.

The boys took off after a hug and kiss from Granny Karla and headed down the road.

It was rare for Sprenger to see the village so quiet. It normally bustled with people attempting to accomplish chores. Now, the only signs of life were the echoing songs of various birds. Unlike the daytime, their voices carried clearly through the crisp and cool morning air. Sprenger did have to concede to himself that this was a much more tranquil way to walk through the village than darting between slow-walking villagers and exchanging pleasantries with people whose names he couldn't remember.

They were not the only ones awake at this hour, however. Overhead, scythe darted across beams and peered down at them from various perches like gargoyles. The village was surrounded by a massive wall, and from that wall were hundreds of thick beams that spider-webbed over their heads, converging in a single tower at the center. The patrol beams were used to easily survey the village and were only accessible by patrol-scythe. They could often be heard at night running over the houses, but people were accustomed to it.

Sprenger watched as a scythe ran across a beam overhead. *I hope I don't ever get stuck doing patrols. How boring.*

"What do you think we're doing today?" Soekka asked him lazily.

"I dunno," Sprenger grumbled. "Probably nothing that we couldn't have waited till the sun came out for. I'm not going to be very happy if he has us meet him so early to do the introductions we were supposed to do yesterday."

"I don't think he's big on introductions, Sprenger," Soekka said. "What do you think? Better or worse than Master Kobei?"

Sprenger thought for a moment. "Better," he finally decided. "Kobei seems kinda annoying to me. He certainly doesn't act like a batennin. I think Kanto will be tough, but that's probably why the Old Man put us with him."

Soekka seemed to agree with that. "Did you notice Warren got put with Master Tarak? Apparently he's the nicest of the master-scythe, which is why Warren had to be with him. Any other master would probably make Warren cry."

The boys laughed and bet on what would happen with the new squads as they headed for the gates at the front of the village, where Kanto had requested they meet him yesterday evening. They were a bit surprised to hear that, as the training grounds were at the back of the village, and that should be where most of their learning took place.

After several minutes walking along the grass and dirt roads that wove between the moss-covered roothomes, they arrived at the giant gates of Durado. To their surprise, the heavy wooden doors were wide open. Tenni was standing in the road in front of one of the towers to either side of the gates, eating the last bites of her breakfast.

Their group greeting was a bit awkward, as it was clear to all of them that Tenni was not particularly happy to be on a squad with them. Rather force pleasantries, Sprenger asked, "So where is he?"

Tenni shrugged. "I only just got here before you two showed up."

Sprenger put his hands behind his head and stretched. "Well, I guess he's late then."

"Or perhaps," Kanto said as he stepped out of the guard tower next to them, carrying something against his chest, "he was early and you just didn't see him." He gave Sprenger a stern look that Sprenger only responded to with an awkward smile.

The three of them lined up and gave him a small bow from the waist.

"So what's that?" Sprenger asked once they straightened, pointing at what Kanto was holding.

"This," Kanto responded while unfolding his arms, "is your first assignment." A mangy cat was laying in Kanto's arms, which tried to push its head back into the crevice of his elbow when he exposed it to them.

I sympathize, Sprenger thought with his warm covers in mind.

All three of them looked at the cat with disgust. It had mats of fur in some places and bald spots in others. Sprenger could hardly tell what color it was anymore.

"So what do we do with it?" Sprenger asked skeptically. "Put it out of its misery?"

"No," Kanto said flatly, clearly not amused. "This is Taxxis. He may not look like much but he's trained more scythe than anyone else in the village." He began scratching Taxxis on top of the head and the cat began purring. "You lot are going to catch him."

Sprenger suddenly became excited and shared a brief smirk with Soekka, who excitedly smirked back. This couldn't have been more perfect of a first assignment for them; Soekka and Sprenger had been catching Granny Karla's cat since they could run. It was one of their favorite competitions and had continued to be for years. Peter was his name, and though he was a bit of a heavy cat, he was in far better condition than this one was. This should be an easy first assignment for them.

"The task is simple," Kanto explained, "bring him back to me by sundown." He gave Sprenger a look, "alive please, Sprenger." Sprenger gave him another awkward smile. "If," Kanto said with diction, "you don't bring him back to me by sundown, then you will be sent back to the academy to join the class below you and wait another year to become pentin."

Everyone's eyes widened a bit. *That's a bit harsh,* Sprenger thought in shock.

"Any questions?" Everyone shook their heads. "Good." Kanto slowly put Taxxis on the ground in front of him, and they all watched as the cat stretched lazily and stared at them with large, curious brown eyes. Its tail flicked from side to side behind it, but it otherwise stood unmoving as it stared at them. Kanto began walking away. "You may begin."

"Ok guys," Tenni whispered, apparently not wanting to spook the cat. "We should-"

Sprenger dove for Taxxis.

"Sprenger wait!" Tenni yelled, but it was too late. The cat hissed and pounced to the left of Sprenger, leaving him sliding on his stomach in the dirt. Taxxis began to run towards the main gate of the village.

Soekka darted in front of the cat and stopped with his arms outstretched. Instead of stopping, as Peter normally would, the cat turned sharply to the right with impressive speed. Soekka wheeled on his hand to the side, and once again landed in front of the cat, but this time it bolted straight between his legs. Taxxis continued running through the gate and disappeared in the tall grass at the edge of the forest.

The three of them groaned and looked up at Kanto, but he stared back unsympathetically and gave a faint nod towards the forest.

Sprenger slowly got his feet and tried to avoid Tenni's glare. He forced a smile. "Sorry guys. I guess it was a little faster than I thought it would be."

Soekka just rolled his eyes and stared at the spot in the grass that Taxxis disappeared into.

Tenni, on the other hand, looked like she was about to hit Sprenger in the face. "You idiot! Did you really think it would be that easy!" She shook a fist at him.

"I said I was sorry," Sprenger defended, raising his hands in case she actually attempted to hit him. "I promise I won't underestimate that disaster of a creature again."

"Well now we have to find him in the forest! You think that's going to be easy too?!" She continued getting closer with her clenched fists, and Sprenger began to step back.

"Both of you be quiet," Soekka said flatly, still staring at the spot that Taxxis had disappeared. "We need to get after him quickly, before he really gets lost in there."

Tenni seemed to calm a bit when she finally turned away from Sprenger. "You're right. Let's go, but this time we need to wait for everyone to be ready before we try and grab him." She gave Sprenger an irritated glare over her shoulder.

He came up and stood next to them. "This time," Sprenger joked, "I'll wait for one of you to tell me to go."

"Okay," Soekka said impatiently, "let's go." He began running for the forest, and Sprenger and Tenni followed him.

“We need to be as quiet as possible,” Tenni yelled up to Soekka. “So when we get in the forest, just stop and wait.”

Soekka nodded back to her.

-<>-

Kanto watched as the three of them disappeared into the bushes and giant trees. He nodded to himself, recalling when he had to chase Taxxis into the forest as a new pentin. Taxxis was little more than a kitten back then, but the events of the day unfolded in a similar manner as they were now.

Kanto started to make mental notes of the first assignment. *Soekka seems to be taking charge,* Kanto told himself. *He focused on Taxxis even as Tenni and Sprenger were bickering. This lot will need focus like that. Tenni seemed to have a plan, but Sprenger was too overly-eager to wait and hear it. But then, when they went after Taxxis again, she was still trying to implement a strategy.*

Soekka’s focus, Tenni’s strategies, and Sprenger’s boldness to act... this group could become very reputable indeed. They just need to practice it more.

Kanto hoped that a day of chasing Taxxis in the trees would give them a chance to learn about one another’s strengths, aside from what they knew from being at the academy together. Working as a team was something not even Master Cerri could teach, and some squads never master it completely.

Kanto turned away from the gates and headed for a grassy spot to the side of the wall. He had all day to wait for them, so he figured he might as well clean his blades.

He sat down in the grass and recalled going through the stress of this day when he was first assigned to train under Jacob. It had taken him and his squad all day to find Taxxis, and it was not for lack of trying.

What they didn't know back then, was that no squad was ever sent back to the academy for this assignment. Taxxis never stayed outside the walls past sundown, and he would seek out scythe to bring him back in when it was time for his supper. The guards of the gate towers deliberately fed him each day right before sundown for that very reason. He would spend the day enjoying himself in the forest, but then would make sure pentin would find him and take him back to the gates so that he could eat. *By the end of the day,* Kanto smirked to himself, *Taxxis will literally crawl into their arms, and insist on being taken back to the village. Until then, they better learn to work together.*

-<>-

Tranis fell to the ground, accompanied by an assortment of leaves and the branch that had just given way underneath him, and laid in the dirt, winded for a moment. It had been too long since he had traveled in the canopy, and his lack of practice led him to choose poorly on sturdy branches to use. He also was beginning to show physical signs of his tussle with a young scythe guarding the wall. Tranis was able to take him by surprise, but the young man still managed to get a few hits in before Tranis knocked him out. He could feel his lip and eye swelling from where the young scythe had hit him.

He slowly stood and looked around. There were no scythe from what he could see, but that certainly didn't mean they weren't there. He straightened himself against the pain in his side and began running. He would brave the mossy roots of the forest floor from this point on. Another fall like that could end in much worse injury, and that was a mistake he could not afford right now. He had to be at the meeting point soon, or he would never get out of this cursed forest.

Tranis started to fill with dread the more he imagined reuniting with Lord Demaedura, especially if he kept him waiting. *An escape is pointless if it just leads to him killing me in the end,* he reminded himself.

Chapter 7

The Runaway

Sprenger loved the rare opportunities he was given to spend time in the forest. He loved the smell, the look, the sounds, everything. Today, however, something felt different about the forest. There were no birds, no squirrels, no sounds of life. Just silence. Each of his steps would echo with cracking twigs and debris, making him feel exposed amongst the tall moss-covered roots all around him. He had the odd feeling that something was waiting for him around every gigantic tree and hidden in every shadow.

They had decided to split up to look for Taxxis, since they had no idea which way he went in the trees. Tenni and Soekka went off in opposite sides to search the treeline, while Sprenger moved deeper into the forest. He pressed forward, ignoring his nerves, and noticed the trees were gradually getting larger and the underbrush was thinning out; a sign that he was a good distance away from the village, where the trees were smaller and denser. Now, each tree was wider than a house, and the tall, winding roots made walking and looking around perilous to do simultaneously. The sun was almost completely blocked out by the canopy and nothing could be heard except Sprenger crunching twigs under his. *Where are all the birds?* Sprenger thought suspiciously.

He walked around for what he felt was a half an hour or so, but it was hard to tell with the sun hidden behind the thick leaves. He wandered in every direction looking for any sign of their feline target, but nothing caught his attention. Sprenger stopped and looked up at the leaves above him. *If I were a cat where would I go?* He thought over and over again to himself.

A branch cracked behind him, and he spun around to face the direction it came from. A large group of bushes between two large roots was the only place he could think the sound came from.

Of course you're hiding in the thick and scratchy bushes, Sprenger complained to himself. He knelt down and began to make kissing noises and encouraging the cat to come out of his hiding spot, hoping to not have to go in after it. The bushes began to shake as something moved forward.

Sprenger smiled, *I can't wait to see the look on Tenni and Soekka's face when I show up with the cat.*

It was not Taxxis that emerged from the bushes, however. Sprenger's smile disappeared quickly as a man in tattered clothes emerged from the bushes. His hair was quite long and matted, and his heavy breathing revealed a poorly treated mouth. Blood and grime coated his teeth and lips, as well as what looked like emerging bruises on his face. Despite his poor hygiene, his thin shirt showed a well-muscled body underneath. Sprenger jumped back but kept his eyes on the man and stood his ground.

"Oh sorry," he sputtered in surprise, "I thought you were something else. I lost my cat, you see. Have you seen it by chance?" Sprenger tried to stay calm, realizing that this man was not supposed to be out here. Any scythe would be in the canopy, and any travelers would be on the road. A cold prickle ran down his neck as he realized that the tattered outfit he was wearing was the kind given to prisoners in Durado. Sprenger stared at Durado's symbol on the right shoulder of his outfit.

The man looked at Sprenger then at the symbol on his shoulder, and back up at Sprenger. "What're you looking at, boy?" He started walking forward, and Sprenger took a stance to fight if he should attack. The man smirked at him. "You really think you're capable of fighting me? As much fun as that could be, I'm in a bit of a hurry, so why don't you just head back to the village? Quietly," he said in dark warning.

Sprenger did not respond and continued to hold his ground, unable to think of anything to say.

"You're in training, aren't you?" the man continued when Sprenger didn't speak. "I'll give you a hint on your training then. Don't try to act noble or brave just because you think that's what makes a good dura-scythe. Dying rarely does any good and they won't care if you do. You should choose your fights wisely. Now, for example, would be a bad time to stick around." He started to slowly take steps forward. "I don't want to hurt you, boy, but I can't afford to be slowed down right now." He gave Sprenger a menacing look. "Last chance to leave." Sprenger didn't move. This man was not meant to leave Durado, and scythe never run away from serving their village. Even scythe at Sprenger's age were trained enough to know that. He steadied his fighting stance. "Fine," the man said decisively and jumped at Sprenger.

Sprenger fell back as someone in black dropped down from the canopy between them and spun the man around before he got to Sprenger. Before the prisoner even realized what was happening, he was struck with rib-cracking blows to his side, causing him to hobble over in pain. The man in black jumped up and put his full weight into bringing his fist down on the man's shocked face, slamming him to the ground with a strong thud and cloud of dust. Suddenly, it was silent once more.

Sprenger sat on the ground, stunned with surprise. His savior stood with his back to Sprenger. He wore a similar vest to dura-scythe, only his was black and not tan. Underneath it was a black silk shirt where most dura-scythe wore green. In his vest was a short sword that lay down the middle of his back and pommel stuck up behind his head of short-cut brown hair. There was no doubt in Sprenger's mind that this was a scythe, but he didn't know if he was a dura-scythe or not. If he wasn't, then he, too, was not supposed to be in the forest.

The man gave Sprenger a brief look over his shoulder then looked back down at the prisoner, seeming uninterested that Sprenger was behind him.

Sprenger jumped to his feet. "Who are you?" This man may have just saved him, but he could still be an intruder. "Are you a dura-scythe?" The man didn't answer him, he didn't even appear to be listening. Sprenger wasn't sure what exactly to say, so he just said the first things that came to mind. "If you're not from Durado, you need to leave this forest."

"Do you plan on being the one to enforce that?" the man finally said, without turning around.

Sprenger retook a fighting stance. "If I have to."

The man snorted, unimpressed. "Go away," he grumbled, half-amused. He knelt to the ground and reached for the unconscious prisoner. Slowly, he began to search the man's tattered clothing.

This man isn't supposed to be here, Sprenger decided. "I said leave!" Sprenger swung his foot around, but the man grabbed his ankle before it slammed into the side of his head.

He gave Sprenger a dangerous look over his shoulder with menacing brown eyes as he held his ankle in place. Slowly, the man rose, pulling Sprenger's foot up with him. Sprenger was flexible, but the man lifted his foot to its limits. Sprenger began to panic, not sure how to get out of this now.

The man kept giving him a dangerous look and tightened his grip on Sprenger's ankle. "It's difficult at times to tell if someone is bold or just stupid." He gave Sprenger's leg a push, knocking him back a few steps. "I can't decide which *you* are." He turned around again. "Go back where you came from and leave the fighting to scythe." He knelt by the prisoner again and began searching his clothing.

He's a thief, Sprenger realized. Sprenger ran at him. "I am a scythe!" he yelled and punched at the man's head from behind, but he ducked and Sprenger's punch missed by inches. The man spun his leg around and smashed it into Sprenger's lower back as he passed, causing his feet to leave the ground as he flew straight forward into the dirt. Sprenger pushed himself up and twirled up to his feet to face the man again.

The man stood to likewise face Sprenger for the first time. "Only the stupid continue after being warned."

Sprenger ran for him again and swung at his stomach, but it stopped short as he grabbed Sprenger's wrist.

Sprenger couldn't believe it. *He's fast.*

The man bent over slightly so he was eye level with Sprenger. "I won't warn you again," he said darkly.

Sprenger swung with his free hand, and the man jumped back to avoid it. Sprenger kept swinging and kicking, attempting to move as fast as he could to land a hit, but every attack was lazily knocked away by the man. After a while, Sprenger could feel his arms getting heavy, and he was getting short of breath. After another failed string of attacka, the man pushed him backwards.

"You have skill for your age," he said lazily and unphased by the fight. "I'll give you that."

The man was taunting him now. Sprenger shook off his fatigue and retook his stance. The man gave him an interested look.

Sprenger ran at him again, but this time the man darted at him as well. His sudden advance took Sprenger by surprise and caused him to flinch. The man slammed his palm into Sprenger's chest, stopping his advance completely, knocking the wind out of him and causing his head to flop forward. When Sprenger looked up to take a desperate breath, he found himself staring at a bent middle finger between his eyes. When the finger uncoiled, its small force and Sprenger's faltering balance was enough to knock Sprenger on his back. Sprenger lay there, gasping for air.

"I hope someday," the man said as Sprenger attempted to push himself up, "you will have the talent to back up your bravery. Until then, don't be overconfident." He started to walk forward but stopped as something else made noise behind a giant tree next to them.

Both Sprenger and the man looked over as Soekka came nimbly tumbling over a root and ran at the man. When he was close enough, Soekka spun to kick him, but the man leaned back as Soekka's foot flew inches from his face. Soekka landed and continued to spin, attempted to hit him with the back of his fist, but the man grabbed his wrist and threw Soekka to the side. Soekka managed to correct himself in midair and stay on his feet. He ran at him again, kicking and punching wildly. Again, the man grabbed his wrist and as Soekka attempted to knee him in the gut, but the man grabbed him by the knee as well. Soekka couldn't move, the man pulled him in close, raised his foot and sharply kicked Soekka in the stomach, sending him tumbling across the ground several times before skidding to a halt, gasping for air next to Sprenger.

Soekka held his stomach in pain, but slowly started to get up. Sprenger moved over and put a hand on his shoulder to get him to stay down.

The man stared at them curiously. "You two are something else," he said with amusement. "But you can relax. I am from Durado."

"You don't look like you're from Durado," Sprenger growled angrily.

The man shrugged. "Then don't believe me. It's not as though you're succeeding at stopping me if I weren't."

Soekka began to push himself up again, but Sprenger pulled him back down. "Don't," he whispered to Soekka.

The man smirked at them but turned when the unconscious prisoner moaned and began to move. The grimy man slowly pushed himself up and held a hand to his head. He looked around confused, then tumbled back with a gasp as he looked up at the man in black. The prisoner stared at him wide-eyed and frantically started to try to push himself backwards in the dirt.

He recognizes him, Sprenger realized. *And he's scared of him.*

The prisoner desperately tried to stand and run back into the bushes, but he wasn't quick enough before the man pulled him back by his shirt, knocked his feet out from behind, and flipped him back onto his stomach with a thud. The prisoner groaned in the dirt.

"Where you off to in such a hurry, Tranis?" The man asked. "Are you not happy to see me?"

The prisoner jumped up and attacked the man. They exchanged blows briefly, but the prisoner was moving too slow to hold his own, and when he stalled a defense, the man kicked him across the face, knocking him back to the ground, where the prisoner laid unconscious once more.

Sprenger and Soekka exchanged brief looks of amazement, but then flinched when the man turned back to them.

"What all did he say to you?" he asked Sprenger.

"Um," Sprenger sputtered for a moment. "Nothing. Just that he was in a hurry and I should move. We're out here trying to find a cat."

The man, clearly not interested in Sprenger's answer, turned back to the prisoner. He knelt down, pulled the prisoner up and flung him over his shoulder with a grunt. He began to walk away with the prisoner hanging limply over his shoulder, but then turned back.

"Cats like to lie in the sun," he said randomly. "There's a clearing over in that direction," he pointed with his thumb behind him. "I'd wager that's where you'll find your cat."

Without another word, he turned and continued walking away. It was not long before he had disappeared behind the winding roots and towering trees.

Sprenger and Soekka exchanged another look. "What just happened?" Soekka finally asked, confused.

Chapter 8

With Time to Spare

Soekka and Sprenger walked over the winding roots of the looming trees, now keeping a cautious eye on everything around them. The fear of more scythe lurking somewhere nearby kept both the boys silent as they worriedly searched for signs of Tenni. Their nerves shaken, they seemed to start at any signs of life in the forest as they walked along. They almost fell off a tall root when a deer went bounding past them up ahead, causing both boys to give a heavy, but embarrassed, sigh of relief.

Suddenly, Soekka stopped on the root they were traversing, almost causing Sprenger to run into him. Soekka looked off to their right, listening. Sprenger listened and began to hear it too. Someone was calling their names.

"Tenni," Soekka called back, "we're over here."

They slid down the root they were following and headed towards her calls. Eventually, all of the students rounded a tree at the same time, causing everyone to jump slightly.

"There you two are," Tenni said with a relieved huff. "Did you find any sign of Taxxis? I didn't."

"No," Sprenger said in a quick whisper, "but I-"

She turned away from him in thought. "Well maybe he went another direction."

"Tenni," Sprenger began again.

"Or maybe he climbed a tree?" she asked herself. She looked up at the boys. "Do you think he could climb a tree?"

"No, but-" Sprenger sputtered.

"Me either," Tenni decided.

"Tenni!" Sprenger blurted angrily.

"What?" she responded, annoyed.

"Something just happened in the forest," Soekka said.

Sprenger and Soekka took turns recounting their encounters with both the prisoner and the black-garbed scythe. Tenni's expression went from skeptical and annoyed to shocked and nervous.

"Perhaps we should return to the village and tell Master Kanto," Tenni suggested worriedly.

"We can't," Soekka protested. "We would be abandoning our first assignment. Scythe don't quit missions, no matter what. If this were a real mission, we would be expected to complete it or die trying. I'm sure that's the lesson Kanto's trying to get across. And," Soekka added, "he seems like the strict, no-excuses, type to me."

"Don't you think this is a bit more important than finding an old cat?" Tenni pressed.

"I do," Soekka admitted, "and that's why we should hurry up and finish finding him, so we can move on to more important things. I also think," Soekka argued, "scythe don't abandon missions, no matter what. This may not be that important, but it's still our first mission under Master Kanto."

"But we're no closer to finding Taxxis now than we were an hour ago," Tenni argued.

"That may not be true," Sprenger interjected. "The man that said he was a dura-scythe told us to go look in the glade that's nearby." Sprenger shrugged. "Better than just walking around like idiots out here."

"Fine," Tenni reluctantly agreed, "but if he's not there, then we have to go back."

The boys agreed with some hesitation.

They backtracked the direction they had come and headed deeper into the forest once again. The glade was not difficult to find, as it was the only area that the sun was showing through the trees. Sprenger stepped out of the shade with Soekka and Tenni, and the three of them looked around silently.

The glade was a decently large, sun-soaked area with ankle-high grass. Even around where the three of them were standing, there was an abundance of deer droppings. This was probably a favored and rare grazing area for the animals. They carefully examined the area before moving, not wanting to spook anything away.

"Look," Tenni whispered. "On that rock." She pointed to a boulder in one of the far corners of the glade. There was something on it that was not the right color to be part of the rock. "Is that Taxxis?" she asked quietly.

Neither of the boys could quite tell, so they shook their heads unsure. Then everyone jumped with a bit of excitement as they saw a tail flick out to the side before being curled back under the napping animal.

"That's him," Soekka whispered eagerly.

"Okay," Tenni said with authority, "this time, we need to approach him quietly and calmly. You two go stand in the trees closest to him, so that if he starts to run you can scare him back into the glade. I'll go and try to get him."

"Why do you get to be the one to grab him?" Sprenger complained.

"I said *get,* not *grab.* And that's exactly why," Tenni snapped. "This needs to be handled delicately."

Sprenger crossed his arms resentfully. "I can be delicate," he grumbled under his breath.

Soekka rolled his eyes at him and then gestured for him to follow. "Come on, let's go get behind him."

The two of them went back into the trees and slowly made their way around the glade to just behind where Taxxis was laying on the rock, but by the time they got there, Tenni was already standing by the rock. When she turned around and smiled at them, the boys saw Taxxis in her arms, flexing his back as she petted him.

Somewhat surprised, Sprenger and Soekka pushed their way through the bushes and into the sun.

"How did you do that?" Sprenger asked.

She smirked at him coyly. "A woman's touch."

Doubt it, Sprenger pouted.

"Okay, we have him," Soekka said anxiously. "Let's get back to Master Kanto, and quickly." He turned and headed back into the forest.

"Good job, Tenni," Tenni said mockingly to herself. "We couldn't have done it without you."

Sprenger turned to her and smiled. "You did great Tenni," he said genuinely. "You were definitely team leader today."

She smiled at him. "Thank you Sprenger." She walked past him with a haughty smile. "Remember that for the next mission before you go jumping after things."

They all headed back through the forest, though not at a pace that Soekka would have liked. He often stopped and told them to hurry. Sprenger understood his urgency, he felt it too, but he stayed with Tenni in case she slipped or tripped on a root and Taxxis suddenly decided to make a run for it again. Tenni was clearly becoming irritated since she didn't want to move too quickly with Taxxis and give him a reason to abandon her, but Soekka's insistence pressured them all along faster.

After an agonizingly stressful march through the forest, the trees began to get smaller and denser. One by one, they popped out of the treeline and into the tall grass by the road. With Soekka at the lead, they hurried back towards the looming white wall and into the village.

Once inside the still-open gates, they stopped and frantically looked around for Kanto but couldn't see him.

"He's under that tree over there," a voice called down to them. They all looked up behind them at a guard in one of the towers. He pointed to their right. "Over there," the scythe repeated.

They all yelled their thanks up to him and ran in the direction he pointed. They soon saw Kanto sitting in the shade of a lone tree, an array of different blades spread out around him in the grass. He was carefully cleaning one when he looked up at them as they approached.

Though he was very good at hiding his emotions from his face, Sprenger couldn't help but think that he wasn't expecting them so soon.

"Master Kanto," Soekka yelled as he ran up to him.

"Do you have," Kanto began as Sprenger and Tenni joined Soekka, but he stopped when he looked at Tenni. He gave Taxxis a short stare before returning his attention to them. "Well done," he said not entirely enthusiastically. "Well done indeed." His voice seemed more surprised than impressed.

"Master Kanto," Sprenger began.

"And who," Kanto interrupted, "was the one to catch him?"

"Uh, Tenni," Sprenger quickly answered. "But-,"

"Well done, Tenni." Kanto congratulated in the same stoic voice.

Sprenger threw his head back in frustration. *Why won't anyone listen to me today?*

“Master Kanto,” Soekka said urgently, “something happened in the forest that you need to know about.”

Kanto gave Soekka a questioning stare. “And?” Soekka gave him a quick recap of the events, and Kanto thought about it for a brief moment before responding. “You’re sure they were both from Durado?” he finally asked.

“Well, no,” Sprenger admitted. “The first man was definitely from our prison, but the second man didn’t look like any scythe that I had ever seen. Though he did head off in the direction of the village after he caught the man, which I doubt he would do if he wasn’t a dura-scythe.”

“Not all dura-scythe wear the typical apparel,” Kanto explained. “Some choose their own wears. But even still, we should go to report this to Lord Scythrith in case it does turn out to not be legitimate.” Everyone moved out of his way as he began gathering his blades. Once everything was collected and hidden away in different areas of his vest, he headed past them for the main road. “You may leave Taxxis here, Tenni.”

She gave the cat one last pet and then lightly tossed him to the ground before following along with the boys behind Kanto.

To speak to the Scythrith, one would most often have to seek him at the Rithhold; Durado’s center of important business. Within its wooden walls were the elders, treasuries, council chambers, and of course, the office of the Scythrith. Unlike the roots that originated from it, the Rithhold was an ancient trunk that towered several stories high before abrubptly stopping. No one knew what happened to the ancient tree that was once attached to the giant remnant, but the remaining structure was still the grandest of Durado’s natural buildings. There were windows aplenty caved into the thick bark, and a large balcony where the Scythrith often made important announcements. From various places on the outer wall, the occasional branch grew with small proud leaves, hinting the life that still existed in the structure and the roots that made everyone's homes. Over the entrance of the Rithhold was a large carving of Durado's curved symbol.

The new squad hastily made their way up the road towards the Rithhold, and upon arriving, were stopped by the two scythe guarding the doors.

"What is your business, Master Kanto?" one of them asked.

"My students have just had an encounter with two men in the forest, one of which was wearing the apparel of the prison."

The guards exchanged a brief look with one another. "Very well," the tall one said with a nod.

The entrance opened into a large corridor that only hinted at the vastness of the building within. There were hallways in each direction on the opposite side of the open entrance hall, with staircases growing from the walls to either side, leading up to the offices above. Sunlight bathed the interior from the countless windows around them, but there was a plentiful supply of candles and torches throughout to light the building during the evening or stormy days.

The squad moved through the doors and up the stairs to where Jacob's office was. Sprenger and Soekka had been in the Rithhold more times than they could count growing up. They had played in most of the corridors as children and even found ways of climbing to the roof when they got older. This was unique to them, however, as none of their classmates had ever even been inside. Granny Karla told them that this was because it was a building for important matters, and it was only because of their relationship with Scythrith Jacob that permitted them to spend time here.

Kanto led them up the wooden staircase to the right and onto the second floor, where a long hallway had doors spaced all along its length. Halfway down the hallway was the only door Sprenger and Soekka had ever been through in this hallway. The door to Jacob's office, and the only door worth noting in the entire building. It was hand carved with intricate designs and artwork of fierce creatures and scythe. Jacob once told Sprenger that it told a story, but Sprenger didn't remember most of it.

Without thinking, Sprenger burst through the door. "Hey Old Man, we have to tell you something!"

To Sprenger's regret, it was not just Jacob in the room. A tall, stern man with greying hair and wearing the same apparel as Kanto and all other dura-Scythe was standing in front of Jacob's desk. The scythe turned and glared at Sprenger, who just stood in the doorway.

"The door was closed for a reason, boy," the scythe growled sternly at Sprenger.

Sitting on the other side of the large desk was Jacob, who seemed to be slightly amused by Sprenger's entrance. "Wait just a moment, Sprenger," Jacob said calmly before he returned his attention to the man. Sprenger crossed his arms and leaned up against the wall next to the door to wait until they finished. "Please continue Shoran," Jacob said politely to the scythe, but he was still glaring at Sprenger. Jacob looked over at Sprenger and back at the man. "I seriously doubt it is of any concern if Sprenger hears the rest of your report," Jacob's voice began to sound more authoritative. "Continue, please." The man turned back to face Jacob and continued where Sprenger had interrupted him

"Tranis was the only escapee. All other prisoners were accounted for. Lord Juriah was returning from his travels at the time and noticed Tranis from the canopy. Had he not, we would not have found him in the forest without the hounds."

They're talking about the prisoner in the forest, Sprenger realized excitedly.

Jacob looked down at the papers in front of him. "Aside from the unconscious guard on the wall, there were no casualties with Tranis's escape?" The scythe shook his head. "That was lucky of us, but still very strange. How did Tranis manage to escape with such a small ruckus?" He sat back in his chair and tugged on his pointed gray beard at the end of his chin. "We are very lucky indeed that Juriah found him. Tranis was a gifted spy and renowned for his ability to avoid his opponents." Sprenger looked around the room and pretended not to be listening. "In any case," Jacob said, seeming to move on, "it seems the threat is over. Thank you, captain." Jacob straightened up the papers in front of him and handed them back up to the scythe. "And I want you to personally make sure Juriah gives me his report as well. I do not care if he just returned from his travels."

The man gave a small bow, then turned and walked out of Jacob's office without another word nor glance at Sprenger. As soon as he left, Master Kanto walked in with Tenni and Soekka close behind.

"Where were you guys?" Sprenger whispered to Tenni as he joined them.

"Waiting outside," she snapped in a whisper, "like you should have, you idiot."

Jacob smiled at them as they stood in line in front of his desk. "Now, I hear you have something to tell me?" he said with a hint of amusement to Kanto.

Kanto gave Sprenger a disapproving look after bowing deeply to Jacob. "I apologize for the interruption." He looked back up at Jacob. "We have had an odd occurrence in the forest this morning that I wish to report."

"That seems to be the theme of the morning," Jacob joked. "And from the look on Sprenger's face during the captain's report, I would say our two stories have an overlap."

Sprenger began rubbing the back of his head, embarrassed. "You're not wrong," he admitted.

Kanto, Tenni, and Soekka gave them both confused looks.

"Captain Shoran just finished giving me the details of an escaped prisoner," Jacob explained, "when Sprenger here decided to join us. Though his report is limited to what occurred in the village, so I would greatly appreciate more details of what happened in the forrest." He leaned back in his tall-backed chair. "Please, say what you were going to say."

The boys, for the third time, began telling their story again. Jacob listened silently as each of them spoke.

"Well I have to admire you boys' bravery," Jacob said when they were finished. "You acted like scythe should in that situation. Though I hope it is easier to distinguish friend from foe in the future."

"Who was that man then?" Soekka asked.

Jacob's face darkened a bit. "His name is Juriah. He is indeed a dura-scythe, and certainly not one to be trifled with. He spends a great deal of time away from the village, travelling for various missions. I cannot hold it against you this time since you did not know any better but stay away from that man in the future. He can be dangerous and I do not always trust *his* judgment in those situations either."

"We didn't do that bad in the fight," Sprenger mumbled to himself.

Jacob smiled at him. "No, I'm sure you didn't." Jacob looked around at each of them. "So," he said a bit more questioningly, "did you abandon your assignment to give me this news? I know for a fact what Master Kanto had planned for you today."

"Actually," Kanto answered, "they did not."

Jacob's eyes flashed with genuine surprise, before chuckling deeply to himself and giving his desk a playful slap. "Truly? My word, children. That has never happened before."

"What hasn't?" Tenni asked skeptically.

"Catching Taxxis so quickly," Jacob clarified. Jacob shook his head in disbelief. "Not in all my years has that task been completed before midday, and very rarely by then."

The students all exchanged proud looks.

"Well it was Tenni that actually caught him," Sprenger added.

"Well done, my dear," Jacob whispered with a wink.

Sprenger noticed Tenni beginning to shy away. Not something he was used to seeing her do.

Jacob leaned back in his chair once more with a large grin. "So, not only did you lot set a new record in your first assignment today, but you did it while aiding in the capture of one of Durado's criminals." He chuckled again. "I dare say that this was quite a start to your training as scythe. It makes me eager to see what will come next." The three of them smiled proudly at one another again. Jacob looked up behind them at Kanto, who was standing quietly through it all, and said, “Do you think they’ve earned a meal, Master Kanto?”

The three of them turned around and stared at him eagerly. He gave them an unchanged look. “I have nothing else planned for today. I would say they deserve a reward, assuming that they don’t expect all their missions to go so smoothly.”

Each of them gave a small, silent celebration.

“Well speaking of your first mission,” Jacob said, “I have it here.” He opened one of the drawers to his desk and produced a small scroll, which he handed up to Kanto. “You lot, and all of the other new squads, will be retrieving the patrol reports from the last week and bringing them to me. Master Kanto will give you the details over your meal.”

“Getting reports?” Sprenger whined. “That’s boring.”

“Sprenger,” Kanto snapped. “A scythe does not choose their missions. They accept them without question or complaint.”

Jacob just smiled again. “Don’t worry my boy, someday you will be on missions that are just as daring as you are.”

“Until then,” Kanto added sternly, “be grateful for any mission. Now, all of you thank Lord Scythrith for his time and let’s be off.”

They all gave a deep bow of thanks, which Jacob retuned with a nod, then began to follow Kanto out of his office and into the hallway. Once they closed the door behind them, Kanto stopped and turned to them. “You lot truly should be proud of what you accomplished today,” he said softly. “I think it is safe to trust you with these now.” He reached into the inside of his tan vest and took out three blades.

Sprenger kept it from showing for the most part, but he wanted nothing more than to scream with excitement. *We finally get our blades!*

Kanto handed them each an identical blade. They were a narrow diamond-shape of shimmering silver. The handles were just long enough for a single hand to grasp it before tapering off into a silver spike.

The three of them admired their reflections in the blades after Kanto handed them out. They were brand new, without a single flaw on any of them. They were all used to using extremely old and dull blades in Cerri's class, and they were not permitted to keep them after the sessions, but these were theirs.

"Let me be perfectly clear," Kanto said after letting them admire their blades for a time, "these are tools, not toys. They are never to be used lightly and having one is an honor. Abuse that honor, and you will never be gifted one again." They all nodded their understanding. "You may someday choose to use a different weapon," Kanto continued, "and if so, then you will have to seek out a teacher. But I will teach you to use a scythe's blade, for it is the weapon of choice for most scythe. Take care of them. They will someday mean the difference between life and death."

They all nodded their understanding once more, and Kanto nodded to them.

"Now," Kanto said with a bit softer tone, "let us go celebrate a job well done. My treat." He turned and headed back down the hallway.

Before the three of them followed, they all exchanged excited looks at receiving their new blades.

"Come," Kanto called impatiently from down the stairs.

-<>-

The sun was only an hour or so from setting and the forest was already becoming dark with shadows from the looming trees.

Phenex crouched silently on a giant branch above their hideout, eyeing everything around them. He could see why Durado was so difficult to attack in the last war. There was a perfect view from the canopy of the root-labyrinth below. Intruders would have an extremely difficult time moving around undetected here.

Phenex did one final sweep of the area as far as he could see in the fading light. *He's not coming,* he decided impatiently. That was greatly aggravating to Phenex; He had not approved of this plan from the start, and now his time had been wasted by a cowardly, worthless man.

He dropped to a branch below him, then to the ground before heading back into the hideout. At the bottom of the stone stairs, everyone was waiting patiently and silently. Surprisingly, even Peatra held his tongue in Demaedura's presence. They all looked at Phenex as he emerged from the stairwell, and noticing he was alone, gave individual looks of irritation.

Phenex walked up to Demaedura, who was rereading a small leather journal in his makeshift stone chair. As Phenex approached him, Demaedura did not look up from his reading, but said, "It appears Tranis will not be joining us." Phenex didn't answer, he just stood and waited for whatever was next. He truly hoped it was to abandon Tranis. "No matter," Demaedura said pleasantly. "We will simply have to go and retrieve him ourselves."

That was *not* what Phenex wanted to hear, but he didn't say so aloud.

"Just leave the idiot," Peatra protested. "You already have *that* journal. That's more information than we had to start with." He crossed his arms stubbornly. "Let's just take it and go."

For once, Phenex agreed with Peatra and was glad for someone to voice the complaint.

Demaedura chuckled softly. "Are you nervous being in Durado's forest, Peatra?"

Peatra glared at him. "I don't get nervous."

That was Demaedura's goal, to play on Peatra's arrogance. *Idiot,* Phenex thought angrily, *you completely fell for his taunt.*

"I'm nervous," Grogin admitted in his thunderous voice. Everyone turned and looked at the giant man, surprised by his statement. "We are close to hundreds of dura-scythe," he continued. "Each of us has a large price on our heads from various villages across the land. We should all be nervous."

"Grogin is right," Ajax agreed from in the corner. His dark skin hid him well in the shadows. "Though we are well-hidden and clear of any patrols, our luck will not hold out. Eventually, someone will find us. We cannot stay here much longer. There are bandits running around this forest. We've all seen glimpses of them when we're on watch, and that means the patrol-scythe are probably getting anxious looking for them."

"Then we must empty the forest of the bandits," Demaedura said casually, turning a page in the journal. "If intruders persist for too long within Durado's boarders, then they release their vicious hounds to smell them out. Should that happen, the hounds will also lead them to us."

"But," Hexis interjected, in his eerie voice, "killing the bandits wouldn't do any good if the patrol-scythe didn't know they were dead."

"Plus they would begin searching for the ones responsible," Ajax added from the corner.

Phenex thought a moment. "Not if the patrol-scythe were the ones to find them," he finally said.

"Well they're clearly having some difficulties with that at the moment," Peatra scoffed.

"So we will assist them and move it along faster," Phenex replied. "If we herd the bandits into a patrol..."

Phenex could see Demaedura's lips curl into a larger smile. "They would stop searching," he sneered, "and give us enough time to plan our invasion of Durado." He looked over at Phenex. "Find them," he said flatly to Phenex, "and push them onto the patrol-routes. When they are killed, the dura-scythe will cease their combing of the forest."

"And what are *we* supposed to do?" Peatra grumbled irritably. "We've been in this hole for long enough."

"You will be patient," Demaedura replied simply. "My servants in Durado will supply us until we leave." He rose from his seat. "Make yourselves comfortable," he grinned at them, "we will be here for a while."

Chapter 9

A Simple Assignment

As he woke, Sprenger could see fresh beads of glistening dew clinging to the outside of his window. The moisture fogged the early light as the warm glass fought against the chilled morning air outside. The sight only made him less interested in leaving the comfort of his bed. His stomach made and interesting noise as he laid back lazily and the lurch of his stomach reminded him of their large dinner the night before. The squad's meal yesterday was by no means disappointing, and it showed a very rewarding side to Kanto that Sprenger did not think would be there. He wasn't particularly talkative over the meal, but he spared no expense for food. The students also learned that he was not quick to complement and would quell any boasting as soon as he heard it.

Later that night, Soekka and Sprenger ran into Master Cerri, who took a great deal of interest in hearing about their first assignment. Sprenger made the mistake of mentioning that he was ready for more exciting missions. Cerri, seeing his overconfidence, seemed to worry about Sprenger's intentions. He offered to walk with the boys as they headed home, and used the time to discuss a very disheartening topic with them.

"I've have already trained you to fight well enough to stay alive," he said as though in the middle of one of their lessons, "and I hope that I have given you the strength to do what is right when faced with hard decisions. The hardest one you will have to make is knowing when it is your place to take another's life."

"I don't think you have to worry about that on this mission, Master Cerri," Soekka joked.

Cerri raised a finger to him. “You can never been certain of that. The times that wrong decisions are made are often because the person making the decision is caught off guard. The only way to prevent that is to always expect things to go wrong.” The boys nodded to him. “Now, if you are forced to kill, and I strongly hope you aren’t until you are older, then there is one thing and one thing only that I want you to remember.”

“What’s that?” Sprenger asked.

“Don’t look into their eyes,” Cerri said. “The eyes reveal pain, suffering and life. If you watch them as someone dies, the memory may haunt you. All else you can learn on your own, but this I feel the need to warn you of.”

The boys exchanged apprehensive looks.

“Well hopefully,” Soekka said, “we won’t have need of your advice for a while.”

“I truly hope not,” Cerri agreed. Content with his brief lesson, the old teacher bit them a good night and asked they give his regards to Granny Karla.

Sprenger was slow getting out of bed this morning. He had stayed up most the night thinking about the talk with Cerri the evening before. In addition to his poor night’s sleep, the mission at hand today was not one that drew Sprenger’s motivation. The idea of walking through the forest all day to retrieve reports was not something Sprenger was interested in.

The sun was just starting to illuminate the treetops in sight over the wall. Sprenger groaned inwardly to himself. It was a bit earlier than he needed to get up, but he was restless so he began to prepare for his day with a quick splash of cold water on his face to press the lingering sleep from his mind. He allowed the cold water to dribble down both sides of his slender body before lazily wiping it off. Still not refreshed, he pulled his shirt over his head and began to prepare his pack. He became grouchy with himself for not putting it together the night before while his mind was in a state of unease.

Kanto had told them to pack for a full day's worth of provisions so Sprenger did so, hoping their mission wouldn't really take all day. Downstairs, Granny Karla seemed surprised at his earliness without her persuasion. Since he had time to spare now, Karla asked him to go fetch rolls for him and Soekka before heading to the gate. Sprenger agreed, having nothing better to do, so Karla gave him a few coins and sent him on his way.

The streets of Durado were in their early stages of the day. Carts with goods were being opened and rolled to their normal spots by the streets and doorways were being swept out of shops in roothomes. Sprenger actually enjoyed the early part of the day; it was quieter and more peaceful than the majority of the time. He was rarely awake early enough to experience it, but every once in a while it served to remind him of the tranquil beauty that Durado was capable of.

Sprenger made his way to the bakers, which was already emanating delicious smelling fumes from within. Since Sprenger hated waking up early, he often wondered how early the baker had to wake up in order to have fresh goods ready to sell in the morning. Much like the other shops next to it, the bakcry was carved into a single-story root with several stumps on top spewing white smoke from the ovens within. To keep the heat and smoke to a minimum, the door to the bakery was always open and had clay trays of cooling goods sitting outside.

As he approached the doorway, he could make out a familiar voice within the bakery. Standing at the back counter was Tenni, who was busily asking Sloan the baker about which of the sweet rolls was the best. As Sprenger stepped through the doorway to join her, he nearly tripped when the person standing next to Tenni came into view.

Korran was standing quietly to the side, waiting with a pleasantly warm expression as Tenni fumbled with her order. Sprenger had to take in the sight of her for a moment, since the only thing he recognized on her was her typical headband holding back her dark brown hair. She was wearing a brand-new silk shirt with sleeves that, like Tenni's, didn't extend fully down to her wrists and barely covered her elbows as she stood there cross-armed. Over the new shirt, she had a thin leather vest that was clearly never worn before and so had not been broken in yet, so the fresh leather clung tightly against her. Her bottoms were brand new silk as well, and hung loosely just above her ankles, exposing her leather sandals.

Too busy looking at Korran, Sprenger caught his toe on the doorway as he stepped through. He only barely caught himself from falling on his face by taking several large stumbles into the bakery. Korran turned and looked at Sprenger as he made his ungraceful entrance into the shop. Clearly hearing his stumble as well, Tenni turned around and gave him a curious expression.

"Are you alright?" Tenni asked confused.

Sprenger straightened and gave an awkward smile. "Yah, I'm just a little tired is all."

Tenni was about to say something else, but Sloan interrupted her from behind the counter. "So the glazed buns then?" he asked, trying to finalize Tenni's apparently long-winded order.

"Oh," she said turning around. "Um, I can't quite decide," she continued to ask about all the different types that Sloan had to offer.

Sprenger walked up to Korran, who gave him a warm, if not sympathetic, smile.

"New clothes?" Sprenger asked casually, hoping his cheeks were not red.

Korran nodded. "My parents got them for me as a graduation gift. What do you think?"

"You look like a scythe," Sprenger answered, trying to keep his mouth shut beyond that.

She smiled at him again. "Well thank you. That is the hope after all."

"So you guys been here long?" he asked, to draw out conversation.

Korran smirked at Tenni, who was busy examining a basket of honey glaze rolls. "I guess you could say that."

Tenni turned to her. "Well I can't decide which are the best," she defended.

Korran just snorted a small giggle, then looked back at Sprenger. "So where's Soekka?"

Sprenger shrugged. "At home still, probably. I was up early today so Granny Karla sent me to get some rolls."

"Don't bother," Tenni said as she bent over and examined another basket of sweet rolls, "my parents are buying a batch for us as a 'good luck' gesture for our first mission."

"That's nice of them," Sprenger said, but Tenni didn't seem to really be listening anymore.

She popped up excitedly. "These ones," she said, pointing to the basket she was just examining. Sloan gladly took them away and began stacking them into a square basket and then wrapping it all in a cloth.

Tenni placed several coins on the counter and gratefully took the cloth of rolls from him.

'Finally' Korran mouthed to Sprenger, who smiled at her.

The three of them exited the shop and casually headed down the road towards the gate.

"So where are you headed Korran?" Sprenger asked, trying to spark conversation again.

"I have a mission today, same as you guys," she said pleasantly. "It's just our two squads leaving this early. I heard Master Tarak doesn't like doing things too early in the day." Now Sprenger wished he was assigned to Tarak instead. Not really thinking it through, Sprenger asked what their mission was. Korran gave him an amused look while Tenni gave a slight sigh. "The same as yours. Tenni said you didn't pay attention when Master Kanto explained things." She gave him a friendly smile. "Your squad is headed to the southern patrol base, while mine is headed to the northern one."

"Oh, that's right." Sprenger shrugged as if it were of no consequence. "The mission is just so boring I didn't take the time to remember details." Tenni gave a disapproving grunt but Sprenger ignored her.

The two of them continued making pleasant conversation that Tenni rarely made comments on, and continued on their way to the village gates. For once, Sprenger wanted the distance to the gates to be farther away, so he could keep talking to Korran, but without fail, their destination appeared.

Kanto stood near the tall wooden doors of the front gate, wearing his usual apparel and unreadable expression. Next to him, a good deal taller and bulkier, stood Master Kobei, wearing the same apparel as Kanto, and most Dura-scythe, but a far different expression. While Kanto stood with his arms crossed, watching vigilantly from under his brow, Kobei stood with his hands in his pockets while looking down his nose at everyone. The way he was standing made him look like he was trying to appear taller, but all it did was make him look rather amusing to Sprenger.

When they reached the gates they gave each of their masters a respective bow, and continued talking amongst themselves. They were the first to arrive, but after a short time Soekka joined them. He handed Sprenger his pack and gave him a look that reminded Sprenger that he was supposed to return with rolls before going to the gates. Sprenger took the pack and smiled awkwardly at him. The four of them stood with the masters and talked casually as they waited for others to arrive.

It was several more minutes before Caymen joined the group, but as usual, he stood silently by himself. Caymen was not particularly friendly, and was renowned for focusing more on his training than on making friends. He often voiced his disapproval of Soekka and Sprenger's lack of discipline, but could never manage to best them in training, which only made him all the more bitter towards them.

Sprenger began getting anxious after a while and asked Kanto when they could begin.

Kanto shot Kobei an annoyed glare. "When all of us are here." Kobei did not notice Kanto's comment, and continued to absentmindedly look down his nose at everyone walking by.

A short time later, Rejeno strolled up, not looking entirely awake, and gave each master a respective bow.

Kanto ignored him and looked over to Kobei. "If there are no more members of your squad that we must wait for, then I would like to finally begin."

Rejeno slunk to the back of the waiting group, his face turning red with embarrassment.

Kobei gave him an undeterred smile. "Of course. I am ready whenever you are."

Kanto gave a heavy sigh. "All right, listen up!" Those around Sprenger that hadn't already, immediately straightened their backs. They clearly weren't used to Kanto's demanding personality. Master Kobei didn't strike Sprenger as the type of teacher that put much energy into the discipline of his students. "We have been given the task of retrieving the week's reports from the northern and the southern patrol bases. This will be the first time for both squads to go as far as our borders, so make sure you don't forget your training." He raised his finger. "Stay vigilant at all times-"

"That's right," Kobei interrupted, "there could be bandits in our woods. There have been sightings of them of late." Suddenly Sprenger felt more excited to begin. The group became a flurry of excited whispers.

Kanto continued his irritated glare at Kobei out the corners of his eyes. "Yes, but should there be any encounters, Master Kobei and myself will handle them. You are not to engage them unless forced to. Remember, your training has only just begun. You will not see combat for a long while yet." The group all gave eager and frantic nods of confirmation, still clearly more interested in the thought of encountering bandits. "All right then." Kanto turned on his heels and led them all through the gates and into the shadows of the looming trees to each side of the worn dirt road.

"This is where our squads separate," Kanto said almost anxiously. "We will meet your squad back here, Kobei, when you've finished your part."

"Of course, Kanto." Kobei gave an indifferent wave of his hand. "I remember. We will see you in late afternoon if all goes well." Kobei continued by giving his students a quick review of some of their training, but Kanto gestured to Soekka, Sprenger, and Tenni to follow him. Sprenger and Tenni gave a silent wave to Korran and followed Kanto along the side of Durado's massive wall. The grass wasn't particularly high here, about an inch or two above Sprenger's ankle, but it was the absence of trees that made this twenty feet of surrounding land unique.

If there were ever young saplings found growing within a certain radius of the wall, they were immediately removed. Jacob once told Sprenger that it was one of the most important jobs in the village: tearing up new trees, as well as keeping the larger ones trimmed back from the walls. By keeping the looming branches away from the wall, it prevented unwelcome scythe from entering the village undetected. Younger trees and bushes needed to be cleared early, so as not to hinder scythe doing patrols on the outside of the wall.

The group followed Kanto single file, all the way around to the back of the village. Once there, Kanto led them through the trees to a path that resembled a large game trail. On Kanto's word, Sprenger and Tenni dropped back and walked to either side of Soekka, who walked directly behind Kanto.

"This would be the formation we would use if we were escorting someone," Kanto explained. "Sprenger, Tenni, you watch the side of thc path that you are on. Soekka, you continue watching both sides, and I'll keep watch ahead of us."

Sprenger didn't see much point actually looking around. The borders of the forest were well-guarded and trespassers were usually expunged quickly.

The surrounding towns and cities all turned their criminal announcements to Durado and paid nicely for certain outlaws. Other scythe villages also gave portraits and information on scythe that had either been banished or left unlawfully. These rogue-scythe were killed on sight when found within the borders of another scythe village. Bandits often tried to hide from soldiers in the woods, but never were seen as much of a threat since they were rarely trained fighters. Another scythe, however, especially a rouge-master-scythe, was cause for carefully laid out plans of attack and much worry. Depending on their skill, a master-scythe could do a great deal of harm before they are finally brought down. Luckily, such incidences were very rare.

Sprenger tried to entertain himself by twirling his blade through his fingers, but a look of warning from Kanto forced him to put it away. Kanto told them to keep all talking to a minimum, so not to inform any unwanted ears about their presence. *Another paranoid precaution,* Sprenger thought. If there was one thing Sprenger was not good at, it was keeping quiet. He hated silence between people and would always try to fill it with some conversation. It was something that Soekka hated, as he preferred to be left alone rather than speak with other people.

Sprenger watched the various animals as they made slow progress over the roots and around the trees. Occasionally, they would walk through an area where the sun was breaking through the canopy, and and the warmth made Sprenger long for the mission to be over so he could sit out in the sun.

After four hours of nonstop walking, they finally reached their destination. A square stone building, which looked only large enough to be a single room, stood in a sunny clearing. It had few windows, enough for someone Sprenger's size to squeeze through, but certainly not an adult.

Standing atop the flat roof were two cross-armed scythe standing back to back, each watching the opposite direction. The one facing them watched the group warily as they approached. Undeterred by the guard, Kanto continued forward without an upward glance. Sprenger assumed that if they were not expected, they would have been stopped.

Inside the building it was dim and cool. The watch warden sat behind a wooden desk that was loaded with many piles of papers. He continued to scribble vigorously onto a piece of paper as the group entered and didn't raise his head but said "Master Kanto and his new team." They were expected or they would have been stopped before ever getting the chance to enter the building. "Please wait a moment. I need to finish writing these reports so I can send them with you." He didn't look up from his work as they approached his desk but said, "Master Kanto, and his new team," without any doubt in his voice. "If you would be so kind as to wait a moment. I need to finish writing these reports before I send them with you."

Kanto politely held up his hand to halt his explanation. "Please take your time, Commander Reise. We are in no particular rush, and I would prefer to wait a minute or two, rather than have the reports not be as thorough as possible."

Commander Reise allowed himself a small smirk as he worked. "Not much to report I'm afraid. A few footprints the other day is the most to rcport this week. But I wouldn't let your guard down in the least. We have yet to find the trespassers."

"Really?" Sprenger asked excitedly. Kanto let out a small, annoyed sigh.

The man gave a dismissive wave of his hand. "Nothing more than a group of runaways or bandits. Nothing to concern yourselves with. But they keep moving, making it hard to find them. Soon I'll have to call in some hounds from the village."

Sprenger pitied any man that would get caught by the hounds of Durado, bandit or not. The hounds were vicious when they were loosed to hunt intruders. They had been known to leave such carnage that the number of men killed would be difficult to determine from the remains.

"I do appreciate your patience," the man continued politely. "Perhaps your students would like to see more of the base while you wait?" Sprenger found it hard to believe there was more than what could be seen with a half rotation of his head. Kanto agreed that a tour would be a good use of their time.

Soekka skeptically raised an eyebrow, "How much more is there to see?"

"Well, for example," Kanto walked behind them to the corner of the building and lifted up a trap door. None of them even noticed it was there. The trap door itself was roughly the size of a table but in the dim lighting looked nothing more than a weathered corner of the stone floor.

Underneath the door was a steep staircase of stone steps. Kanto held out his arm in invitation. "Shall we?"

At the bottom of the stairwell, the group entered a surprisingly well-lit room. Torchlight flickered off the stone walls of the square chamber. Three doors, one to each wall with the exception of the wall beneath the stairs leading down, told Sprenger that this patrol base expanded further still. They all followed wide-eyed as Kanto moved to the first door.

"The whole purpose of a patrol base is to have a meeting point for the scythe patrolling our borders," Kanto explained. "Since the village is too far to run from our borders, scythe need a place in which they can quickly deliver reports and rest. Since a scythe assigned to patrol may have to be here for long periods of time," he yanked a torch from its place in the wall and opened the first door, "they may desire to train to keep their abilities honed." He held the torch up and stepped inside to allow the three of them to enter the room.

Under Kanto's torchlight, Sprenger could see a sparring circle on the ground in the center of the room and to the far walls were targets for blade throwing. They were so heavily used that Sprenger could hardly see any remnants of the painted circles. Across from them were four sparring dummies, two of which had extensive cracking down the middles. A sharp kick seemed to be all that would be necessary to snap the dummy completely.

The smell of the room was all too prominent of a feature as well. The thick musky sent of sweat and body odor caused Sprenger to hold his breath for short times before taking a quick gulp of air through his mouth.

Tenni put a hand over her nose and mouth. "Charming," she murmured as best she could from under her hand. "No wonder the sparring grounds in the village are outside." When Kanto gestured to do so, the group gladly walked back through the doorway. Kanto replaced the torch on the wall and moved to the opposite wall. The group took a collective sigh of fresh air as they reentered the open room.

Kanto pushed the second door open to reveal an already illuminated room. On the walls were shelves of scrolls and books, cramped to the max in most cases. In the center of the room, a large wood table held nothing but a huge map spread across the top, covering the entire surface. On the map, Sprenger could see miniature replicas of patrol bases in each of the four directions, as well as a miniature version of Durado at its center. Looming over the map were two scythe. Each bowed their heads as Kanto entered the room.

"Master Kanto," a well-groomed man greeted politely from across the table.

"Please, continue about what you are doing," Kanto said casually. "I was just giving my students a tour of their first patrol base."

The scythe nodded understandingly and returned to their spots at the map and continued their conversation while pointing out places in the forest.

Kanto lowered his voice and bent down to the group's level, so not to disrupt the two men's conversation. "This room is used to hold significant reports, as well as to discuss patrol reports or defensive strategies should the village ever be threatened. The patrol routes change at random times, and the routes themselves are closely guarded secrets. This way, an enemy scythe in our village cannot simply watch our patrol cycles and learn to avoid them." Kanto rose to his full height and said, "Come, let's leave them to their work."

Once Kanto and the team moved back into the center of the main room, he informed them that the third area is the living quarters including a dining area. "We won't go into it, as it is likely someone is resting, but it is the largest section of the patrol base. There are near fifty bunk beds for scythe to be garrisoned if needed."

Sprenger stared at the wooden door. "Why so many beds?"

"The forest is vast and the village is not always a convenient distance from where scythe are needed. Scythriths of the past have had to defend against armies from multiple fronts in the Ancient Forest and those scythe needed a place to recover after long battles with soldiers."

Soekka was rotating his head, looking in every direction, examining the underground room. "Who would be stupid enough to attack a scythe village with soldiers?"

Kanto gave a humorless snort. "You lot have not known a time of chaos like that." The three of them ceased their curious stares and looked at Kanto. "There was a time when this land knew nothing but war. Soldiers against scythe, and scythe against other scythe. No one believed peace was even possible until a treaty was finally agreed upon." Kanto stared at the back wall, lost in thought.

"What ended the fighting?" Tenni asked shyly.

Kanto returned his attention to them, as if he forgot they were there. "That is a story that is too long to tell in the time we have left to finish our mission. Come," he beckoned with his hand for them to follow. "Let's see if those reports are ready for us."

The group headed back up the stairs and emerged into the cramped study. Sprenger, Soekka, and Tenni returned to their original spots in front of the desk, while Kanto closed the trapdoor.

Commander Reise ceased his frantic scribbling and looked up at them for the first time since they had arrived. He had a kind smile on his face as he asked, "Did you enjoy the tour?" The students each gave him an amused nod. "Good, I'm glad." He grabbed a small scroll and envelope from the side of his desk and reached across to hand it to Sprenger. "Here are your reports. Apologies for the delay."

Sprenger gave his thanks and took the reports. Both the envelope and the scroll were sealed with black wax, bearing the symbol of Durado. Sprenger looked up at Kanto, not sure what to do with the reports, but Kanto did not say anything so Sprenger put them in his own pack. Kanto thanked the man again and led the group back through the door and into the open air.

Kanto gave them the option of eating their lunch at the base or in the forest. They agreed on eating at the base to enjoy the nice day, and to avoid the bugs in the shade of the trees. They found a spot and sat on the ground in a circle. Tenni pulled her loose braid over her shoulder and nervously stroked it before sitting. A habit, Sprenger noticed, she did when she was uncomfortable with something.

Kanto pulled a square piece of leather out of his pack and placed it in the middle of the circle. A bit larger than a doormat, the brown leather was just large enough for the four of them to spread out the food they brought for the trip.

Sprenger unloaded his four apples and pile of jerky Granny Karla had wrapped in a cloth. Soekka had identical jerky, but also unwrapped a respectable pile of rice patties that Granny must have been in the process of making when Sprenger left for the rolls.

Kanto untied several pouches of dried fruits and placed them in the center. Sprenger could see apples and grapes, but there were two more pouches that he couldn't see into. Tenni unloaded a large bag of baked goods. The sweet buns, covered with honey and sugar, looked particularly good to Sprenger.

Each eagerly started taking mouthfuls of food, offering what they brought to others, as well as requesting a sample of something another had brought.

It was a quick and satisfying meal break, and Sprenger reluctantly prepared to leave when Kanto said it was time to be off. After having a sample of rest, Sprenger's legs protested at beginning another long walk, but he silently complied and took his place next to Tenni in the formation. *Can't we just walk in a line?* Sprenger pouted to himself. *It's not as though we're going to see anyone anyway.*

-<>-

Phenex felt the snap of the man's neck in the crook of his arm, so he released his hold and allowed the body to fall to the ground. This body added to the four already lying at his feet.

Phenex crouched as the yelling man behind him attacked, and as he ducked, a club sailed over his head. Using the man's shadow as his guide, Phenex knocked the man's feet out from under him with a swing of his arm, and before the man had even hit the ground, brought his flail's heavy end down on the back of his head, slamming him into the dirt.

Idiots, he thought, unimpressed. *It makes it easier to keep track of where you are if you're always yelling before you attack.*

Phenex eyed the monstrous trees around him. The majority of the group fled over the twisting roots instead of fighting. *Cowards. But you did what you were supposed to do.* With a quick dash, Phenex scaled a root and ascended the nearest tree. He would have to drive them into a patrol squad somehow and remain hidden himself. Just killing them all would do no good.

He almost hoped Tranis was lying about having information. *Just so I have an excuse to kill him for this trouble,* he thought as he jumped to a larger branch.

Chapter 10

An Unexpected Encounter

After leaving the sunny area around the patrol base, the shade of the trees felt refreshingly cool and caused Sprenger to notice he was covered in a glaze of sweat from sitting out in the sun.

Though Sprenger never wanted anything more than to be a scythe, and he knew that could only be accomplished by completing missions, this was a mission he wanted to be done with. He was becoming bored with it all, and it was only their first mission. Sprenger hoped this was not the extent of what their years of training added up to. Walking through the forest, gathering reports, staying quiet all day, it was all a bore. Sprenger imagined a much more exciting life as a scythe. One with adventure and dangerous missions. Things he could be proud to say he accomplished. He caught himself wondering if the Old Man would give them more exciting missions if Sprenger asked. Jacob gave them gifts as children, so Sprenger did not see why missions couldn't be considered the same.

These thoughts continued even once they were back on the trail, surrounded by massive trees and their giant roots. Kanto instructed them to reform the escort formation that he taught them on the way over. Soekka again took the lead of the squad. Sprenger thought about asking why they couldn't change the order but thought better of it.

Again, they were discouraged from talking and told to watch their assigned directions. Sprenger didn't put more effort into watching the trees than counting birds and squirrels lazily in his head. After he lost count for the third time, he just let his mind wander while he looked to be attentively scanning the tree line.

Without warning, Kanto stopped so abruptly that the three of them had to use each other for support to keep form running into him.

Soekka pulled his arm from Tenni's grip, which she used to balance herself after nearly colliding with Kanto. "What's wrong?" Soekka asked, more irritated than worried. "Why are we stop-"

Kanto shushed them and held up a hand to exaggerate his command of silence. He sharply eyed the brambles of bushes and heavy roots to their right. "Do you hear that?" he whispered.

Sprenger strained his ears but couldn't make out anything distinct. Then he heard it. Then another. Twigs were snapping just beyond the path and getting louder. Someone was running towards them.

Sprenger felt his heart beginning to race, whether out of fear or excitement, he didn't know. The snapping twigs became louder and greater in number. The huge trees around them made it difficult to see far into the forest. Each tree was as wide as a house, and anyone could be behind them and not be seen until they were right on the trail.

Kanto stepped in front of them and dropped his narrow diamond-shaped blade from his sleeve. "Get ready guys," he said softly to them. "Stay behind me, remember your training, and stay calm."

The three of them each dropped their blades from their sleeves, and huddled back to back, blades raised just under their eye-line, each watching a different direction.

"Couldn't it just be a patrol squad?" Tenni whispered hopefully, though Sprenger thought she already knew the answer.

"No, they're coming straight over the roots," Kanto answered in a hushed voice, without taking his eyes off the trees in front of him. "A patrol squad would have paths to follow in the canopy. They would have no need to use paths on the forest floor." He slowly raised his blade to just below his chin in preparation. "There's more than a squad, too. Get ready."

Tenni resumed her readied stance and watched down the trail in the direction they were headed, while Sprenger watched where they had come from. Soekka stood between them, facing where the intruders were making the most noise, like Kanto.

Everyone's heads turned as a series of shuffling steps echoed not far in front of them. More soon followed. They grew louder, until they were less than ten feet away.

The three of them tensed as a bald man in basic traveling clothes came running around the nearest tree. Before the man had realized they were there, Kanto jumped forward and drilled his fist into the man's gut, stopping him abruptly. Kanto swung his leg, kicking the man across the face and sending him flying backwards. He fell at the feet of ten more men, who slid to a halt as best they could before tripping over their comrade. All of them were wearing basic garbs, some with leather caps, others with thin cloth covering their mouth and nose.

Bandits, Sprenger realized.

Kanto glared at the group of winded, filthy men. "You are intruders in Durado's territory," he announced. "Go back to where you came from. You can have no refuge in our forest. Leave or die."

The group then looked behind them as if considering their chances of retreating back the way they came. Apparently deciding against it, they turned their attention back to Kanto.

The first man to come from the trees slowly stood, while rubbing his jaw where Kanto kicked him. "More scythe," he grumbled.

More scythe? Sprenger thought. *What does that mean? Maybe a patrol squad is already following them.*

The bald man looked back the way they came, as the others had, but he too decided against whatever retreat they were hoping for. “Aright boys. It’s either them or him.” He pulled a knife from his belt and ran with an inspired shout at Kanto.

Kanto twirled his blade through his fingers to regrip it. The man raised his knife to stab Kanto, but before he could bring it down, Kanto swung faster than the man had time to react to. His eyes went wide as his throat emptied of blood, and he fell to the ground.

Others drew their weapons and repeated the bald man’s actions, yelling wildly as they ran at Kanto. Kanto killed two before they even brought their weapons down. The next two forced him to avoid their swinging weapons and knock them back with a knee and a kick. Not a single man exchanged blows with Kanto for long. They either missed their attack or died in the effort.

In a short time, there were six bodies at Kanto’s feet. While Kanto was moving around the frantic swings of a man’s club and another’s sword, the three remaining bandits turned their attention to the three students. Sprenger’s grip tightened on his blade and a knot formed in his stomach.

Tenni threw her blade over Soekka’s head and hit the middle man in his left shoulder, dropping him to a knee in pain. Now without a weapon, Tenni moved to stand behind Sprenger and Soekka, who crouched at the ready in front of her.

The two remaining bandits raised their weapons; one a very dull sword, the other some sort of hooked farming tool. As they brought them down, Soekka parried the sword to the side and ran his blade under the man’s sternum. Sprenger stopped the hooked weapon with his blade and when they pulled their weapons apart, he thrust it into the man's gut. Without a moment's hesitation, Tenni punched the man with the sword in the nose, causing blood to spill onto Soekka's arm. Then she turned to Sprenger's assailant and struck him so hard in the jaw that Sprenger saw it pop out of place. The two men fell backwards, and as soon as they hit the ground, Sprenger and Soekka leapt on top of them and thrust their blades into each man's heart, ensuring they would not make a final effort to keep fighting. Sprenger made sure to avoid looking at the man's eyes as Cerri had explained to him, and he hoped Soekka remembered the same.

Both breathing heavily, Sprenger and Soekka looked at each other from atop their victories. Sprenger forced a smirk through his shaken nerves, which Soekka returned. Soekka raised a bent arm and fist, which Sprenger mirrored, and the two knocked the sides of their fists and forearms together as a silent congratulation.

Soekka looked over his shoulder. "You alright Tenni?"

Tenni was squeezing her right hand. The skin was torn off one of the knuckles and was bleeding slightly. Her fingers were twitching, as if in pain. "I'm fine," she panted, "just caught that last one's tooth a bit." She forced a smile at them. "I think we did pretty good." The boys smiled back at her.

Sprenger looked over to where Kanto had been finishing the last two bandits, but Kanto was already walking towards them. He held out his hand to Tenni. "Let me see what damage is done, Tenni." She slowly and gently placed her hand in his and flinched when he pulled it closer for a look. After a few moments of looking over the entire area of her hand, he released it with a sigh. "I don't think you broke any bones, but you certainly jammed some fingers. Though it sufficed this time, I would not recommend being so blunt in future fights. I can tell we need to spend more time on weaponless combat."

Tenni gave a shy nod. "Sorry, Master Kanto. I was not thinking. I should not have been so reckless in my actions." Kanto grunted his agreement.

"And you two," Kanto said to Sprenger and Soekka. "I never want to see you celebrating a death again."

"Yes, Master Kanto," the boys said together. Sprenger and Soekka pushed themselves up from the two bodies they had been crouching over. Kanto was clearly not going to grant any of them praise, so at the very least they wouldn't give him a reason to scorn them further. They moved to stand next to Tenni as Kanto bandaged her hand.

Then, Sprenger saw something move in the corner of his eye. The bandit Tenni had hit in the shoulder with her blade had yanked it free and was pushing himself to his feet. Before Sprenger could turn, the man started running.

"Hey!" Sprenger shouted at him, causing everyone to jump. Sprenger started off after the man before Kanto could grab and stop him. Sprenger could hear Kanto calling after him, but Sprenger would be ashamed to tell Jacob that he had let one bandit escape. Sprenger jumped over bushes, and darted over the intricate roots and low branches of the trees, following the trail of broken soil the bandit left behind. The trees began to widen, and soon their roots were larger than streams. Only the occasional footprint in the dirt showed which way Sprenger's chase should take him.

A short, deep scream brought Sprenger to a halt. He waited for a moment but heard nothing more. *The man must've tripped and fallen,* Sprenger decided. He continued following the trail, sensing his opportunity to close the gap between him and the bandit.

Suddenly, Sprenger caught himself on a branch as his foot hit something. It was a pair of boots sticking out from behind twirling roots of the tree next to him. As he peered around the trunk, he saw the bandit looking wide-eyed at the canopy, dead. His chest was horribly smashed and bloody. A chill ran up Sprenger's back, causing the hairs on the back of his neck to prickle. Sprenger could make out the slight sound of the chain rattling, then Sprenger ducked as bark and wood erupted all around him. He couldn't stop a small yell from escaping his mouth.

He heard the chain clicking above his head before it was pulled back in a second shower of bark and splinters. Heart racing, Sprenger looked over the root that was concealing him. Not ten feet away stood a man with dark, unruly hair, wearing a loose black cloak. In a swift metallic swirl, the chain wrapped around his body for another attack. A large silver end-piece came closer and closer with every twirl, before the man readily snatched it from the air. Several shiny loops of chain now hung over his left shoulder and under his right arm. In his right hand, Sprenger could see the end-piece: four bladed pillars held a metallic sphere in their middle before coming together into a sharp, pointed end.

"You will have no honor hiding like a coward." The man's voice was calm but harsh. "Face me as a man should."

Sprenger quickly realized that the man must think he's a bandit. *He must be a patrol scythe,*

Sprenger thought hopefully. Sprenger slowly stood, but he had a gripping nausea in his stomach that would not dissipate, no matter the number of times he told himself that this was a scythe looking for bandits, and that he had nothing to worry about.

The man gave him a curious look as Sprenger emerged from behind the root that was concealing him. A shiny white scar was now visible on his face, running from his left temple to under his chin. He didn't say anything at first; he just eyed Sprenger with emotionless curiosity.

Sprenger tried to swallow the lump in his throat when the man finally spoke. "No wonder I missed. If your head stood a bit higher from the ground..." He let his voice trail off. He made his point, there was no need to finish that sentence.

Before Sprenger could say anything in response, the chain began uncoiling once more. An arm reached around Sprenger's chest and pulled him over backwards as the flail went soaring over his face. Sprenger recognized the arm around him as Kanto's, but before he could not say or do anything before the end-piece was above them, hurling down. Kanto rolled them over before it landed, smashing the root where they just laid.

Still clutching Sprenger around the chest, Kanto sat up and threw three throwing blades at the man, who slid to the side, readily avoiding them. With a strong pull and a burst of splinters, the man yanked his flail free of the ground and remnants of the tree root.

Kanto, still holding Sprenger, stood and threw himself behind the nearest tree. Finally, he released Sprenger. "Stay here," he ordered quickly. Sprenger nodded, not trusting his mouth to speak.

Kanto pulled six throwing blades out of his vest and held three in each hand. He drew a deep breath, then threw himself out from behind the tree and loosed one hand of blades, then the other. Sprenger quickly peered around the tree with one eye.

The cloaked scythe was now slowly twirling himself around, intricately pulling his flail all around him protectively. The chain was spiraling all around him like a metal tornado. Kanto's knives were harmlessly knocked down by the twirling chain, each clanking as they hit before falling to the ground. Kanto drew a sparring blade instead readied himself.

With a midair spin, the man flung the flail straight at Kanto, who leaned to the side, allowing the end-piece to pass by his chest. With a yank, the man pulled it back and with another spin and sent it hurling back again, this time far faster. Kanto again tried to dodge it, but it clipped his shoulder, leaving a thin, bloody gash.

Kanto grimaced, but didn't falter. Instead of waiting this time, he ran towards the man, blade in hand. The cloaked man again began intricate spins and twirls commanding the chain around him into a swirling vortex of metal, forcing Kanto back again. Then, the flail's heavy end came whirling around and narrowly avoided colliding with Kanto, forcing him backwards. Once far enough back, the man sent the end-piece hurling down on Kanto who barely avoided it again. Kanto suddenly slammed his blade through the chain, pinning it to the ground through one of its links, yanked another blade from his vest, and ran for the man again.

Using the chain in his hands, the cloaked scythe blocked all of Kanto's assaults. Kanto kicked and swung, and finally struck the man in the chest with his foot. Before Kanto could strike again, the man gave a quick spin and pulled his chain free from the blade holding it to the ground. Another spin and the end piece came around, smashing into Kanto's ribs. Kanto gritted his teeth in pain but still managed to kick the scythe away again. As the scythe faltered from the kick, Kanto nimbly threw himself back in three handsprings clutching his bloody side with one hand. He once again stood next to the tree Sprenger hid behind, breathing heavily, and holding his bloodied ribs.

Kanto squared off with the cloaked scythe across the way, who was watching him wearily, casually twirling his mace next to him. There was a pause as the scythe prepared for another bout, both waiting for the other to move first.

Suddenly, Sprenger could hear someone yelling at them. Tenni and Soekka were not far behind calling his and Kanto's names, but Sprenger didn't dare call back.

The cloaked man gave an irritated grimace at Tenni and Soekka's calls. Then, with a quick swing of his arm, sent the chain wrapping back around his body, before snatching the end-piece from the air. He bolted to a tree behind him and hopped from one low branch to another until he was near the top. A quick leap to another tree and he was gone.

Chapter 11

Interrogation

Sprenger remained frozen in disbelief behind the tree. He stood transfixed, watching the canopy where the cloaked scythe disappeared. He could hear Kanto breathing hard next to him, also not willing to look away from the spot the man was last seen.

"Master Kanto." Tenni came bursting through the bushes shortly followed by Soekka. Each was carrying either Kanto or Sprenger's packs in addition to their own. As they freed themselves from the underbrush, Tenni's eyes immediately were drawn to Kanto's bloodstained side. "What happened?" She gasped.

Neither Kanto nor Sprenger answered. They both continued watching the canopy for any other sign of their assailant.

Finally, Kanto let out a reserved breath, then looked over his shoulder at Tenni. "If you would be so kind, Tenni, retrieve some bandages from my pack, and keep your voice down."

Tenni looked shocked at first, then gave a nervous nod and began rummaging through Kanto's pack.

Soekka stepped past her, towards Sprenger. "Sprenger, what happened?" he whispered nervously. Sprenger heard Soekka's words but couldn't wrap his tongue around the answer to give him. Soekka leaned in closer. "Was it the bandit?" Soekka pressed. "What happened?"

Sprenger's mind suddenly flashed with the events of the last few minutes. He shook away the shock of what he had just seen and just let everything come out. "No, it was a scythe!" he finally blurted. Soekka recoiled from Sprenger with wide eyes.

Sprenger finally found his voice and now he couldn't seem to contain it. "I chased the bandit, but he was dead." He pointed to where the man's body lay on the other side of Kanto. "The scythe killed him! Then he attacked us! I've never seen a weapon like that. It had a long chain, and Kanto couldn't hit him because-"

Soekka grabbed him by the shoulders. "It's okay, Sprenger. Relax, get your head together first. You're fine." He tried to force a comforting smile but there was no mistake, Soekka was scared.

After some assistance from Tenni, Kanto gently held his freshly bandaged side as he grabbed his pack from the ground. "We need to get back to the village, and quickly. Lord Scythrith must be told about this as soon as possible."

Soekka pulled Sprenger's pack over his shoulder and held it out to him, which Sprenger took with a small nod of thanks. Before any of them had time to respond, Kanto began climbing and hopping among the roots. Soekka waited for Sprenger to pass before following Kanto.

They were not running, but Kanto still set a difficult pace to follow in the intricate roots of the towering trees. In a short time, they were back on one of the trails to Durado. Kanto did not stop, but rather increased his speed.

Tenni waited for Soekka and Sprenger to catch up to her. "Do you want front, Soekka?"

"No, I'm going to stay next to Sprenger."

Tenni gave an understanding nod and ran off to catch up with Kanto, who was already waiting a distance ahead of them. Though Sprenger didn't acknowledge it, he felt a warm wave of relief to have Soekka close. The two of them set off after Tenni, and when they reached Kanto, he gave them no chance to stop before he took off at a swift pace.

The distance and Kanto's breakneck pace seemed to take an eternity to overcome, but finally they entered an area Sprenger recognized. They were not far from Durado. After about an hour of running, Sprenger's legs were burning, and toes constantly dragged on the ground or threatened to catch on any rocks or roots they passed. They felt as though at any step, they would give way beneath him. Throughout the whole time, Soekka rarely took his eyes from Sprenger. Sprenger pretended not to notice it, but anytime Sprenger would falter, even for a moment, Soekka's eyes returned and stayed on him for a long time afterwards.

Tenni was having a hard time as well, but just when Sprenger thought she was going to have them stop, she would increase her speed and push forward even harder.

Kanto periodically looked behind him to make sure they were all still there, and only slowed his pace when the distance between them had grown too large to ignore.

The trees around them gradually began narrowing their path, until they were forced into a single-file line, Sprenger following Tenni, and Soekka him.

Sprenger almost hoped that the brush hiding the trail from view would force Kanto to halt, or at least slow him enough to allow the group a moment of reprieve. They didn't.

Kanto hardly missed a stride as he barreled into the final obstacle of bushes. Tenni was nearly slowed to a stop by the branches, but with a helpful push from the boys, she forced her way through. They shortly followed, but not before a coiled branch Tenni was holding out of their way snapped Sprenger across his nose. Soekka had to place a bracing hand between his shoulder blades to keep them from stumbling backwards. Through the pain, Sprenger could feel beads of blood mixing with beads of sweat on his cheek. He swore silently and forced himself forwards into the comforting shadow of Durado's wall.

They had no chance to appreciate being free of the forest at last, however. Kanto was already yelling from several feet away to not slow yet.

Once again, the three of them took off after their teacher, and once again, he did not wait. Sprenger forced himself with all his might to catch up with Kanto and Tenni, but the effort nearly caused him to stumble to the ground. Luckily, he managed to find his footing before he fell and closed the distance between them.

The open gates quickly came into view around the walls bend, a sight Sprenger could have wept with joy at seeing again. The scythe posted at the gates quickly moved out of Kanto's way, lest they be trampled by him. One began to run beside him asking for orders. Kanto sent him off to close the gates as well as to double the wall patrol, all without slowing a step. The man veered away to ensure the orders were fulfilled.

Onlookers crammed to the side of the road to make room for them. Parents pulled children from their path. No one needed explanation to make way for a batennin in a hurry. Kanto called to unaware villagers to clear the way, who quickly did so.

Anxiety built as the Rithhold came into view. They were close to being able to stop. Sensing the urgency, the guards quickly opened the doors to allow Kanto and his squad in, and Kanto bounded up the stairs, clearing several steps with each stride.

In an attempt to keep pace, Tenni missed a step, but Sprenger and Soekka each grabbed her by an arm and pulled her upright before she hit the wooden stairs. Her arm was so glazed with sweat that Sprenger nearly lost hold of her, but she recovered fast. She voiced her thanks as best she could through her panting and started upward again.

By the time they reached Jacob's office, Sprenger could handle no more. He fell onto all fours as he entered the office, trying desperately to catch his breath. His side exploded with a sharp pain, which only added to his lack of breath. Soekka dropped to a knee next him while supporting himself on Sprenger's shoulder. Tenni stood to his other side, hunched over with her hands on her knees. Her loose braid, now unruly in several places, hung over her shoulder. All Sprenger noticed around him was his side cramping in pain, and all three of them desperately trying to catch their breath while fighting the urge to topple to the ground.

"Roughly five miles south," Kanto panted to Jacob.

Jacob stood from where he sat behind his desk. "Parken!" He shouted out the doorway. Within seconds, Jacob's big guard pushed his way past the three fatigued kids and dropped to a knee in front of Jacob's desk. "Send squads out to escort Kobei and Tarak's teams back to the village. They are headed to the northern and western patrol bases. I want them back as quickly as possible." The scythe nodded his understanding and rose to his feet. When he turned to leave, Jacob added, "And someone find Juriah. Tell him to see me with the utmost urgency." Parken again nodded and weaved his way back out the doorway and started running down the hall. "Claudia!" Jacob barked back through the doorway.

A short, plump woman wearing an apron bustled down the hall. She did not try to force her way into the office but remained standing behind them. Jacob gestured to Sprenger and the others. "Can you please bring these weary children some water?"

She looked down at them with motherly-concerned eyes, then back up to Jacob. "Of course, my lord." She hurriedly shuffled her way back down the hall and stairs.

For the first time, Sprenger realized how dry and cracked his throat felt. Even so, the idea of taking a drink of anything seemed impossible through his desperate heaves.

Jacob turned his comforting eyes to the three of them. "If you are able to, perhaps it would be wise to clear the doorway. You've had a trying day, and I would hate to see you trampled by a rushed scythe." He gave them a gentle smile, and opened an arm to where Kanto stood, holding his now red-bandaged side. "Please."

Tenni rose to her full height, while sucking in a large breath. After a large exhale, she walked over to stand by Kanto. Sprenger didn't want to move. His whole body protested the very idea of it all. Soekka seemed no more inspired either. Sprenger looked up, realizing Jacob's gentle gaze was on him. He couldn't appear weak in front of Jacob. He had to move.

His side felt as though it was threatening to tear open and his legs groaned with the action of moving from their resting position. Seeming to use all the strength he could muster, he rose to a knee. His side caused him to clench his teeth and squeeze an eye shut, but he continued to rise. He was finally on his feet.

Soekka's hand began to slide off Sprenger's shoulder, but Sprenger grabbed it and the underside of his arm. With a scream of pain from his side, Sprenger helped Soekka to his feet.

Supporting their weight on each other, they too joined Tenni next to Kanto. They weren't breathing so hard anymore, but none were able to breathe solely through their noses yet, except Kanto of course, who began to explain the whole story to Jacob in greater detail.

After a few minutes, Claudia returned carrying a tray with four wooden cups of water. She placed the tray on the corner of Jacob's desk closest to them, crushing several papers underneath. She gave a small bow as best she could, without popping the buttons on her dress, and asked if that would be all.

"Yes, thank you, Claudia." With that, the plump woman scurried from the room. Soekka and Tenni grabbed a glass from the tray, and greedily gulped them down. Sprenger didn't feel up to it. His side was cramping so fiercely that it was making him nauseous. Even water sounded like too much for his stomach at the moment.

"What do you want now?" someone growled irritably from the back of the office. The three of them started at the new voice in the room. They turned to the open window behind Jacob's desk. Crouching on the windowsill, was the man who had been the center of many of Sprenger's and Soekka's conversations of late. Wearing his black leather vest, black shirt, as well as his short sword down his back, was the scythe they had fought with in the forest.

"Juriah," Jacob sounded relieved but kept the rush in his voice. "We have an emergency."

Juriah looked at him for a moment, but it didn't seem to grasp the situation. "Shocking," he grumbled. Apparently uninterested, he looked over at Sprenger, who was still squeezing his side. "Put your hands on your head and stand up straight. It'll help the side-ache to go away."

Jacob turned to see who he was actually talking to, then shot a glare back at him. "Juriah, this is important."

"Better be," he grumbled back at Jacob.

"So rude," Tenni said under her breath so no one would hear.

After Juriah had turned his uninterested gaze back to Jacob, Sprenger did as he said. Soekka and Tenni watched him with interested expressions, as he straightened and put his hands on his head. It didn't ease his pain by any means, but at least it didn't make it worse.

"Juriah," Jacob continued, "there could be Adimortis in the forest. Kanto and his squad were attacked on a transfer mission today." Gesturing over his shoulder to the four of them, but Juriah cut him off before he could finish.

"Considering they're standing here before me, I'm not inclined to believe you. I doubt underlings would survive an attack from elites."

"By a man in a black cloak, wielding a bladed flail," Jacob finished. Now Juriah's expression went from uninterested, to darkly serious.

Juriah looked over at Kanto. "Did he have a scar?"

Kanto shrugged. "Couldn't tell. He was constantly moving when I saw him."

Juriah opened his mouth to add something but Sprenger interrupted. "Yeah. It was on the left side of his face. A big one."

Juriah swore under his breath. He turned his attention back to Kanto. "Can I assume that since you are standing here, that you hurt him enough to drive him back? Or, though I seriously doubt it, kill him?"

"No," Kanto grumbled, disappointed in his own answer. "He fled when he thought we had more scythe with us."

"You mean to tell me he escaped unscathed?" Juriah raised an eyebrow as he looked down at Kanto's bleeding side. He gave a humorless snort. "Good work." He looked back up. "Thought you were supposed to be one of the best?"

"Enough," Jacob snapped, ending the childish banter.

"How did you know he had a scar?" Sprenger asked.

Juriah turned his attention to him. "Because I put it there. Over a month ago." He smirked at Sprenger. "Side still hurt?"

Sprenger had completely forgotten about his side. It was true, it didn't hurt anymore. Surprised, Sprenger silently shook his head.

Jacob turned and stood in front of them, blocking Juriah from view. "Kanto, you can give me a full report after you visit the healers." He dropped his gaze down to the three of them. "You three should spend some time in the Healer's Quarters as well. A hot soak will help your muscles from turning to stone overnight." They all gave a bow and thanks. Sprenger tried to look around Jacob at Juriah, but Jacob insistently hurried them out the door. Apparently wanting them out was something he could only silently insist on. Sprenger caught Soekka's gaze and they both gave an understanding smirk and nod as Kanto forced them towards the door.

Kanto closed the door behind him. Once they were all out in the hallway, Sprenger noticed something small in Kanto's expression. He looked somewhat angry to Sprenger, which he assumed was because of what Juriah said, though it was strange for

Sprenger to see Kanto lose any of his composure. Kanto took a deep breath which seemed to lighten his frustration. "I want you lot to know something." He looked each of them in the eye to make sure they were listening. "I feel you should know how proud of you I am. You were very brave today, but even more importantly than that, you didn't give up. I understand that what I expected of you was not easy in the end, but you took it head on with the determination of scythe far beyond your years and you did it without complaint. You showed me today how strong of a squad I was given."

He leaned forward and lowered his voice. "Let us be thankful that it wasn't Kobei's squad out there, or things may have gone horribly wrong." The group smiled a bit and nodded their agreement. Kanto smirked, a rare sight, then rose to his full height once again. "That being said, we still have much to work on, but not for a bit. Let us visit the healers, and tomorrow we will rest. Come." He began walking away, Tenni turned to follow, rubbing her injured hand.

Sprenger and Soekka exchanged frantic looks. They had to do it now.

"Master Kanto," Soekka hastily blurted. Kanto stopped and looked over his shoulder at them. "Sprenger and I didn't take any serious injuries like you or Tenni, and I would like to tell Granny Karla about today. She's here seeing the elders. Would you mind Sprenger and I going to the healers later?"

Kanto pondered it for a moment. "I suppose not." He raised a finger in exaggeration. "But make sure you see the healers. You'll regret it if you don't."

"Of course, Master Kanto," they said together.

He gave an approving nod. "Very well then."

Sprenger waited until he couldn't hear Kanto and Tenni's footsteps anymore, before looking over at Soekka. "Nicely done."

He gave Sprenger a self-satisfied smirk. "That's why you should always let me do the talking. You would just screw it up."

Sprenger gave a small shrug. "Probably."

"Come on, we're missing it." Soekka walked up to the wall just to the right of Jacob's door. Above the height of the door, and each side, were two vents, meant for preventing the crawlspace above Jacob's office from becoming damp and growing mold. The vents were made with intricate spirals and designs and most people just disregarded them as mere decoration.

Soekka stood just underneath the one to the right. He gave a few lazy stretches, then laced his fingers and squatted. Sprenger quickly stepped into Soekka's hands and braced himself on the wall as Soekka lifted him up a bit, until he was eye level with the vent. He stuck his fingers into as many holes as possible, and with a small push, popped the vent inward. Soekka raised him a bit further, and Sprenger placed the vent silently to the side on one of the support beams in the crawlspace. With a hand to each side of the crawlspace, Sprenger pushed his upper body through the vent. Using the main beam in front of him, he pulled the rest of him through the hole.

As quietly as he could, Sprenger turned around and poked his head back through the vent. The top of Soekka's black hair was pivoting side to side, watching for anyone walking up the hallway.

With a small whistle from Sprenger, Soekka looked up, took a few steps away from the wall, then ran at it. With a quick push from the wall, he jumped up and grabbed wrists with Sprenger. Sprenger pulled him up until the first half of his body was through the vent.

Soekka pulled himself in, and replaced the vent cover, in case of any passersby.

Sitting on the largest support beam in the middle, the two of them looked down through several cracks in the ceiling boards of Jacob's office. Soekka and Sprenger just happened to chance upon this hiding spot one day when they were desperate to hear Jacob punish a young group of scythe for pestering a younger squad of boys.

Since then, they came up here to listen in on conversations that they normally would not be allowed to hear. It required no conversation between Sprenger and Soekka to decide a private audience between Jacob and Juriah was one worth listening in on.

"Phenex would have no reason to concern himself with clearing out bandits," Juriah's voice said. He had moved from the windowsill to in front of Jacob's desk. Sprenger could not see much of him through the ceiling, but he could see enough to tell Juriah was crossing his arms.

Jacob's face and shoulders could be seen sitting behind his desk, tugging on his pointed beard. "Kanto said they were running from something."

There was a silence as Juriah thought it over. "How long have you been hunting that group of bandits?"

"A while. Why? What are you thinking?"

"If we have been hunting them for a while with no results, then that would mean we would need to go to the next step."

"By loosing the hounds of Durado," Jacob finished.

Juriah did something that Sprenger assumed must have been a nod. "Phenex must have known that somehow. It makes sense that he would want us to find the bandits to stop our search. If we loosed the hounds, then Phenex would more than likely have been found as well. It must have been sheer luck that Kanto stumbled across him at the time."

Jacob's voice became more stern. "I hardly consider what happened today luck, Juriah. It could have been much worse."

Juriah gave a lazy wave of his hand in disregard. "Whatever. The point is we have a chance to stop them before they do whatever they're planning now that we know they're here."

Jacob ceased the tugging on his beard. "Them?"

"Adimortis never work alone. I got rid of Phenex's partner when I gave him the scar on his face. Demaedura probably has already paired him with another scythe by now."

"Juriah, what if it's Demaedura himself? If they know our procedures well enough to avoid them, then they must know more about the village than I care to admit." Jacob's expression became sharper. "Someone from the village must have warned them of the hounds. Someone like Demaedura."

"It's unlikely. Demaedura would not put himself in harm's way like this when he has plenty of vassals to do whatever needs to be done."

"Unlikely, perhaps, but if it were the case, could you think of any other reason why he would return? Perhaps he finally plans to confront you?"

"It's possible I suppose." Juriah paused again to think. "The only reason to do that is if he has something big planned that he doesn't want me interfering with. You should reinforce your border patrols until I can be sure who all is here. I'll confront them myself if there are more."

Jacob nodded. "Very well." He once again started tugging on his beard. "Do you think Tranis is involved in this?" Juriah didn't answer. "What with his recent escape attempt and his past history with Demaedura? Perhaps it's something to look into."

"It would make sense if Demaedura thinks that Tranis has more to give him. If Demaedura is up to what I think he's up to then it would mean Tranis could have useful information for him. That could be enough to send Phenex to break him out."

"Juriah, we may have already interfered with their plan. Tranis had successfully escaped already, but you stopped him." Jacob leaned back in his tall chair and crossed his arms. "If I were to guess, this sounds more like an escort." Again, Juriah remained silent, so Jacob continued. "What else would an Adimortis be waiting for? If they are truly are as skilled of scythe as is told, then they wouldn't have waited so long to attack, only to lose their advantage of surprise. I would be willing to bet that they were waiting for Tranis to meet them but are unaware that he's already been recaptured."

"Makes sense," Juriah grumbled in agreement, "but that's not necessarily a good thing."

"No, it's not." Jacob closed his eyes in thought. "It would mean, especially now that they've been discovered, that their escort will turn into an abduction."

Sprenger and Soekka turned to each other in the darkness above the office. Even in dim light, Sprenger could see the reflection of his own fear in Soekka's face.

Chapter 12

Recuperation

Soekka and Sprenger made slow progress to the Healer's Quarters once they left the doors of the Rithhold. Though directly behind the Rithhold, the short distance to the healers was a dragging effort for both of them. There were several things that they wished to talk about, considering what they just heard and what they just experienced, but the thought of a conversation seemed too taxing at the moment, so they walked along slowly in silence.

The day's activities had taken all their will power and strength. Squatting above Jacob's office only reminded them how tired their limbs were. Sprenger's legs were becoming shaky as they tried to silently listen to the conversation between Jacob and Juriah below, and now they seemed to have no ability to raise themselves higher than a couple inches off the ground with each step.

Now that rest was only a short distance away, their bodies seemed to collapse under the challenges of the day. Exiting the crawl space was an entirely different matter from entering it. *More a fall and a tumble than a climb down*, Sprenger thought tiredly.

Their fall made enough noise that Jacob came to the door to see the cause of the commotion. Luckily, the contents of Sprenger's pack were spilled all over the floor, including the reports from the outpost. Sprenger snatched the reports up to hand them to Jacob explaining that he had tripped running up the stairs because of his hurry to deliver the reports. Jacob seemed convinced, took the reports, and returned to his office. The boys inwardly gave a huge sign of relief as the vent cover above was still open.

Soekka had collapsed under Sprenger's weight before the cover could be replaced.

The Healer's Quarters was one of the jewels of Durado. Though not appearing so grand while shadowed by the Rithhold, it was still a beautifully crafted building and several times larger than most other buildings in the village. Unlike the other buildings, the roots of the Healer's Quarters' foundation was made up of several smaller roots that left honeycombed gaps between them, which were all filled with clean sparking windows.

Sprenger knew that, as a scythe, he would be spending many nights of his life in the Healer's Quarters. He had not expected to be here so suddenly, having only finished his first real mission, but no scythe can do their duty to the best of their ability without losing some skin or blood here and there.

To help scythe heal faster and better, all manner of studies are conducted behind the walls of the Healer's Quarters. Herbalists and physicians were constantly experimenting with new plants and remedies that could hasten the healing process of an impatient scythe. Sprenger once burned his hand on a boiled rock. The healers removed the blisters and wiped a brown paste on it that immediately ceased the throbbing burning on his palm. It was just one of many stories that could be told about the impressive abilities the healers of Durado.

Including sewing wounds, tending bruises, scrapes, and cuts, Sprenger and Soekka were quite familiar with visiting the healers. This, however, would be the first time they visited to recover from a mission.

The grand building stood two stories high, plus a basement underground. The multitude of shimmering windows cast reflective light from the sun all around the surrounding area. There was constant bustling of people going in and out of the doors, and many of the windows had people peering out of them or walking past. The healers themselves were trained early as scythe, like all in Durado, but then left scythe training for training in the healing arts for the next few years. They studied herbs, wounds, poisons, and anything that could be applied to rejuvenating a fallen scythe. They were distinct from the scythe by their egg-white robes, often with a pack on their backs or hanging at their sides filled with assortments of their healing ingredients.

Because of the vulnerability of the injured scythe here, the Healer's Quarters was heavily guarded to allow secure and peaceful recovery. Scythe stood watch at every entrance and the roof, vigilantly watching the surrounding area. However, the Healer's Quarters could not be accessed from just any direction. A small wall closed off the Rithhold and Healer's Quarters from surrounding buildings. The only entrance to the huge courtyard was from the main road, so any intruders bent on attacking the Healer's Quarters would first have to make it past the Rithhold's guards, and less directly, the Scythrith himself. The combination of guards, a wall around the back and sides, and Scythrith Jacob watching the front, made the Healer's Quarters one of the safest places in the village.

Sprenger and Soekka were so tired they stumbled through the double doors and up to the massive front desk. The desk stood at the intersection of two hallways veering off in opposite directions. Behind the desk stood a slender old woman with graying hair tied back into a messy bun. She had a long crooked neck like a vulture, which was all the more useful for peering over the desk at people looking for information. She was bustling around looking for something, momentarily glancing at papers before setting them aside again.

Every time Sprenger and Soekka came to the healers, this woman was in the same spot. Sprenger wondered if she ever truly left. He gently cleared his throat to grab her attention, and she stopped her frantic search and looked down her hooked nose at them.

"Hello, boys," she said in an old but firm voice. "What can I do for you this afternoon?" She asked, as though they were the same boys that showed up from time to time, with Jacob's blessing. Today, however, was different.

"We're the rest of Master Kanto's squad, ma'am," Soekka replied.

She gave a giddy bounce. "Ah, yes. Master Kanto has been taken to top-priority healing to clean up his wounds. He will have to stay overnight. A very damaging hit to his side like that will take time to heal." She turned around and snatched up a piece of paper from a pile behind her and turned back to them. "Your fellow squad member is having her hand worked on and should be done shortly." She moved the paper closer and farther from her face, as in an attempt to bring it into focus. "Master Kanto instructed to have you boys receive basic post-mission care." She lowered the paper and looked back down her nose at them. "No injuries I presume?". The boys shook their heads. "Then perhaps thc good hot soak will be all you need." She put the paper on the desk and scribbled something quickly onto it with a feather quill. Without looking up, she pointed a bony finger to the hall on her right. "You boys know where to go. Enjoy."

They both gave a bow of thanks and slowly made their way down the hallway she had indicated to them.

The Simmering Pools, as they're called, were fed from hot springs high in the mountains to the south of Durado, and were used solely for the purpose of therapy, despite many civilian attempts at a hot bath. Having a special pull with Jacob and being the children of Lady Karla, Sprenger and Soekka often were allowed in without any real need but for a relaxing soak.

The hallways were bright with sunlight, as they always were. Windows all down the first half of the hallway drenched the floor with glares from the sun. A right turn down another hallway led to the pools, at the back of the Healer's Quarters. Once close, the boys recognized the smell that was hard to ignore. As if eggs were rotting, there was no mistaking the smell of the Simmering Pools.

A thick wooden door at the end of the increasingly dim hallway kept the majority of steam and smell locked away behind it, but not all.

Soekka took a deep breath and released it in anticipation as Sprenger pulled the door open.

A cloud of hot, moist steam engulfed them and instantly caused their clothes to cling to their skin, as if shrinking in the hot air. Now the rotten-egg smell went unchallenged by the fresh air of the rest of the building. It wasn't particularly unpleasant, but it had taken Sprenger some time to get used to when he was younger.

Inside the dim room were several, round, steaming water basins in the wooden floor. A tall wooden fence separated one half of the room from the other for women and men, so not to be exposed to unwanted eyes. Each basin was large enough to hold five or so men or women comfortably. Such numbers were rare and more often than not, avoided. In the rafters of the ceiling, skylights were cut into the woodwork to allow some of the steam to escape into the air outside.

Sprenger and Soekka stripped and threw their clothes into baskets on the near wall. Standing naked in the dim room could be an unnerving experience, but the boys had it to themselves, and they had no care between one another.

The wood floor was hot and slick under Sprenger's toes, already giving his sore feet a taste of the relieving heat to come. He didn't know what was sweat from the day and what was only steam clinging to his exposed skin, but he anxiously awaited being rid of it all the same.

They agreed on their usual spot, the one near the middle where the water was the freshest and so the hottest. Sprenger's legs seemed to cramp in anxiety and cry out for some form of comfort.

After what seemed like hours since they came falling into Jacob's office, the boys slowly slipped into the simmering, milky water. At first, the hot water was almost too much of a shock for his body, but then it gradually started to give comfort as Sprenger lowered into it one inch at a time. Once he was fully submerged, Sprenger let out a heavy sigh. As if bliss itself was caressing his naked body, Sprenger forgot the world around him. Today's troubles became a distant memory. Even Jacob and Juriah's concerning conversation took no sway of interest with him. He was in ecstasy in this pool and nothing else mattered while he was in it.

-<>-

Phenex bowed his head as he knelt at Demaedura's feet.

"It is not like you to fail such a simple task," Demaedura said with a coy smirk of amusement, that everyone knew was hiding his annoyance. "Now our presence is known, as well as our animosity."

Phenex remained silently staring at the floor. There was nothing he could say to excuse his mistake.

"I told you I should have done it," Peatra boasted, but froze when Demaedura suddenly threw a blade at him that stuck in the beam Peatra was leaning against, inches from his ear. Peatra gave the blade a surprised look then pouted silently.

"Our plans have now been moved up," Demaedura snapped at them all. He peered down at Phenex with a contemplating look.

"There may be a way around attacking so quickly," Ajax said from the far side of the room. "The wall and borders will no doubt be even more heavily guarded now that they know we are in the forest. We can time it for when they let their guard down."

"Tell us what you are thinking, Ajax." Grogan grumbled from across the room to his partner, curious what the nomad was getting at.

"The scythe only saw Phenex," Ajax explained from his place against the back wall, "which means they will only be looking for one man. If they were to see that one man leaving the forest-"

"Then they would stop their search and lighten their guard again," Peatra finished once he realized the point. He looked over at Phenex with a grin. "Bye, Phenex."

Ajax nodded. "Phenex can easily get through the patrols by himself, then after everything has calmed again, sneak back in and assist us in retrieving Tranis."

Demaedura thought for a moment then looked down at Phenex. "Leave," he said plainly. "And let them see you leave." Phenex rose and gave a nod of understanding. “When it is safe to do so, return. Your return will mark our time to act.”

Chapter 13

Jacob's Bold Decision

Durado was in the early stages of a soft evening, lightly lit by the sunset behind the towering trees. Everything was calm and peaceful, despite the excessive scythe guarding the wall. Jacob sat behind his desk and slowly tugged his pointy beard and puffed on his pipe, lost in thought. He hardly noticed Errand as he opened the door and began sorting papers on the table to the side of the room.

"Where would you like the scouting reports?" he asked, then turned around when Jacob didn't give an immediate answer. "My Lord?"

"Oh," he said, coming back to his senses, "just leave them there please. Thank you, Errand."

Errand eyed him curiously. "Is something troubling you, Lord Jacob?" He stepped up to the desk.

"Sprenger and Soekka killed two bandits today," he grumbled.

"Truly?" Errand said in disbelief. "Doing what?" He began to scan his reports, searching for the answer himself. "Doing a reports transfer," he confirmed as he lowered the reports again. "Not a typical first mission."

"Not typical at all," Jacob agreed casually as he took another deep pull from his pipe and stared off to nowhere in particular.

Errand stared at him curiously. "What are you thinking about then?"

Jacob looked back up at him, then removed his pipe from his mouth. "The Exerptus Exams."

The answer was clearly not one that Errand was expecting. "They are in a few months. What of them?" he asked, not seeing the connection between the two topics.

The Exerptus Exams were the tests put in place to decide whether or not a squad was prepared to move on to more advanced training and missions. The exams consisted of three parts: blade throwing, sparring, and then the Exerptus Routine. If they pass, pentin are promoted to the rank of junettin. Until all members of a squad pass the exams, they are not permitted to be assigned to anything higher than low-ranking missions.

"I'm contemplating something that I need you to talk me out of," Jacob finally said.

"I wasn't aware such a thing was possible," Errand joked, "but I'll do my best."

Jacob gave him an apprehensive look, before taking another heavy pull from his pipe. "I'm going to call a meeting," he said softly through the smoke. "A meeting that has not been called for, neigh a decade."

Errand had to think a moment, but then gave an expression of sudden realization, but said nothing.

"I want to call the meeting," Jacob said again, as if to emphasize that it was not a mistake the first time, "and discuss putting all our in-training scythe through the Exerptus Exams." He stared through the smoke with a definite look. "*All* of them."

-<>-

It was well into the night when they all finally arrived. Sitting around the crackling fireplace in Jacob's office was a congregation that had one purpose and one purpose only: to save Durado's future. Among them was Master Cerri, Master Kanto, Lady Karla, Elder Bakkon, Elder Jaydon, and of course Jacob and Errand. There were some from the original group that were no longer in this world, but the majority sat silently in the flickering firelight.

"What a gathering," Elder Bakkon finally said. "The likes of which we have not seen in a long while."

He was a fierce looking man, with oiled-down black hair that went past his shoulders and a long, wiry black beard. Not an emotional man by any means, he stared at them all from under his fuzzy black eyebrows with no expression to be read.

To his right was Durado's second elder, Elder Jaydon. He was Bakkon's visual opposite; he had an impressive head of white, full-bodied hair falling down his back that he did little to contain. Only a leather headband with Durado's symbol kept the masses of hair from covering his clean-shaven face. "It makes us curious as to the nature of this meeting," he added to Bakkon's comment, but in a softer tone.

Jacob leaned forward in his chair. "The reason I have called this meeting," he began softly, "is because I see a need, and an opportunity, for our plans to be modified."

"Modified how?" Karla asked, just as skeptically as the rest of them.

"The Exerptus Exam," Jacob replied. "I see no reason to wait another two years for it to happen again before we test our young squads."

"What do you mean 'no reason'", Cerri contested. "Time itself is the reason. Students need a chance to train under their masters and learn to work together as a team before we ready them for dangerous contracts and missions. Escorting rich lords on the roads and delivering reports may not be glorious, but it teaches the basics of being scythe."

"Indeed," Elder Bakkon agreed. "It defeats the whole purpose of having the exams if we just throw students into them whenever we feel like it."

"That would be true," Jacob replied, "were it any other group of students."

"You cannot tell me," Elder Jaydon said quickly, "that you believe this class is that unique."

"I can, and I am," Jacob said flatly.

"Really?" Jaydon asked skeptically.

"I am," Jacob repeated.

"I will admit," Cerri interjected, "that I have never had a class come remotely close to the skill I see in this new class, but that is in training, not the field."

"What is the point of their training if not to reflect their potential in the field?" Jacob pointed out, to which Cerri had no reply.

"Does this have anything to do with what happened today?" Kanto asked in his composed voice. He was gently holding his side but did not allow the injury to inhibit his posture in any way. Technically, he was still supposed to be in the Healer's Quarters.

"Yes, it does," Jacob admitted to his former student.

"What do you mean?" Cerri asked, looking from Kanto to Jacob. "What happened?"

"A mission gone horribly wrong," Karla grumbled. "The boys ended up having to defend themselves from a group of runaway outlaws and unfortunately, both took a life."

Cerri became a bit frantic. "What?" he looked around for someone to explain more. "How did this happen? How are they coping?"

"Fine," Jacob said raising a calming hand. "They are doing fine. It was a group of bandits that attacked them. They each killed one, and so far, neither seems shaken up by it. It was an unfortunate event, but they handled it well enough."

"Among other events occurring," Kanto grumbled.

"Speaking of which," Jaydon said, seeing his opportunity. "What is being done about the Adimortis in our forest?"

"The man Kanto encountered, whom we have reason to believe is none other than Phenex of the Adimortis," Jacob replied, "was seen exiting the forest earlier this evening. We believe he was meant to escort Tranis out but deserted after Tranis was recaptured." There was little else he could provide and Jacob had the haunting feeling that he was missing something. Unfortunately, he could only know what was reported to him.

Jaydon nodded his understanding but was clearly going through the scenario in his head as well.

"Back to the topic at hand," Karla said, a bit impatiently. "Why the sudden desirc to put such inexperienced scythe in the Exerptus Exam?"

"Why else?" Kanto answered for Jacob. "To allow them to go on higher-ranking missions."

"And what is the benefit to that?" Karla pressed.

"To push them all to their full potential," Jacob responded. "This class has been setting new records left and right," he raised a finger, "and not just the boys. All of them. We should be doing everything we can to challenge them and force them to grow. Such talent would be wasted otherwise."

Each of the group contemplated the idea for a moment. It was an interesting concept, but not without its risks. Each of them was no doubt weighing all the risks they could think of in their minds. Jacob hoped they saw his logic and the opportunity in front of them, but he also called upon these people for their opinions. They were each sharp-minded and rarely overlooked problems when they all contemplated the same ideas.

"An interesting proposal," Jaydon said after a moment of silence. "It will not come without a great deal of concern and contestation, however. We still have yet to pass the two classes before them. What tension do you think that will cause between the older classes and the younger ones?"

"That may yet be another test," Cerri pointed out. "If this all goes the way we hope, then a petty squabble of rank will be exactly what we need them to solve on their own. That is, after all, the point of everything." Jacob understood both points, but trusted Cerri's opinion of his students above any other's. If his teaching-master believed that the students could overcome the situation, then Jacob believed him.

"I agree with Cerri," Bakkon added. "Tension amongst the ranks is a problem that all scythe must face at some point. I leave it to their individual masters to maintain discipline among them. This will be a great determining gamble in our plans, however," his gaze became more stern, "if we start sending inexperienced scythe into the field, there's no guarantee that they'll return. Should either Soekka or Sprenger be killed, this will all have been for not."

"And the entire class entering the exams?" Jaydon asked. "That is hardly justified. I am willing to believe that a handful of the students are skilled enough to pass, but find it difficult to believe they all are. These exams have failed plenty of students that *had* proper time to prepare."

"They do better when they are together," Jacob said sternly. "These students thrive off one another's energy. I want to see how far we can take that combined strength, and the exams are a harmless way to test those waters. Waiting for a true situation may not give us the answer we hoped for at a time that is most inconvenient. All or none," he said conclusively. "That is my proposal." Though he was Scythrith, he did not have the power to make such a large decision as this. He needed the cooperation of his advisors if he had any hope of even testing his theory.

Everyone around the fireplace thought it over for a moment in silence, each leaving their faces blank to whatever thoughts were occurring in their heads. Jacob had to wait patiently for an answer.

"We have trusted you this far," Karla whispered. "I think it would be foolish to stop now." She and Jacob locked eyes for a moment and he gave her an appreciative nod.

Gradually, everyone began nodding their agreement.

"Very well then," Jacob said. "I will call for Kobei and Tarak, as well as yourself," looking over at Kanto, "tomorrow morning. I will tell them of what is happening, and hopefully they will not protest my decision."

"If they see the same potential in their students as we do," Cerri stated, "then that should not be a problem."

Chapter 14

The Next Level

It was a chilled and damp but beautiful morning in Durado. After two days free of training, all the students were happily and eagerly buzzing with excitement. All three new squads were gathered together in front of the gate of Durado's wall. They had received word the day before that, should their students be willing, their teachers were going to begin training them for the Exerptus Exams. The students had no reserves about accepting, but many of their parents were skeptical when they heard the news.

When they first arrived at the gates for the announcement, each squad looked the others, confused to see them. They hadn't all been together like this since graduating Master Cerri's class, and they eagerly began to exchanged stories and discuss what kinds of training they were doing. Sprenger and Soekka's story of finding a prisoner in the woods was quickly the dominating topic of conversation.

Sprenger wanted to tell everyone about what happened on their report-transfer mission, but Kanto told them the information was not to be shared. It was officially classed as a mission to not be shared without direct permission from Scythrith Jacob. They were forced to lie and say that their squad was escorted back by scythe, like Kobei's squad was. Sprenger enjoyed the conversations nonetheless. It was nice to be able to socialize with everyone else again. Soekka, on the other hand, seemed impatient to back to training. He never enjoyed questions or socializing. For this reason, Nabi, the lanky girl in Tarak's squad, always preferred to pester Sprenger with questions and admirations. Affections, Sprenger could not help but feel, he would have preferred come from Korran and not Nabi.

"What's with the cluster of frontline distractions?" someone behind the young squads said. Everyone stopped talking and turned to see Kimimaro and his two squadmates walking towards them. The three boys were from the year above, and had been bullies from a young age.

In the center of the trio and leader of the despised group, was Kimimaro. The boy had a long face with a disproportionately tall forehead and bushy black eyebrows that matched his bowl-cut black hair. Behind him was Parker and Schaum, who were notably bigger and stronger built compared to Kimimaro. One with shoulder-length greasy brown hair, and the other short red hair. Schaum, the redhead, had ears that stuck straight out and teeth that were overly large and crooked. Overall, he reminded the boys of an overgrown rat that seemed to strut about, thinking himself undeniably attractive. They had never encountered someone that agreed with this thought, however.

Several people in the younger squads mumbled disapproving comments under their breath. 'Frontline distractions' was a very dark joke that referred to people that could not fight and would only serve as a distraction for the enemy in a battle. During the war, prisoner of rival villages were rumored to put captured scythe out as bait for ambush to test if enemies were hiding somewhere. Joking about the horrid tragedies of the past was strongly frowned upon in Durado, and saying such things in front of someone of rank could subject one to punishment. These boys used the phrase all the time, however, especially towards the members of Sprenger and Soekka's class.

"Nothing would be more distracting than you three's ugly mugs, Kimimaro," Sprenger rebutted. Everyone began giggling.

Kimimaro gave him an irritated look. "Still think you're so amazing, don't you, Sprenger?"

Sprenger shrugged. "I don't really have an opinion of myself. I think *you're* amazingly stupid sometimes, but luckily that doesn't normally bother me." Everyone giggled again.

"Now Sprenger," Soekka said coming up to stand next to him, "be nice. You know that they're just upset because they were constantly getting shown up in training by the class under them." Everyone began making taunting noises.

This had been the relationship between the two classes for the past several years. It was obvious that the older class lacked the discipline that Cerri's class received, and they never missed an opportunity to start a fight. As the younger class grew and gained more skill, Kimimaro and his friends were forced from physical bullying, to verbal. The transition had not served in their favor.

"You guys are still as cocky as ever," Kimimaro said bitterly.

"The arrogant ones," Caymen said, to everyone's surprise, "are the ones that seek out confrontation when none need be had." Of all the students in their class, Caymen was the least outspoken of them. He believed keeping a calm head and focus was the greatest measure of a scythe. He was Sprenger and Soekka's greatest rival within the class, but never managed to surpass them, despite his unrelenting training. Something that he outwardly resented the boys for. It was rare when Caymen said anything, even more so in an argument. Whenever Caymen did speak up in an argument, the way he spoke always surprised

Sprenger. His voice was monotone and collected, and he seemed to pride himself on using large words.

Kimimaro was about to say something else, but someone behind him interrupted.

"I could not agree more." The classes all shared a smirk as Masters Kobei, Kanto, and Tarak came up behind Kimimaro and his squadmates, who turned nervously with poor grace. "My student has a very good point," Kobei continued as he towered over the students and crossed his heavily-muscled arms. "Perhaps that was not a lesson you have learned well enough yet."

Kimimaro and the others bent at the waist into deep bows. "Masters," they said together. "We were only catching up," Kimimaro lied desperately.

Kanto's expression read as being deeply unconvinced. "Which master are you training under?" he asked sternly when they rose from their bows. "I would like to 'catch up' with them as well."

"Master Baunic," Schaum replied nervously.

"Well," Kanto continued. "I will have to insist upon some added training to Master Baunic with you boys' discipline. You are disturbing my students and I consider that an insult to myself as well as them."

Tarak gave an amused look to Kanto. "Be sure to mention something about humility with that too, Kanto."

"Indeed," Kanto said sternly, glaring down at the boys.

"Now," Kobei added, "I'm afraid you are cutting into our training time. Perhaps you should be on your way."

The boys all gave a pathetic bow before hurriedly scurrying away. All of the classes quickly formed their lines and stood at the ready, but still couldn't help smirking a bit at each other.

The masters all turned their attention to them and Tarak gave a very satisfied look. "See?" he said to Kanto. "Discipline. Our squads are eagerly waiting to begin."

Kanto nodded his agreement. "Now," Kanto announced, "you have all been informed of what is next, yes?" Everyone nodded. "Good. If there is any among you that do not wish to participate in the Exerptus Exam, then speak now." None did. "Excellent."

"Some of you," Tarak announced next, "may be wondering why this is happening. Why would we want you to take the exams so early? Well, the answer is simple. You have all shown a common strength, and this strength is one that we feel should be taken advantage of sooner rather than later."

"That strength," Kobei elaborated, "is your lot's ability to rise to the occasion; to not back away when a challenge is met, but rather to push yourselves to overcome it."

"That is why," Kanto finished, "we want you to take your training to the next level. It will be difficult and it will be frustrating, but if you are the students we think you are, we have little doubt in your ability to impress. Will you prove us right?" Kanto said, raising his voice. "Will you rise to the challenge?"

"Yes sir!" all the classes yelled at once.

"Wonderful," Kobei said with a grin, then clapped his big hands together eagerly. "Then let's begin. If you all would please follow me through the gates." He walked through the line of students and everyone turned to follow except Tenni, Sprenger, and Soekka.

Tenni turned to Kanto as he and Tarak approached. "Master Kanto," she whispered, "we're going back into the forest? Is that safe?" She was asking the question that Sprenger and Soekka were also wondering. They were the only squad that knew about the intruder in the trees and had no desire to have another unexpected fight.

"The man that attacked us was seen leaving the forest a couple days ago, and no more sightings have occurred," Kanto assured. "However, we are not so reckless as you seem to think, Tenni."

Tarak smiled at her from the other side of Kanto. "Remember, Tenni, you are being watched by three dura-masters. Few scythe would take that challenge." He gave her a reassuring wink.

She smiled at them, seemingly satisfied with their answer, and then followed the group along with Soekka and Sprenger.

The three squads were led a short ways into the forest to an area where the trees were medium-sized and more spread out.

"Now, today," Kobei announced as he approached an open area, "we must practice a skill that is one of the most crucial to the scythe of our great village." He looked up. "And that is moving in the trees instead of the ground."

Everyone began whispering excitedly, until Kanto snapped at them sternly to be quiet from the back of the group.

"Moving in the trees may seem an exciting task," Kobei continued, "but there is a reason why it is not normally trained to such young squads. It can be dangerous."

Obviously, Sprenger thought, *none us forgot that falling out of a tree is a bad thing.*

"So I don't want anybody to be doing anything reckless today. We will start with the basics, and only when they are perfect will we move on. Let's begin," he announced again. "Each of you needs to find a tree of your own, preferably one with low branches. I want you to start by running up the tree as far as you can get, and then carefully returning to the ground as smoothly as possible. If you lose control, lower your height until you find it again."

Kobei demonstrated on the nearest tree to him, making it a respectable distance up before sliding back down the bark. "The trick," he explained, "is to keep fast feet the whole time, and don't push out, but up. Go on and give it a try." He raised a cautionary finger. "But remember, carefully."

Everyone spread out and stood in front of their own trees, some larger than others, and some with intricate roots that had to be moved around. Sprenger, Soekka and Tenni all shared one large specimen, with plenty of room for all three of them to have a place. Sprenger hoped that Korran would join them too but she went to a tree elsewhere. The students were spread out all over the area of the forest, and the masters paced amongst them, watching diligently and giving advice where they saw it needed.

All of them were only able to take a few steps up the tree before being forced to drop back to the ground. Gradually, they were able to add more steps, but their slow progress was not as encouraging as Sprenger hoped it would be.

Scythe make this look so easy, Sprenger thought in irritation. He watched Soekka try again, but he was no more successful than Sprenger. When he turned his attention to Tenni, he noticed that she was making swift progress in gaining height before sliding back down.

Sprenger tried again, but made it no farther up than before, and this time he skinned his knee on the tree's bark when sliding back to the ground. He cursed under his breath when he rolled up his pant leg to see tiny beads of blood beginning to form where the skin was just removed. He almost flinched when he noticed Master Tarak standing behind him, watching. Sprenger hoped he didn't hear him curse, but Master Tarak just smirked and then approached him.

"Is that the only way you can think to dismount?" he asked Sprenger. Sprenger didn't really know how to answer, so Tarak elaborated. "The tree just hurt you. That would make it like an opponent, yes?"

Hardly, Sprenger thought to himself, but nodded anyway.

"Then would you want to remain directly in front of your opponent when you just failed an assault?"

"No," Sprenger admitted. "I'd try and get back so that they couldn't counter."

"Exactly," Tarak said with a nod of his bald head. "So now show me how you would do that." When Sprenger hesitated, Tarak added, "Just do what comes naturally in the mindset of getting away from your opponent."

Sprenger nodded, then after a second of thought, ran at the tree again. When he reached the max of his height, instead of just dropping, he pushed off and flipped backwards, landing close to where he started.

Tarak nodded. "Perfect."

Tenni and Soekka watched with curiosity, then tried it for themselves. Soekka managed to get it on his first try, but Tenni hesitated a couple times before finally trusting herself to do it.

When they turned back around, Master Tarak had already begun to move on to watch others. Sprenger, Soekka, and Tenni all continued flipping away from the tree, realizing it was quicker when making multiple attempts at climbing higher.

Eventually, everyone began making gradual progress and was able to get close to the lowest branches of their trees. Tenni was the only one of their group that was able to make it high enough to at least touch a branch with her fingers, before she was forced to descend.

"The next step," Kobei announced, "is getting up your trees, and then staying in the tree. In other words, get a hold of the lowest branch and pull yourself up. Once you've accomplished this, carefully drop down and do it again. Keep in mind that this action must be swift. If you are trying to evade an enemy, they will pull you down if you do not get on to the branch quickly enough. Focus on making it one fluid action."

Sprenger, Soekka, and Tenni shifted around their giant tree to a slightly lower set of branches. Though it still took time to get high enough, all three make steady progress towards their target branches.

Finally, Sprenger was able to wrap his arm around his branch and twirl over it. This part proved to be much easier for Sprenger than climbing. After he was able to reach a branch, spinning around it to sit on top was a much less complicated task due to his dexterity. Only a few people were having trouble reaching their branches but some were higher than others. Once they all finally did, they too were able to pull themselves up, but not always with grace. A few falls drew everyone's attention, but each seemed to be harmless, once their classmates rose from the dirt.

Even after accomplishing their accents multiple times, they were told to repeat the exercise until it came naturally. For the whole morning, the squads completed the task time and time again. Finally, Kobei called for them to stop.

Sprenger and most of the others dropped to the ground from their trees, and then just sat down in the dirt, exhausted.

"Return to the village," Kanto announced. "Get something to eat, then gather at the training grounds. There, we will continue this lesson for the remainder of the afternoon."

The break was far too short-lived for Sprenger's liking. He and Soekka went with most of the others to the market and got some fruits and small snacks before heading to the training grounds, where dozens of young students were in their orderly lines of basic training; a sight that Sprenger was all too sympathetic of.

He spotted Master Cerri pacing amongst the lines of his new class, and every once in a while he would correct someone's posture with a light smack of his oak rod that he constantly carried. Cerri once explained the rod to Sprenger and told him it was called a *doclo,* a tool used for training and teaching since the first Scythrith.

I hate that stupid stick, Sprenger thought bitterly, remembering countless occasions where he was smacked with it.

Once everyone had gathered, Kanto led them to the back corner of the training grounds, where there was an area of beams and logs of varying heights and thicknesses. Some beams were the size of a path that two people could pass on without much struggle, while others were hardly the width of a man's foot. Not all the beams were straight paths either. They spiraled around one another, rising and falling, often at steep inclines, like wooden waves frozen in time. Sprenger became extremely excited when he realized what the next part of training was before Kanto's explanation confirmed it.

"Here," Kanto said, gesturing to the variety of beams behind him, "is where we will be practicing our balance. We will devise a series of drills that will require you to run and alternate beams in a similar way that you would in the canopy. For obvious reasons, we will not move on with this training in the trees until it is perfected here."

Tarak stepped up next to Kanto. "Now, I want you all to contemplate something while you are doing this." He looked around at each of them. "In the exams, you will be tested in blade throwing while standing, running, and moving in the trees." Some students began whispering to each other, not knowing that the exam involved the forest. "You will have to hit targets while maneuvering the canopy, so use this time to practice that mindset. Keep in mind that the test will not give you a second chance if you fall from the trees, so practice with that same motivation while you are here." When he was sure that everyone had thought about his advice, he finished by saying, "Let us begin."

This training turned out to be to Sprenger's favorite. He didn't find it particularly difficult to run along the beams, even when they were the narrower ones. The beams themselves were not new for their training, however. Cerri often incorporated them into training of somc kind, though never more than one at a time, and never of different sizes.

This training was far more demanding and complicated than Cerri's had been, but Sprenger loved the acrobatics of it all. Jumping from one beam to another without falling was a bit more difficult than the running, but not incredibly so that the students were discouraged by it. The masters kept introducing new challenges and new drills to make things different and more difficult, but really they just felt like acrobatic games to Sprenger.

Why can't all our training be like this? Sprenger thought happily as he finished the course yet again without a single misstep and returned to the line of waiting students.

For the entire afternoon, the students trained on the beams, and all eventually got a feel and balance for them. By the end of the day, everyone was exhausted, and when their performance began to falter, the masters finally called for the end of the day's training. Warren was the only student that couldn't finish the final drill before the day was out, but he was close enough that Sprenger was sure he would get it the next time they practiced.

Soekka and Sprenger both wondered if Warren would manage to pass the exams, but so far, he was able to complete all the tasks asked of him. *It's not very pretty,* Sprenger told himself, *but he always gets it done.*

"A very successful first day of exam training," Kobei said with an overly large grin. "A couple more months like this and you'll be ready for the exams."

Many of the students exchanged apprehensive looks, forgetting that this was only the beginning. They had not been worked so hard since Cerri's exams, and this was just the first day of many more to come.

Sprenger couldn't help but groan a bit to himself as the thought struck him.

Chapter 15

The Exerptus Routine

For the next week, the squads focused primarily on learning to use the canopy. Gradually, they were introduced to throwing blades while standing and moving on the beams. Everyone was now able to complete all of the drills and could even maneuver in the actual canopy at a cautious pace, but being in the trees proved to be far more intimidating than the beams.

Pillas froze one day in the canopy, too nervous to move from the branch he was on. He was a heavily muscular boy, and he didn't trust many of the branches with his weight, nor his own ability to successfully move among them. Sprenger wasn't sure he needed to be so nervous. Most of the branches were larger than the beams they practiced on, but Pillas showed no signs of being convinced by his classmate's encouragements. With Master Tarak's blessing, Master Kobei spent a good part of the afternoon with him alone, teaching him tricks to being a large scythe that needs to use the canopy. It wasn't long before Pillas rejoined them and seemed to be able to move more readily among the branches, if not still slightly hesitantly.

One morning after they all successfully completed a full day of drills in the canopy, they were told that they would be returning to their individual squads. Sprenger was somewhat disappointed by that. He liked everyone being together; it made things seem more fun when everyone was doing it and reminded him of when they were all in Cerri's class together not so long ago.

Now he, Soekka, and Tenni waited for Master Kanto as he searched for a quiet spot in the training grounds. With the exams in the looming future for more than just the new squads, the grounds were flooded with the young scythe of older classes that were diligently training with strong hopes to pass. When Kanto returned, they followed him to one of the back corners of grass.

"Take a seat," Kanto said and the three students did so, curious what was next. "Now, this is the part of the exam that is the main determining factor of whether or not a student passes; the Exerptus Routine. It is extremely intricate and far more complex than any routine you've learned thus far."

Isn't that the point? Sprenger thought impatiently, but luckily managed to keep it to himself.

"Pay close attention," Kanto said as he took straight-backed and focused stance, closing his eyes, and inhaling a deep breath.

As Kanto began the routine, it seemed fairly straight forward, but then it grew faster and faster. It began incorporating spins and kicks that would not normally be done in series with one another. Sprenger caught himself staring with nervous shock and quickly tried to regain an unintimidated face.

For its intensity, the routine was a very long one. Endurance itself was going to be a challenge, let alone the moves. Most of the routines the students were trained were brief and focused more on the control of the moves. This routine never seemed to end as Sprenger watched it with wide eyes.

When Kanto finally slapped his palm to the ground to signal the end, everyone just stared at him, gawking. Kanto rose to his full height, only slightly winded. "Now stand, and let us begin," he said with conviction.

Slowly, everyone stood and took the beginning stance. Step by step, Kanto went through the beginning moves with them, then added one move after another, making them start from the beginning each time. He taught a routine the same as Cerri would, making sure that the parts already learned were perfect before adding another.

At least Kanto doesn't use a stick, Sprenger thought.

The three of them worked on the routine for the entire morning, practicing the moves slowly and precisely. Kanto separated out the most complicated spins and kicks to work on them separately. The complexities of the moves were, as Sprenger thought they would be, incredibly difficult to do in combination with one another.

Around midday, Kanto finally called for a break.

"A good start," he said with a proud nod. "You have the rest of the day to practice it on your own. Tomorrow morning I will meet you here and help again, but after that, you must continue practicing it without any assistance from anyone."

"What!" they all exclaimed together.

"How are we supposed to do this without a teacher?" Soekka protested.

"The same as you would on a mission as scythe," Kanto replied calmly, "by helping one another. Scythe do not have their masters there to hold their hands when things get tough. They can only call upon what they were taught, trust their teammates, and act on their own. Rcmember, this is an exam to separate those that are ready to accept greater challenges as scythe, and those that are not."

"What if we forget part of the routine?" Tenni asked.

"Then you will not pass the exam," Kanto said plainly. "You have most of it committed to memory already, and tomorrow morning I bet you will have it all committed. After that, focus on the speed, precision, and timing of things. The order will eventually come naturally." He raised a finger. "I will give you some advice, though. Practice the order everyday so that you don't forget anything. If you have to stop and think during the exam, you will likely panic and lose your place." Without another word, he walked away and left them standing there in a slight panic.

"Okay," Tenni said a bit skeptically, "we can do this." The boys looked at her apprehensively. "Let's focus on memorizing the order today, and then tomorrow we can spend our time with Kanto working on the difficult moves while he can still give us advice for them."

Soekka shrugged. "Sounds like a good idea to me. If we only get one more day with him, we had better use it to focus on the difficult parts."

Going with Tenni's idea, the three of them focused on the order of things, and when parts of intricate moves came up, they did a very lazy version and just focused on what came next. They got tripped up a few times, not sure if they were remembering it correctly, but eventually they would come to a consensus of what was next, agreeing that they would watch Kanto carefully tomorrow to confirm if they were correct or not.

They took breaks and quizzed one another verbally on the order. The three of them sat there and said the steps out loud in a sort of chant and found that saying everything aloud was very helpful when performing it for real.

The sun started to set behind the looming trees outside the wall of the village and the training grounds quieted as scythe departed. In the fading light of the evening, they decided to stop for the day.

"I think that's as good as it's going to get today," Tenni said through short breaths.

"Agreed," the boys said, equally exhausted

"And to think," Sprenger added, "we all used to complain about Master Cerri's routines."

"That's what we were just saying," Korran said as she and Caymen walked across the now empty training grounds. She stopped and gave the lot of them an amused look. "Have you guys been practicing the routine this whole time?"

"Have you not been?" Tenni asked surprised.

Korran shrugged. "We took a break a while ago since we couldn't remember the last steps."

"Master Kobei said he would only show us once more tomorrow," Caymen said annoyed. "As if the routine itself wasn't hard enough to do, now we have to do it without a teacher."

"Us too," Soekka agreed bitterly.

"I imagine that's the way it's always been," Korran pointed out. "But I still wish they told us that at the start so I knew to pay closer attention when watching Master Kobei perform it. If I had known that we could only watch a certain number of times, I would have paid much closer attention. By the end of the routine, I was too intimidated to remember what he was doing."

"We can help you guys with the last part," Sprenger suggested.

Caymen gave him a suspicious look. "We don't need your help. We'll see it again tomorrow."

"Sorry," Sprenger grumbled. He should've known better than to suggest help to Caymen; he never liked doing things with others. *Probably because no one likes doing things with you.*

"I may have to take you guys up on that tomorrow," Korran said much more kindly. "I wouldn't mind having others around to help jog my memory when I forget parts."

"We should all practice it together," Sprenger suggested. He gave Caymen a hesitant look. "Or at least everyone that wants to, I guess."

"Yah," Tenni agreed. "It would be good for all of us to help each other out. That way someone is bound to remember if we forget parts."

Soekka gave a hardly interested shrug. "It could work. I'd rather not be at the training grounds though. It gets too crowded and we would need more room if we are all going to practice together."

"There's not really anywhere else in the village with enough room," Korran said disappointedly.

"We would have to go into the forest then," Tenni pointed out. "Oh," she exclaimed excitedly, "we could use that glade that we found Taxxis in."

"Who?" Korran asked confused.

"That would actually be perfect," Soekka agreed.

"The cat Kanto made us catch on our first day," Sprenger whispered to Korran, who was still giving them a confused look.

"Oh," she giggled. "That sounds good to me." She looked at Caymen. "Are you in?"

He crossed his arms resentfully and gave no indication that he was going to answer.

"Oh come on," Sprenger pushed. "It'll only help you."

"I'll think about it," he said flatly.

"Well I'm definitely in," Korran said eagerly. "I'll let Rejeno know too, and anyone else I see before then."

Tenni nodded her agreement. "Us too. Meet us at the gate when you guys finish tomorrow. Tell the others too."

"Will do," Korran said. She and Caymen waved as they started to leave. "See you guys tomorrow."

"Is this allowed?" Soekka asked curiously as Korran and Caymen walked away. "Kanto didn't say it was just him that we couldn't get help from. He said we had to do it without assistance from *anyone.*"

"Dunno, don't care," Sprenger grumbled tiredly. "My philosophy with rules is that if they want us to follow them, they should make them more clear."

"Good luck explaining that to them if they consider what we're doing as cheating," Soekka grumbled at him.

Chapter 16

The Next Generation

The next morning started the same as the last for Sprenger, Soekka, and Tenni, on the practice field with Kanto demonstrating the routine again. This time everyone watched more, determined to commit it to memory this time. Out of the corner of his eye, Sprenger thought he noticed a few older students stop their practice and watch Kanto as well, but he refused to take his eyes from Kanto. When he looked over, the older student resumed whatever they were doing, and Sprenger wondered if it had been a year or more since they were last shown the routine.

Kanto answered more questions, then helped them with difficult areas for the rest of the morning. When midday came around, he left them again and wished them luck with the routine, but instead of staying at the training grounds, the three of them headed to the gates to wait for the others.

It was not long before Korran, Caymen, and Rejeno showed up. Caymen still wasn't fond of the whole idea, but since the other members of his squad were joining, he would either have to train with everyone or by himself. Sprenger was sure he would have elected to train by himself if he thought he could remember it all without his squadmates.

Kobei's squad was shortly followed by Tarak's squad, who all seemed unsure of the idea with the same reservations that Soekka had pointed out the evening before.

Pillas gave Sprenger a skeptical look. "I'm not so sure squads are supposed to train together for this. Tarak told us that he couldn't help anymore so that we would learn to do things on our own as a squad." He looked around at them all. "This seems to defeat that purpose, if you ask me."

Sprenger noticed Tenni and Korran exchange guilty-looking expressions, as if they hadn't considered they weren't allowed to train together. Everyone seemed to be contemplating what Pillas just said and were not quite sure what to say back to it.

"I like the idea of working together," Pillas pointed out, "but our masters practically told us not to. If we get caught, they might not let us take the exams and we would be letting all our teachers and Lord Scythrith down. I heard he was the one that pushed for us to be here at all."

Seeing the chance to better prepare slipping away, Sprenger thought of what to say to save it. "I suppose you're right, Pillas," he said casually, "but consider this." Everyone looked over at him, probably hoping he could ease their guilt. "Our teachers don't want us becoming dependent on them, which is understandable. I mean, they won't be around forever right? But we're not depending on them by practicing this way. We're depending on one another. I don't know about you guys, but I personally would like to think that we will all be able to call on each other when we need help, no matter how great of scythe we become." Sprenger shrugged. "I guess I've never really seen the logic in depending on only the squad you train with. Which would you rather have in a battle; two people watching your back, or eight?"

"But that's a battle," Caymen protested, still unconvinced. "Battles don't have rules that we have to follow. This is training for an exam. One that we may not be allowed to take if they think we are breaking rules."

"We have not been told that this is breaking rules," Sprenger said smugly. "And I agree that this isn't like a battle by any means, but that doesn't mean we shouldn't always be training like it is." Sprenger noticed Tenni nod encouragingly for him to continue and smile in agreement. "I can't help but think that there is more we are supposed to be getting out of this test then just some fancy new moves. I think we're taking a test of sorts right now; a test of team cooperation." He looked around at them all. "If you want no part in it, then I understand and there is no shame in leaving."

Korran came and stood next to him, making Sprenger a bit excited. "We all were asked to take the Exerptus Exams together," she announced. "Not by squad, but by class. We were asked as the class of Master Cerri to take this step together. I say that since we all began this together, we finish it together. If we are breaking some rule, then they can punish us as a class, and we can take it as a class."

"I agree," Tenni said stepping forward to join them.

"Me too," Soekka joined as well.

"And me," Rejeno added.

One by one, each of the students stepped forward and agreed until it was only Caymen and Pillas left. They looked at each other before giving a sigh and nodding reluctantly.

Sprenger beamed. "Alright then, let's go."

"Halt!" a guard called down from the tower. "Students are not permitted to leave the village without a parent or master's permission."

Sprenger almost stumbled and fell in surprise. "What!" Sprenger yelled back at the guard. "Why didn't you say something earlier?" *As in, before I talked everyone up, you jerk.* The guard gave no reply to his question.

"Well this is a bit of a deal-breaker," Rejeno grumbled as he scratched the top of his blond head. "For some reason I always forget about that rule."

Because they rarely care, Sprenger thought, bitterly crossing his arms.

Caymen grouchily pushed himself to the front of the group with a particularly sour expression and looked up at the guard. "We are now training for the Exerptus Exam. Our masters have given us permission to go wherever we need to in order to accomplish our training. As you know from taking the exam yourself, our masters are not allowed to assist us after a certain point, hence they cannot accompany us."

The guard was silent for a moment. "Very well," he finally called back down.

The group gave a variety of excited exclamations to one another.

"Nicely done, Caymen," Rejeno said surprised.

"Let's just go before someone else sees us leaving," Caymen said quietly.

"Aright follow us," Sprenger announced as he began walking down the road through the gates.

"Where are we going?" Naibi asked eagerly.

"We're not going to the Shattered Hill are we?" Warren asked shyly.

"Course not," Soekka scoffed. "Going there would definitely get us into trouble."

The Shattered Hill was a small mountain of broken and free-standing boulders deeper in the forest. It was a forbidden area that no one was allowed to visit due to a battle that was held there long ago. It was said that so many had died that there was no rock nor blade of grass that wasn't coated in a dura-scythe's blood. To ensure that the dead would never be disturbed and their sacrifice honored, the Shattered

Hill became a sacred area without forgiveness for trespassing.

“We found an open glade in the forest,” Sprenger explained. “No one will bother us there.”

Sprenger, Soekka, and Tenni led everyone into the forest, and after a short ways, relocated the familiar glade that they once caught Taxxis in. Nervous deer darted away as the students began emerging from the trees, looking around with surprise.

“I didn’t know there were any open areas like this in our forest,” Naibi said as she looked around.

“Our forest is so large,” Caymen said uninterestedly, “that there are probably dozens of areas like this scattered all over the place.” Naibi gave him an annoyed look for his condescension but didn’t say anything back.

They all headed out to the center of the glade together and piled their unnecessary items off to the side in the grass.

“So,” Korran said looking around at them all, “should we just give the whole routine a try and then focus on areas that are weak?”

“I think that would be the easiest way to see where everyone’s at,” Rejeno agreed.

They all faced the same direction and took the starting stance. “Ready,” Sprenger said, “start.” They all began going through the motions of the routine together. Sprenger was mumbling the steps under his breath, as they did the night before, and noticed Tenni doing the same to his left.

It did not take long for the class to begin to fall out of sync with one another, but they continued on through the whole thing without stopping. At their own intervals, they smacked their hand to the ground to signal the end.

"Okay," Sprenger said, a bit short on breath, "where do we need the most work?"

"After the first set of left blocks," Pillas said through deep breaths. "We all fell out of unison when we began kicking."

"And," Rejeno added, "a few of us don't remember all of the steps near the end."

"Let's start with the middle," Tenni said, "since those moves will require the most work."

"Who's already pretty good at those moves," Sprenger asked, "and can show us or help us?"

No one spoke up at first, then Korran looked over at Caymen. "Caymen is," she announced. "He can do the first set of kicks and spins really well."

Caymen just stood there cross-armed.

"Perfect," Tenni said. "Caymen, would you mind showing us or explaining what you do?"

Caymen looked around at everyone from under his long black bangs, almost irritably, then sighed and took his stance. He did a few of the steps leading up to the kicks then performed the first set and stopped. "I still haven't figured out the transition from the first to the second set of kicks."

"Let's just focus on the first then." Tenni said.

They all attempted to mimic Caymen as he went through it again and asked for advice here and there, and much to Sprenger's surprise, Caymen began to loosen up a bit around everyone as he did his best to help them with the moves. Once Sprenger and Soekka had figured out the first part, they began to work on the transition to the second part while others continued to perfect the first. Caymen joined them after a while, and between the three of them, they were able to work towards a smooth transition.

"You have to keep your kicking leg close," Sprenger explained when he managed the transition, "then spin on your toes. I lose balance if my kicking leg is still out while I spin."

"Oh, I see," Caymen nodded before mimicking Sprenger's stance.

Caymen was always competing at the top of the class with Soekka and Sprenger, and Sprenger had somehow forgotten that he was actually a rather skilled student.

Sprenger smirked to himself as other students joined them to practice what they had figured out. *We'll have this down in no time.*

-<>-

Kanto watched the students over the trees from his thick branch high in the canopy. He could see Sprenger, Soekka, and the boy with shoulder-length black hair all attempting to transition from the first set of spin kicks to the next, one of the hardest obstacles of this routine.

Kobei stood next to him, staring out at them with a childish grin. "I don't believe it," he said. "You were right, Kanto. How did you know they would all work on it together? I thought maybe two squads or some students from each, but not all three of them."

Kanto just continued to stare out at the glade. "Because this class is different. They realize how valuable it is to have friends that will help you succeed."

Leaves began to fall around them, and then Master Tarak dropped from a higher branch to the other side of Kanto. "Well, what happened?" He asked as if he missed something important.

"Kanto was right," Kobei said, looking around from Kanto's opposite side.

"Really?" Tarak asked in excited disbelief, stretching his bald head out to try and see where they were staring.

"Take a look for yourself," Kanto said softly as he pointed out to the glade.

"Well I'll be," Tarak said jokingly. "I have to admit that I didn't think they'd end up doing it. I have never heard of an entire class practicing together after they graduated from basics." He looked around Kanto at Kobei. "Remember when our squads tried practicing together and Andreas threatened to tell Scythrith Danko?"

Kobei laughed slightly. "Oh ya, she was really scared that everyone would be kicked out of the exam for working together." He shook his head while still laughing. "She was a bit of a nut."

"Unfortunately for her," Tarak added, "the time that she cracked like a nut was in the middle of the battle for the Shattered Hill. I feel sorry that she never got to see us emerge victorious from that. She would've been named a 'Yearling Master' too if she had survived."

Kanto remembered her. *She was a bit... odd.* Kanto never got to know many of the people in his class. His squad decided early on that they would look out for each other and that would be enough. He also remembered when Tarak's squad asked them to help with a section of the routine that they forgot and Kanto's squad refused to help for fear of being called cheaters.

"It surprises me," Tarak said, "that this class wasn't worried as well, or at least that someone amongst them wasn't worried enough to refuse."

"Oh they were," Kanto assured. "Shamolt is on wall patrols, and was listening in on their conversation before they left and told me what they were saying. They all had a bit of a debate, 'but the spiky-haired kid managed to convince them'." Kanto smirked slightly to himself. "Apparently, Sprenger said they should treat this like it was training for a battle and watch each other's backs. One of the girls in you two's squads talked about succeeding and failing all together."

"That would be Korran," Kobei beamed. "She's a good one to have around. Very little will dampen that girl's spirits. Proud to have her."

Tarak was shaking his bald head slightly. "They're a brave bunch, willing to put their necks out for one another and risk their chances at the exam."

"But there is no risk of that," Kobei scoffed. "We just imply it, like our masters did with us. This is the first class to not fall for it, as far as I know. I still don't understand why we do it that way."

"Of course you don't," Kanto said softly, still watching the students. He could see both men give him a surprised look as if he was intending insult, but he continued to stare out at the kids. "We were never willing to risk it," he explained. "But that's why we do it; to teach scythe that there is always going to be risk involved with trusting someone, but the benefits of that trust outweigh the risks." He finally looked over at Kobei. "That is why it is so important that squads feel as though they are doing something wrong. It is a test to challenge them to do it anyway. To force them to choose the right thing, even if someone is trying to convince them that it's wrong." He looked back out at the glade. "Our generations have all failed that test."

Tarak nodded. "The Wars seem to have robbed us all of our trust for one another, as well as the attempted coup of the village. I'll admit just as much fault in that as anyone. The Yearling Masters have stayed true to one another, but we don't seem to trust outside of our own rank."

Kanto nodded. "Our village has lost much of its trust amongst scythe, but hopefully it will be generations like this that rectify that." *By design,* Kanto reminded himself.

Chapter 17

A Familiar Name

"No way, you idiot," Soekka protested. "Lord Scythrith is probably just doing it so that Kimimaro and the idiots from his class aren't the only pentin taking the exam." He kept his voice calm but there was a bit of a haughty flare while he spoke, something that he often did when arguing. It did, admittedly, add a sense of confidence to him that made him hard to argue with.

It didn't, however, hold any sway when arguing with Sprenger. "Soekka, think about it. We'll be the youngest master-scythe ever!" Sprenger pulled his arms behind his head, in a self-satisfied pose as the two boys walked down the main road of Durado. "It makes the most sense. If I were the Old Man, then that's why I would put us in the Exerptus Exam so early in training."

"Or maybe it is simply because Jacob knows we can complete it now and doesn't see the need to wait two more years for it to be held. If it was because he wanted *us* to take the Master Trials next year then why would all the other squads be in the exam too? Huh?"

Sprenger gave a continued self-satisfied smirk and shrugged. "I dunno, probably because he doesn't want to hurt their feelings."

Soekka sighed, a sign he had given up. "Sprenger, some days I wonder how your mind works to come up with the things you do. All I know is that all of us are going to be the youngest scythe there, and quite possibly the youngest ever. I just hope Jacob knows what he's doing."

Sprenger blew air through his closed lips. "The Old Man always knows what he's doing."

The argument had lasted most of the morning. Sprenger and Soekka weren't the only ones in debate about Jacob's decision to send the young squads into the Exerptus Exam so early in training. It had been over a month since they were all informed about starting training for the Exerptus exam and today was their first day off. Since Jacob's decision to have Cerri's class start training was a confidential decision that was urged to be kept secret, word spread through the village like wildfire: Durado was simply buzzing with the news.

Several people had already offered their congratulations as well as good luck, while others gave very poor efforts in keeping their glares in check. Many believed there was some sort of conspiracy underway. Sending new squads into the exams with scythe years farther ahead in training was not something most people overlooked.

Sprenger understood their concern. Some people saw it as Jacob lowering Durado's standards of training by allowing such young scythe to enter. The exams were a way of demonstrating the scythe that had completed their training and were ready for dangerous missions. Sending inexperienced scythe out of the village could lead to their deaths and allow the world to think that Durado was losing its strength.

Though not unheard of, pentin at Sprenger's stage were rare in the Exerptus Exam, let alone an entire class. Not many would refuse an early opportunity at the exams though, since it was the only way to move on to becoming respected scythe with more interesting missions outside the village.

The routine was immensely complex compared to what they were used to, but Sprenger was confident that having all of them training together would be enough for them to pass. All of them had already begun to discuss what missions they were hoping to be sent on as soon as they were allowed.

For the entire week, the nine of them were meeting after morning training, and helping one another to get the routine down. Sprenger always found it helpful to learn if he helped someone with a routine. That way, he forced himself to think about it in different ways that would later improve his own technique. It was also nice to have people who were better at different parts to help explain difficult areas.

The two boys, despite flustering opinions on the matter, continued their walk in silence, watching people go about their day. It was midday, so the village was in full bloom. Every store had bustling people hurrying in and out with baskets full of goods. Villagers shopped and gossiped up in the second stories of the giant roots that held shops, as well as down below, where the larger shops drew the biggest crowds. Children, squirrels, rabbits, and birds all darted over the roots, chasing one another.

Sprenger took a quick glance into Spinners, the finest clothing store in Durado, and as far as Sprenger knew, anywhere. In broad, prominent gold letters over the front door stood the proud words FINEST SILK SOUTH OF THE DANKIRK, and to no exaggeration. The owner, Todd and his wife, Cherr had drastically expanded from Todd's father's old establishment. By means few know of, the family successfully runs their own silk shop. Next door in the same root-building, was the home of the precious worms, and its dozens of workers that care for them and harvest the fine threads.

The clothing was a bit expensive, but in Durado's hot weather it was somewhat necessary to procure. Both Sprenger and Soekka wore silk outfits from Spinners, along with the majority of Durado's residents. During the rainy seasons, Spinners closes and uses the slow business time that the cold weather brings to restock their inventory with piles of silk roles to later fill orders when they reopen. It was often a stop for traders coming through the village who wanted to take it back to the kingdoms and sell it for an even higher price.

Just past Spinners was their destination: the Steaming Pot, Durado's largest eating establishment. It occupied a large portion of a giant roothome, and produced copious amounts of steam and smoke through the branch vents above. The smell of cooking foods would radiate through most of the village on busy days.

In front of the root-building stood Tenni and all the members of the other two squads. They had figured since they all had a day free of training that they should share a lunch to celebrate their taking the exams. The group was already deep in conversation about the different parts of the exam, hardly noticed Sprenger and Soekka join them.

Korran and Tenni pushed their way through a friendly argument between Pillas and Naibi.

"Finally," Tenni complained. "We've been waiting for you two so we could eat." She gave Sprenger a sharp poke to the chest. "Be on time next time." As was typical, Tenni's voice drew everyone's attention. Even Pillas and Naibi, whose argument was about which of them would have higher scores on the exam, had ceased for the time being.

Pillas smiled at Soekka. "I see what you mean about her."

Tenni spun around to look at him, her hands clenched into fists. "What did you say?"

Pillas held up his hands in defense. "Nothing," he said quickly. The rest of the group burst out laughing. Sprenger noticed Soekka give Pillas a confirming nod.

Annoyed passersby on the street began grumbling at them to clear the way, so Warren suggested they head in and eat.

Just as they were about to enter the Steaming Pot, something on the street changed. The buzzing sound of chattering people quieted. People pulled back from the road, as though nervous. Children running nearby were grabbed by their parents.

Sprenger and Soekka noticed the change and looked around for the cause.

Down the road, coming towards them in slow, steady strides, was Juriah. Scythe bowed as he passed, but he paid them no attention; he paid no attention to anyone and continued on his way. He walked with an undeniable presence. His expression was not a welcoming one and his eyes were anything but kind. It set an unseeable aura about him that warned all to be weary. His black leather vest made him a noticeable figure amongst the light-colored outfits in the crowd, and was adorned with his shortsword down his back, the pommel raised behind his head.

Sprenger got a bit excited. He was hoping to see Juriah again since their last interaction, but he also remembered the warning that they received from Jacob about him.

Their group gladly parted to each side of the road as he approached, giving him a deep bow and a wide birth, as all the others had. Juriah didn't give any of them so much as a sideways glance as he passed.

Just before he reached the boys and Tenni, Sprenger slid out in front of him, to the shock of many onlookers, especially the other pentin. Juriah simply stopped and raised an eyebrow at him.

"You again?" He said curiously. "It would seem very difficult to be rid of you lately." He had no anger in his voice, nor did he look upset. Sprenger wanted to see what Jacob was talking about with this man and why people treated him differently.

"I just wanted to let you know that I've been training," Sprenger said haughtily. "I thought I should warn you that I won't go easy on you next time I bump into you in the forest."

Juriah gave a simple snort of humor. "You think so, huh?" He gave Sprenger a stern poke on his forehead. Many students flinched, not sure what he was going to do. None but Sprenger and Soekka knew the meaning of it. "We shall see." Juriah gave him a small smirk, and then continued past Sprenger down the road, seeming fairly amused by Sprenger's joke.

Sprenger rubbed his forehead, not for pain as much as to attempt to rub away the embarrassment of Juriah's last contact with his forehead. Sprenger had almost forgotten how demoralizing it was to be knocked over by a flick to the forehead. He was off-balance to begin with, but still.

Everyone around stared wide-eyed as Juriah continued down the road. When he was a good distance away, people continued to go about their business, but all the students remained gawking at Sprenger. Soekka was the only one who didn't look as though they had just witnessed a murder.

"What?" Sprengcr finally asked, starting to become a bit uncomfortable under the unwavering stares.

"Sprenger," Korran whispered in shock.

"Are you mad!" Tenni blurted. "Do you have a death wish? You think because you saw him in the forest that you can do that? I know you're a bit slow, but I didn't think you were truly stupid."

Sprenger began nervously rubbing the back of his head, not sure what to say to Tenni's overreaction.

"Sprenger," Korran began in a tone that was far more pleasant than Tenni's. "Do you know who that is?"

Soekka stepped up to Sprenger's defense and to draw the unwanted attention from him. "He's a scythe that Sprenger and I ran into during our mission with Kanto's cat. His name's Juriah." Their expressions didn't soften. "Don't worry," Soekka assured them, "Sprenger was only joking with him. He's not *that* big of an idiot to really challenge a batennin yet." Soekka looked away for a moment. "I hope," he mumbled to himself.

Warren began to speak, but hesitated when Soekka moved his attention to him, something many did around Soekka in an argument. After a moment's pause, Warren started again. "Don't you know who Juriah is?" He looked back and forth between Soekka and Sprenger. "Did your parents not tell you the stories as children?"

"Well considering we're both orphans," Soekka snapped, "we missed out on such bedtime stories, so please enlighten us."

That's why people hesitate talking to you, Sprenger thought.

Instead of continuing, Warren fell back behind Pillas, who also looked unnervingly away from Soekka as well.

Korran moved in front of them, giving Soekka a fierce scowl. "That's not what he meant to imply and you know it."

Sprenger put a calming hand on Soekka's shoulder. "Granny Karla told us plenty of stories growing up, but none with someone named Juriah. What stories are you talking about?" He asked Korran.

She took a deep breath and spoke in a calmer tone, but not before looking around them for any eavesdroppers. "Have you ever heard of the village of Corundo?"

"Yah, the Blood-village," Soekka said coolly. "They were the strongest scythe-village entering the last war." He crossed his arms. "Until Durado destroyed them and became the strongest village."

Korran shook her head. "Not us. *Juriah*."

"Meaning what?" Sprenger asked.

"Meaning Durado was credited with the victory against the Corundo Village, but my parents told me that it was only because Juriah and his partner laid waste to the village themselves and without anyone else's help. The damage was so great and their losses so large that Corundo ended up losing the war." Neither boys spoke, nor did any of the other students. Only Sprenger and Soekka looked surprised. "He is not just a scythe, Soekka, he and his squad were the legendary Hessiets of Durado. My parents told me that he's no longer referred to as a dura-scythe, but the Dura-*reaper*." Both boys' jaws dropped.

"*That's* the Dura-reaper?" Sprenger asked in shock.

"The Reaper of Durado," Pillas clarified. "I'm sure you've heard *that* before."

Of course they had, everyone had. There wasn't a single person that didn't hear at least one story over their lives about the Dura-reaper. Once, Granny Karla was speaking to one of her old friends in the market and she told them that there was a fight in one of the taverns the night before. A squad of new scythe was celebrating their new independence from their master, and got a bit too rowdy. "One of them must have said something to the Reaper, because a fight ensued." Her expression turned sad, "he sent them to the healers nearly dead." She slowly shook her head. "They were out of control, I agree, but they were young. What's worse is that some older scythe stepped in to stop it and ended up getting badly hurt as well. That man should be locked up."

Sprenger didn't say so, but he now realized why the name had sounded so familiar when Jacob first said it in his office. There were always stories spreading about missions gone wrong, but none more than when the Reaper was sent out to finish a task. Rumors buzzed of the death that accrued on missions with the Reaper and how his companion dura-scythe didn't always return with him from missions. Soekka and Sprenger never gave it much thought, and certainly had never seen the man before, or if they had, they didn't know who he was.

Soekka and Sprenger shared the same flustered look. Not only had Sprenger just taunted one of the greatest scythe in the village, but both boys had fought him. Had he wished it, Juriah could've killed them with impunity, for simply being an annoyance to him.

"How could two scythe have destroyed an entire scythe-village?" Soekka asked skeptically, after a moment to process everything that Korran had just said.

Korran shrugged. "That's all my parents told me."

"My parents said that because of Hessiets' actions," Warren shyly added, still looking at the ground, "the wars ended. If they hadn't destroyed the Corundo village, we probably would have lost the war."

Such a thing didn't seem possible to Sprenger. It couldn't be possible. To attack a scythe village meant certain death, no matter how skilled the scythe is.

Naibi spoke in a low voice. "You should not speak of this. The Dura-reaper is an idol to draw respect but speaking of him will only bring problems and bad luck." She was nervously clutching something that hung from a leather necklace around her neck. "It's a bad enough omen that he crossed our path. We should stop speaking of this." She was wearily looking at people passing by, as though she expected one of them to attack.

"Naibi is right," Pillas agreed calmly. "Let's go eat before someone gets mad at us."

The students gave Sprenger and Soekka one last look of concern, then filed through the entrance of the foodhouse. Once inside, the group decided on a roasted goose to share. Normally such a thing would be far too costly, but between the nine of them it was only a bit more than what a meal would cost each of them normally.

Their table was a bit of an oddity in a scythe village. Normally squads kept to themselves, worrying only about their own affairs. To have three squads sharing a meal was something people hardly expected to see, and some passersby looked at them as such.

Granny Karla once told them that experienced scythe of Durado kept few ties to the other scythe outside their squads. Something Sprenger had never understood. "All dura-scythe are of the same mind and spirit," Jacob once told him, and Sprenger had always thought that would be enough to bring people together. They all fought for the same home, and the same lives. They all grew up together and should be able to trust one another with their lives. In fact, Sprenger saw much of the village as his family. Many knew him, and many of those folks were very kind and generous while Sprenger was growing up. Though Sprenger was not related to any of them, they all took part in his upbringing. Jacob especially.

Durado was his family.

Jacob was Durado's father, and as good as any Sprenger ever had.

This was Sprenger's whole premise for uniting the other new pentin. And now, here they sat, gossiping and giggling around the same meal. Arguing and harassing one another for it all to end in a laugh, as a family should.

But Sprenger was numb to it all at the moment.

His mind continued to wonder and fall back to what Korran had just them. *Two men destroyed a village, an entire scythe village, much like Durado*, and Sprenger had just openly mocked one of those men on the street. *The Reaper of Durado*, he repeated in his mind.

Jacob should have told him when Sprenger first met Juriah. The Old Man should never have kept something like that from them, knowing what a dangerous man he was. Then again, he did warn them to stay away from him. Sprenger just didn't take heed at the time.

Sprenger thought he could feel his forehead throbbing where Juriah had flicked him, and more recently poked him. It was probably not sore at all, his mind was just teasing him, but now Sprenger truly understood the point of poking him on the forehead. *It's a reminder of what little effort it took for him to beat me.*

He forced himself to push the troublesome thoughts from his mind when Soekka gave him a strange look for his silence. Sprenger forced a smile and jumped into the conversation. He was at a celebration of sorts, afterall. There wasn't a moment of the meal worth missing.

Chapter 18

Breach

Jacob listened politely as the emissary spoke to him from the other side of his desk. The young man had been there for days trying to convince Durado to send scythe to his town, but there were many issues that had arisen with his proposal. Though Jacob admired the emissary's persistence, he was getting tired of having this debate and something else was making Jacob uneasy at the moment, making him all the more impatient with the situation. He didn't know what it was he was feeling, but something didn't feel right. He spent the entire morning looking out the windows, searching for some sign that something was wrong, but never found it. He convinced himself that it was nothing, but he still had this haunting feeling as he sat in his office.

"Lord Jacob," the man continued, "if you were only to send a handful of scythe, it would be enough to quell the violence from Viramon's thugs."

"My friend," Jacob said kindly and sympathetically, "I have already told you. These thugs are the men of your lord and though you and I may not agree with their methods for tax collection and law enforcement, it is not Durado's place to stop it. We cannot counter the men of your lord because he is a man of title and has rights to the land you're on. If you wish something to be done, then you must tell your king. The lords of the Southern Kingdom are in his charge. Durado cannot step on toes wherever we'd like, especially if it means impeding on a king's prerogative."

"We have sent word to the king," the man continued to plea. "The king is ill and little is being done due to the focus on his health. Thrice we have sent word and messengers and thrice we have returned empty handed. We now ask Durado to do something. People are dying," he said with complete seriousness. "Viramon's men kill innocent people and say that they're just enforcing the law. We all know perfectly well that they're killing people that don't line their pockets well enough, but it's our word against theirs. Viramon will do nothing unless confronted by someone with more strength than he. With the king ill, there is no one that he will answer to. Please, Lord Scythrith, we need help."

Jacob had heard that King Pryon was sick a while back but he thought that he would have either improved or passed by now. An illness that has been lingering this long is probably very concerning for the crown and royal court. *I suppose that if they have tried getting the king's attention and failed, the situation may be more dire than we originally thought.* He tugged on his pointed beard, contemplating a scheme that would serve everyone involved in the predicament. "My friend," he said politely again. "I may have a solution, but it will take some time and no small amount of politics."

The emissary perked up excitedly. "Yes of course, my lord. Whatever it is, I will do anything to assist you. My town can pay as well. I've been given permission to give you whatever you ask of us."

Jacob liked this man. He was so passionate for his people, and had wonderful manners. Many of low birth in the kingdoms were poorly educated and could hardly hold their own in a conversation, but Jacob could tell that this man had done his studies to become his town's emissary. He spoke clearly and was literate. It was no mistake that he was the man selected to come bargain with Durado. Jacob hoped his solution would provide help for his people.

"My solution is this," Jacob said. "Since King Pryon has more pressing matters than hearing the pleas of his people at the royal court, I will send him a message personally. Not even a king can ignore a Scythrith." Jacob gave the man a friendly wink, which caused the man to smile eagerly. "I will put all of your concerns into my letter and ask that either he sends forces to quell the violence himself, or grant Durado permission to see to the matter. If he gives us permission, then I will send two squads of scythe to your town at *your* command. They will serve as guards for your people and assure that your lord's enforcement of laws are being justly upheld. If the king chooses to send his own troops to assist, then there is nothing I can do, but either way, something will be done. Would you be willing to accept my proposal in replacement of your request to immediately send scythe to your town?"

The emissary bowed. "Yes, my lord. My town and myself are in your debt."

"You understand that this will likely take some time," Jacob warned. "Politics are an agonizingly tedious thing. Though I have no doubt that the royal court will eventually respond to me, I cannot promise that it will be soon. Your people need to stay strong for a while longer, but find comfort in the fact that something will be done eventually."

"That is all I ask," the man said gratefully. "I will return to my town and deliver the news."

"Very good," Jacob said with a nod. "I will send a messenger to you as soon as I receive word from Billingdor. Please allow me to send a scythe to escort you back to your town and your home, free of charge of course. A gesture of good will between your town and Durado." *Arriving with a dura-scythe at your side may also be enough to prove your lord that you have powerful friends.*

The man bowed again. “I am forever in your debt, Lord Jacob. I hope to see you again and look forward to receiving word from you.”

Jacob nodded kindly at him and watched him leave the office before letting out a sigh. *If he had told us that the king didn’t respond to their pleas already, we could’ve finished this conversation days ago.* Jacob supposed it didn’t matter. He was glad they found a reasonable solution to the problem. He hated turning away good people in need, all in the name of politics, but there were facts of life that he couldn’t ignore.

He stood and turned to look out the window behind his desk once more. His anxious feeling was growing. His old eyes scanned his village, but nothing appeared wrong. He could even see scythe patrolling on the wall in the distance. Despite what his eyes told him, Jacob knew he was missing something. He couldn’t explain it, but he knew that something was amiss and that he needed to do something. Problem was, he didn’t know what the problem was, so couldn’t possibly know what to do for it.

Your old mind is getting the best of you, Jacob convinced himself. *Everyone is safe and happy.*

-<>-

Five...six...seven...eight...nine, the young scythe turned back around and walked slowly along the top of the wall. *Nine seconds,* Phenex thought, *not enough time to move onto the wall and into the village undetected.* Phenex stifled his frustration as he contemplated any other option that they had, but none came to mind. *Even young scythe in Durado are well-trained enough to maintain a steady patrol.* Any other area of the wall will have a more experienced scythe and this was the closest the trees came to the wall.

The young scythe looked right at him for a moment before continuing to scan the heavily leafed trees. Phenex had been watching him for almost an hour from the same branch. There had been no change in the young scythe's patrols the entire time. With the setting sun behind him, and the leaf-full branches all around, all but Phenex's eyes were shadowed from view.

Phenex had watched the whole wall all day. This was the most weakly guarded area, and now there was an inexperienced scythe on patrol. There would be no better opportunity to enter the village, but it was getting to the wall undetected that was the difficult part, and nine seconds wouldn't be enough time.

Phenex pulled back from the outer edge of the branches; he had seen enough. He dropped from one branch to another, until he landed on the ground with a thud and a jingle from the chains surrounding his body.

Grogin, Peatra, Hexis, and Ajax were all standing around him in the shadow of the large tree. The tall, mangled roots and black cloaks concealed them from surveying patrolling eyes.

"It won't be possible without some sort of distraction," Phenex explained to them in a soft voice. "But we need to do it now so that I can be ready come tomorrow."

Hexis gave him a cruel smile. "I have an idea." He pulled a small clay orb from within his cloak; one of many that Phenex knew the man had hidden away underneath the folds of his black drapings. On top of the orb was a cork stopper, that told Phenex it was full of one of Hexis's many concoctions. "If Ajax breaks this on the wall, close enough to where the patrol-scythe is standing, it will be enough to immobilize him for a bit, probably even make him sick. Though it is not as strong as Lord Demaedura's topcill oil, it will have the same sort of effect."

Peatra stepped forward, offended. "Why Ajax? And why is it *you* entering the village, Phenex?"

Phenex didn't respond with more than a glare to Peatra's arrogance. The man always wanted to do everything himself, if for no other reason but to caress his own ego.

Hexis answered first. "Ajax's aim is undoubtedly the best amongst us, and this," he held up the clay orb, "needs to be broken close, otherwise it will not have the desired effect. Like I said, it is not as strong as what Lord Demaedura carries. The clay will make noise when it shatters and if my oil doesn't have the desired effect, the noise might be enough to raise an alarm."

"And I am entering the village," Phenex growled to Peatra, "because Lord Demaedura ordered me to be the one to break into the prison tomorrow. Nothing can be left to chance anymore."

"Do you really think yourself more skilled than me, Phenex?" Peatra challenged. "Don't forget, I killed my Scythrith and escaped my village unscathed. Killing guards at a jail is no more a task for me than it would be for you."

"You are too hot-headed to wait all night in an enemy village, Peatra," Ajax said in his low voice. "Phenex was chosen by Lord Demaedura himself for this task, so it is not your place to question it."

Peatra crossed his arms and looked away with a grunt of irritation.

-<>-

It worked; Phenex quickly pulled his flail free from the branch he used to swing across the gap between the trees and the wall. He could hear the young scythe getting sick a short ways down the patrol path atop the wall, but Phenex didn't stop to look. He trusted that the man was too indisposed to see him hastily land on the flat surface.

He wrapped the chain around himself and dropped silently to the rooftop on the other side, and then into the ally below. He froze in the shadow of the building, waiting to hear if someone was going to raise an alarm.

There was a bit of a commotion on the wall as other patrols noticed their companion falling ill, but none indicated that they suspected someone entering the village. Hexis's oil would no doubt raise questions, but none that could be answered anytime soon. Phenex only needed until tomorrow and the rancid oil was not enough to give scythe reason to think they had an intruder.

With it being mid-sunset, the shadows were perfect to remain hidden for the remainder of the day. Phenex would have to use them all night to avoid unwanted eyes, but stealth would be easy enough now that he was within the village. He pulled up the hood of his black cloak and disappeared farther into the shadowed spaces between the many moss-covered buildings.

Chapter 19

A Returning Threat

The day following the shared lunch between all the squads, everyone seemed to have a long list of tasks to perform for families on their day off. For some, however, it was obvious that they wanted to spend a relaxing day in the bright sunshine and to give their battered bodies a reprieve from the constant training for the exams. Sprenger was having trouble concentrating on the Exerptus routine today. He had been up most of the night before thinking about what he had just learned about Juriah.

No wonder everyone is so hesitant around him, Sprenger thought as he went through it all in his mind again. *Perhaps I should be more careful around him as well.* But that didn't make sense to Sprenger. He, admittedly, remained more awestruck than frightened by Juriah, and Juriah didn't show any signs of aggression towards Sprenger, with the exception of the brief sparring match they had. *But that was my fault,* he reminded himself. *He actually seemed quite amused with it until Soekka showed up.* His mind continued to churn with the ideas all morning, until finally Soekka broke his train of thought.

"Sprenger!" He shouted as Sprenger yet again forgot a step in the routine. Sprenger's attention returned to the glade where he, Soekka, and Rejeno were practicing on their own. Soekka was glaring at him and Rejeno was giving him a quizzical look. "What's with you today? You're fumbling all over the place, and places that should be simple to us by now."

"Sorry," Sprenger grumbled. "I'm just a little tired. Don't worry, I'm ready now."

A skeptical grunt was Soekka's only response. The three of them took their stances once more to begin again. They were the only ones available to train today; everyone else seemed committed to something else this morning. Rejeno seemed happy enough to join them without the other members of his squad and neither Sprenger nor Soekka could think of a reason why it should matter.

Shaking the images of Juriah and his black outfit from his mind, Sprenger focused on what he was doing, trying to concentrate on the routine.

Only a few steps into the routine, however, the lot of them froze. There was a foul scent on the air of the glade. It was the strangest thing that Sprenger had ever smelled. He couldn't even begin to think of something that smelled so odd. Something burning? Something rotting? They all noticed it and their noses wrinkled with disgust. Silently, the three boys looked around for anything that had changed.

Then, a faint hum was audible somewhere close by. It was a somber melody and it only added to the confusion of what was going on. Sprenger felt an odd feeling sweep over him as the smell became stronger. His face became hot and his fingers began to twitch. The feeling dominated everything going through his head and the humming echoed endlessly in his ears, as though it was forcing itself within his mind. Soekka and Rejeno had a similar dumbfounded response, standing with wide eyes and paling skin as something seemed to take them over as well. All three of them looked around shakily, searching for the source.

"What-" Sprenger began but stopped. Emerging from the trees at the opposite end of the glade, was a man garbed in a sleek, dark green robe and tunic, slowly walking towards them from the shadows of the trees. His eyes were slightly curtained by his slick, black shoulder length hair. With a small smirk curling the corner of his thin lips, the man coolly strode towards them, humming the eerie tune. Sprenger could see twisting gold flames erupting from the pommel of the sword draped across his lower back and a young man with dirty blonde hair and dark brown eyebrows following closely behind. The young man looked only a few years older than them, but taller and a bit more filled out in his features. *Scythe?* Sprenger wondered nervously.

As the two of them slowly made their way out of the shadows of the trees and into the open glade, the smell became more and more potent. Like an invisible smog that was suffocating them, the boys began to wheeze and shake. Sprenger's stomach lurched and his face was becoming flushed and feverish. His head filled with an uncomfortable pressure as the humming throbbed in Sprenger's mind, echoing in his skull as though it were trapped inside an echoing cave. Sprenger's eyes began to water, his stomach churned, and he fell to his knees, unable to keep his balance any longer. His mind was screaming at him to run, but his body seemed to be disconnected from the rest of him. He could only watch as the two strangers gradually approached.

He noticed to his left that Soekka was in a similar position, hardly able to keep from falling completely to the ground. He was kneeling and shaking and began to drool slightly before he vomited on the grass in front of him. Soekka grabbed his stomach as he became overwhelmed by tremors. Rejeno was kneeling as well, and clearly fighting back similar urges as his body began shaking slightly.

Without warning, Rejeno threw one of his sparring blades at the robed man, who raised his hand in front of his face and stopped the blade between two of his fingers. His smirk widened greater still, but then he ceased his humming and just smirked at them silently.

How the heck did he do that? Sprenger thought in frantic shock. He had never seen a blade caught before. Next to Soekka, Rejeno had the best aim in the class, and that throw should have been fatal.

The two strangers now stood a short distance away and then stopped their advance.

"Young dura-scythe in training," the robed man said in a mocking and amused sort of tone. His voice caused a cold prickle to run down Sprenger's neck. "So far from your protective walls, you foolish children. Don't you know it is not safe outside your village?" He chuckled at his own joke. "Yet, you may serve in a greater purpose today." He held up the blade Rejeno had thrown at him and examined it in the sunlight while he spoke. "You have a *great* role to play today, actually. I have a favor to ask of you." He turned his gaze towards the three of them. "You see, I'm trying to get someone's attention. An old friend of mine. He should be patrolling somewhere nearby, but I find I would rather he come to me. So, if you would be so kind, I need you to make some noise for me." He gave them a wicked grin. "Preferably a scream," and with that, he sent the blade hurling back at Rejeno.

Sprenger flinched as the sound of metal striking metal echoed in the glade as another blade came soaring over Rejeno's head and collided with the blade directed at him, causing both to ricochet in different directions.

The young man behind the intruder quickly pulled out a sparring blade of his own and held it at the ready. For the first time, the man's smirk temporarily was replaced by a scowl, clearly disappointed his attack was interrupted, but his smirk gradually returned as he watched someone approaching from behind Sprenger. Sprenger's body wouldn't allow him to turn to see who it was though.

A hand clasped on to Sprenger shoulder and the sensation that bound his nerves seemed to dissipate and his head became clearer. Sprenger took a much desired gasp of air as his discomfort lessened.

"Come back to your senses," Juriah whispered from behind him, before striding out to stand in front of them, glaring across the way at the intruders.

"Juriah," the robed man said, with a tone that almost sounded glad to see him.

"Demaedura," Juriah replied with the sound of disgust. "You finally crawled out of whatever hole you have been hiding from me in."

Demaedura! Sprenger recognized the name immediately. *This is the scythe that Juriah was talking to the Old Man about.*

Demaedura began to chuckle to himself. "Come now, brother, you simply have not been looking in the right places."

Brother? Sprenger's mind was racing, trying to make sense of what was going on.

"But in any case," Demaedura continued slyly, "I am home now." For a moment there was silence as both Juriah and Demaedura stared at each other. As if someone gave some sort of signal, Juriah ripped the sword from the sheath on his back, and Demaedura did likewise with his flame pommeled sword. They sprinted at each other, swords trailing behind them, until they met with a clash of steel in the center of the glade.

Like opposite gusts of wind, the two men became engulfed in an indiscernible spiral of swordsmanship. Only for brief moments did they separate before re-colliding. Their feud was long-lasting for the intensity that it was being held at but neither seemed to gain the advantage over the other, nor did they ever show signs of slowing in their battle. If anything, the intensity grew as it progressed. Every move of their fight was flawless, and Sprenger held his breath in disbelief.

Their movements became so intricate that Sprenger could hardly follow which razor edge belonged to whom. At first, Sprenger considered helping, but knew he would serve no purpose in a fight of this level. *I would just get in the way,* he reminded himself.

Across the way, the blond boy seemed to be having a similar debate about entering the foray to help his companion. He clearly felt the need to join the fight but could find no visible opening in which to enter. His eyes darted from the fight over to Sprenger and the others. Sprenger panicked when he saw him look over and began to shake Soekka, who had not yet recovered, but at Sprenger's touch seemed to suddenly snap out of his disorientation with a desperate gasp. Both Sprenger and Soekka clamored for a weapon of any kind as the blond boy ran at them.

Sprenger readied himself with a sparring blade, but as the boy attempted to cross the grassy field, he veered too close to the fight raging between Demaedura and Juriah. As he passed, Juriah spun around Demaedura, swung out his leg, and smashed the top of his foot under the boy's brow, sending him tumbling backwards. After rolling several times, the boy laid seemingly unconscious near the spot he and Demaedura once stood.

Apparently unconcerned about his young accomplice, Demaedura took advantage of Juriah's temporarily shifted attention. With his sword above his head, Demaedura attempted to bring down a devastating hit to Juriah's shoulder.

Juriah barely got his sword up to stop the attack, but Sprenger could tell that he struggled to maintain his control under the force of the blow. Though the attack did not land, it was enough for Demaedura to take control of the fight, and through events that happened too quickly for Sprenger to see, Juriah's sword went spinning from his hand, and stuck in the ground pommel-up in the grass out of Juriah's reach. For several agonizing moments, Juriah was forced to avoid Demaedura's attacks with no protection. Sprenger flinched during several strikes that he was sure would be Juriah's last, but no matter the attack, Juriah somehow was able to maneuver around them.

Even throughout the fast-paced movements of the fight, Sprenger could see Demaedura becoming frustrated that he was losing his chance to end the fight. He swung faster and faster, trying to land any sort of injury on Juriah, but Juriah maintained his evasiveness.

Suddenly, as Demaedura attacked, instead of avoiding, Juriah moved in closer to Demaedura and grabbed the wrist of his sword arm as it came at him and sank his other fist into Demaedura's stomach. Demaedura's slick black hair fell forward as the wind was knocked out of him. He swung his leg in an attempt to knock Juriah away, but Juriah ducked it and struck him again in the side. Demaedura frantically tried to regain control of the fight, but wherever he opened up to attack, Juriah would deliver a crushing blow.

Demaedura finally succeeded in knocking Juriah back far enough to use his sword again and lunged with his shimmering blade outstretched at Juriah, but Juriah evaded it so narrowly that it seemed to skid along the top of his shoulder.

Arching his arm back and loosening an intimidating roar, Juriah smashed his fist into the side of Demaedura's jaw, knocking him to the ground and causing him to skid on his back across the grass before Demaedura rolled over and hopped back onto his feet, with fingers dragging on the ground to balance himself. After spitting out a mouthful of blood, still smirking menacingly, he slowly and unsteadily rose to his full height to face Juriah again.

-<>-

Phenex looked up at the sun's position. *Mid-day,* he thought as he crouched in the shadows of two small bark-covered houses, *it's time.*

Chapter 20

Distracted

Juriah and Demaedura eyed each other dangerously as they recovered from their intense bout. Demaedura's sword was shimmering at his side, while Juriah's remained imbedded in the ground between them. A breeze blowing through the wide leaves of the trees and the grass of the clearing was the only movement around them. The silence was only broken by a groan from the blond-haired boy as he attempted to push himself up while holding his hand to his head. His face shot upward as a deep growl began emanating from behind the treeline. Through squinting eyes of pain, the boy looked at Demaedura, who continued to face Juriah but also wearily eyed the shadowed trees around them.

"You bring a boy," Juriah said to Demaedura as he watched the trees nervously, "but I bring a beast."

Sprenger's heart was pounding to the point that he felt the pulses would cause his chest to explode. *What was that?*

Soekka, too, began looking wide-eyed around them, but Rejeno was lying on his side, arms wrapped around his stomach, groaning in discomfort. Drool was starting to emerge in the corner of his mouth and he seemed unaware of everything that was happening around them.

"Shake him or something," Sprenger whispered to Soekka. "That's what snapped you out of it." Soekka leaned over to Rejeno. Once Soekka laid his hand on Rejeno's shoulder, his eyes snapped wide open, and he shot up gasping for air. Soekka recoiled in surprise, not expecting such a violent awakening.

Sprenger dared not move; he neither wanted to miss the fight, nor remind Demaedura and the blond boy that they were there. Soekka and Rejeno clearly had no compulsion to leave either and knelt next to Sprenger nervously.

A second booming noise began to reverberate through the air, but this one Sprenger recognized...

"That's the alarm bell," Rejeno exclaimed, looking behind him in the direction of Durado. "The village is being attacked!"

Demaedura's smirk widene, and, quick as a fox, he whipped around and sprinted back in the direction he had come from in the forest. The blond boy pushed himself up and did the same, trailing close behind Demaedura.

"Get back to the village now!" Juriah yelled over his shoulder. Without another word he ran over and snatched his sword from where it remained imbedded in the grass and sprinted after Demaedura and the boy.

The three boys exchanged looks of overwhelming disbelief, not sure what to do. Finally, Sprenger clenched the grass beneath his hands and then stood before saying, "Come on, we need to go see what's going on at the village." Soekka and Rejeno were both pale, and still appeared to be in shock from what they just witnessed, but both nodded and stood. They each got a sparring blade at the ready; Rejeno reluctantly took the one that came so close to threatening his life. When they were ready, the three of them went running in the direction of the village.

As they approached the wall, Sprenger could hear the clamor of scythe yelling orders back and forth, echoing from the other side of the massive barrier. Just before the three of them broke through the last bramble of branches concealing the wall, Sprenger heard something whistling through the leaves and jumped back just before a blade imbedded itself in the ground where he had just stood. Soekka mirrored his movements almost in perfect sync as a blade landed in the center of his old footprints. Rejeno jumped to the side the same time as them, but no blade appeared in front of him.

"Wait!" Sprenger shouted through the leafy coverage, hoping his assailants would hear him.

"Stop!" answered a voice shortly after. It did not come from the direction the blades were thrown from, but from near the treeline to Sprenger's right. Sprenger started to push his upper body through the brambles as another set of blades came from the wall. Sprenger flinched, unable to pull himself from the clawing branches around him.

Someone slid in front of Sprenger and with a fell swoop of his arm, knocked away the incoming throwing blades with a sparring.

"I said stop!" Kanto screamed at two scythe standing on the wall, who immediately ceased their attack. "Get down here now!" Kanto demanded of the scythe on the wall. The two scythe hesitated, but reached behind them and each threw a spiral of rope over the edge of the wall. The ropes uncoiled as they fell, with the tips whipping wildly ten feet from the ground as they reached the limit of their length.

Kanto turned around and looked at Sprenger, then Soekka and Rejeno as they emerged from the brush. "Are you lot alright?" he asked with surprising concern. They all nodded, not trusting themselves to speak. "Good," Kanto lightly responded, then his expression hardened once more as the two scythe slid down the wall with both hands clasping their individual ropes, their feet gliding on the surface of the wall in a wide stance to slow their decent. They both hit the ground with a thud then dropped to one knee, supported themselves on one knuckle, and bowed their heads as Kanto turned around.

"You idiots," Kanto barked, "I ought to have Lord Scythrith send you back to training for that! Never attack unless you know exactly what it is you're attacking! You could have killed my students! And I assure you that your deaths would shortly follow theirs if that were the case." The two scythe flinched at his final words. "I want you two to finish my patrol of the wall. Make haste!"

"Yes sir," the two scythe replied before setting off in a brisk jog down the base of the wall.

When they were out of earshot, Kanto released a heavy sigh before turning back to the three of them and saying, "Come. We need to get into the village. It's not safe out here." Sprenger wanted to ask what was going on but he refrained, knowing he would find out when they were no longer in danger.

The group followed Kanto to the front gate. The three of them had to jog from time to time to keep up with Kanto's brisk pace. Inside the gate there were dozens of scythe frantically darting all around them. A few approached when they noticed Kanto.

"Master Kanto," a bald scythe leading two others said.

Kanto nodded. "Captain," he said in reply.

"I was worried you wouldn't find them soon, but now that you have I will close the gates again."

"Thank you for waiting," Kanto said with a nod. Both men bowed slightly to each other before the captain and his men moved around them and shouted to close the gate.

Sprenger looked around. There was no one but scythe on the streets. Everyone else was safely hidden in their houses, as they know to do when the village is under attack.

"Master Kanto," Soekka desperately said, "what's going on?"

"I'm not entirely sure," he admitted. "All I know is that we were attacked on more than one spot on the wall, and there were casualties at the prison."

"Who was it?" Sprenger asked.

"It happened so quickly that I never saw who the enemy was." Kanto slowly shook his head. "They attacked and then they were gone. Whoever it was, there wasn't very many of them. There were very few casualties on the wall which leads me to believe that those attacks' main purpose was to be a distraction."

"What do you mean there wasn't very many?" Soekka asked skeptically. "As in there were only a few squads?"

Kanto shook his head. "A few scythe. Five at most."

"That's impossible," Rejeno said in disbelief.

Kanto was going to respond but someone behind him called his name. A scythe that Sprenger recognized from around the village was running towards them. He stopped in front of them, panting slightly.

"Master Kanto," he repeated. "Lord Scythrith has asked for you. He is at the prison, and requests that you join him there as soon as possible."

Kanto turned to the three of them. "Go home and stay there."

"Actually," the scythe interjected before Sprenger could argue. "Lord Scythrith has asked that they join you as well."

Kanto turned skeptical. "Why?" he growled. "They would be safer at home."

The scythe did not waiver, unintimidated by Kanto. His voice was just as sure as when he started. "He asked that if you had found the missing students, which you have, that I should summon you all." He bowed slightly at the waist. "And not to argue with you sir, but there is no safer place than with the Scythrith himself."

Kanto seemed to have no response to that for a moment. "Fine," he finally said.

The scythe then turned to the boys. "I will inform Lady Karla," he looked at Rejeno, "and your parents as well, that you all are safe and where you are."

Sprenger smirked slightly. "That's probably a good idea."

"I'm surprised she isn't standing at the gate herself," Soekka agreed.

The scythe nodded at them, turned to Kanto, bowed, and then headed off.

"Come," Kanto ordered as he began running down the main road to the prison that was near the back of the village. The boys took off after him.

Rejeno came up close to Soekka and said, "We need to tell them about what happened in the clearing."

"I'll tell Master Kanto when we get to the prison," Soekka said. "That way Lord Scythrith can hear as well."

Rejeno nodded. For the first time since the glade, Sprenger realized how pale Rejeno was. His face looked as though he was still feeling sick. As Sprenger watched him for a moment he noticed Rejeno was swallowing frequently, even while running. Sprenger realized he must still be fighting the urge to vomit.

Odd, Sprenger thought, *I felt fine after Juriah snapped me out of it.* He looked over at Soekka and noticed nothing out of the ordinary. The color had even returned to his face, and Soekka was the only one that actually got sick from whatever caused it. *If anyone,*

Soekka should still look sick. It seemed to affect him the most for some reason.

Sprenger's line of thought was interrupted as they ran by the Rithhold. There were no guards at the front door like there usually were, which meant Jacob wasn't there. Sprenger knew that, but it was not very often that Sprenger had seen the front entrance without guards.

After several minutes of running down the empty road, Durado's prison came into view. The drab square building was a very gloomy sight. With no windows or extending features, it was truly the most depressing place in Durado. The building's front was surrounded by a high spiked fence. The gates bore the symbol of Durado, but at the moment it was split up the middle by the parted doors. Several scythe were visible in the courtyard, but what they were doing Sprenger could not tell.

As they passed through the looming opened gates, Sprenger noticed Jacob's unique black robe adorned with white pattering along the seams, and Durado's emblem embroidered in white on his back. Sprenger could also see he was holding his uniquely long blade. The blade was of the same look as all scythe blades, but Jacob's was a bit longer and forked near the base to produce a second small blade just above the handhold. He was standing in the center of ten or so scythe clustering around him and something Sprenger could not see.

The group stopped on the outskirts of the crowd. Sprenger began to walk forward to speak with Jacob, but Kanto put his arm out to stop him, and shook his head. Sprenger crossed his arms impatiently but did as Kanto instructed. No one in the courtyard spoke. Many of the scythe were bowing their heads, while some, including Sprenger and the others, were still attempting to get a look at what Jacob was standing over.

Finally, the crowd parted enough so those behind could see. At Jacob's feet lay three bodies, which were saturating the ground with thick pools of blood. The chest of the man closest to them had been completely smashed inward with, what Sprenger assumed to be a large mace or hammer of some kind. The next had a similar injury, but it lay in the curvature of where his shoulder met his neck, which in this man's case, had clearly been parted from the spine it once held onto. The third lay flat on his stomach, no clear source of his bleeding was visible, but Sprenger could imagine what injuries he held on his down-turned front.

Jacob turned to face the onlookers; all raised their gazes to their aged leader. His expression went from somber to fierce. "Do not let their sacrifice be for not. Secure this village!" he roared, swiping his hand through the air. "Send word throughout the ranks that, if found, this enemy is only to be confronted by batennin. Go!" All of the surrounding scythe, with they exceptions of Jacob's four guards, Kanto, Sprenger, Soekka, and Rejeno, gave a small bow and sprinted past them through the open gates to their backs.

Jacob gave a heavy sigh as he gave the dead scythe one last look before turning his attention to the group. His wise eyes fell on Sprenger and for a moment, Sprenger could see relief wash over him before he looked up to Kanto. "What news?" he asked Kanto.

Kanto didn't hesitate to report all that he knew with a surprisingly stoic face. "There were at least five that were in the village. Four attacked the wall from each direction. I believe to draw attention away from here. There were about four more casualties during the attack, apart from these three," he indicated to the bodies behind Jacob. "The assailants were highly skilled, but quickly overwhelmed with patrol scythe throughout the village. They each fled in opposite directions into the forest when confronted in force. Masters are leading squads in pursuit of them now."

Jacob tugged on his pointed beard, pondering the information he was just given. "We already did a sweep of the prison," he said calmly but gruffly. "Tranis and his partner are missing. That must have been the reason behind all of this. I'm sorry to say that I know who these five men were, and it worries me that they converged on Durado."

"There were seven," Sprenger added. Kanto and Jacob looked at him. "There were seven attackers." Sprenger clarified.

"What do you know Sprenger?" Jacob asked, stepping closer.

"There was another man in the forest with a boy that was a bit older than us. With the others, that makes seven." When their expression didn't change, Sprenger began to become frustrated, not sure how he could be any clearer. He was about to try and explain again but before he could, Jacob spoke.

"Where were these other two?" his voice was becoming more anxious as he spoke. "Were they in the village?"

"No, Lord Scythrith," Soekka replied. "It was in a glade in the forest, where we were training." Jacob's eyes flickered to each boy as they spoke. "Juriah was also in the forest and drove them off. He was headed into the trees after them, last we saw."

"Is there anything you boys can tell me that could help us find out who these men were? Can you describe them? Where they wearing black robes?"

“It was Demaedura,” Sprenger said surely, skipping all the questions.

Though expressionless and sturdy, the color drained from both Jacob and Kanto’s faces. Clearly Sprenger had said something more significant than he realized.

“How do you know that name?” Kanto demanded quietly.

Sprenger’s stomach lurched. He forgot that he wasn’t supposed to hear anything after their first mission.

Soekka’s face remained calm, but his eyes widened and began to look over at Sprenger, but he caught himself and returned his gaze to the ground. Both boys knew that if Sprenger wasn’t careful, Jacob would realize that they had eavesdropped on his conversation with Juriah.

Sprenger could feel himself begin to panic. Nervous dread started to build in his stomach. Then, much to his surprise and enormous releif, Rejeno spoke up.

“My Lord,” he said weakly and everyone looked at him. “Lord Juriah knew him. He called him by name.”

“Yah, that’s right!” Sprenger blurted excitedly, but quickly shied away as everyone gave him an odd look.

Jacob didn’t seem completely convinced for a moment, but Sprenger held his innocent expression. He knew from experience that the trick to convincing Jacob was to hold composure under his powerful gaze. Even the hardest scythe can break beneath it, but Sprenger had years of practice with lying to Jacob that few others had. The few seconds of silence seemed to drag on, and Sprenger was beginning to doubt his luck, but still he stood there innocently. Finally, Jacob looked away. Sprenger and Soekka both let out a silent sigh of relief.

He shifted his attention to Kanto and said, "I want you to go rescind my previous orders. No one is to leave these walls. I want all scythe that aren't patrolling the village or taking head counts on the wall. Pull all patrols on the outside of the wall and ring the bell, call back those pursuing squads. Send out one messenger to the patrol bases and tell them to move all activity to surveillance. They are only to report sightings, not engage. I want to hear of no more deaths today." Kanto nodded his understanding.

"And Kanto," Jacob added. "I want you to find Master Skyle. You two track down Tranis, and if at all possible, kill him. Juriah is in pusuit of Demaedura. All patrols are to assist in his hunt, but none but Juriah are to confront him. All Adimortis are to be avoided unless absolutely necessary."

"Understood," Kanto said with a quick nod. With that, Kanto ran off.

Jacob's voice softened once more. "You," looking down at Rejeno, "look paler than a corpse. Go see the healers. I'm sure they can settle your nerves." Rejeno gave a bow, and without saying anything, gladly headed through the gates.

"I would like you two to stay with me for the time being," Jacob said once Rejeno had disappeared. Jacob ushered them forward, but Sprenger didn't move.

"You're not just going to leave Juriah out there without reinforcements are you? If you call everyone back then there will be no one to help him."

For the first time since Sprenger had arrived at the prison, Jacob's wrinkled forehead relaxed and his face regained its warm composure to comfort Sprenger. "I have learned time and time again not to waste my worry on Juriah of the Hessiets' survival." He leaned in closer and whispered softly, "The man is impossible to kill." He gave Sprenger a quick wink and rose to his full height again. "He prefers to work alone anyway." Sprenger forced a smirk, though he still wasn't completely comforted. "Come now." Jacob gestured for Sprenger and Soekka to follow him as he also headed for the gates of the prison's courtyard. "You boys should stay with me for a while, until the village is no longer on lockdown." Sprenger clung closely to Jacob's side. For the first time since he heard the eerie humming and smelled that putrid odor in the glade, Sprenger felt safe.

Chapter 21

A Legend Long Since Silenced

Soekka and Sprenger quietly stared out the windows behind Jacob's desk, staring out across the village, looking for any sign of commotion. There was no one on the streets, which Soekka had only seen once as a child. That had been when a group of rouge scythe trying to steal from the village. They came in like any other travelers looking to shop or trade, but were caught in a few minutes with something that was not theirs. They tried fighting their way out, but the dura-scythe kept them at bay while the village was locked down. This time, Soekka could see the eerie effects of a lockdown on the village, as opposed to just Granny Karla constantly shushing them in the back room of their roothome.

Every once in a while, a scythe would come and update Jacob about what was going on with patrols and surveillance. Jacob mostly just sat behind his desk and tugged on his little beard and nodded stoically to the reports. They hardly gave any news worth noting, which Soekka was a bit anxious about. There had been two in the last hour, but nothing about Master Kanto's search, which had begun over five hours ago.

Worriedly, Soekka stared over Durado's roothomes and green structures at the wall. Dozens of scythe were visible on the wall that Soekka could see, and hundreds more where he couldn't. Those that he could see appeared to be very small statues shadowed in the setting sun. They all stood tall and unwavering. None of them had moved since the village had been locked down. Nothing had moved.

"Look," Sprenger said suddenly, "someone's coming."

Soekka lowered his gaze from the scythe on the wall to the main road. Sure enough, someone was making their way up the road. “I don’t think it’s a messenger this time. They’re just walking.” It was impossible to discern one person from another with their backs to the sun.

“Boys, come away from the windows for now,” Jacob said from his chair behind them.

Soekka was too anxious to know what was happening to want to leave the windows, but he dared not ignore his Scythrith. Both boys reluctantly pulled away from the windows and moved to in front of Jacob’s desk.

Sprenger leaned up against one of Jacob’s tall armchairs by the fireplace. “How long are you going to keep the village locked down for, Old Man?”

Soekka used to find Jacob’s nickname funny as a child, but he had since become numb to it and was accustomed to hearing Sprenger say it. Jacob, likewise, never seemed to mind.

“Until I’m confident that the threat on our village has passed,” he answered calmly.

“Well, when’s that gunna be?” Sprenger demanded. Soekka gave him a small nudge with his elbow to remind him to stop being a pain, though Sprenger did not seem to grasp the hint.

Jacob just gave them a kind smile. “Once I’m sure the enemy has crossed our boarders, but that may not be their intentions. It’s bcst to just be patient so that we can be safe.”

Sprenger crossed his arms, clearly not satisfied with Jacob’s answer. Jacob gave a warm laugh at Sprenger’s discontent. “Oh my boy, I know you don’t like being cooped up but it’s not for much longer.”

“Jacob, do you think Master Kanto is alright?” Soekka asked. It wasn’t very often that Soekka got to call Jacob by name. He only did it when they were all alone, like when they were children, but he called him by title when others were around. A courtesy Sprenger never grasped.

Jacob shrugged slightly. "It's impossible to tell at this point. They could be engaging the enemy as we speak, or even be returning to the village. There is simply no way to know." There was a third option that Jacob was kind enough to leave out. *They could be dead.*

Something Soekka was doing must have revealed his worry to Jacob. "Don't fear child. There is reason why I choose Master Kanto and Master Skyle for this mission, and that is because they are extremely skilled scythe. They would never get into something they couldn't get out of. Have faith in your teacher, Soekka."

Soekka forced a smile, though his worry hadn't really lightened.

Suddenly, the door behind them burst open, causing both Soekka and Sprenger to jump. Juriah came storming into the office, and the boys quickly moved to get out of his way.

"Have you gone mad!" Juriah barked. "Has your age finally made you senile, or are you simply a cowardous fool?"

Soekka noticed Sprenger preparing to say something, but Soekka quickly nudged him and shook his head in a desperate plea for Sprenger's silence.

Jacob simply propped his elbows up on his desk and laced his fingers in front of his mouth, waiting for Juriah's yelling to end, and after a few moments, it seemed it finally had.

Despite the sudden energy in the room, Jacob spoke calmly. "I assume you are about to explain what you mean, but if you require me to ask the question, I will."

"The border patrols! You called them back and told them to stay hidden. Why!"

"They would serve no purpose aside from aiding your pursuit," Jacob answered plainly. "I take it you didn't manage to catch Demaedura?"

"You know as well as I that he is too quick to chase through the forest, especially when he gets into the canopy. If I'm going to catch him, I need something to slow him down. If you pull the patrols then there's nothing to keep him from fleeing even farther."

"You are asking me to use scythe as reckless distractions against someone they could not hope to defeat. You cannot ask me to sacrifice good men and women for such a chance of long odds."

"Oh yes I can!" Juriah clenched his fists and stomped towards Jacob's desk angrily. "Considering that is their job as scythe!" He certainly wasn't as composed as a scythe should be. "If you asked me," Juriah growled angrily, "I'd say you were scared."

Jacob, on the other hand, remained calm. "We have already lost enough lives today, Juriah. I will not pointlessly lose more."

"It wouldn't be pointless if it meant me finally catching Demaedura. Your priorities are horribly mangled if you truly think the lives of your patrols are worth more than catching and killing Demaedura. Think of the lives he's already taken. Do they mean nothing?" Juriah paused to let his last words sink in for a moment before continuing. "What I'm hearing you say is that the Adimortis can attack a great scythe village with impunity? They can come and go as they please? You're allowing them to desecrate your village and then just walk away. So I ask again... Have you gone mad?"

Jacob continued to patiently watch Juriah as if he were watching a child throw a tantrum, and simply waited for him to settle down. When Jacob was sure Juriah had finished, he leaned back in his tall-backed chair. "We had no way of knowing this would happen. This was a bold move by any scythe's standards. They surprised us and caught us unprepared. I am protecting my remaining scythe so that next time someone thinks it possible to attack Durado, we can crush them." Juriah's attitude didn't soften, but he remained silent. "Be patient, Juriah. Someday he will make a mistake, and someday you will catch him when he cannot run."

Juriah looked away from him, as if he wanted to start yelling again, but was fighting to keep quiet.

"Juriah," Jacob finally said, "have you thought of any possible reason why all this happened?"

"No," Juriah grumbled. "All we know is Tranis and Cellic were among Demaedura's vassals before he went rogue. They were locked up for it, but that wouldn't bother Demaedura. They were simply tools that he no longer had any use for. To come back for them now makes no sense."

"You must have some idea of what Demaedura has been up to?" Jacob pressed curiously.

"I do, but it doesn't answer any of our questions."

Jacob began tugging on his beard. "What has he been doing?"

"He's searching for Nymphigori."

Jacob stopped tugging his beard. "What? How can that be? He must know there are none left, there hasn't been for over a decade."

"He knows what we know, and we know how very possible it is for a village to protect a Nymphigori in secret."

Before Jacob could respond, Soekka's worst fear came true. "What's a Nymphigori?" Sprenger asked. Juriah and Jacob looked over at them as if they had not realized they were there. Soekka wanted to hit Sprenger for drawing attention to them.

Almost immediately, Juriah's gaze fell on Sprenger's spiky hair. Something many people did, and something Sprenger hated.

"Why are they even here?" Juriah snapped at Jacob.

"Don't worry yourself with them," Jacob replied. "They are not your concern."

"I could say the same to you." Juriah and Jacob glared at each other for a moment.

"I invited them to stay with me while the village is locked down. I would appreciate it if we finished our conversation after they have left."

"Then send them home already. This is far more important than babysitting."

Soekka and Sprenger both crossed their arms in resentment.

"They were fine here until you barged in," Jacob snapped, clearly losing patience, "and I don't want them listening to conversations about our current situation. I momentarily got caught up in the discussion, but now this conversation must wait."

"What's a Nymphigori?" Sprenger repeated impatiently. Soekka gave him a quick hit to the chest for not staying quiet, but Sprenger just gave him a resentful look before continuing to stare at Jacob.

"Never mind that Spre-" Jacob began, but Juriah cut him off.

"It was the name given to those who were companions to Feral Beasts."

"Juriah," Jacob hissed angrily, but Juriah ignored him.

Sprenger's nose wrinkled with confusion. "To *what?*"

Soekka stood quietly but was also curious to hear the explanation as well.

Juriah turned on Jacob. "You haven't even told them that much?" The two exchanged fierce glares yet again.

"It wasn't time," Jacob growled from behind his desk. Soekka had never seen someone get under Jacob's skin before. He had seen him angry but this wasn't a situation that Soekka expected him to get upset about.

Juriah curiously looked back at them for a moment, then returned to Jacob. "Well I guess it's time now." He gave Jacob a taunting smile. "You're welcome. Always happy to take the first step." Juriah took a step back and extended his arm towards Soekka and Sprenger, as if he was ushering Jacob through a door.

Both boys looked over at Jacob, awaiting a response. Jacob finally pulled his glare from Juriah and took a calming breath.

"The Feral Beasts were powerful creatures of intimidating size and intelligence. Long ago, the first wars broke out between scythe villages and nations ruled by kings. In order to expose the villages, soldiers began destroying the forests and mountains in which many were built. But the destruction of the natural world brought forth something the kingdoms had never seen before. It had awakened mighty beasts that dwelled in the trees and soon scythe and beast had a common enemy. After realizing the power and strength of these beasts, the five Scythriths of the time began investigating ways to use Feral Beasts as weapons and allies.

"They discovered that some beasts were willing to form bonds with certain scythe. Not all were willing to help of course, but those that were became powerful friends. The scythe who were able to form a partnership with a Feral Beast were known as Nymphigori. Each Great Village possessed at least one Nymphigori, and even some of the smaller scythe villages that had no Scythrith came to possess some."

"So we had a, uh-" Soekka struggled with the word.

"A Nymphigori," Jacob finished.

"We had several over the years," Juriah answered. "In your lifetimes, we had four. They were one of the reasons we became such a powerful scythe village." Juriah seemed about to say something else, but Jacob harshly cleared his throat, signaling to Juriah to be quiet.

"Then where are all of them?" Soekka asked as politely as he could.

Jacob took another deep breath. "After the last Great War between the five villages, the damage and death toll across the land was horrifying, so a treaty was agreed upon. One of the demands for peace required all the Feral Beasts and their Nymphigori to be destroyed." Soekka could tell that saying this was causing Jacob some sort of pain. He had never seen him so riled up before. "Not doing so would have meant fighting alone against the newly allied villages that did agree on it, and no end to the wars."

"All four of them were killed?" Sprenger whispered sadly.

Jacob and Juriah exchanged a look, as if they were having a silent conversation.

"It's not time, Juriah," Jacob whispered.

"You're right. The time has long past," Juriah rebutted. "This should have already happened long ago, but you have lost sight of what's important. Tell me I'm wrong."

Jacob was silent. The boys just looked from one man to another, waiting for an explanation.

Apparently having come to a decision, Jacob gave Juriah a slow nod and lowered his gaze to his polished desk.

"All but one was killed," Jacob mumbled.

"Me," Juriah said impatiently, in answer to the question both boys were about to ask. "I was once a recognized Nymphigori." His raptor gaze fell on Sprenger. "Along with your mother." Sprenger's jaw dropped. Then Juriah landed his gaze on Soekka. "As well as both your parents." Soekka's stomach lurched.

Soekka didn't know what to say. Sprenger likewise seemed to be at a loss for words. The two boys stared at one another in shock, as though just seeing one another for the first time.

"H-how..." was all Soekka could force out.

Jacob refused to look up at them. "Don't concern yourselves on 'how' or 'why' right now. Try to understand what we're telling you."

Soekka understood just fine what they had been told, but it was the reasons behind all of it that he wanted to know more of. *Why keep such things secret? Why tell us now? How did they die?* Soekka dared not ask any of them though.

"If it helps," Juriah said, "just know that they died for the village's protection, as a scythe should." Soekka scowled at him. There was no sympathy in his voice. His tone had not softened like Jacob's had. Telling them this was clearly not causing him any inner-turmoil.

"I don't understand," Sprenger said in a shaking whisper. He mouth continued to move as though trying to form more words, but nothing further came out.

"I don't expect you to understand all of it at one time," Jacob said in a calm whisper, as though he was expecting either boy to erupt at any moment.

"When?" Sprenger finally said, his voice shaking. Soekka looked over at him. Sprenger's eyes were wide and beginning to gloss over. He was in shock, but Soekka could sense something inside him churring to come out.

Juriah raised a curious eyebrow to him. "When did all this happen? About eleven years ago. You would not have been more than a couple years old." Juriah turned his head and looked out the windows behind Jacob's desk. The sun had nearly completely set. "It was around the exact same time that the Shattered Hill was declared sacred."

What a strange thing to add, Soekka thought.

"No!" Sprenger shouted, causing Soekka to jump and both Jacob and Juriah to look back to him. "When were you going to tell me this?" Sprenger demanded, glaring at Jacob. "No one has ever spoken to me about my parents until now, and it was only because *he,*" he pointed at Juriah, "made you. When were you going to tell me? Did you think I didn't deserve to know? Did my mother do something wrong? Did you just think we couldn't be trusted to know why our parents are gone? Tell me," Sprenger pleaded with a mixture of sadness and anger, seeming to lose control of all the emotions these questions caused him.

"Sprenger," Jacob whispered calmly. "There is more to this than you know."

Juriah snorted. "Obviously," he scoffed. "We've barely scratched the surface of our village's secrets."

Jacob suddenly slammed his fist down on the desk, causing Soekka to jump. "No more Juriah," he growled. "Parken!" In moments Jacob's tall, square-jawed guard came through the doorway and dropped to a knee in front of Jacob's desk. "Take them home. I'm sure Karla is having a fit not having them close during a time like this."

Now he cares about that, Soekka thought bitterly. He was avoiding Sprenger's questions and Soekka had never felt so shunned before in his life.

Parken nodded his understanding, rose and began ushering Soekka and Sprenger out the door. Jacob turned to look out the windows and clasped his hands behind his back so he wouldn't have to watch them leave.

Soekka followed Parken's lead, not wanting to fight the big scythe, but Sprenger seemed to have other thoughts.

"Why didn't you ever tell me this!" Sprenger shouted at Jacob, desperate to learn more. "Why hasn't anyone ever told me this!"

Juriah crossed his arms and watched as Parken scooped Sprenger up in one arm and urged Soekka out with the other. Jacob just continued to gaze out the window, unresponsive.

Sprenger flailed frantically but his large captor didn't waiver. Sprenger continued to scream at Jacob, to receive no reply. Soekka could hear Sprenger's voice beginning to shake once again, almost as though he was about to cry. Soekka understood the pain he was feeling, but knew there was nothing to be done to help it. Hearing Sprenger yelling in such pain nearly brought Soekka to tears as well. He could feel his eyes becoming damp, but he blinked it away. He couldn't let such damaging emotions out at a time like this.

Soekka could only listen to Sprenger's pleas as they were escorted out of Jacob's office.

-<>-

Jacob just stared out across the village. It had been years since he had felt this heartbroken. It was the fear of such pain that kept this moment at bay for so long. He could still hear Sprenger's cries outside.

When that boy becomes determined about something, he is not likely to stop. The thought gave Jacob no joy at the moment.

He could feel Juriah's hawk-like gaze staring at him. At least the man was remaining quiet for now, probably because he knew there was nothing he needed to say. He was a smart man; he would wait for Jacob to make the first move.

Jacob just stared out the window a while longer, dreading the reality he must now face. Finally, he forced himself to begin the conversation that he knew he would eventually have to have. Juriah apparently knew as well, or else he would not still be here.

Jacob took a bracing breath. "That was not how I wanted them to find out." He remained looking out the window. He didn't want to see Juriah's 'told you so' look.

"If you wanted it to go better, then you should have told them before now." Juriah's voice remained strict, but he had softened since the boys left.

"I know."

"You allowed yourself to become too close to him. You made this difficult on yourself."

"Can you really blame me, Juriah?"

"Yes," Juriah snapped. "We all have our parts to play in your little plan and-"

"*Her* plan," Jacob corrected.

"Whatever, the point is that you came dangerously close to letting it all come apart. And for what? Because you were afraid he would hate you?" Jacob just remained silent. "If it gives you any comfort, he would have hated you no matter when you told him."

"No, Juriah. That gives me no comfort." Jacob took another calming breath to keep his pain from surfacing. "I would still like to thank you."

"For what?" Juriah asked suspiciously.

"You did what I was not strong enough to do." Jacob finally turned around and looked over at Juriah, who stared right back. "Do you think he will forgive me if given the time?"

Juriah came over and looked at the sunset next to Jacob. "I don't much care." Jacob smirked at that, though he knew Juriah was completely serious, pretending it was a joke made him feel a bit better. "What I'm more concerned about is what you plan to do when they start asking questions. Especially the dark-haired brat."

"Let me handle that." Jacob turned a very serious look to Juriah. "And I want you to make no mistake. Soekka is not his parents."

Juriah didn't look away from the sunset. "Let's hope not."

Chapter 22

The Danger of Curiosity

After Parken had dropped them off, Sprenger and Soekka said very little to each other or to Granny Karla. They sat around the table, mulling over what they had just been told in Jacob's office. Each boy stared listlessly into a hot bowl of soup that Granny Karla had made for them. She could tell that they were upset, and after Parken informed her of what had happened, she did not bother asking questions. She allowed them to contemplate things on their own.

It all seemed so strange, so unreal, that neither boy completely believed it. To find out so much so soon was overwhelming. Neither boy ever inquired much about their parents growing up, not that they ever got much of a response when they did, but they didn't care. It was common for there to be war orphans in a scythe village, and the boys had accepted that truth a long time ago.

Now, however, they didn't understand why their parentage had been kept a secret from them. The idea of Feral Beasts was daunting enough, but to throw their parents into the mix with them was too much for the boys to completely wrap their minds around at once.

They kept exchanging looks with one another, as though they needed to talk about it, but neither seemed able to find the words to say. What comforts or questions do you ask someone that is just as confused as you are? Every time one of them would open their mouth to say something, they would close it again awkwardly and the other would look away, disappointed that the silence wasn't broken.

They sat at the table in silence while Karla was cleaning dishes at the counter. Suddenly, Sprenger realized something that now seemed obvious: Granny Karla. Surely she would know what was going on. Parken told her that they knew, and she didn't need any more explanation than that. She was in on whatever was happening.

Soekka noticed Sprenger's change and gave him a silent but curious look. Sprenger gestertured with his chin to Granny Karla's back. Soekka turned to see what he was referring to, then turned back with realization dawning in his eyes. He nodded to Sprenger, then took a bracing breath.

"Granny Karla," Soekka said softly.

She looked ovcr her shoulder at him. "Yes, dear?"

Soekka hesitated, looking to Sprenger, who nodded back encouragingly. "What do you know about our parents and their feral beasts?"

The moment that followed Soekka's questions made Sprenger suddenly nervous, as though they had just deliberately broken a rule of some kind. The boys looked at one another through the corners of their eyes as they waited for her response.

Granny Karla ceased whatever she was doing at the time and slowly turned around. Sprenger watched her nervously, though her expression was not stern, nor did she seem particularly upset. If anything, her face seemed more stoic than ever.

Granny began to say something, but stopped, as if she reconsidered whatever she was going to say, then started again. "Children, what you have to understand is," she stopped again. She was clearly struggling with what to say, or how. She let out a frustrated breath.

"Very well then," she said, coming to some sort of decision with stern conviction. She came over and sat down at the table. "You boys have been through so much. More than you remember, I'm afraid." She folded her hands in her lap, then looked both boys in the eye to make sure they were paying attention.

"First of all, the reason why these things have been kept from you boys wasn't for petty or cruel reasons. It was because there was no other way." She paused for a moment, considering her next words. "After the war between the five scythe villages, there was a great deal of tension between the remaining scythe. The war had ended, but we were still far from peace. Three years after the treaty between the Scythriths was signed, an additional treaty was made to ensure that the scythe world would be balanced, and that a village's strength would only be determined by the skill of their scythe. They ordered the death of every Nymphigori and known Feral Beast. The villages that did not agree to follow the treaty would become the enemy of the newly-allied villages."

She took a bracing breath. Soekka and Sprenger took the opportunity to exchange sidelong glances.

After a brief moment, she sturdied her posture and cleared her throat. Sometimes Sprenger forgot that Granny Karla was a scythe in a past life. She was trained to suppress her emotions while others were around. "Scythrith Jacob was forced to agree to the treaty. He handed all of the village's Nymphigori over to the scythe of the newly-allied villages. They were never seen again."

"What did they do with the Feral Beasts?" Soekka asked gently.

"Why would they go?" Sprenger added.

Karla's voice was softer now. It showed her respect while speaking of honored dead. "Most Nymphigori understood that their sacrifice would mean safety of their village. That is the true duty of a scythe, after all. They went willingly, and their beasts followed them to their deaths. That is what it meant to be a Nymphigori: to fight and die alongside the Feral Beasts that were bonded to them."

Frustration and confusion was beginning to boil in Sprenger. "But Juriah was allowed to live?"

Granny gave a lazy shake of her head. "Your mother willingly presented herself to die, along with her and Juriah's companion beasts but Juriah himself was never handed over, nor did the new allied villages come to claim him."

"Then why would she do it at all then?" Soekka asked.

Granny's gentle voice took on a sharper edge. "Probably because she knew that Juriah would not go willingly. He would have fought to his last breath before being taken, or before he allowed them to take his giant white beast. Such defiance would have brought all of the other villages down on us." She looked over at Sprenger. "Your mother couldn't allow that to happen."

Sprenger still didn't understand. "But they knew that Juriah was a," Sprenger chewed on the word for a moment, "well, they knew what he was," he said, finally giving up on it. "So why was he allowed to live?"

"It is a well-known fact throughout the scythe world that Juriah of the Hessiets is an extremely dangerous man. But another quality of Juriah is that he does not put his village before himself, and that was true even then. Had they tried to take him, he would have brought his full strength against them. After the war, Juriah and the other members of his squad, Demaedura and Lucas, had become legends of the fearful sort. They were given the name 'Hessiets' by the scythe world to mark their lethal abilities.

"That name is still feared to this day, but it was especially feared then. They allowed Juriah to live, but only because they were not sure the results of condemning him would be in their favor. Does that make sense?"

Both boys nodded.

Granny smoothed out the wrinkles on her gray cloak. "Good." She looked over at Soekka. "Now, you wanted to know about your parents' Feral Beasts?" Soekka nodded again. "They were magnificent creatures. All Feral Beasts were. They were called 'Pysliths'." She looked at Sprenger. "And your mother's beasts were called 'Pantrores'." She looked away in thought for a moment but kept a straight posture. "The Pantrores are massive black and white cats that are covered in shimmering hair. There could only be one Pantrore for every Nymphigori. The Pysliths were quite different. They were huge serpents that could grow as large as a river, if given the time, and they had a very different kind of Nymphigori. There was always ever one male Pyslith, and several females. It was only with the males that a Nymphigori could be bonded, but once they were, the Nymphigori could also influence the females as well. It was a different sort of bond; one male would be willing to bond to more than one Nymphigori at a time. Like your parents, Soekka. Their massive male's name was Sassor and he was the most magnificent thing I have seen in all my years."

Sprenger still could not entirely believe what he was hearing was real. "Sassor," Soekka whispered to himself. Soekka wanted to ask something else but it got caught in his throat. He and Sprenger just sat there in silence once more.

"You poor boys have been given enough to think about for one night," Karla said finally. "I will answer more questions tomorrow, if I can." She rose from the table. "I'm so sorry that you had to find all of this out like this. It was my intent to tell you sooner, but I'm afraid time got away from me, and now it is you boys that suffered because of it. I'm so sorry." She returned to the counter to resume whatever she was cleaning.

The boys looked at one another again, but still neither seemed to know what to say to the other. Eventually, Soekka looked away and back down to his soup.

Sprenger let out a disappointed breath, knowing that Soekka was going to prefer to think about things on his own before he was ready to talk about it. Sprenger always wanted to talk about things, but Soekka was more reserved in times like this. Sprenger would leave him be, knowing that's what he wants, but it never helped quell Sprenger's frustration to not have someone to talk to.

That night, lying in bed in silk bottoms, Sprenger stared up from the flat of his back at the intricate swirling patterns that formed in the wood of the ceiling. Even in the darkness, he knew the curves of the ceiling he had spent years staring up at from his bed. He could plainly hear Granny Karla snoring down the hall, but that wasn't what was keeping him awake tonight. In fact, Sprenger had become accustomed to the near-roars that echoed from Granny Karla's room almost every night.

It was Sprenger's mind that would not allow him rest. His whole life, he had accepted that he was without parents, and that information on his parents would be little to none. Sprenger felt overwhelmingly guilty as he realized he couldn't even remember his mother's name. Granny Karla had told him once, and Sprenger had only asked because he wondered where *his* name had come from. The thought made him very sad that he had not cared enough to even commit her name to memory at the time.

Being without parents had never bothered him. He was not without a family. He had Soekka and Granny Karla, and Jacob, and many people from Durado he considered family as well. Durado *was* his family, and there was no interest in wanting after something he already had. It had always been the harmless wonder that had ever driven Sprenger to ask questions about his parents, and he could tell that it made some people uncomfortable to talk about it for some reason. It had taken Sprenger a very long time to accept that he did not have parents and that he would know very little of them, but eventually *did* accept it and had moved on.

Now, after all these years, he not only found out a great deal about his mother, but that she was a significant figure in Durado. It would have been different if people had not really known her and so could not answer Sprenger's questions, but now it was clear that everyone knew of her. Everyone would have known their village's Nymphigori. So why did everyone feel they had to keep that from Sprenger?

Sprenger realized that he was clenching his teeth so hard that his cheeks were beginning to hurt. He took a few deep breaths through his nose and calmed himself.

She was a great scythe, a Nymphigori, a companion to a Feral Beast, Sprenger kept thinking to himself over and over again. Jacob tells him nothing of his parents for years and now expects him to shrug something like this away?

Jacob told him the beasts were all destroyed many years ago. That was a lie too. Sprenger knew they were somewhere in the forest. Neither he nor Soekka said anything to Jacob about the very clear and very large growl that even had Demaedura and Juriah watching the trees. Rejeno had not likely recovered enough yet to realize what was happening, and Sprenger and Soekka didn't say anything because they weren't sure what it really was, but they were sure now.

Somehow, a Feral Beast managed to stay hidden all these years, and it was out there. If Sprenger knew where to start then he would not be lying in bed, but sadly, the forest was endless, and this beast had avoided people for years. It would be impossible for Sprenger to even begin looking.

All of it still seemed strange to Sprenger. Even in a massive forest, it should have been seen by someone at some point, at least a glimpse. The borders were heavily patrolled, so Sprenger doubted it moved past them. That at least narrowed his area to Durado's territory. That, however, made it seem all the more unlikely that an animal of any size could live undetected for so long. There was nowhere in Durado's territory that a scythe cannot go, especially when there are emergencies and the forest has to be swept. Sprenger could think of several occasions where squads and hounds were sent out to run off trespassers, and surely they would have also flushed out a beast in the process. There was simply nowhere to hide that scythe couldn't search.

Where scythe couldn't search...

Sprenger shot upright. *Where scythe couldn't search,* he almost said aloud.

Juriah had told him where the beast was hidden, or at least in his own way. He wanted Sprenger to know. Jacob clearly didn't, and he probably stopped Juriah from revealing far more than he could have, but Juriah still managed to tell Sprenger what he wanted to. Sprenger began repeating what Juriah had said under his breath, making sure he remembered it correctly.

"It happened about eleven years ago. It was the exact same time that the Shattered Hill was declared sacred." Sprenger hadn't given the statement much thought originally, but there had been too much going on for it to sink in. Now, however, Sprenger realized that he was giving hints in front of Jacob.

The Shattered Hill, Sprenger though excitedly. That was where it was hiding. That's why it was forbidden. Sprenger would not wait to have someone else lie to him about it.

He hopped out of bed and began putting on his clothes. He would uncover these secrets himself.

He pulled his silk shirt over his head.

That's where he would hide something like a giant beast. The Shattered Hill was certainly large enough, and the punishment for going near it was almost that of treason, which in some cases could be death. They were always told the place was forbidden to respect the lives lost there in a battle of the last war. It was meant to leave the dead in peace.

What a brilliant lie that was. Threatening to insult someone's ancestors by trespassing on their resting place was a perfect way to keep people's curiosity at bay.

Sprenger slowly opened his window and hopped up onto the sill, but hesitated. He looked back into his dark room in the direction of Soekka's room. Should he tell Soekka what he had figured out, or should he leave him alone? Soekka was always the more calm-headed one of them, and though he enjoyed adventures with Sprenger to a certain degree, he was also the voice of reason many times.

Sprenger looked away and prepared to leave.

Sorry, Soekka, he though with a bit of guilt. *I'm going to find out for both of us.*

Chapter 23

An Unguarded Escape

The cool night air felt good after the last few restless hours in bed. Sprenger waited until a patrolling scythe moved away before he sprinted down the patrol beam above their house, towards the wall. Sprenger made sure to stay light on his feet so any nearby patrols would not hear him.

The wall was getting closer, and oddly, he didn't see any scythe patrolling atop its wide ramparts.

Good, he thought with relief. He worried he would have to sneak around all the patrols to get over the wall, and admittedly had no idea how he would do that.

He leapt from the beam onto the flat of the wall, and with a wide stance, slid to a halt in the quiet darkness. He ducked low and moved to the edge of the wall, looking around in the darkness for guards. There was no one there.

Why can't Kanto ever be around when I do something right? Sprenger thought as he admired his accomplishment.

Sprenger grabbed a rope and hook from one of the many places they were kept on the wall, nestled the hook into the corner of a holder, but not all the way so he could pull it free at the bottom, and threw the rope over the edge of the wall. Careful not to pull the hook free prematurely, Sprenger grasped the rope in both hands and slowly began sliding down the side of the wall. He had seen scythe do it before, but it was much harder than it looked, and Sprenger's hands nearly gave way more than once, making his descent anything but graceful.

Sprenger was still ten feet off the ground when he reached the end of his rope, forcing him to stop and balance.

That's a problem, he realized as he looked down at the ground, while struggling to keep his feet from slipping off the wall.

Sprenger forgot that the ropes were only meant to get people down, not up.

He clenched the rope as hard as he could to stay where he was while he turned to face up towards the sky. Standing straight on the wall, looking up at the top, Sprenger gave the rope a whip. The slack caused Sprenger to lose his footing and smash flat into the smooth side of the wall with a dull 'clunk' from his head, but the hook remained in place and somehow Sprenger managed to not release his grip.

Now he was glad Kanto was not there to see this.

While he grumbled complaints under his breath, Sprenger shook his head, replaced his feet on the wall, took a deep breath, and gave the rope another whip. This time, the hook gave way and Sprenger fell to the ground, thudding to the flat of his back with a gasp of pain. The landing knocked the wind from him and caused his vision to go white for a moment.

The rope began falling all around him until the hook landed with a thud by his head.

Sprenger lay on the grass for a moment, looking up at the starry sky attempting to suck air back into his lungs and blink away the tears in his eyes.

Now he was truly very glad that Kanto was not here.

After a few moments of ashamed recovery, Sprenger stood and began quickly collecting the rope. If a patrol scythe saw it, they would know someone had left and raise an alarm. It was treason for a scythe to leave the village without permission. To cross the border without permission deemed you rogue, and you would be hunted by your village and killed on sight near any other scythe village.

He tossed the rope and hook into the trees as he moved away from the wall. The way Sprenger saw it, Jacob betrayed Sprenger's trust by lying to him his whole life. Sprenger was entitled to a little betrayal of his own tonight.

He ran up the closest tree until he reached the thickest branches and began running through the canopy. He had never run in the canopy before. The training for the Exerptus Exams was the closest he had gotten, and now he felt himself getting nervous trying for the first time in star-lit darkness. He started slowly at first, but steadily gained confidence. Some of the branches he used were thicker than the patrol beams in the village, making his movements easier than he expected. He moved from tree to tree towards the Shattered Hill, determination replacing his fear.

The trek took a while, but it was almost tranquil above the ground. The moon illuminated the branches and Sprenger only mis-stepped once. He found the canopy to be rather peaceful compared to the mangled roots below. He wished he was trained how to do this before their mission to the patrol base. The journey back would have been much easier.

After a steady but long run, the trees began thinning out. He was close to a treeline. Sprenger gradually lowered himself to the branches below, then dropped to the ground and started walking towards the clearing ahead.

Running in the canopy had calmed him more than he would have thought, but now that he was here, he became immediately reinvigorated. Sprenger was tired of people lying to him, now he would find out for himself what the truth was.

Gradually, starlight filtered through the leaves overhead, until Sprenger was completely out in the open once more. Ahead was a mountain of jagged rock-splinters of every size, as though something had exploded from the ground itself. *So this is the Shattered Hill,* Sprenger thought as he admired the unique terrain. He had never been this close before and only every seen the side of it through the trees from a distance.

Unlike the rest of Durado's ancient forest, the Shattered Hill was made of solid rock. Other than the bushes and grass filling crevasses at the base, it was bare of plant life, making it clearly distinct amongst the forest's lush green surroundings. The hill rose sharply until the very top where it leveled off, overlooked by only the tallest of the ancient trees around it. It spanned to both limits of Sprenger's field of vision on either side.

Not far ahead, one of several wooden signs stood proudly in the grass in front of the mountain. Even at night, Sprenger could make out the message in the starlight:

'WARNING
FORBIDDEN AREA
TO HONOR THE ANCESTORS OF A BATTLE SINCE PASSED,
TRESPASSERS SHALL NOT BE FORGIVEN
IN MY OWN HAND,
SCYTHRITH JACOB OF DURADO'

The old post of the sign snapped with a loud crack as Sprenger punched the center of the message, knocking it to the ground. Sprenger began rubbing his hand contently, then froze. The air was grumbling with a deep growl all around him. He could not tell where it was coming from at first, but his eyes quickly landed on the source amongst the rocks.

Up on a rock ledge ahead of Sprenger, silhouetted in the glowing moonlight, stood the largest cat Sprenger had ever seen. Claws and oversized canines were fully exposed, lips pulled back into an intimidating snarl. It had a pure white underside, but a black top, as if ink had been poured down its head and back, trickling into its glowing white fur underneath.

Sprenger froze. His breath caught in his chest and his stomach filled with a hot mix of dread and excitement. He wasn't sure if he believed what he was seeing, even as he stared at it. Now that he found it, Sprenger realized that he hadn't truly expected to.

The giant cat's growl intensified as it took a step forward, lowering its black and white head. Its shoulder blades moved up and down anticipatorily, looking ready to leap from the edge. Heavy muscles clenched in its black-topped shoulders, looking fully capable of closing the distance between them in a very short amount of time.

Sprenger recoiled a few steps, only just realizing what situation he had just put himself in. This seemed like a very foolish idea now. Not truly considering the odds of encountering any creature, Sprenger had not considered what he would do if he did come across something. *This thing is going to kill me,* he realized with dread.

Despite Sprenger's certainty that he wouldn't be able to get away from this animal if it decided to attack, the cat didn't move. It stood staring at him with eyes as bright as the moon behind it.

In a shower of pebbles and dirt, the mighty cat jumped to the ground in front of Sprenger and continued to snarl dangerously as it slowly stepped towards him in the grass.

Sprenger didn't know what to do. Should he run? There was no way he could outrun it. Should he attempt to fight? He had his blade up his sleeve, but he doubted it would do him any good. Sprenger just stood there holding his breath and staring, paralyzed with fear.

Appearing to lose interest in their staring contest, the massive feline snorted at him as it raised its head. It turned and leapt back into the boulders and began hopping from one rock to another until it had disappeared behind enormous rock slabs near the top.

Sprenger gawked stupidly. After staring at the place it had disappeared for an unknown amount of time, he finally released a heavy, shaking. *This would be why people think I'm slow. I could have just been eaten and no one would have even known where to look for me.* Now driven by fear, Sprenger started to turn back into the forest, but couldn't force himself past the first step. He clenched his fists in frustration, feeling so conflicted about what to do.

He had come so far to find out what was being hidden from him and now he knew. Was this all there was to know?

No, he decided. *I'm not finished yet.* His body and his mind were fighting one another, as he stepped forward but couldn't will himself away from the Shattered Hill.

This was the only link he had ever had to his family. If he left now, the pain of not knowing would cause him to return. He knew it would.

Sprenger spun around and headed for the mountain once again. *Granny Karla always says I never know when to stop,* he reminded himself stubbornly, though she usually was talking about his mouth. *Besides,* he thought as he pulled himself up onto the first boulder, *no one else is going tell me anything.*

Sprenger made his way up the rugged mountainside, pulling himself atop jagged boulder after boulder. It was a difficult climb, but he was so lost in thought that he hardly noticed the scrapes and bruises he was accumulating. He would occasionally stop, his raising heart convincing his mind that something was watching or preparing to leap down on him from above. Every time he dislodged a rock from the side and sent it bouncing off the boulders below, he cringed at the echoing racket in the quiet night air.

Finally, he pulled himself over one final boulder and reached the top. Only, much to his surprise, there was no top.

Sprenger looked over the edge of the rock slab that he was standing on. The Shattered Hill was no hill at all, it was a bowl. Just as steep as the side he had just scaled, the rocky siding descended into a vast open space below. There was a grassy glade in the center of a giant caldera. Sprenger looked around in amazement. The glade was an oasis trapped within a rugged wall. There was a pond against the far side, and Sprenger could make out a small glistening creek flowing in and out of the glade through crevasses in the rock.

Sprenger couldn't see the giant cat anywhere, but the glade was not exactly untouched by its surroundings. Everywhere, there was evidence of rock slides and several large boulders lay scattered throughout the lush green grass below, some larger than Sprenger's room. There were plenty of places for the cat to hide, even something that big. The thought made Sprenger deeply nervous, but his stubbornness pushed him forward.

The climb down into the glade was even steeper than the climb up, so Sprenger kept to the large boulders as much as possible. A few times, he chose his footing poorly and sent rocks crashing down to the grass below with echoing bounces. *Well, at least it won't be surprised that I'm here,* he joked to himself nervously.

When Sprenger dropped down to the soft grass, he paused. The only noise around him was the trickling of the creek through the rocks across the glade. Sprenger suddenly felt very exposed standing in the shadow of the surrounding cliffs. He had a feeling that it would be all too easy for that giant cat to watch him from behind any of the rock faces without Sprenger having any idea it was there.

Sprenger recalled a time when he watched Granny Karla's cat jump down on a mouse from the windowsill. The thought urged Sprenger away from the towering cliffs. Instead, he moved inwards, towards the still pond on the other side. He passed several house-sized boulders, which he gave a wide berth in case something was waiting on the other side.

He hadn't made it halfway across the glade before the air began grumbling deeply again. Sprenger spun around. The giant black and white cat had just dropped to the grass from somewhere in the cliffs, canines fully revealed in a continuous snarl. Again, the two stood staring at one another.

At this point Sprenger realized that if it was going to kill him, it would have probably done so already, but that didn't even come close to taking the terror from the situation.

Sprenger took a deep breath and sturdied himself. Jacob said that Feral Beasts were intelligent, so Sprenger did the first thing that he could think of. "Great beast," he said as respectfully as possible, though his voice was embarrassingly hoarse and shaky. "I have come looking for answers, and I found you." He felt somewhat silly for talking to it but continued anyway. "I wonder what other answers you may be willing to give about what I'm looking for. I need to know about my mother." Sprenger wished he could even remember her name.

It didn't seem to matter. Sprenger's words changed nothing about the cat's disposition. "Though, now I'm starting to think that you don't understand a word I'm saying," Sprenger said more to himself than to the cat, and he started to back away nervously. "I'll leave you be then." The black and white cat made no move as Sprenger turned away.

Sprenger stopped dead as he spun around. A second massive black and white cat had been standing behind him the whole time. It was identical to the other in almost every way, but this one wasn't growling, just staring silently with glowing blue eyes that reflected the moonlight.

Sprenger's body shivered as a chill ran up his spine. The beast puffed air out its nostril at him, causing him to flinch slightly. There was nowhere for him to go now.

"About time you showed up," a casual voice said above him, causing Sprenger to start. He looked up to see Juriah casually sitting on top of the towering boulder next to him, cleaning his sword and giving Sprenger a very amused look. The boulder was so tall that Sprenger hadn't seen him when he was passing by and he had to arch his neck to look at him. "Wasn't sure you were ever going to come," Juriah continued as he looked away from Sprenger and continued to clean his sword. "I've been waiting for most of the night." He put his sword on his lap as he looked down at Sprenger. "I heard you were bit slow but I didn't think it would take you all night to figure out what I told you."

Sprenger was too dumbfounded to say anything back. Juriah didn't seem to care as he replaced his sword in the sheath on his back and stood. With a lazy hop, Juriah descended from the boulder and landed in front of Sprenger with a light thud.

Juriah casually strode past Sprenger, as if he wasn't talking to him at all. "So, you finally disobeyed Jacob, eh? Wasn't sure that would ever happen either." Sprenger remained silent as Juriah strode over to the snarling cat, and once he was close enough to it, Sprenger saw how truly massive the creature was. Able to look Juriah square in the eye, the great beast must have reached six feet tall at its jet-black shoulders. The creature continued to snarl at Sprenger and didn't even acknowledge Juriah standing beside it.

Clearly unintimidated by its display, Juriah gave it a sharp smack on the nose with the back of his hand. "Be quiet," Juriah said in an irritated grumble.

The cat recoiled slightly with a wrinkled nose and gave Juriah a sharp hiss before continuing to snarl at Sprenger.

Sprenger continued to gawk, unable to put words to what he was seeing.

Juriah sat down cross-legged in front of a particularly large boulder. He looked over at Sprenger with a somewhat entertained look. "If you're going to leave your mouth open like that, then you might as well let some words out before bugs get in."

Sprenger realized he was staring slack-jawed and quickly closed his mouth.

"Well let's get on with it then," Juriah said impatiently. He gestured for Sprenger to come sit down, so Sprenger slowly did so.

Juriah gave him a quizzical look. "All the other times we've encountered one another you wouldn't *stop* talking. Now suddenly you're-"

"What is going on!" Sprenger finally blurted.

Juriah cringed at the abrupt interruption and noise, then relaxed and looked at Sprenger again. "That's more of what I was expecting, I suppose," he grumbled, "and an easy question to start with."

"Well first off, these are Pantrores. The dumb looking one is Setdo." He gave a nod towards the cat that was behind Sprenger, who was watching them curiously while its tail playfully twitched behind it. "And the one with the personality problems is Satra." The second cat was still continuing to snarl at Sprenger without pause or breath. "Jacob told you about the Feral Beasts of old, and these are them... or at least, one kind of them," he corrected after a moment of thought.

Sprenger stared over his shoulder at the two creatures behind him. Now that he was sure they were not going to eat him, Sprenger appreciated their majestic beauty. "They're amazing," whispered. He looked back at Juriah. "They're the biggest animals I've ever seen."

Juriah snorted in amusement. "You'll take that back in a moment." Sprenger looked at him incredulously, but Juriah continued without explanation. "In any case, these are hardly like any animals you've ever encountered. Feral Beasts have always been far more than mere animals."

They look like animals to me, Sprenger thought, but managed not to say. "How so?" Sprenger asked skeptically.

"Well for one thing," Juriah explained, "you can walk up to an animal and insult it to its face and it would never even know. If you tried such a thing with a Feral Beast, you would not likely survive the encounter."

"Are you saying they can understand us?"

"Not all, but many can, depending on if they trained with a scythe or not. The Pantrores have spent their entire lives around scythe. Their numbers were so small that even if they were not companion beasts, they still spent much time around those that were and the scythe they were paired to."

"Can they talk?" Sprenger asked eagerly.

"No," Juriah said, almost annoyed by the question. "Can you bark like a dog or sing like a bird?" He shook his head. "But after a while we learn to interpret such noises."

Sprenger was about to ask another question but stopped. A shadow was being cast over them. Even in the night, the stars and moon gave enough light for Sprenger to notice the change.

Juriah noticed as well and looked over his shoulder. "Ah, there you are," he said to the creature casting the shadow. Two glowing platter-sized eyes peered around the massive boulder Juriah was sitting in front of. As it moved out from behind the boulder, Sprenger resumed his slack-jawed staring.

A third Pantrore now stood over the two of them, however this one was large enough to look into the second story window of Granny Karla's roothome.

Unlike the other two, this Pantrore had grey hairs sparsely placed down the black of its back. Around its neck, the white hairs had outgrown the rest of his body hair, giving it a small, proud mane. Its face was scarred in many places, and pieces of its ears were missing as well. Its massive canines protruded from its top jaw and down both sides of its chin, easily the size of Spenger's legs.

The huge creature moved around the boulder and regally laid across the grass behind Juriah, who appeared no bigger than one of its paws. The creature kept its neck upright and peered down at Sprenger with its wise old eyes. Its gaze was pulled away to Satra, who had yet to cease her insistent snarling. The towering cat gave a sharp roar that echoed through the hollow mountain, and nearly sent Sprenger tumbling backwards in surprise.

For the first time since Sprenger had seen her, Satra reluctantly fell silent. She moved in closer to sit next to Setdo, who continued to coyly watch them from behind.

Juriah arched his neck to look up behind him at his giant companion. "You're getting old, my friend. You never used to sleep through important events like this... or Satra's tantrums." The massive cat chuffed down at him in reply. Juriah turned his attention back to Sprenger. "This is Konn, my companion beast."

Sprenger was still gawking up at Konn and had no interest in looking away.

"Well," Juriah continued, "if you don't have any more questions, then I have a few for you. Like how you got out of the village, for one thing."

Sprenger finally dropped his gaze from Konn and looked at Juriah. A nervous knot was beginning to form in his stomach. "I borrowed a grapple and rope on the wall."

"Did you leave it there?"

Sprenger shook his head. "I pulled it down."

"Fair enough," Juriah said plainly. "Now, how were you planning on getting back into the village? As you may have noticed, those hooks are not long enough to reach the top of the wall from the ground."

"Well," Sprenger tried to think of anything that wouldn't make him appear so ill-prepared, but Juriah didn't give him the chance.

"So let me see if I have this straight," Juriah began rubbing his chin in mock thought. "You unlawfully left the village, a treasonous act, to search for a beast that you know nothing about and could easily kill you, while the most dangerous scythe in the land just finished attacking our village, led by one of the deadliest men in the world himself, and you have no way of getting back into the village?" He snorted in amusement. "And I bet you wonder why people call you slow."

Sprenger felt a bit embarrassed to have it all put to words like that, but then he remembered the reason for it all, and his temper began to flare. "Well no one else was going to tell me about any of this. What was I supposed to do?"

Juriah smirked at him with interest. "You really are something else." That was not the response Sprenger was expecting. "Clearly I was hoping that you would do all that, hence why I was waiting. But I can't help but point out the stupidity behind it, even as expected as it was."

"Oh," Sprenger said, taken aback. *Did he just call me stupid?*

"Frankly, it's refreshing to see that not everyone is so brainwashed nowadays."

"What do you mean?"

Juriah shook his head a bit. "Not important. But tonight was a good example of why scythe train to put their emotions aside and see through them. Look at the dangerous situation you put yourself in because of your anger. However,"

"But if I hadn't," Sprenger interrupted, "then I never would have learned all this."

Juriah rolled his eyes. "That was going to be the 'however' part." He gave Sprenger an annoyed look. "You really have a hard time not talking, don't you?"

Sprenger shrunk a bit. "Sorry."

Behind Juriah, Konn made several strange snorting sounds.

Did that thing just laugh at me? Sprenger thought as he looked back up at Konn, who quietly stared back.

"You're just like your mother," Juriah grumbled.

Sprenger sat upright.

"Ah yes," Juriah said in realization. "I forgot that you originally came to learn about your mother." He leaned back on Konn's white stomach. "I had already forgotten that you've had a very confusing day in terms of what you thought you knew about your own life. I suppose you have more questions about your past than about Nymphigori tonight." He sighed a bit. "That wasn't *my* priority tonight, but I imagine it's fairly important to you."

Sprenger ignored his rambling. His mind was focused on only one thing at the moment. "Can you tell me anything about her? About my mother." Sprenger couldn't help but feel that he sounded like he was pleading. He cleared his throat. "Please."

Konn lowered his massive head and laid it next to Juriah, who began scratching the side of his nose. "I expected as much." Juriah stared into one of Konn's eyes as if they were coming to some sort of decision. For a moment, Sprenger wasn't sure he would answer, but then he spoke.

"People will tell you about her skills as a scythe, and the hair that you both share as a family trait, so I will leave it to them to explain such trivial things." Juriah stopped scratching Konn's nose and looked up at the night sky. "Sasha had the ability to bring warmth to the dreariest of situations. Everyone loved her because there was no mood that you could be in that she couldn't improve, even if only slightly. But most of all," Juriah looked down at Sprenger, "she was unnaturally kind to everyone around her. A trait that is not common amongst people anymore." He returned to scratching Konn's nose. "I found it annoying at first," he said indifferently. Then his voice softened. "She is the reason Konn, Setdo, and Satra are still alive. Probably myself as well. The final act of her life was to save ours."

Sprenger had dozens of questions in his mind earlier, but he suddenly couldn't remember any of them. He could feel warmth inside him and tears forming at the brims of his eyes. It was as though an entire lifetime of wondering had just been satisfied, and for the first time in his life, Sprenger had an image of his mother in his mind. He didn't know her face but he could see her beautiful smile, and he could see it making others smile as she passed them. Sprenger couldn't help himself from smiling, even through his blurred vision.

Juriah interrupted his bliss, clearly unaware of the impact he just had on Sprenger. "If you plan on inquiring about your father next, I would take such questions to someone else. I'm a bit," he thought a moment, "biased." He swatted the air as if to shoo away a fly. "In any case, describing people in the best light is not exactly one of my skills. Ask Kanto to explain that mess to you."

"That's okay," Sprenger said softly with a smile. "I appreciate what you told me about my mother."

Juriah eyed him curiously, as if Sprenger had said something confusing. "Well that was easy. However, now would be the time for questions if you have them." He looked off to the side, appearing disgruntled. "I bet Jacob will make sure you don't have the chance to ask *me* any more questions," he grumbled.

Sprenger was fully content with what he had just heard. It confirmed everything he hoped his mother was like. *Sasha,* Sprenger repeated in his mind. *I will not forget the name again.* But now, sitting in front of this strange man, Sprenger recalled a question that tormented his mind for quite a while.

"Is what they say about you true?" he asked, hesitantly.

Juriah turned back and raised an eyebrow at him. "That would depend on the 'what' and who's saying it."

"Did you really destroy the Corundo village with only one other scythe?"

Juriah suddenly looked entertained for some reason. "Ah, that. It's been a while since that story has been told. Seems like ancient history now."

Not according to all the pentin, Sprenger thought.

"But yes, it's true," Juriah finally replied. "That was before I met Konn, when my life was much different."

"So it's true? How is that even possible?"

"There is a story preceding that one which exceeds the time we have left tonight, but someday, if you're still curious, I will tell it to you." Juriah pushed himself off Konn's stomach and sat upright. "But I suppose that an important part would be the scythe that was with me." His eyes became more serious. "You've just met him." Sprenger gave Juriah a confused look. "Demaedura," Juriah clarified. Konn growled at the name. "The man that led the assault on our village and has us on high alert at the moment."

Sprenger's jaw dropped, something that was becoming a regular occurrence tonight. "But that means he was a dura-scythe."

Juriah nodded. "Demaedura abandoned our village not long after the wars ended and became rogue. The sword he now carries was taken from the Scythrith of the Corundo village. After we killed him, Demaedura took it as his trophy, and has wreaked havoc with it ever since. I have spent most of the last several years hunting him, but he always manages to evade me. On the rare occasions that I do catch him, I can never manage to kill him, and he escapes again."

"Is he really your brother?" Sprenger asked before thinking. Juriah's brow furrowed in confusion. Sprenger quickly tried to justify his question. "I heard him call you 'brother' today in the glade. Is that why you can't kill him?"

Juriah's expression softened at Sprenger's explanation. "Demaedura prides himself in toying with people's minds. He was referring to 'brothers in arms', but I can understand your confusion. That was probably his intent." He gave a humorless snort. "No, the reason I can't kill him is because neither of our skills as scythe have managed to overcome the other's. As has been our relationship our whole lives."

Sprenger could hear Setdo and Satra repositioning themselves behind him, and he had to resist the urge to turn around to look. It was a bit unnerving to have creatures likc that behind him. Juriah seemed not to notice.

"After Demaedura left," Juriah continued, "rumors covered the lands of the rogue-Hessiet. Demaedura used this fear to his benefit. Not only has he constructed one of the most elaborate underground empires in the world, but he has also used the fear and the reputation of his skills to draw some of the most elite and deadly scythe that can be found to his call." Juriah's eyes seemed to be becoming more intense as he spoke. "From what I've learned the past few years, Demaedura and his Adimortis have a village's worth of vassals under their command, as well as someone corrupted by his malice in almost every part of the civilized world. It's difficult to go where Demaedura cannot find you."

Things were beginning to become far more extensive than what Sprenger was expecting. "Why would anyone want to follow a rough-scythe?"

"Most of his original vassals were rogue as well," Juriah explained. "They now make up his Adimortis. The five that lurk directly in Demaedura's shadow have each earned their prowess in the scythe world multiple times over. They are the puppets that maintain Demaedura's secret world. Very rarely does Demaedura call them all together like he did for the attack on the village. They are normally paired up and dispersed, serving some dark purpose. Some are addicted to his power, while others worship him as an untouchable being. In any case, Demaedura only chooses those he is absolutely sure he can manipulate. Something else he's proficient in.

"The man you encountered in the forest, Phenex, is Demaedura's right hand." Sprenger could perfectly see the man in his black cloak, glaring down at Sprenger with his scarred face. Sprenger remembered the chill that man sent up his spine. "This is a scythe who shares in Demaedura's lack of empathy and has honed skills the like of which you will not likely see again. He is one of Demaedura's deadliest servants, and he is also one of Demaedura's most loyal followers."

"But why?" Sprenger finally asked. "Why would Demaedura go to such lengths to build power, and then stay hidden?"

"War," Juriah said flatly. "War is Demaedura's single goal. To bring a sweep of chaos back into the world. War is what Demaedura and I were born into. It was all we knew, and it's what we are most efficient in. Because of it, Demaedura fell into a blood lust when the Great Wars ended and he has been setting the pieces for the next one ever since.

"Those that follow his war-mongering have their reasons. Some share in his perverted vision, some choose it best to remain serving a deadly force than to be in its path, while others do so out of ignorance, or because they are forced into it. Demaedura has the uncanny ability to locate scythe when they are at their weakest and is then able to brainwash them into believing whatever he says." Juriah locked eyes with Sprenger intently. "If you ever see Demaedura again, don't think, just run."

Sprenger flinched when he saw something move in the corner of his eye. It was Setdo, who was slowly walking around to examine Sprenger, but stopped when Sprenger noticed him.

Juriah smirked at him. "You can relax. Setdo won't hurt you. Neither will Konn." Juriah gave the massive creature a friendly pat and he chuffed deeply at Sprenger.

Sprenger looked over his shoulder at Satra, who raised her head from its resting position in response to his stare. "What about that one?" Sprenger looked back for Juriah's answer.

Juriah seemed to be thinking about it. "Well these two definitely won't hurt you." Sprenger wasn't at all comforted by that. "It seems Setdo has taken a liking to you, and I'm sure you've been wanting to see one up close since you've gotten here. So go ahead," he said with a flick of his chin towards Sedto.

Sprenger looked between Juriah and Setdo, not completely sure Juriah was serious, but Juriah's expression showed no sign of taking back the offer. He looked up into Konn's regal eyes, who stared back with encouragement.

Sprenger looked over at Setdo, who laid calmly in the spot where he had stopped, his tail twitching excitedly.

Tonight was not turning out at all like Sprenger was expecting it to.

Sprenger calmly rose, careful to keep his nerves in check, and slowly began walking over to where Setdo lay. At first, the big cat just watched Sprenger coyly, but when Sprenger was within arm's length, he stood. The creature towered Sprenger, looking down at him with glowing eyes.

After a few moments of wordless staring, Setdo crouched slightly so that he was eye level with Sprenger. Without any thought, Sprenger reached out and placed his hand on Setdo's nose. He was surprised at the feel. The hair was not at all like Peter's, which was soft and fine. This hair was thick and course, almost hard. Sprenger gently began stroking Setdo's nose, who closed his eyes and began to chuff softly through his nose.

Sprenger smiled. It was a giant cat's equivalent to purring, he realized.

"Be careful to only move with the grain of his fur," Juriah warned from behind.

Sprenger dragged his hand down Setdo's nose but recoiled with a yelp as his hand flashed with pain. Sedto recoiled a bit at Sprenger's reaction and watched him nervously. Sprenger quickly squeezed his wrist in an attempt to settle the prickling agony that covered his hand. He noticed blood beginning to bead on his fingers and palm, as if he was just stung by a dozen hornets.

He looked over at Juriah, who gave an exaggerated roll of his eyes. "So, of course, you do exactly what I told you not to do."

Sprenger ignored his snide comment. "What was that?"

Juriah reluctantly stood, came over, and stood next to Sprenger. "Their fur is more like a sort of armor. Most blades wouldn't be able to penetrate deep enough to break the skin. But more than that, it makes them nearly impossible to touch if they don't wish it." Juriah put a hand on Sprenger's shoulder and gently pulled him back a step. "Watch."

Seeming to recognize his cue, Setdo hunched his shoulders. In total unison, every hair on Setdo's body shot upwards and stood on end. Even the short hairs on his face jutted outward. The result was a far less regal creature. Now Setdo had a sharp, fierce appearance.

Sprenger once again caught himself gaping at what he was seeing, and quickly tried not to look so surprised.

He looked up at Juriah. "How did it do that?"

"If I recall, Old Lady Karla has a cat, right?" Sprenger nodded. "Doesn't it do something similar when it's angry or frightened?"

"Hardly," Sprenger scoffed. "At most, Peter just arches his back and hisses. The result isn't really anything like this." Setdo, apparently tired of holding his pose, relaxed and gave a lazy shake, causing his fur to return to normal. "I've never seen anything like that before."

Juriah playfully flattened Sprenger's hair under his palm, and watched it return to its original spikes. "Perhaps you should see your reflection then."

Sprenger put a hand on his hair protectively and glared at Juriah through the corners of his eyes. *I hate when people talk about my hair.*

"And Peter's fur," Sprenger continued, attempting to move the conversation away from his hair, "doesn't make my hand bleed when I pet him the wrong way either."

Juriah smirked. "A mistake that is hardly ever made twice." He turned his head to look at the skyline above the ridgc of the Shattered Hill, where the black sky was slowly being encroached by a dim red light. "I'd say that you've had quite a night tonight. We had best get back to the village now." Juriah smirked coyly. "Let's see if you've been declared a rogue-scythe yet."

Chapter 24

A Simple Explanation

Light was beginning to creep its way back into the wet air of Durado's forest. The leaves on the trees and the blades of grass between roots all glistened with fresh dew. The calamity of chirping birds echoed all through the forest, each trying to gain attention over the next.

Sprenger stopped on a thick branch in the canopy and took one last look over his shoulder towards the Shattered Hill, even though he could no longer see it through the trees. He had not been able to see it for some time now, but he still had the urge to stare at it a bit longer. It had been the only place where Sprenger felt complete; where he didn't feel bogged down by unanswered questions.

"You will see it again," Juriah called back from a branch up ahead. "That I promise you." His voice echoed in the calm morning air. It seemed gruff compared to the peaceful songs of the birds all around them. He hopped from the branch he was standing on to the next and continued forward. Juriah didn't keep a particularly difficult pace, but he didn't seem very willing to wait when Sprenger stopped.

Apparently he's not a very patient man, Sprenger noted to himself.

After a short while, they were at the end of the treeline and about to re-enter Durado to face whatever results were in place for Sprenger's actions. It was possible that no one noticed his absence, but Sprenger doubted that Granny Karla hadn't already discovered his empty bed.

He and Juriah dropped to the ground before pushing their way through the remaining layer of bushes that separated the forest from the clearing around Durado's white wall. The air was open and chilled in the shadow of the looming wall and trees.

High above them, Sprenger could hear the scythe guarding the wall begin to shout back and forth as Juriah and Sprenger emerged. It didn't take long to spot people from the wall.

Even as scythe watched them from above, Juriah and Sprenger continued along the wall towards the main gate. Sprenger had half-hoped that Juriah would know a different way into the village so that they wouldn't have to draw attention to themselves by having the gate opened for them, but that did not appear to be the case. The massive doors always remained shut to outsiders until the afternoon, when traders could enter Durado to buy and sell goods. After the lockdown, however, it would be a long time before anyone was allowed into the village. Only scythe of rank could request the gates open, and even then it took convincing.

The more Sprenger thought about it, the more nervous he became. He looked over at Juriah. "What if they don't open the gates for us?" He asked softly.

Juriah did not look back. "They will," he said flatly.

"How do you know?" Sprenger pressed skeptically.

Now Juriah looked over at him. "You don't know what it means to be a Hessiet, do you?"

Sprenger thought about it for a moment. "The only time I've ever really heard of a Hessiet was when Granny Karla told us stories about you guys in the Great Wars. Other than that, not really."

Juriah looked back ahead. "Then just take my word for it. We'll get in."

Though he wasn't completely sure if Juriah was telling the truth, Sprenger was hopeful that whatever it meant to be a Hessiet was sufficient enough to at least get them back in, but more importantly, that his rank was sufficient enough to justify Sprenger's desertion.

I guess I'm about to find out, he thought nervously.

The towers to either side of the gate slowly began emerging from around the bend in the wall.

By the time the two of them stood between the two towers and in front of the massive doors, Sprenger's stomach was in a knot.

Scythe from the top of the wall peered down at them before disappearing from sight. Shortly after, Sprenger could hear the orders from behind the wall to open the gates.

There was a small pause, and then the gates began to open with a deep moan. Now all that was left to do was to survive the punishments of his actions.

To Sprenger's great relief, there was no one on the other side of the gates to greet them. Sprenger half expected to see Jacob or Kanto waiting for him with very disheartening stares, or worse, Granny Karla. But luckily, the road was clear, so Juriah and Sprenger made their way through the gates and into the village. They didn't get far through the gates before they closed with a large boom behind them once more.

All seemed normal on the main road. Life had certainly returned to Durado after the attack. People bustled in and out of shops and homes, children chased cats or each other between houses or over grassy rooftops; everyone seemed to have returned to their lives.

The only thing that didn't seem normal was people's expressions. As they walked past, people gave Sprenger and Juriah some very peculiar stares. It was the sort of look that Sprenger expected to see when people saw a lamb walking hand-in-hand with a wolf.

Sprenger imagined that Juriah did not normally walk with anyone, especially not a pentin, like Sprenger.

Shadows soared past them as scythe ran on the patrol beams high overhead. Then Sprenger realized something: there had been no scythe patrolling last night when he had left the village. He had even been allowed to get onto the wall without being seen. Such a thing should not be possible, especially after the village was locked down.

Sprenger's thoughts were interrupted as someone dropped from a patrol beam right onto the road in front of them. Sprenger attempted not to flinch at the sudden appearance, but he still let out a small gasp before gathering his composure.

The man rose to his full height, and standing silently in front of them, was Master Kanto. He truly had the face of a scythe; his expression was unreadable. Sprenger already knew he was in trouble, so he did not wish to push his already diminishing luck. He stepped forward and bowed his head.

Before he could tell what was going on, Sprenger felt firm hands on each of his shoulders. Sprenger looked up as Kanto held him at arm's length, his eyes boring down into Sprenger's.

"Where have you been?" Kanto asked very sternly

"I, uh-" was all Sprenger could manage. Was he supposed to tell the truth or lie?

Juriah stepped in closer to Sprenger. "He was with me." Kanto released Sprenger's shoulders and shifted his intimidating stare to Juriah. "It seems," Juriah continued, "that after Jacob told the boys about their parents, Sprenger here had a few more questions. He's been rather annoying to tell the truth."

Kanto's face remained unreadable. "And what did you tell him?" he asked, unamused.

"Nothing that he shouldn't already know," Juriah said coyly back.

Sprenger couldn't tell if Juriah was simply toying with Kanto or if such answers were really enough to satisfy his questions.

"You showed him then?" Kanto asked.

Suddenly, Sprenger's temper began to return. "You knew about the- 'them' too?" Sprenger almost forgot that there were other people around, and had to catch himself from saying something important. "Does everyone know but me?" Sprenger threw his hands in the air in agitation.

Kanto just calmly looked down at him. "There are a select few of us that know about the Shattered Hill, Sprenger." Kanto lowered his voice. "I understand why you are upset with everyone, but you have to trust us. Believe me when I tell you that things are far more complicated than they seem."

Sprenger crossed his arms disapprovingly but held his tongue. *Everyone keeps saying that as if it's a good reason to not tell me things.*

Kanto resumed his harsh tone. "How did you even get out of the village?"

"Uhh-" Sprenger didn't entirely know himself, let alone how to explain it.

Kanto looked over at Juriah. "I assume that was your doing?"

Juriah smiled coyly. "I just told all the patrols to return to their homes, and that I was personally taking over their watch. They must have assumed that I was going to stay in the village after they left." He shrugged. "Their mistake."

"What if we were attacked?" Kanto growled, apparently not impressed with Juriah's answer.

"Demaedura got what he came for," Juriah answered casually. "I doubt he'll return anytime soon."

Juriah's tone became harsh as well. "Speaking of which, I assume you didn't manage to catch up with Tranis?"

"No," Kanto admitted. "We chased them all throughout the forest with no luck. At the very least, we had hoped to follow them wherever they were hiding, but we lost them a bit after dark."

Juriah swore loudly, causing several passersby to look over, but a quick glance from Juriah sent them hurriedly on their way.

Kanto didn't seem to notice. "Jacob has assigned several people to look into why Tranis may be of value to anyone, let alone Demaedura. Hopefully such information can give us an idea of their intentions."

Juriah didn't look to be listening; in fact, he looked closer to cursing again than responding to Kanto. Behind Kanto, Sprenger could see someone running towards them, but he tried to stay focused on what Kanto was saying.

Kanto gave Juriah a disapproving look, then looked back down to Sprenger. "Now as for you-"

Kanto was nearly knocked off his feet as Granny Karla shoved him aside and fell onto Sprenger with a deep hug. She held him so tightly, trapping his arms, that Sprenger couldn't even hug her back. It was almost painful. After what seemed like ages, Granny released Sprenger, and before anything could be said, she gave him a fierce smack across the face.

"If you ever scare me like that again I will leave a permanent handprint on your cheek!" she shrieked.

Sprenger cupped a hand to his throbbing cheek and gently rubbed it. The smack caused Sprenger's ears to ring. He just stood there, abashed and at a loss for words.

"And you!" Granny nearly knocked Sprenger to the ground as she pushed past him and pointed a bony finger at Juriah's face. "You may be a Hessiet, Juriah, and the Reaper of Durado, but I warn you now," Sprenger went over and stood next to Kanto who was smart enough to stay back behind Karla and out of the way, "if you ever do anything as reckless as that with Sprenger again, I will personally end your great legacy!" Granny was not nearly tall enough to look Juriah in the eye, so she continued pushing her bony finger closer to his face.

Juriah, at first, seemed very surprised, but now was glaring at Granny's finger, clearly disapproving of its presence. "Careful, old lady, your aged heart may not be able to continue at the rate you're going."

Kanto quickly slid between the two, which Sprenger would never have been brave enough to attempt. "Lady Karla," Kanto frantically sputtered, "perhaps it would be best if you took Sprenger home. I'm canceling training for today due to the recent activities."

Granny Karla straightened her posture and placed each hand in the opposite sleeves of her grey cloak. Deep wrinkles appeared on her cheeks as she gave Kanto a pleasant smile. "Yes, of course, dear. You're right. It's time to be headed home." She gave a quick spin on her heels and began walking towards Sprenger. "Come, dear. I have porridge for you."

Sprenger smiled at her and moved so that he could walk beside her. Granny Karla did not have a short temper, but she certainly was capable of an enormous eruption when pushed too far. The explosion was always violent, but brief.

Sprenger looked over his shoulder at Kanto and Juriah, and they in turn, stared back with unreadable faces. Faces of skilled scythe.

Sprenger had the nagging feeling they were about to discuss secret things that pertained to him. He wanted nothing more than to follow them and force someone to explain things further, but he knew he could not. Even with his slight hesitation to be off, Granny Karla gave him a sharp look of warning that she was not to be tested right now. Sprenger supposed he was fortunate that his punishment was so small and he decided to not push his luck any farther. *I can't wait to tell Soekka about all of this,* he suddenly realized as he hurried to stay close to Karla.

Chapter 25

A late goodbye

Granny Karla placed the remainder of the porridge in a large bowl in the center of the table and took a seat across from Soekka. She hadn't seemed angry since her outburst that morning with Juriah, but the silence in the house was worse in Sprenger's mind.

The whole day had continued with tensions running high after Sprenger's disappearance. Everyone was mad, even Soekka for some reason. They all dealt with it in different ways, but Sprenger knew when his family was upset about something. Granny Karla would pretend like she wasn't angry about what happened, but everyone knew she was. She would not speak unless spoken to, and would hardly give a useful answer the times she did. She did it as her own sort of punishment, and Sprenger hated that it worked. The silence was miserable and made Sprenger feel terrible.

Sprenger leaned over his bowl of porridge, almost in an attempt to hide in the steam to get away from whatever it was he was feeling, but it didn't help. It was either embarrassment or shame, but he hadn't figured out which yet. Sprenger had spent the whole morning explaining to Soekka what had happened, but it was difficult while attempting to finish all of the chores Granny Karla had given him to do as punishment for leaving.

For reasons Sprenger had not figured out yet, things were also tense between the two boys. Soekka had hardly said a word since Sprenger told him about Shattered Hill. Sprenger would have thought the news was exciting, but Soekka offered him no congratulations, no smile, nothing. He just stared at him in shock of what he was saying. It was as if he resented what Sprenger had found out about his mother, which wasn't fair.

Sprenger shoveled as much porridge as he could onto his biscuit before taking a few large bites out of it.

Perhaps Soekka was mad because Sprenger found the Feral Beasts that his mother was paired with. *The Patroars, or whatever they're called*, Sprenger thought to himself as he tried to think of the reason why Soekka would be upset. *That must be it.* Soekka was mad because he couldn't see his parents' Feral Beasts. Soekka hated when things happened for Sprenger and not for him. It was something that made Soekka who he was, and Sprenger wouldn't dare put it to words. Sprenger never understood why Soekka was like that, but he had been their whole lives and Sprenger learned to deal with it a long time ago.

Sprenger finished his biscuit and grabbed another one from the pile on the plate in front of him. He looked over at Soekka, who was eating rather slowly. In fact, he was just moving the porridge around in the bowl instead of actually eating it. Now Sprenger was almost annoyed by his undeserved pouting.

Granny Karla seemed to notice his restrained pace as well. "Soekka my dear, you have hardly touched your food. Are you feeling all right?"

Sprenger shoveled more porridge on his biscuit and took another bite as he waited to see what Soekka would say.

"Not really hungry is all," Soekka mumbled.

Granny Karla still looked concerned, but she didn't press the matter. "All right, dear." She looked over at Sprenger, who was in mid-bite. "You, on the other hand, need to slow down, or you'll be too fat to be a scythe."

Sprenger almost lost the food in his mouth as he held back a laugh. Even Soekka allowed a small, if pathetic, smile to touch the corner of his mouth.

Granny pushed her chair back as she stood, and picked up her and Soekka's bowls. Sprenger wrapped his free arm around his bowl protectively. She probably couldn't carry it with her hands already full, but the woman had a way of being tricky. She just smiled at him and walked over to the fireplace where the cauldron was cooking the porridge, and poured what was left in Soekka's bowl back in. Sprenger was glad there was more left, it was very good.

Granny took her now empty bowls over to the counter next to Sprenger and dropped them in a bucket of water.

"So are you going to be a Nymphigori now?" Soekka suddenly said to Sprenger in the voice he used when he pouted.

Sprenger was not expecting such a question, or any question really, and just stared at Soekka with a mouth full of biscuits. "Umm," was all he could manage at the time.

"No, he's not," Karla answered sternly for him.

Sprenger scowled, *that was not what I was gunna say.* Sprenger forced down his large mouthful. "What do you mean 'no'," Sprenger objected to Karla.

She continued dealing with dishes on the counter. "Just because you managed to sneak away to discover one of our village's secret, doesn't mean you're going to be a Nymphigori. You're lucky you didn't get killed last night, but you won't be testing your luck again. I'm glad you found out some things about your mother, so accept what you've learned and stop wanting."

"But that's not fair!" Sprenger protested. "Juriah wanted me to find them."

Karla spun around with intent. “That man is evil and untrustworthy.” She raised a wooden spoon to him. “You stay away from him.”

“He’s more trustworthy than any of you!” Sprenger yelled back. “At least he hasn’t lied to me! That’s more than I can say about you or the Old Man!”

Karla had no response to that. She looked at him, shocked.

Sprenger, temper now flaring, turned to Soekka. “And you,” he barked. “I’m sorry there’s not more for you to find out about your parents, I really am, but don’t get mad at me because I went out looking for answers. If there was a way to find Pysliths, I would help you without a moment’s hesitation, but I can’t.”

Soekka just pouted, he didn’t even look up at Sprenger.

Sprenger slammed his fists down on the table. “I’m tired of everyone getting mad at me for finding things out that I should’ve known my whole life!” He looked back at Karla. “Not you or the Old Man or anyone else has the right to keep my own family a secret from me.” He looked at Soekka. “And you have no right to be mad at me for digging up those secrets.”

Sprenger pushed his nearly empty bowl away and stood. "I'm going to the pond."

Nobody said anything to him as he left.

Once outside, Sprenger already felt a bit better. Something about Durado just before the sun began to set always made Sprenger feel so happy. He didn't feel happy now, but he felt better at least.

The streets were nearly empty, and only a few places that served food and drinks were still buzzing with noise from within. Luckily, the people were all inside. Sprenger was in no mood to talk or fake a smile to anyone.

He hardly saw a single person by the time he had reached the pond, with the exception of scythe watching from overhead. Sprenger hopped over the waste-high fence surrounding the pond and the grassy area around it. There was only one tree in this small area, underneath which was a stone bench. Granny Karla used to bring Sprenger and Soekka here all the time when they were little, and she would watch them play while sitting on the bench. Once a year, the tree would bloom with white flowers, and Granny Karla challenged them to bring her the most beautiful flower that had fallen off. It was always a tie.

Sprenger walked up to the edge of the pond and looked down into the clear water. There were a few black and white spotted coy fish that lived in the pool, and most eagerly swam in Sprenger's direction, hoping he would drop something in that they could eat. When Sprenger didn't, they resumed their unguided swim through the water.

Sprenger just stared at his reflection in the water for a while. Mostly, he looked at his hair. His eyes started to water.

The stupid spiky hair that everyone says he inherited from his mother.

A slow tear ran down his cheek when he blinked.

Sprenger couldn't picture a woman with hair like this. He couldn't imagine anything about his mother at all. How could he?

Sprenger dropped to his knees at the water's edge.

He had never seen her. Now he would never see her. He could only take people's word for it. *People,* he thought resentfully. People that had only lied to him his whole life.

Sprenger plunged his hands into the water, causing all the fish to scatter. Cupping as much water in his hands as he could, he spilled it over his head. With both hands, Sprenger attempted to flatten his hair, but he could feel his hair rising as soon as he released the pressure from his hands.

He peered back into the pond. Nothing had changed. His brown hair still stood on end, but now in wet, matted spikes. It was no use.

"Sprenger?" a soft voice said from behind.

Sprenger spun around.

Kanto was eying him curiously. "What are you doing?" His voice was gentler than usual. It lacked its normal authority.

Sprenger turned away from him, embarrassed. He frantically tried to wipe his wet eyes and face, both from dumping water over his head and crying.

"Nothing," Sprenger mumbled. "I was just..."

"Bathing?" Kanto almost said like a tease from behind.

"Thinking," Sprenger corrected.

Kanto walked up closer and stood behind him. Sprenger could see Kanto's reflection looming over his own in the pondwater.

"Ah, I see," Kanto said gently. "Thinking about your hair?" Sprenger didn't answer at first, but Kanto held his ground, already knowing he was correct.

"I'm just tired of everyone looking at it and talking about how it looks like 'hers'," Sprenger finally said.

"Is that all that you're thinking about?" Kanto asked stoically.

"No," Sprenger admitted. He stared at his reflection, then cast it an angry scowl. "I'm tired of being lied to." Sprenger struck the water, causing the still reflections to dissipate amongst the waves. "I'm tired of everyone lying to me!" Sprenger rose and faced Kanto, who stayed where he was and allowed Sprenger his tantrum. "I'm tired of not knowing who will tell me the truth, not knowing who I can trust!" Sprenger could hear his shouts resonate in the stillness around them. He lowered his voice. "I'm tired of not knowing anything, and not being able to believe what I hear." Sprenger's eyes were beginning to water again, but he stifled back the tears in front of Kanto.

Kanto stood quietly and patiently, like Jacob did when Juriah was calling him 'mad'. After a moment of quiet, Kanto finally said something. "I have never lied to you Sprenger, nor will I ever. That is the trust that is unbreakable for a master with their students." Sprenger gave him a skeptical look. Kanto shrugged, "I may not always tell you everything, but I won't lie."

"That's the same as keeping secrets," Sprenger grumbled.

"True enough, I suppose," Kanto agreed. "But don't you have secrets as well?"

"Not really," Sprenger said flatly. Sprenger thought about it some more, and the only thing that came to mind was Korran, but that was none of Kanto's business.

"Well, as time goes by," Kanto continued, "you will have to make your own choices about telling someone something that may hurt them or keeping it a secret. It's part of life, I'm afraid."

Sprenger just stared down at the grass between his feet. Kanto had a point, but it didn't make Sprenger feel any better about all of it.

Kanto placed a comforting hand on Sprenger's shoulder. "Come with me. I want to show you something." Without waiting for Sprenger to respond, Kanto turned and started for the street.

Sprenger wasn't entirely sure he wanted to see anymore today, but he followed Kanto anyways. He might as well; he wasn't feeling any better here by himself.

He silently followed Kanto through the empty streets towards the back of the village. They passed the prison where Phenex had killed all those guards and helped Tranis escape. Sprenger remembered what it was like to see that man fight. The way he used that heavy flail was amazing to say the least. Even Kanto, a master-scythe, was almost killed by him, and it was only by sheer luck that Phenex had decided not to follow through and kill both Kanto and Sprenger.

Sprenger pushed such thoughts out of his mind. Kanto had told them, "If you continue to look back at the past and shudder, it will only make you more fearful of the future." Instead, Sprenger returned his thoughts to where they were going.

After a short time, his question was answered. They were at the very back of the village. Somewhere Sprenger had only been a few times. Over to his right, Sprenger could see Korrena's orchards, where he grew all his fruits. There was a great assortment of colorful trees all throughout the small fenced-in area.

To his left was a large area of ground that was given to the training of the hounds of Durado. Most were sleeping now, but during the day there were dozens of hounds that lived on that property. At the back of their enclosure was the Hound Master's house: a lonesome triangular stump that was no longer attached to any of the surrounding structures. From what Sprenger was told, it was a family of scythe that trained these hounds for specific purposes that Durado needed, such as clearing the forest of unwanted visitors. Sprenger wasn't sure he had ever seen the family since they mostly stayed with the hounds. A boy in their class, Garrett, was the Hound Master's son, but Sprenger never talked to him or really knew anything more about him. He was a bit odd and distanced himself from the others. The only clear memories Sprenger had about him, was the times Master Cerri would scold him for saying or doing something defiant or rude. Other than that, Sprenger knew little about him.

Neither one of those things, however, was why they were there. In front of Sprenger, was a stone wall that was about the same height as him. Two massive pillars guarded each side of the entrance. From behind the wall, trees grew in every corner, and periodically emerged in the center of the large area. This was Durado's cemetery.

"Why are we here, Master Kanto?" Sprenger asked.

"I thought that after today you may want to know some things about the past. This place seemed only appropriate to me."

Kanto led Sprenger past the stone wall into the cemetery. It was quite a tranquil place with the surrounding wall blocking the rest of the village from view. Everywhere Sprenger looked there were stone slabs covering the ground in neat, ordered rows. They were not particularly large, about the size of a doormat, but each was polished to a shimmering finish. Each stone reflected the sunset's light in a brilliant display. There were no flowers, no rocks, nothing to take the attention away from the stone slabs. It was truly a beautiful place.

Kanto led him down the center of the cemetery, not slowing to look around as Sprenger had. Despite Kanto, Sprenger still took every chance he could to look at someone's gravestone. On each of them was someone's name and occasionally had additional words like 'Honored in full for committed loyalty'. Each stone was given about a foot of space to every side before another stone was placed next to it. The grass between each stone was kept very short, so not to intrude on the gravestone itself.

After moving to the back of the cemetery, the stones increased in height and size twice. The center stones came up to Sprenger's knee, and ones near the back, closer to his waist. Like the others, these stones were polished to a brilliant finish, and were engraved with the name of the person whom it honored.

Sprenger stopped at one of the taller ones. It was about twice the height as the center stones, and a bit wider than the others. They all had a name engraved at the top but a few, like the one Sprenger stopped at, had titles that were earned during the scythe's life. One that caught Sprenger's eye was "The White Talon of Durado". Sprenger wondered what that scythe had done to earn such a name. At the bottom read "Honored in fullest for their devotion to Durado".

Kanto didn't stop for these either. He continued on to the very back of the cemetery, where they were shadowed by the towering wall of Durado. Kanto stopped at the last row, and by far the largest gravestones. The gravestones there were even wider than the others and came up to Kanto's waist. There were nine in all. Each stone was engraved with intricate designs all around the polished stones. Between each of the nine gravestones was a lush rose bush. They weren't in blossom yet, but the red thorns on the branches still gave more color surrounding these stones than anywhere else in the cemetery.

Sprenger came up and stood next to Kanto, who had stopped in front of one of the gravestones in the center. Sprenger had never seen gravestones like these before. All the words were engraved with gold lettering.

Above the name, carved into the marble, was the face of the man whom it honored, placed in shimmering gold. It was extremely detailed, down to every feature of his face. Only the eyes were left to the imagination, but even so, it was as if they were boring into Sprenger. The man had a strong handsome face, but was more defined by the scars he wore.

Kanto turned and looked back up the way they had come and pointed to the far stones. "Pentin," he said softly. He pointed to the next largest stones. "Junettin." He pointed at the taller ones near them. "And batennin." He then looked back down to the large stones in front of them. "These are Durado's past Scythriths," Kanto explained as Sprenger examined the stone. "Every time one dies, their gravestone is placed in the center of the line of his predecessors. The farther from the center of the line a stone is, the older the gravestone."

Sprenger looked down the row with awe. Each grave was different. Some of the men were similar in age to the man's that Kanto stopped at, while some were Jacob's age, and some of them were closer to Kanto's age.

Sprenger looked up at Kanto. "How are the stones placed in the center without disturbing the other stones?"

"They are carefully moved to the next spot down the line. With the passing of another Scythrith, each gravestone moves farther from the center. When he passes, Jacob's stone will be placed where this one is now, and so on. This is done so that the people of the village still feel closer to the Scythrith that they spent their lives under, and the Scythrith in turn, would want to be as close to the people that they protected. As generations die off, so too does the Scythrith of their time."

Sprenger put a hand on the cold stone of the most recent Scythrith. "Why hasn't anyone taken me here before? I know Soekka hasn't been here either."

"Because you have never known anyone that has passed. You hadn't even been born yet when this Scythrith guarded."

"So why did you bring me here now?"

Kanto looked down the line of past Scythrith. "These are the men who built this village. They protected it, and in many cases, died defending it. Their decisions are what molded Durado into what She is today." When Kanto paused, Sprenger pulled his gaze from the gravestones and looked up at him. Kanto was staring at him intently. "Not all their decisions were easy ones, and they weren't always accepted at first, but eventually, it proved to be for the best. That is why we must always trust in our Scythrith. Even if we don't understand or even agree with them at first."

Now Sprenger understood why they were here. He crossed his arms resentfully. "Do you always try to give the Old Man's apologies for him?"

Kanto looked back at the last Scythrith's stone. "I'm not doing it for his sake. I'm doing it for yours." Kanto placed a respectful hand on the stone as Sprenger had, and stared at the face of gold. "You will regret not forgiving him if you're not careful. Jacob is fully prepared to accept your anger and even your hatred, but you will be the one who suffers because of it." He carefully dragged his fingers over the man's golden name –"DANKO"-. "Eventually, your time to forgive him will run out and you will never again have the chance. Trust me when I tell you that in the end, your anger will mean nothing, and you will only wish that you could take it all back."

Sprenger dropped his arms to his sides. "Is that what happened to you?"

Kanto nodded, all while staring at the stone. "I was born into a war. He had enough to handle, including being a father. I understand that now, of course, but back then I resented him for it. There is no more stressful job than to be Scythrith in the middle of an ugly war, but I still felt that I deserved all his attention." He gave a sad snort. "I was being selfish," he turned back to Sprenger, "and he died thinking that I hated him. Not a day goes by that I don't wish I could tell him how much I loved him, or what a good father he really was."

Sprenger didn't think it was possible, but he felt a great pang of sympathy for Kanto. It was amazing that he could say such things, and still keep his composure. "You were the last Scythrith's son?" Kanto nodded. Sprenger looked over at the stone. "What happened to him?"

"He was killed when our village was attacked by enemy scythe. Two squads attacked the village when they realized that our forces had moved to the borders for a different battle. They took the opportunity to hurt an unguarded Durado." A small smirk emerged in the corner of his mouth. "He killed them all," the smirk faded, "but he was mortally wounded in the process. He died of his injuries a short time after. My father never got to see his village emerge victorious from that war."

"I'm sorry, Master Kanto," Sprenger said gently.

"Don't be," Kanto said flatly. "That's not why I'm telling you this." His gaze became more intent. "Jacob has deep love for you, both of you, and I know you do for him as well. I simply wanted to warn you what will happen if you don't put your petty anger aside and move on from this. It doesn't have to be soon, but the longer you wait, the harder it'll become."

Sprenger gave a grim nod. "I'll try."

"Good." Kanto strode past Sprenger and down the line of gravestones behind them. "But that is not the only reason why I brought you here." Sprenger followed him a short distance before he stopped and stood in front of a batennin-sized gravestone.

When Sprenger came closer, Kanto stepped aside. "Like I said before, I thought you might like to know things from the past, including yours."

On the polished stone in front of Sprenger was something that caused his stomach to clench.

Engraved in shimmering letters was her name: "SASHA".

Chapter 26

Dead Silent

Sprenger stared down at Sasha's grave; at his mother's grave.

He took in every detail of it; every crevasse, every letter, every sparkle. The world surrounding it went black. Nothing else at that moment mattered.

As far as Sprenger knew, this was what it felt like to see your mother for the first time.

Kanto's gentle hand on his shoulder pulled him back to the cemetery at the back of Durado. The colors of the sunset resembled that of a smoldering ember and was starting to cast its light on the village. It was almost enough to make his mother's headstone glow. Sprenger was beginning to feel his emotions welling up inside of him. He struggled to keep them from overflowing in front of Kanto.

"Thank you," Sprenger whispered through his inner turmoil. He finally took his eyes from the stone and looked at Kanto, who was giving his mother's headstone a respective stare. "Thank you for showing me this place."

Kanto didn't look at Sprenger, he continued to stare at Sasha's headstone. "You deserved to see it. I'm sorry it took so long."

Sprenger returned his gaze to the stone. He forgave him. He forgave both of them. It wouldn't be fair for Sprenger to not trust his mother the first time they met. After all, she had trusted him with so much. It only seemed fair that he returned the favor.

Then Sprenger remembered something, something that he became ashamed he forgot. "Master Kanto?"

"Hmm?" was his only response.

"I was told that you might be able to tell me about my father." Sprenger had forgotten what Juriah had told him in the glade until now.

Kanto raised an eyebrow at him. "And who told you that?"

"Juriah."

"Of course he did," Kanto grumbled. "Well that's difficult for anyone to explain, I'm afraid. You see, your parents never married, and your father did not want to play a role in your upbringing."

"Oh", Sprenger groaned disappointedly. He was hoping his father was just as wonderful as his mother was.

"Don't sound so disappointed," Kanto said. "Many scythe, especially master-scythe, don't marry, but that certainly doesn't mean they don't fall in love. Love, however, is difficult for us sometimes. We live dangerous lives, and love can be distracting."

"So did you know him?" Sprenger asked.

"I can't say if anyone really knows who he was for sure, but I think I did. Your mother had many suitors, but she always declined their offers." He looked down at Sprenger. "I suppose you're proof that she didn't decline them all."

Sprenger looked away. He could feel his face turning red. *I really didn't need to hear that about my mother.*

Kanto must have noticed. "But I'm certain she was in love," he added quickly. "She never said so but I still think she was. There was never a time that she was happier then when she was pregnant with you." Kanto began rubbing the back of his head. "I'm not sure what else to tell you, I'm afraid."

"That was perfect," Sprenger said with a smile. "Thank you." He looked back at the headstone and imagined what she looked like again.

Sprenger couldn't help it much at this point, he was feeling too much to hold back. He gave the stone a broad smile and he allowed a small tear to roll down his cheek, but just a small one.

He was going to make sure that she would be proud of him.

-<>-

Jacob looked out over the village as the sun set beyond the view of the trees that surrounded their great wall. He very slowly tugged his pointed beard. Errand came in behind him and dropped a pile of what sounded like reports on his desk. There were no footsteps out.

"You may speak lad," Jacob assured as he continued to stare at the sunset. He always knew when Errand wanted to talk.

This was one of those occasions when Errand was in no hesitation to say something. "Will you be alright, Lord Scythrith?" he asked very gently. He was such a good-hearted lad.

"I'm fine, thank you," Jacob replied as casually as he could muster.

Seemingly unconvinced, Errand continued to press. "It seems like we would never get this far, huh?" he asked innocently. Jacob turned his chair back around as Errand spoke. "It has been so long that we've talked about how this would turn out. I hope we're ready to find out."

Jacob smiled at him. "I know what you mean. The last several years have been quite boring, and now I have a feeling that we are about to have a lot to deal with." He chuckled to himself. "Our days of tranquility are about to become extremely rare occurrences."

That made Errand smirk. "I'll push through it with you as long as you keep pushing through. I think it will take both of us to pull Sprenger back onto the right path from time to time. We both know how stubborn he can be."

Jacob gave him a warm smile. "He got that from his mother. And look how much trouble that's caused."

-<>-

Tranis squeezed the pommel of the blade in his hand, as if to assure himself it was still there. Bark from a branch crunched under his foot as he leapt off it to another. The last time he attempted to flee using the canopy, he had fallen to the forest floor and found by Juriah. Now, he was hesitant with every step, knowing his escort up ahead would not be forgiving if thcy slowed. He could hear Cellic not far behind, following him across the branches. Phenex was in front of him leading the way.

That man made Tranis nervous. He squeezed the blade in his hand again.

Tranis had heard the guards screaming to get help, to raise the alarm, but none did. Tranis had seen the aftermath of this man when he was fleeing the prison. *What carnage he had left,* the thought almost made him shudder.

Tranis eyed the bladed endpiece that Phenex clutched in his right hand. *What a destructive weapon.* It took great skill to wield a weapon like that with such control. Scythe that used chained weapons could be useful in a team: they were able to keep an opponent at a distance, or stall a number of opponents at one time. Such weapons, however, were rarely effective for long. They could easily be tangled or caught up, and it was the scythe wielding them that pays the price for such a weapon choice.

Tranis had never seen Phenex fight, only seen the result of it. He was curious of the technique he used. To keep a weapon like that going, a lot of spinning must be incorporated into the style. If the end is allowed to stop moving, it would take time to build up its momentum again, and any wasted time could be fatal in a fight between scythe.

The three of them were being tailed by dura-scythe since they left Durado, and Tranis wondered if Phenex would stop and fight them, but he insisted they keep moving. *It would have been interesting to see him handle himself,* Tranis thought to himself as he watched Phenex bound from one branch to the next. Tranis much preferred they run though. He was good at avoiding scythe but limited in his ability to fend them off. Not to mention, he caught a glimpse of their pursuers; Masters Kanto and Skyle, two of Durado's top scythe. They had a few close encounters with them, but once it started getting dark, the three of them had the advantage. Avoiding someone in the dark is easier than finding someone. It had been almost a full day of hiding and traversing the canopy to avoid the batennin. The group was exhausted, but none of them let it show. To stop now would mean certain death at the hands of dura-scythe.

Suddenly Phenex dropped through the canopy. Tranis nearly lost his balance trying to stop and do the same. He landed directly behind Phenex on the ground, and not long after, Cellic landed next to him.

They were finally here. Tranis was breathing somewhat heavily, and he could hear Cellic was too. Phenex stood mute, staring ahead. He rarely spoke. He rarely allowed any manner of emotion to touch his face. That was the mark of a true scythe, and Tranis attempted to do the same.

Once all three of them were on the ground, Phenex began walking forward.

Clever hideout, Tranis thought as he examined their surroundings. It was unlikely that anyone would think to look for them here. Few probably even remembered they were still out here. Tranis knew for a fact that they were no longer on the Patrol Squad's maps.

"I was beginning to wonder when you would finally come back," a voice called down to them from a nearby branch.

Out of reflex, Tranis raised his blade in preparation. Cellic did the same. Phenex just looked up at the man on the branch with an expressionless stare.

The yellow-haired man was wearing the same black cloak as Phenex and was sitting on a branch, leaning up against the tree and holding a scabbard across his lap. These were the clear features of Peatra the Treacherous, Tranis knew.

Peatra lazily stood and draped the scabbard across his back. With a quick leap and flip, he landed behind the three of them. "Honestly," Peatra said, "I wasn't sure you even made it out of Durado." Phenex didn't say anything in reply but began walking again.

It is finally happening, Tranis thought with nervous excitement. If he answered the questions that Demaedura wanted, he could be free. Better yet, he could find a place of rank in the world at Demaedura's side. Unfortunately, despite his self-assurances, Tranis became more nervous with every step. He remembered what it was like to be around the Demon Hessiet. That smirk had troubled many of Tranis's dreams through the years and his incessant humming could haunt a man until he died.

Tranis looked over at Cellic who was nervously looking around as they moved underground. Cellic had proposed they run for it after Phenex had broken them out, but they never had the opportunity. Now that they had a second escort behind them, he doubted they ever would ever have another opportunity to flee.

The four men made their way through the wreckage and down the stairs. Tranis could see light flickering up the steps from below. Demaedura's distinctive smelling topcill oil became more and more staggering as they descended the steps. By the time they reached the bottom of the stairwell, Tranis could hardly keep from being sick. His face felt hot and his stomach lurched. There was a time that he started to become accustomed to the effects of Demaedura's concoctions, but that was a long time ago.

They stepped into a dim room with piles of stones crackling with burning oil, that only added to the thick odor of the room. The fires were not the main source of rancid air though. No, Tranis knew what that smell was; it was the herbs that Demaedura used to paralyze people. This was not the first time Tranis had cxperienced it, but it had been so long since he had to endure the effects of Demaedura's topcill oil that his body had lost its resistance to it.

Three men stood in the shadows of the small underground room, watching them as they entered. Tranis had never seen these men in person, only heard of them via rumors and reports.

The closest was dark-skinned and bald, the distinctive characteristics of the nomad clans, so Tranis knew this was Ajax. The next one was sickly and pale and had a bladed gauntlet on his left hand. Hexis of the Toad was what people called him, and Tranis wondered how many poisons he had hidden away in his cloak. The final Adimortis was the most distinct of them all. He stood so tall that his head nearly brushed the stone ceiling that Tranis could hardly reach with his hand. His cloak was so large that Tranis thought it could be used as a sail for a ship. Grogin's eyes were beady compared to the rest of his features, and they watched Tranis like all his compatriots'.

The three Adimortis stood as motionless as statues, almost hidden by their black cloaks in the shadows. With those three, Phenex, and Peatra behind them, that was five of the normally six Adimortis. Such a gathering was proof of how badly Demaedura wanted what Tranis had and he needed to reassure himself of this to muster the courage to continue into the room.

In the center of the room, a boy was shirtless, practicing fighting forms in the light of the fires. Something was different about his face, and when Tranis looked harder as the firelight hit him, he saw that his eyes were heavily bruised, giving him the appearance of wearing a mask or a blindfold. They were fresh bruises, and evident that they would only get worse in the next couple days. *I never thought Demaedura to take a student,* Tranis thought. When the boy noticed their presence, he stopped his practicing and moved to the edge of the firelight. Next to the boy, sitting on a throne of stone slabs, sat the image of Tranis's nightmares. Demaedura of the Hessiets looked exactly as Tranis remembered. His menacing eyes peered out from under his black bangs, and his smirk teased the corner of his thin lips. The dancing firelight shadowed his sharp features, truly giving him the appearance of a demon.

Tranis began shaking slightly. All confidence that he tried to muster before this moment had left him. He couldn't bring himself to face Demaedura again, he decided in an instant. The stench was just too much in such a confined area and it was only exacerbating his anxiety of seeing this man again. He wanted to run but couldn't move. He felt the threat of being sick pushing its way up his throat, and he desperately tried swallowing it back.

"You're looking a bit uncomfortable, Tranis," Peatra sneered from behind.

Phenex, after bowing to Demaedura courteously, moved aside and stood next to the hulking man in line with the other Adimortis.

Peatra gave them a sharp shove from behind, pushing them into the center of the room. Tranis looked over at Cellic, who looked even worse than Tranis felt. He could feel all eyes on them in the darkness. A feeling that only added to his apprehension.

Tranis forced himself to look forward. Demaedura was looking at him as a monster would a meal. He wore a tunic and robe that was similar to the style only worn by village elders. Though Tranis could not see the color, he knew it to be dark green; the color most scythe of an arboreal origin wore. His flame-pummeled sword was leaning against the side of the stone chair. In addition to his apparel, Demaedura was also wearing his usual dark smirk.

"What took you so long, Phenex?" he said with amused indifference.

"We were being followed by batennin," Phenex answered from his place in the shadows. "I made sure we had lost them in the forest before I returned here. I give you my word that we were not followed."

"Did you not think you could handle them?" Demaedura asked curiously.

"It was not my life I feared would be taken." Phenex gave Tranis and Cellic a sidelong glance.

Peatra stepped in close behind Cellic. "I thought we only intended to free one prisoner?" He reached behind him and pulled his sword halfway out of its scabbard. "Should I correct the numbers?"

Cellic's eyes nervously shifted over his shoulder, then at Demaedura.

Demaedura began to chuckle. “Don’t be so hasty, Peatra.” Peatra slowly lowered his sword back into its sheath and gave Cellic a cruel grin. Now Demaedura turned his attention to Tranis. “I kept my part of the bargain, Tranis. Now you’re going to give me everything you know about the Feral Beasts, and their Nymphigori.”

“Now?” Tranis gasped. “But we’re still in the borders of Durado. We are still in danger here, and there is no doubt that every dura-scythe is combing the forest for us.”

“Do you not trust me Tranis?” Demaedura asked coyly. Tranis wasn’t sure what to say immediately, but Demaedura continued. “My Adimortis have gathered so that they can begin their searches based on your information. When we leave this wretched forest, they will each go their own ways. This is the only time we may have while in the same confines.”

This was what Tranis feared; they could just abandon him in Durado’s forest after they get what they wanted. Tranis needed them to get him and Cellic past not only the walls, but the border patrols as well. He looked over at Cellic, who gave him an affirmative nod. Cellic took in a deep breath, then spoke.

“We will give you what you want then, but we humbly ask for something else.” Demaedura’s black eyebrows rose with curiosity. “We are now rogue-scythe, and will not survive long on our own after Durado sends squads to hunt us down.”

“And why is that my concern?” Demaedura asked.

“With your resources, we can remain alive, and of service to you. We served you when you resided in Durado, and we feel we should be rewarded for our loyalty, which did not falter even after we were locked away for it."

"What is it that you want?" Demaedura pressed politely.

"We want you to take us as Adimortis." Several of the men laughed softly, but Cellic ignored them. "We are skilled spies, and we will shortly give you information that will further increase your power." Demaedura's eyes narrowed. "If you do not agree, then we will take our information with us."

Don't say that! But Tranis couldn't say it fast enough.

Flames sputtered, and Tranis and Cellic flinched as Demaedura flew from his seat and darted past them in the blink of an eye. Tranis made the worst mistake a scythe could make: he flinched. When he opened his eyes, there was something shimmering in the corner of his vision. He turned his head to Cellic, who was staring wide-eyed at the ceiling, a sword tip jutting from his chest. He looked as if he were trying to scream, but couldn't. Tranis faltered back a few steps in shock.

"Adimortis do not choose themselves," Demaedura whispered eerily from behind Cellic. "And the world is littered with my spies." Cellic seemed to be choking with pain as Demaedura spoke. "Even now, I have spies in Durado, who are responsible for Tranis's first escape attempt. You are not as valuable as you think." He slid the blade out of Cellic's back, and watched him fall forward and lay motionless on the ground.

No! Tranis felt tears building in him, only seconded by the urge to vomit.

Demaedura gave the sword a quick swing, leaving a streak of blood on the stone floor. He turned his smirk to Tranis. "To be Adimortis, you must be invincible." Without warning, Demaedura lunged at Peatra with his sword, who clapped both hands onto the blade before it entered his chest. Peatra slid back a bit from the force of Demaedura's thrust, but Tranis could see that he had managed to stop the blade with his bare hands. Demaedura began chuckling and pulled his sword free of Peatra's hands, who looked very unhappy about being used to prove Demaedura's point.

Demaedura smirked back at Tranis and held something up in the light for him to see. It was Cellic's journal.

Where did he get that! Tranis was sweating heavily now. That journal contained everything they knew about enemy Nymphigori. Both Tranis and Cellic kept one, along with the third member of their squad, who was still somewhere in Durado's prison. Tranis's journal was well hidden, and he told Cellic to do the same a long time ago, but there it was in Demaedura's hand.

Demaedura strode back to his stone throne and began flipping the journal over his fingers. "The same man that dropped a key to your cell, as well as delivered messages between us, was also kind enough to provide me with this. You know what it is, and you know what it contains. Luckily for you, Tranis, there are holes in his writing that you will fill in for me. So if you play your role well, then I will allow you to go on your way, safely on the other side of Durado's borders. It all depends on how useful I find your information." Tranis seriously doubted that Demaedura would let him live at this point, but if Tranis refused then there was no hope.

Demaedura leaned forward in his seat. "Not to mention, no one else alive was there when Juriah faced and killed Sortan in the mountains. It is that information that makes you unique, Tranis." He laced his fingers in front of his face. "So tell me, what has become of Sassor?"

Chapter 27

Offer

Sprenger casually strode along the market, prolonging his time in the sun before he returned to the house. Their squad was given the day off, and Granny Karla was forcing them to use it to clean the house and do chores. She had sent Sprenger out to get some food, and he had gotten it, but he was certainly in no hurry to return to cleaning. He wandered aimlessly, saying hello to people that recognized him as he twirled the basket of food, testing his skill to not lose a single piece.

The Exerptus Exam was in a week, and Sprenger was glad for the distraction from the recent drama involving him and Soekka's parents. The exams were the perfect thing to keep him from thinking about all of it. All he wanted to do was to run back to the Shattered Hill and see the Pantrores again, but there was no way for him to do that. Thinking about it only made him more upset, so he tried to focus primarily on the exams instead.

As Sprenger left the market, he took the long route back to the house; the one that went past the pond. *Maybe I'll spare a roll for the coy*, he thought, happy to think of something else to kill time. If he stalled long enough, Soekka would finish scrubbing clothes and Sprenger would only have to help dry.

When Sprenger rounded one of the bends, he stopped. Juriah was standing to the side of the road, listening cross-armed to another scythe. Sprenger couldn't hear what they were saying, but Juriah didn't look happy, nor the scythe very confident.

Sprenger couldn't decide what to do. This was the first time he had seen Juriah since they were at the Shattered Hill, and he wanted to convince Juriah to take him back, but then he didn't want to jeopardize everyone getting mad at him again. Especially now that they were so close to the exams and Sprenger was already on thin ice with everyone that knew about his trip to the Shattered Hill. Sprenger clenched his teeth, unable to make a decision about what to do.

Finally, he decided to approach Juriah, if only to ask him a few more questions about the Pantrores. As Sprenger got closer, he could hear that the scythe was explaining the border patrols.

"If they haven't been spotted leaving the forest," Juriah said angrily, "then that means they're still in there somewhere. Find them."

"I understand that, Lord Hessiet," the scythe defended, "but Lord Scythrith has ordered us to not confront the Adimortis if found."

"I'm not telling you to confront them, you idiot, I'm telling you to find them. *I'll* confront them by myself if that's what that senile old bag wants." He pointed a finger at the scythe with an angry glare. "But I *can't* search the whole forest by myself."

"Begging your pardon, Lord Hessiet, but why not request the services of the hounds?" the scythe suggested.

"Because," Juriah snapped, "Demaedura's topcill oil would likely kill them. If you get too close, it'll make you sick and even stun you if you're close enough. It can also be strong enough to kill a dog if they get too close. We release the hounds, they'll run the opposite direction as Demaedura."

Sprenger wondered about that himself, and had forgotten to ask Juriah about it before.

The scythe nodded his understanding as well. "I'll spread the word amongst the patrols. I'll make sure anything strange is reported to you as well as Lord Scythrith."

"Good," Juriah said flatly.

The scythe gave a deep bow then ran past Sprenger, who Juriah noticed standing there as he watched the scythe leaving.

"Eavesdropping?" he asked curiously.

"Just passing by," Sprenger corrected. "Can that smell really kill the hounds?"

Juriah nodded. "Remember what it was like for you to experience?" Sprenger wished he couldn't. "A hound has a far more powerful sense of smell; the side effects would have been amplified with it. It's incredibly dangerous for anyone who hasn't experienced it before, but luckily the effects taper as one is exposed to it more."

"How can oil do that?" Sprenger asked curiously.

"It's a cocktail of herbs and toxic plants, many of which have deadly effects on their own. Demaedura has learned to recreate many of their effects in an oil that he always carries around with him. You're lucky you were exposed to it outside. In close quarters, it can cause people to have violent hallucinations." Juriah turned and began to walk down the road, so Sprenger walked next to him. "So," Juriah said casually, "I hear you're already training for the Exerptus Exam."

"Yah, the Old Man asked our entire class to do it. No one is quite sure why."

"Why indeed," Juriah mumbled. Sprenger gave him a quizzical look but Juriah didn't look down at him. "I certainly hope you learned the routine well enough," Juriah said. "The Pantrores can be awfully choosy when it comes to that routine."

Sprenger stopped, and Juriah turned and gave him a coy look. "What?" Sprenger said in shock. "What does the routine have to do with the Pantrores?"

Juriah raised an eyebrow at him. “There is always something that is required to becoming a Nymphigori.” Juriah gave an uninterested shrug. “If you want to be a Nymphigori, then I suggest you make sure that your routine is perfect.”

A chill ran up Sprenger’s spine. He wasn’t sure what to say, he wasn’t even sure he understood what he just heard.

Juriah turned back around and continued to walk away. “Perhaps I can tell you more when, or if you pass the exam,” Juriah yelled over his shoulder.

Sprenger just stood in the road awestruck holding his basket of food.

Juriah had shown him the Feral Beasts and now had just told him what it takes to become a Nymphigori. He wanted Sprenger to become a Nymphigori for some reason.

Chapter 28

Higher Stakes

Soekka and Sprenger slapped their right palms to the ground, signaling the end of their routine. A small group of children clapped and cheered for them as they finished and stood. It was becoming a regular occurrence for the pentin to attract an audience in the training grounds, especially when it was Sprenger and Soekka training. Usually the group was mostly young ones taking a break from their basic training, but now the crowd had added some girls that were in Master Cerri's class with them but didn't continue on to be pentin. They were by far the loudest members of the crowd.

Ever since Demaedura's failed attack on the village, no one was allowed to train outside the walls until the Adimortis' whereabouts were discovered. All of the pentin were forced to share the training grounds with other scythe of the village that came to practice their skills.

Soekka was tired of being cooped up in the village, especially when they were trying to train for the Exerptus Exam. He heard a couple girls in the group of young admirers yelling his and Sprenger's names, but Soekka ignored them. The children he didn't mind so much since they were there because they liked watching the routine, but the girls were probably more interested in the fact that Sprenger and Soekka trained bare-chested. They continued to shout at them for a short time before quieting down into annoying giggles and whispers. He preferred quiet when he was training, and he had not had that since they were forced to continue training inside the village.

Sprenger, on the other hand, seemed to relish the attention. He would always turn when someone yelled his name and wave at them, which only encouraged them further. Soekka just pretended not to notice.

They would get reprieve from the annoying girls when Tenni would join them. Like Soekka and Sprenger, Tenni was top of their class and was very intimidating to many of the other girls. It only took an annoyed look from under her sandy bangs to silence their former classmates. One girl was so loud, Tenni stormed up to them with clenched fists, and they darted away like mice in the grass.

Sprenger was annoyed when Tenni would silence their audience, but Soekka appreciated it. Today, however, Tenni was off with Korran somewhere, and the boys were training without her.

Soekka had to keep reassuring himself that the interruptions from the onlookers wouldn't make a large difference to his training. As far as he was concerned, their routine was practically flawless at this point and they didn't need to be so disciplined in practicing it anymore. Soekka was thankful that they got the time they did in the glade to train, otherwise their progress would have been much slower here in the village.

"We seem to be quite the attraction," Sprenger beamed as he waved at another nameless girl.

That's exactly what I don't want to be, Soekka thought irritably.

Sprenger looked over his shoulder with a childish grin. "Did you see how many people were watching us, Soekka?"

Soekka didn't look at him when he spoke. Instead, he just headed for the shade. "We used to come and watch the scythe train here when we were on break from Cerri's class too." Sprenger wasn't listening though. He just continued to smile and wave until he noticed Soekka walking away.

Sprenger ran up next to him. “Well I think that’s enough of the routine for a little while. What else do you want to work on?”

Soekka knew that Sprenger was trying to act like there was nothing going on between them, but it wasn’t that easy for Soekka. He was slower to forgive than Sprenger was, and things had been a bit tense since Sprenger snuck off to the Shattered Hill.

“We should take a break,” Soekka mumbled, “and then, since we threw yesterday, we should spar today.”

Sprenger put his hands behind his head. “Sounds good to me.”

The two of them sat down under one of the trees on the edge of the training grounds. It felt good to be out of the sun for a bit. Sprenger lay back in the grass, and Soekka rested his arms on his knees.

“You may be sparring with Juriah eventually,” Soekka said, trying to match Sprenger’s care-free attitude. “If he ends up training you as a Nymphigori, I mean. You should really get some more practice before then.”

Sprenger didn’t answer at first, a bit surprised Soekka brought it up again. Soekka wanted Sprenger to realize that he was happy for him. Soekka wished he could find a similar opportunity to connect with his dead family, but that didn’t mean he wasn’t excited for Sprenger. He knew he wasn’t good at showing it, though. Talking about it was Soekka’s way of proving to Sprenger that it didn’t bother him.

“I don’t think those will be long matches,” Sprenger joked. “Not if our match in the forest is any idea.”

“But still,” Soekka continued, “if you become a Nymphigori then learning to fight from a Hessiet will be unlike anything you’ve ever done before.”

"I doubt it," Sprenger grumbled. "Considering me and Juriah's last fight, I'll only learn to take a hit better than before. Unfortunately, delivering them is what wins fights."

"Kind of," Soekka said skeptically.

"What do you mean 'kind of'? How can you win if you don't make any hits?"

"Well if *you* prevent your opponent from making any hits, then technically they can't win either. Remember Cerri telling us fights between master-scythe can take so long to finish. They can fight non-stop for hours. The best for a whole day."

Sprenger thought about it for a moment. "Makes sense to me," he agreed. "Can you imagine being in a fight like that?"

Soekka shrugged. "I doubt I could fight someone for more than a few minutes without tiring myself out."

"Pillas's parents told him that when he went rogue, Demaedura's fight with Juriah started in the village but took them all the way to the mountains before the fight stopped, and obviously neither one killed the other so it could have gone even longer, but Demaedura fled."

Soekka looked over his shoulder at Sprenger, who still had his hands behind his head, looking up at the leaves of the tree. "The mountains? That's an entire day's journey." Soekka couldn't even picture such a thing happening. It would be impossible to go for such a distance and still be able to fight.

Sprenger shrugged. "That's what he said. And really, if you think about it, if they were fighting the whole time then it probably would have taken even longer than normal."

Soekka looked back to the training grounds. "That's amazing. I definitely couldn't do that."

"Well not yet at least," Sprenger teased.

Soekka watched a pair of scythe sparring in one of sparring circles close by. They were fairly impressive with their skills, and far more developed physically than Sprenger and Soekka. He watched them for a time and wondered how a fight like that could go for hours. *Someone is more likely to just die of exhaustion after a certain amount of time.*

"I wonder how long my parents were fighting for before they were killed," Soekka said softly, and was almost surprised that he said it out loud.

Sprenger sat up next to him. "What?"

Soekka didn't look at him, wishing Sprenger hadn't heard him. "I just wondered if my parents' final battle was as grand as that."

"I thought they were taken because they were Nymphigori?" Sprenger asked, confused.

Soekka shook his head. "Remember how when we were kids and we would ask Granny Karla about this? She told me that my parents died when there was an uprising of traitors in the village."

Sprenger became slightly somber, seeming to remember now. "Yea, and when I asked she would say 'Your mother likewise died protecting the village, as scythe should.'" He gave a forced snort of amusement. "I guess she wasn't lying to me."

"She didn't lie to me either," Soekka said.

Sprenger's brow wrinkled. "How do you know?"

"I asked her again that night that you went to the pond." Soekka began picking dirt out from under his fingernails. "She said that it was that uprising with Demaedura that killed my parents. Not long after that the Nymphigori in all the villages were condemned." Soekka finally looked at Sprenger. "My parents were killed by traitors. I can't help but wonder if they even got to die fighting."

"Of course they did," Sprenger reassured.

Soekka looked back at the sparring scythe, who were still keeping a strong and steady pace. "I'm not so sure, Sprenger." Sprenger tried to say something else reassuring, but Soekka interrupted. "Think about it. My parents were Nymphigori, and everyone says they were great scythe. How could they be killed in a readied battle by scum scythe? Shouldn't the Pysliths have protected them? There's no way all of the Pysliths were killed in a small uprising, so where were they and where did they go after? The only way scythe would kill my parents is if they were taken by surprise and didn't even have a chance."

They were both silent as Sprenger gave it some thought. Finally, he said something. "I see what you're saying, but I think there could be more to it than you think."

"Like what?" Soekka grumbled.

"From what Juriah has told me about Demaedura, he likes to recruit the best scythe he can find. That means that this uprising may not have been as small as you think. It could have been made up of skilled masters. And we know that a key part to a successful infiltration is isolating a village's masters and taking them out individually versus giving them a chance to assemble. Your parents probably were among the scythe targeted early because they were such a threat."

"I suppose that's true," Soekka admitted. "But that was kind of my point. They were probably hit before they even knew there was trouble. That's not how I think good scythe should die."

"You're forgetting one other thing," Sprenger pressed.

Soekka looked at him skeptically. "What's that?"

"Demaedura himself," Sprenger said, as though he was saying something obvious. Soekka raised an eyebrow at him. "We have absolutely no idea how things happened that night. For all we know, your parents fought Demaedura himself before Juriah got there. And it sounds like it would take the best scythe in our village to hold him off."

Soekka smirked. "It's a nice thought, but one man can't kill two Nymphigori and all of their beasts."

"Do we know that for sure?" Sprenger asked temptingly.

"I think that's a pretty safe bet, Sprenger," Soekka grumbled.

"Just like how it's impossible that he and Juriah destroyed an entire scythe village?" Soekka perked up slightly, and Sprenger gave him a very smug smile. "See? We can't assume we know anything about how big or small battles involving Hessiets are. If I were to bet, I'd say your parents were the reason Demaedura didn't kill more people that night. I bet they were at the forefront to stop him because, besides Juriah, they were the only ones in the village who stood a chance against him."

Soekka's smile broadened. He had not thought about it like that before. "Leave it to you to cheer me up when I didn't want to be cheered up, Sprenger."

Sprenger lay back down with his hands behind his head again, now with a smug expression. "It's not easy being your brother, but frankly, you'd be a wreck if I wasn't." He closed his eyes contently.

Soekka smiled at him. Soekka knew the truth of that. "Honestly, if changing the past and getting our parents back meant not having you as a brother, then I wouldn't even consider it, Sprenger."

Sprenger just continued to smile with his eyes closed. "Can't say I blame you."

Soekka smiled even bigger, something he had not done for a while. Soekka smacked Sprenger's exposed stomach, causing him to lurch into a ball. He groaned from the hit while giggling at the same time.

"Jerk!" Sprenger tried kicking Soekka but it was very half-hearted and Soekka grabbed his ankle. Sprenger jumped on him and the two began rolling around the tree, trying to grapple the other into submission. Sprenger managed to get Soekka in a tight bear hug from behind, and Soekka struggled to break free.

Soekka heard a thumping noise behind him, and suddenly Sprenger's grip released. Before Soekka turned around, a sharp pain erupted on the back of his head.

The two boys rubbed their heads and looked up to see Master Cerri shaking his head at them, his oak rod in his hand. "In a few days you two will be recognized scythe," he snapped. "There is already controversy about allowing you to take the exam so young, and you're not helping by rolling in the dirt like toddlers."

The boys stood. "Sorry, Master Cerri," Soekka and Sprenger grumbled together.

"Old habits, you know," Soekka joked.

"I need no reminding of that, Soekka," Cerri pointed out. Soekka and Sprenger smiled at the memories of being hit by that stupid stick during class.

"So," Cerri continued more pleasantly, "how is the training going? Many of my new students have told me you are quite impressive with the routine."

"We are," Sprenger said flatly. Soekka rolled his eyes.

Cerri raised his rod to Sprenger's face, and pointed it right at his nose. "Not only can overconfidence be annoying," he jabbed Sprenger in the nose, "it can be deadly," he jabbed him again.

"Okay, sorry," Sprenger said as he rubbed his nose.

Cerri smiled at them. "But I do look forward to seeing my pupils advance into the ranks of scythe. In fact, I plan to be watching it with Scythrith Jacob, so I'll be at the very front of the crowd."

"We will do our best to not disappoint you," Soekka assured.

"You rarely do. But that is not why I'm here." He began twirling his stick over his fingers. "I have not talked to you boys much recently, and I want to know how everything is going before the exam gets too close."

"That would be good," Soekka said. "A lot has happened recently, and your advice would be much appreciated."

"Of course," Cerri said kindly. "A true teacher never tires of helping their students. I'll see you tonight then at the Steaming Pot. My treat, of course." He spun on his heels and began walking away, twirling his rod through his fingers. "And save the sparring for the sparring circles please," he called over his shoulder.

"Think he'll tell us anything new?" Soekka asked.

Sprenger shrugged. "He's bound to know something. After all, he's older than Durado itself." The two boys began to laugh again.

Chapter 29

Cerri's Favorites

The day of training in the sun left both the boys tired and hungry. They continued in the training grounds until about mid-afternoon, where they decided that was enough and they should let Granny Karla know they wouldn't be home for dinner. Upon their arrival, Karla made sure to force them to clean themselves before meeting Master Cerri, and was quick to silence the protests from each boy. After splashing water over themselves and changing into nicer clothes, they took off through the village once more.

As evening fell, many of the shop were closing their doors, but several places of food and drink were as busy as ever. The air started to fill with the smells of cooking from within the roothomes. Smoke billowed out of hollow branches of homes and shops alike.

Sprenger and Soekka walked into the Steaming Pot and looked around for Master Cerri. Behind the counter, Nellan noticed them and started waving. He was a small boy and surprised no one when he decided to end his scythe training after the basics and took work in his parents' foodhouse. Sprenger and Soekka waved back with smiles at their former classmate, then Nellan pointed to one of the back corners. Soekka struggled to peer around people, but then noticed Cerri's shoulder-length grey hair sitting at one of the back tables.

The boys gave Nellan a small, polite greeting and then headed to Cerri's table.

Soekka noticed how Cerri sat with excellent posture at the table and was slowly sipping a small wooden cup of something they could not see.

"Evening boys," he said with a small smile as they came around to sit at the table. "I took the liberty of ordering us all the pork and noodles." He lowered his voice. "It's Nellan's specialty," he said with a wink.

"That sounds perfect," Soekka said.

"Yah," Sprenger agreed. "I'm starving so I hope he makes a lot."

Cerri smiled at that. "So," he said casually, "do you boys think you're ready, for the exams?"

Soekka shrugged modestly. "The new training takes us time to learn, but eventually we figure everything out. The canopy and routine are the hardest parts for most, but it seems like everyone will do well enough to pass."

"Even Warren," Sprenger joked.

"Warren has potential," Cerri said plainly as he took another sip of his drink. "He tries harder than most, but for half the results, I'm afraid." Cerri raised a finger. "But mark my words. Warren's hard work will eventually pay off and he will blossom into a great scythe."

I seriously doubt that, Soekka thought, but kept his mouth shut.

"You've seen us all training for the exams," Sprenger said. "What's your opinion about everybody's likelihood of passing?"

"Very good, from what I can tell. I worry about Pillas and Naibi in the throwing tests, though. They've always struggled with stationary targets, let alone while moving or in the trees."

"I guess I haven't noticed that," Soekka admitted.

Cerri chuckled. "No, I imagine you haven't, Soekka."

What's that supposed to mean? Soekka wondered, not sure if he should be offended or not. He looked over at Sprenger who looked just as unsure about the comment.

"You have, however," Cerri continued, "probably noticed Rejeno's abilities with throwing, haven't you?"

"Oh yah," Sprenger huffed. "I think he's getting better than ever. Better than Soekka even."

Soekka gave him an annoyed look.

"Well, Soekka?" Cerri asked curiously. "What do you think?"

Soekka shrugged. "He was always neck and neck with me in your class with the stationary targets, but he really seems to have a knack for throwing in the trees and while running. Since we're not scored in our squads, like we were in class, we don't know if he's passed me or not."

"Well," Cerri said over his glass, "the exams are scored. So I guess we'll find out." He took another drink. "Speaking of finding out," he said as he put his glass back on the table and looked at Sprenger. "I hear you've been trying to do an awful lot of it lately."

Great, this again, Soekka thought annoyed. *When are we ever going to stop talking about Sprenger and his Feral Beasts?*

Sprenger gave Cerri a shy smile. "I've been a bit curious lately," he admitted.

Soekka snorted, and Sprenger briefly gave him an irritated look.

"And has that curiosity been satisfied, or has it led to more questions?" Cerri asked.

"A bit of both I think." Sprenger gave him a suspicious look. "How much do *you* know, Master Cerri?"

Cerri gave him a coy smile, then slicked down his thin mustache with his fingers. "Hopefully more than you still," he teased.

"That's not what I-" Sprenger began.

"I know what you meant," Cerri said with a smile. "I am well aware of your families' secrets, and the Shattered Hill." He looked at Soekka with curiosity. "And have you been digging into your past as well?"

"No," Soekka said flatly. "I've been repeatedly informed that stories will be all that I get from my family."

Cerri continued to stare at him for a short time, but luckily for Soekka, Nellan came over carrying three wooden bowls of steaming food.

"Here you guys go," he said as he put them on the table. "I made it all myself," he said proudly, "so let me know what you think."

"It smells amazing," Cerri said kindly. "I wonder how good you would be at making us a plate of cocoa rolls."

Nellan smiled. "Those are easy. I'll go start them now." With that, he headed back to the counter and out of sight.

Cerri turned back to the table with an excited smirk. "They're my favorite," he said eagerly.

"I wish coco wasn't so expensive," Sprenger said. "Everything at the bakery with it is too much for what Granny Karla gives us to spend."

"Well it does have to come from very far away, so the traders are quick to bid it for more than it is probably worth. One of the few downsides of living in our beloved village. Still worth every bit it costs," Cerri defended sternly.

The boys smiled at him, then started into their meal, which Soekka had to admit was very good.

"So, Soekka," Cerri said between bites of noodles, "why do you seem disheartened by everything that you've discovered? Are you not excited to learn that your parents were reputable scythe?"

Soekka stopped eating and looked back up at Cerri. He was getting tired of this topic continually recurring, but he answered anyway. "I am not disheartened, I'm actually very happy to learn about my family's past. What makes me sad is the manner in which I lost them, and the fact that I will never get anymore from my family but legends."

"Ahh," Cerri nodded his understanding. "And to what manner to which you lost them are you referring?"

Soekka gave him a confused look. "Them being killed by traitors," he said bluntly.

Cerri nodded again. "I see."

"What do you know about that night?" Sprenger asked through a mouthful of noodles.

"I know quite a bit, unfortunately," Cerri said somberly. "It was one of the worst nights of my life. War is one thing. Watching comrades killed in battle, killing anonymous foes, but this was not like that. These opponents were people we knew, people we had fought and lived with, and some were even people we had trained. Trust me, Sprenger, I know a lot about that night, and none of it is knowledge I wish upon you." He finished his drink.

"So do you know how my parents died?" Soekka finally asked.

Surprisingly, Cerri gave him a fierce look. "You know they were killed, and that should suffice."

Soekka was dumbstruck, that was not any sort of answer that he was expecting. Of course it didn't suffice. "But-"

"No, Soekka," Cerri said firmly. "There should never be comfort in how a person died, especially in our world. Your parents died in the way they should have, in defense of our village. Knowing that should be enough to satisfy your curiosity."

Soekka didn't know what to say, he looked over at Sprenger, who was also so shocked that there were un-chewed noodles hanging out of his mouth as he just stared at Cerri.

Cerri took a lower tone. "I fear that you boys are going through a very natural step of losing a loved one, and that is the desire for revenge or closure. *That* is why these things were kept from you for so long. It was hoped that you could be spared such dangerous emotions."

Soekka stabbed his fork into his noodles with agitation and continued eating. He knew this would happen. Everyone refused to just tell him about what went on with his parents 'for his own sake', while Sprenger was being handed secret after secret.

Apparently, Sprenger noticed Soekka's frustration and continued asking questions casually on Soekka's behalf.

"So you knew about the Pysliths and the Pantrores then?" Sprenger whispered to Cerri.

Cerri's eyes narrowed at Sprenger, as though he were considering if what Sprenger asked was out of line or not. "Of course," Cerri finally replied. "Villages used to celebrate the Feral Beasts that shared in the defense of their home. But after the war, it was decided to wipe away the memory of such things and people." He took a small bite of noodles then lightly dabbed his lips with a napkin. "You boys are not the only ones that lost loved ones under mysterious circumstances when it happened. Remember, many scythe villages had Nymphigori, and all were gathered and destroyed."

"But Soekka's parents died before that," Sprenger pointed out. "So what happened to the Pysliths?"

Soekka stopped his eating and waited for Cerri's answer, who thought about it for a moment.

Cerri looked up in thought. "They disappeared right after that, actually; I believe killed." He shook his head. “But I can’t say for sure. Only a handful of people knew about those circumstances and I was not one of them.”

“Then no one knows what happened to the Pysliths?” Soekka whispered softly.

“No one that I know of,” Cerri admitted. “But like I said, I believe they were killed before the extermination of Nymphigori.”

But you don’t know for sure, Soekka reminded himself.

Nellan came around the tables and dropped off a saucer with small doughy rolls. They were still hot and smelled like cocoa beans. Cerri gave them a hungry smile and thanked Nellan. Nellan then gave each of them a small glass and filled it with milk.

“You have to have milk with these,” he said excitedly. “The milk is on me.” They all thanked him as he filled their cups.

After he left, Cerri raised his tiny cup of milk. “I would like to wish you both luck in the upcoming exam. I have never been disappointed with the two of you, and I don’t expect to be now.”

They all took a sip of milk and grabbed a cocoa roll. Soekka didn’t really listen to too much of the conversation that followed. He just stared into his glass as he swirled the milk around.

No one knows what happened to the Pysliths, he continued to repeat to himself. *They’re still out there, I know they are.*

Chapter 30

The Exerptus Exams

The day of the exams seemed like any other at first. Granny Karla forced the boys out of bed for an early breakfast and instructed them to do their stretches early to make sure they were ready for their tasks. Then, seeming worried they would be late, she rushed them out the door, moving her short legs quickly through the village. The sun was shining in Durado, and most people continued about their business as normal, but worry started to build in Sprenger's stomach the closer to the front of the village.

He could see up the road where people were gathering for the exams, but Master Kanto stopped them, Tenni at his side, before they were able to join the group. Tenni gave both boys an encouraging, yet nervous smirk as Kanto and Karla exchanged quick pleasantries. After giving both boys a hug and kiss on the cheek, Karla left them to go stand in the waiting group of people to see the students off.

"I will not be permitted to speak with you again until the exams are finished," Master Kanto said to them once Granny Karla had gone. "If you make a mistake, do not waiver from the next task. It is more important to keep focused than to try and correct a mistake that has already happened." They all nodded their understanding. "And remember," he said more gently than normal, "breathe." They each took a long, slow breath. "You lot can already do everything they are going to ask of you. Push any doubt of that from your mind. Your only task now, is to show the elders. Simple enough." He nodded reassuringly again. "I will see you when it is all over. Good luck." They bowed to him as a team, then started apprehensively to join the rest of the waiting students.

Within a few moments, the three of them stood amidst their six companions from Cerri's class, as well as five others from the class before theirs, and two from the class before that. All stood silently in organized rows in front of the main gate, surrounded by dozens of expressionless scythe, as well as eager members of the village, who came to wave and encourage individual students.

In front of the students stood the village elders: Elder Jaydon and Elder Bakkon. Sprenger had only seen them on rare occasions before this, as they were not often found wandering the village and only tended to show up for important events, like graduation. Now the two men were here to score every student on their exams and determine whether or not they were ready to proceed to the next level of training.

Jaydon was clean shaven but had an eccentric head of cotton white hair that fell down to his lower back and was only held out of his face by a leather headband that bore Durado's symbol. He wore an impressive silk outfit consisting of a green sleeveless tunic over a white long sleeve silk shirt that was wrapped by green silk straps on each arm up his forearms.

To his right stood Elder Bakkon, who looked to be his exact opposite. He had a long black beard that was peppered with graying hair, and bushy black eyebrows to match. His hair was thinning and was greased back over his shining scalp. His outfit mirrored Jaydon's, but instead of green, he wore dark grey silk over a white shirt.

"Today," Bakkon finally announced when Sprenger thought his patience would take no more, "you will show us what you've learned as pentin. If we deem you worthy, you and your squad will then be permitted to travel the land and represent our village on missions of far greater difficulty, danger, and reward. If you so choose to continue your training at its current level, and not proceed to take the exam at this point in time, please step forward and humbly depart. Keep in mind that it will be two years before this chance will come again."

There was an awkward pause as everyone wondered if someone would let their nerves get the best of them and leave. No one did.

"The exam then," Jaydon announced after a short pause, "will consist of three parts. The first is blade throwing, the second is sparring, and the third is the Exerptus Routine demonstrated all together. If there are no questions before we start, then you will all be escorted to the forest where we will begin the blade throwing portion of the test. These scythe around you," he said, gesturing to the dozens of scythe standing all around the students, "will be spread amongst the trees to ensure your safety while outside the walls." Many students couldn't help but look around at all the stoic faces of scythe around them. "We will test you each individually in a series of challenges, then you may return and join your comrades. When everyone has finished, we will regroup at the training grounds and continue from there. Unless you have questions, you are not permitted to speak unless spoken to from this moment on."

He gave a small bow. "Good luck to you all."

Everybody bowed back silently.

"Let us begin," Bakkon said, then turned with Jaydon and led the mass of scythe and students through the gates and into the forest.

The walk was uncomfortably silent for Sprenger. The only noise was the dozens of feet on the ground, and the silence was only making Sprenger's nerves worse. His stomach was starting to lurch and palms beginning to sweat, but he wiped them off and took a calming breath. This is what he had been training for nonstop for the last couple months. He was ready, he knew he was ready.

They were all stopped amidst a shaded clearing surrounded by giant twisting roots and looming trees that blocked their view from any of the surrounding forest. Almost immediately after arriving, Jaydon and Bakkon called the first name on their list to follow them. It was one of the students from the oldest class, and they were led past some bushes and out of sight. In a few minutes, Sprenger could hear the sound of blades hitting wood, and knew that they had begun to test.

Everyone waited patiently as Jaydon and Bakkon returned, the older boy in wake with a content smirk on his face and called someone else's name to follow them. Another of the older students disappeared and the process was repeated three more times.

Soekka was finally called, and Sprenger listened as hard as he could, though he didn't exactly know what he was listening for. He heard several blades hit wood and so assumed all was well, imagining them being targets.

When Soekka came back, he had a very discreet smirk on his mouth and gave Sprenger a small thumbs up as he passed him.

"Sprenger," Bakkon called out.

Sprenger took another breath and then stepped out and followed the elders around the brush and into an area that had targets in several creative places. Some were on stumps or trees as Sprenger had expected, but others were up in branches or even swinging on ropes from the trees.

Sprenger was led over to a small table, where a map of the course was drawn out as well as a small hourglass full of sand. The map showed all of the trees, stumps, and rocks that were in the immediate area, but more importantly, it had a black dot in all the areas that a target was located.

"Take a moment to determine where all of the targets are at," Jaydon explained. "There are fifteen in all. Blades are in a box in the center of the grounds. We will tip the hourglass when you are ready, and if you do not hit all of the targets before the sand runs out or you run out of blades, you do not pass."

Sprenger nodded his understanding, then stared intently at the map for a few moments, periodically looking up and around to make sure he had an idea of where in the clearing the map was referencing.

Nervously, Sprenger turned back to the two men. "Ready," he said.

They nodded and then Bakkon came over and grabbed the hourglass. He made sure Sprenger was prepared to start, then flipped the hourglass over. "Begin."

Sprenger ran for the wooden box in the center of the area and grabbed out four throwing blades. He started with the easiest targets on the stumps and trees, of course. He flung the blades effortlessly across the ways and landed them in the center of each of the four targets. He then grabbed a new set of four from the box, and ran to his right, hitting the three targets that were tucked away in the small branches. He ran back across the grounds and snatched up three more blades and headed to his left. There were three more targets in the branches as well as one that was being pushed on a rope by a scythe sitting on a branch above. Sprenger hit the three in the branches but his first attempt to hit the moving one missed and he was forced to return to the box and get more blades.

Upon his return, he hit the moving target on his first try and caused it to spin on its rope wildly.

That's eleven, Sprenger reminded himself, and frantically tried to remember where else to look. He knew that they were supposed to be in front of him but he couldn't see where. Then it dawned on him and he looked up into the canopy. He immediately spotted two more targets on higher branches, and as he ran to the tree, noticed a target directly underneath one of the branches.

Sprenger knew what he had to do. He ran up the tree and threw a blade at the target on the underside of the branch, it stuck with a 'thud', but then Sprenger grabbed a hold of the branch and pulled himself on top of it. Once up, he spotted the two targets that he was looking for and managed to hit them on the first try.

He looked around. He had one blade left in his hand. *One more target.*

He spotted it in a tree across the way, being flung around the tree on a rope by a scythe. *They must have hidden that one until the end.*

Now Sprenger realized he had a choice to make. He could either drop to the ground and get more blades, or stay in the canopy and risk only having one blade. He decided to risk it then began moving from branch to branch towards the target that was spiraling around the tree.

Sprenger stopped on the branch in front of it and focused, allowing the target to wrap around the tree a few times, so that he could get a feel for its pattern. The scythe allowed the target to spin around the tree to the full length of rope before he would send it wrapping around the opposite direction.

Sprenger waited until he was sure he had the rhythm down, then threw his blade.

It barely stuck the edge of the target but it was enough to interrupt its lap around the tree.

I did it, Sprenger realized excitedly. His first instinct was to just lay back on the branch and give himself a well-earned break, but then, remembering where he was, quickly found a way down and dropped to the ground. As soon as he was back in the center of the glade, the first thing he looked at was the hourglass. Much to Sprenger's relief, there was still sand falling from the top half.

Bakkon and Jaydon walked up to him from behind the table. "Well done," they said together. "Let's return and get the next student."

Sprenger gave them a bow and a smile, and spared no effort keeping his excitement in check as he followed them back to where everyone was waiting.

As they came into view, everyone gave him questioning looks, which Sprenger responded with a quick thumbs up like Soekka had. Then Sprenger retook his place amongst the other students as Jaydon called for Tenni.

She let out a nervous breath and followed Jaydon and Bakkon around the bushes.

Now that Sprenger knew how many targets there were, he tried counting as he heard the sound of metal striking wood. There were a few times that he thought he heard something, but didn't, and times that he was sure he should have heard something but couldn't. The task proved to be no more useful than just waiting so Sprenger gave up trying to count.

After a long while, Tenni returned and gave them all a quick smile of excitement.

Everyone was doing well so far. Only a few that came out did not seem happy with the results. Caymen either didn't do well, or didn't care that he did well, since he gave no indication that he was happy or not. Warren gave a small smirk and a shrug, which Sprenger wasn't sure how to interpret, but he seemed content with himself.

One after another, each of the students was led away and then returned to wait for all of the others to finish. Finally, there was no one left, so Jaydon and Bakkon began reviewing something between themselves.

Bakkon stepped forward. "A good start," he announced. "Everyone managed to pass, and so is able to move on to sparring."

Everyone smiled eagerly, but they all remained silent.

"Let us return to the village," Jaydon said to everyone.

Again, everyone silently followed the elder's lead. No one spoke. Surrounded by the accompanying scythe, the large group headed down the road and then to the training grounds.

As they approached, they all exchanged confused looks. The training grounds were not as they had been the day before. There was a thin wall erected all around the grounds, keeping everyone out and any curious eyes from viewing. Sprenger forgot about the wall; he had seen it many times before, but never knew its purpose, and even got into quite a bit of trouble with Cerri when he and Soekka tried climbing over to watch the exams as children.

The wall was there to give the participants some privacy, as well as keep the Exerptus Routine somewhat of a secret. Sprenger was disappointed that the exams were not open to everyone to watch. He liked it when there was a crowd of people cheering him on.

Jaydon and Bakkon led them through the opening of the makeshift wall and onto the training grounds. Once inside, Sprenger was surprised to see a small crowd of people inside seated up on a small balcony. Among them was Jacob, Cerri, Granny Karla, all the masters, and several others that Sprenger didn't know.

There was one man sitting to the other side of Jacob that had an interesting head of yellow hair that would normally be shoulder-length, but it practically stood straight out; the length of hair caused it to droop down, but not enough to reach his shoulders.

Next to that man was another that Sprenger had never seen before, though this one he had a pretty good idea of who it was. He had an expressionless, yet strict face. His black hair went down nearly to his lower back, and he wore finer clothes than anyone else there. *That must be Caymen's father,* Sprenger decided.

There were no other families, parents, or young students within the wall. The viewing was apparently restricted to scythe that already knew the routine, or members of rank in the village. Sprenger didn't have a chance to look around the crowd completely before Bakkon called for everyone's attention once more.

"Soon we will begin the second portion of the exam," he announced. "As before, you will wait until your name is called, then step forward and face your opponent. Each student will be picked at random, as well as their opponent. Once chosen, the task is simple; three direct hits to the body, or one to the head and the body. The first student to accomplish this will be declared the winner of the match. After a strike, you will have five seconds to recover before your opponent may strike again. Do not take losses as a sign of failure," he assured. "We will be grading the whole fight, so even if you suffer a loss, make sure you do so while demonstrating your abilities."

Not really inspirational, Sprenger thought.

Jaydon stepped forward carrying a small sack with something inside. "When we have finished all of the matches, then you will end the exams by demonstrating the Exerptus Routine to our Lord Scythrith. Now," he said, holding the bag out to Bakkon, "let us begin the first match."

-<>-

Granny Karla smoothed her grey cloak over her legs before straightening her back and replacing her hands in the opposite sleeve. She looked over at Sprenger and Soekka, who were standing apart from one another, paying close attention to what Jaydon was saying.

Cerri sat to her right and Jacob to his. Karla casually peered around them at the yellow-haired man down the row of people. She was surprised that Lucas had come for the event. His visits to Durado nowadays were rare and brief. She wondered if Jacob had asked for him to come personally.

Both men were behaving well enough, but Karla was no fool. They never looked at one another, nor ever spoke. If Jacob called for him as a sign of peace, then it clearly wasn't going as smoothly as he had hoped.

Those two, Karla thought disapprovingly.

"Rejeno and Barton," Jaydon announced. Karla looked back to the students, who werc now clearing the center sparring circle, with the exception of two boys; the handsome blond boy from Sprenger's class, and an awkward looking older boy. Karla watched Jaydon toss the two tiles he had removed from the sac to the side, as the boys took their places and assumed their fighting stances.

"You may begin," Bakkon growled.

The two boys hesitated for a moment, then the older one attacked. The two exchanged basic moves with one another, not risking anything complicated yet. Then, Karla saw Rejeno's foot slip, and apparently so did the other boy, since he quickly kicked Rejeno in the chest, knocking him backwards.

That's one hit, Karla looked over at the classes of students across the way. Those of Rejeno's class were looking worried, while some of the older boys looked amused. Karla noticed that there were no girls in the older classes. That either meant that they had already passed the exam or possibly were waiting longer to take it, both of which Karla doubted. *There were likely none in these classes to compete.* That idea worried Karla and made her angry at the same time.

Suddenly, excited expressions began to spread amongst Rejeno's classmates. Karla looked back to the fight and saw the older boy holding the side of his face.

Karla smirked a bit. *Well done Rejeno.*

The break was short before the boys reengaged. One strike after another and neither seemed confident enough to truly attack, until the older boy threw a daring punch at Rejeno that missed completely as Rejeno rolled around it.

Idiot, Karla scoffed at the older boy's attempt.

Rejeno spun around the boy, then swung his arm and backhanded the older boy across the face, knocking him to the flat of his back. A small wave of cheering echoed from the students.

That's two hits to the head, Karla realized. *Rejeno won.*

The boys stood, faced the elders and gave a small bow, all while Rejeno tried to contain his smile. The older boy looked more embarrassed than anything as they returned to the group of students.

Kobei leaned past Kanto towards all of them. "He's my student," he said proudly.

Kanto, who was standing next to him with his typical cross-armed, serious posture, sighed and rolled his eyes. "Yes Kobei, we know."

The next few matches were equally impressive. The younger class seemed to have a stronger motivation than the older ones. Many of the older students, Karla noticed, were getting impatient with their attacks and by so doing, were making foolish mistakes.

Pillas and Warren were the most recent fight, following a series of several others, from which Kobei made sure to claim each of his students as they appeared. Now that most of the students had gone, Karla was getting impatient. She looked over at Kanto, but the man's expression hadn't changed a bit since they started, not that she really expected it to. She assumed he was becoming anxious as well; none of his students had been called yet and they were nearing the end of the sparring. Only six students remained, including Kanto's entire squad.

Karla looked over at the boys, who were clearly in very different mindsets. Sprenger was smiling and whispering to Warren and Pillas as they returned, congratulating Pillas on his victory, while Soekka stood silently staring at the elders as they began to draw for the next names.

Soekka's getting anxious. Karla sympathized; waiting until the very end was the worst thing you could do to a boy like Soekka, who was always so focused and driven with his tasks.

Jaydon pulled another tile from the sac. "Kimimaro," he announced, and one of the older boys stepped forward with a very confident expression. Karla recognized him immediately, as he and the boys had gotten into a number of fights at the academy. Jaydon pulled the second tile out. “And Tennirria,” he exclaimed.

Tenni slowly stepped forward, looking at Kimimaro, then nervously stroking her braid over her shoulder.

Chapter 31

Final Matches

Tenni and Kimimaro stepped out to the center of the sparring ring. Tenni looked very apprehensive to Karla, while Kimimaro looked extremely eager. This wasn't making sense to Karla. From what the boys had always told her about Tenni, the girl was never scared, especially when it came to sparring. Karla wondered if it was because the boy was from the older class and she found that intimidating. The boy, on the other hand, seemed to expect an easy win based on his eager smile. He gave Tenni a cocky wink, which she pretended not to notice.

The two faced each other; Kimimaro took his fighting stance, but Tenni just stood there shyly petting her braid.

Everyone exchanged confused looks, and even Bakkon gave her a curious expression before yelling "Begin!"

Kimimaro waited a moment, not sure if he should attack an ill-prepared opponent, but then jumped at her with his fist back, preparing for a heavy hit.

Suddenly, Tenni bolted forward and repeatedly slammed her fists into Kimimaro's stomach, then pulled back and slammed him across the face, knocking him to the ground hard so hard that he yelped like an animal as he toppled over.

Everyone became a fluster of giggling excitement. Tenni stood over Kimimaro with one hand on her hip as he pushed himself up a bit, looking very dazed.

"Don't ever wink at me again," she said sternly.

Karla couldn't help but smile a bit. *What a clever girl, tricking her opponent into lowering his guard like that.* It was a shame to think that only the first hit would count, but Tenni didn't seem too upset by it. She returned to the center of the ring and took a fighting stance as Kimimaro slowly got to his feet. His smile had disappeared.

By the time Kimimaro took his stance, the five second break after a hit had passed but Tenni waited patiently. Hesitantly, Kimimaro approached her again.

The two reengaged, exchanging basic attacks, not willing to do anything too bold and create an opening.

The two grabbed each other's wrists and became locked in a tussle. Normally, since neither could do anything in such a position, opponents would separate and then reengage, but when Tenni went to do so, Kimimaro gave her a quick backhand across her cheek. It wasn't enough to really faze her; she just slowly raised her head again, revealing her now red cheek.

Several people stood up in anger, and many students took a step forward with disapproving scowls. Everyone looked at Jaydon and Bakkon for their response, but the two exchanged apprehensive looks with one another.

"It counts," Bakkon finally said. "But another like that will not. I remind you," Bakkon warned sternly, "you are graded on technique more than hits."

Kimimaro smirked arrogantly anyway, seeming very pleased with his attack.

What a pompous boy, Karla thought angrily. Hitting an opponent like that would serve no purpose in a real fight but to demoralize or to anger them. In this case, it was only used for an easy headshot. *What a coward.*

Tenni rolled her neck a bit before taking a fighting stance again. She just stared at Kimimaro with hate but otherwise kept her composure.

Again the two reengaged, but this time Tenni pushed forward with gusto. Even as Kimimaro would block her assaults, she made sure to deliver the hit on any part of his body he chose to block with. Nothing was breaking through, but it was obvious that each hit was doing damage to Kimimaro's arms.

As he raised his arms to block another punch to his face, Tenni suddenly crouched to the ground and delivered one between his legs. Kimimaro began to crumble in a shock of pain, but as he fell forward, Tenni shot up and smashed her fist up under his chin. Kimimaro's feet left the ground for a moment before he fell onto his back.

Several students cheered and whistled excitedly as Kimimaro rolled over and spit blood onto the ground. He just laid there in agony while Tenni turned with a hand on her hip to Jaydon and Bakkon.

They smirked at each other for a moment, then Jaydon stepped forward. "The first hit was neither to his body nor his head so does not count. The second, however, was to his head and counts. Tennirria wins."

Tenni gave them a respectful bow, then turned and joined the other students, who stepped forward to congratulate her on her fight. None even tried to keep their laughs subtle.

One of the scythe guarding the event came out and pulled Kimimaro to his feet and took him over to a healer that was waiting with a small cloth. The old woman forced herself into his mouth and looked around briefly before handing the cloth to him to hold to his bleeding tongue.

Karla couldn't seem to push her smile back, nor did she want to. She peered around Cerri and

Jacob to look at Kanto, but the man's expression had not changed. He just watched the students with emotionless curiosity.

Karla looked over at Jaydon anxiously as he pulled two more tiles from the sac. One of them either had to be Soekka or Sprenger's since there were only two matches left. Two boys from the older class remained as well, which meant that Sprenger and Soekka would each have to spar with older students.

They'll enjoy that, Karla thought excitedly.

Jaydon held the two tiles out to read them. "Areos," he announced and one of the older boys stepped out, "and Bardin." The other boy from the older class stepped out.

Around Karla, Jacob, Cerri, Lucas, and Kanto all perked up with surprise. Jacob looked as though he wanted to say something but couldn't. He and Kanto exchanged a look as Karla looked down to Jaydon and Bakkon, who were watching the two older boys begin to spar.

That couldn't have been by chance, Karla realized suspiciously. Now Sprenger and Soekka were the only students left; they would have to fight each other. Everyone knew it too, even the boys. They looked shocked, but not necessarily disappointed. They both began to stretch a bit while everyone watched the current match.

Karla looked down her row of those involved; they too stared back with silent acknowledgment of their mutual feelings. Even Kanto's expression had broken before Kobei patted him on the shoulder and said something jokingly to him, oblivious to Kanto's shock.

Karla glared back down at Jaydon and Bakkon, who still had no sign of making eye contact with any of the agitated onlookers. They watched the match with stern posture as they had for all the others. Karla knew that they had done this on purpose.

There will be a lot of questions those two will have to answer when this is done, Karla assured herself. *Questions being asked by some dangerously protective people.*

Distracted by what had transpired, Karla didn't even realize the match had started and ended without her watching for a moment. Everyone clapped lightly as one of the older boys delivered the winning hit, and then they bowed and exited the ring.

Sprenger and Soekka both stepped forward eagerly as soon as the boys returned to the side. The crowd tensed as they took opposing stances, as though this was the main event of the entire exams.

Karla noticed Bakkon look up to Jacob for a fleeting moment before yelling, "Begin!"

As they had done countless times before, Sprenger and Soekka collided with a flurry of assaults. Unlike the entirety of the students before them, these two had no apprehension between them. They held nothing back as they became intricately interwoven between one another's movements.

It was a match that belittled all that came before them; youngest class or not. Karla was not surprised. These boys knew how the other fought, and today they both had something to prove. Though their attacks would have been plenty to best any other opponent, there was little they could do to fool each other.

People gawked at their speed and agility, their technique and their form, but mostly they gawked in surprise at the equality of skill between the two.

Suddenly, Karla saw Sprenger slip in the dirt and loose his footing. Soekka spun and kicked him in the chest, knocking him back several steps.

Sprenger hardly faltered and jumped right back into their match, not even allowing himself the five seconds of reprieve after a hit.

Again, they became endlessly locked with one another, unable to surprise the opponent that knew their fighting style better than themselves.

Sprenger swung his leg around, but Soekka ducked it. Again and again, Sprenger swung his leg but Soekka ducked it, until Sprenger dropped to the ground and swung at Soekka's feet. Soekka saw it coming and jumped over it, but Sprenger sprang from the ground and slammed his fist into Soekka's stomach before his feet even touched back down.

Soekka winced as he was knocked back in midair before hitting the ground. He stalled for only a brief moment before whirling up to face Sprenger again.

"That was an impressively thought out move by Sprenger," Cerri whispered to Karla. "The timing and agility that took was beyond anything I ever trained him to do. That was pure talent."

Now Soekka began swinging his leg at Sprenger, but astonishingly, Sprenger jumped up and rolled over his kick. Now behind Soekka, Sprenger spun again and kicked him in the side. Soekka crumpled slightly but spun away to put space between them.

Karla was squeezing her cloak in both hands. *One more hit and Sprenger wins.*

The crowd, and even the students, were silent with awe. No one had any time to catch their breath before they were holding it again.

The boys were continuing to hold nothing back, but Soekka seemed to be winded from the hits to his abdomen. He had shifted to being more defensive, and focused on avoiding Sprenger's attacks. As he ducked another kick, Soekka shifted to his hands and began spinning his legs around to force Sprenger back.

"Soekka worked for a long time to perfect that move," Cerri whispered, "but I've never seen him use it in a match before."

Sprenger jumped back as Soekka continued to twirl his outstretched legs around and around, dancing on his hands.

Boldly, Sprenger moved to engage him. He jumped into the twirling kicks and caught one of Soekka's legs to stop him.

Karla gawked as she watched what happened next unfold as if time had slowed around them...

Soekka pushed off his hands and continued to spin in the air. Now only supported by Sprenger holding his leg, he slammed his free foot into the side of Sprenger's head. Sprenger was knocked completely off his feet as his face was slammed to the ground. Soekka finished his spin, barely landing on his feet.

People shouted and cheered, still gawking over what they had just seen.

Karla and Cerri just sat there silently staring, along with most others sitting in the balcony.

"That was incredible," Cerri said in shock.

"Soekka wins!" Jaydon exclaimed, and the crowd erupted with cheers.

Soekka slumped and took in heavy sighs, but then knelt to the ground as Sprenger began to stir in the dirt. Soekka leaned in close and put a comforting hand on Sprenger's back and whispered something that no one could hear.

Slowly Sprenger began to push himself up with Soekka assisting him. As he raised his head, Karla could see the cheek that had hit the ground was raw and bleeding, as well as the eyebrow above it. Sprenger put his arm around Soekka and allowed him to support most of his weight.

When the boys finally reached their feet they each bowed together at Jaydon and Bakkon, the crowd cheered even louder.

The healer woman ran over and examined Sprenger briefly, before ushering him to follow her to the side of the ring, where she began to clean his face.

Karla couldn't take her eyes off him. Astonishingly, even as he sat there with blood on his face, Sprenger was smiling.

Karla's eyes began to water as she gazed at her boys with pride. They not only proved that they were the most gifted scythe of a generation, but they did so with smiles and love for one another. They had just proven far more than Karla, or anyone else, could have hoped for them.

Remembering something, Karla turned a hateful glare to Jaydon and Bakkon who were discussing something amongst themselves. Karla looked down her row at the others; they too were staring with anger and hate across the sparring circle at the two elders.

Chapter 32

The Exerptus Routine!

Jacob continued to contemplate in disbelief what he had just witnessed. Never before had he seen such raw talent in such young scythe. He expected great things from those boys, but his expectations never even come close to what he just witnessed to be their true level of skill. Despite his excitement, however, his mind was distracted by the circumstances that led to the fight.

Jaydon and Bakkon had just undertook a risky endeavor by pitting the boys against one another. Jacob knew it to be for their own twisted curiosity, but they had just risked a spark in a dangerously flammable place. Their risk turned out to be quite the development, but it was not for them to test it, and Jacob would make a point of reminding them that. His irritation only grew as he realized that the conspiracy of the situation was distracting him from the amazement of it all. Despite himself, Jacob forced to his focus back to the children and their accomplishments.

Slowly, Jaydon and Bakkon made their way across the sparring ring and stood just under the balcony where Jacob and the village leaders were sitting. “Students,” Jaydon called out. Everyone turned their attention from the excited whispers of Sprenger and Soekka’s match to him. “Students, come here please.” Everyone quietly shuffled over to him and spread out into their neat lines yet again.

Jacob stood and peered down at them all from over Jaydon and Bakkon’s heads. He looked over to the side where Sprenger was still being cleaned up by the healer and Soekka was sitting next to him, patiently waiting.

Jacob said nothing at first. He just stood there silently, looking over the organized lines before him. He would wait until Soekka and Sprenger joined them, and this would be a test of patience for the others as well. He looked over each and every one of the students individually. They all stared back with confidence, except the smaller boy in Sprenger's class, Warren. He had lost his fight to a fellow squad member, and now he seemed to be holding shame in that fact. *He will need confidence as time goes on*, Jacob noted.

The one who should be ashamed was the older boy to the left of the group: Kimimaro. Jacob was disgusted by his cowardous actions, and the attitude that followed was equally disgusting. The boy was now pouting with a deep scowl on his face. Not only did he fail to win admirably, but now he was refusing to lose with dignity too.

That scowl will only deepen when you discover what I have in store for you, Jacob thought staring down at Kimimaro, who didn't even bother to look up at him.

Finally, Sprenger was released from the healer and he and Soekka came running over and stood at the back of the group, apparently aware that Jacob was waiting for them.

Jacob took a breath to begin speaking, but he stopped as the group of students began to shuffle and move. The lines were slowly stepping aside and forming a path up their middle. Rejeno, who was standing closest to Sprenger, turned to him with a smile and nodded up the opening.

Jacob smiled with pride that he had not felt in years. Sprenger and Soekka, on the other hand, did not seem entirely sure what to do. Slowly, the students all turned and silently ushered the boys forward, encouraging them to the front. Hesitantly, Sprenger began to move forward, up the center of the crowd of students. Soekka followed him with a smirk.

As they passed, the group closed the gap behind them and resumed their structured lines. Now Sprenger and Soekka took a postured stance at the front of the group, smirking humbly, if not a bit embarrassed.

Jacob beamed down at them and took a breath again. “My dear students,” he said proudly to them all. “It seems like such a short while ago that many of you stood in front of me to receive your new masters. I knew then that you would all be the start of great things to come, and now here you are, proving me right.

“There was talent demonstrated here today, the likes of which I have rarely seen in my many years. But it was not talent measured by one’s skill with a blade,” he shook his head. “No. It was the talent to hold your head up with pride, even when faced with a loss.” He made sure to look at Warren. “And the ability to win, but with humble composure and grace.” He locked onto Tenni’s strong gaze. “It is these things that make a scythe worthy of legend. I believe that many of you will have a grand tale being told long after you are gone, and it is that future that makes you worthy to be called dura-scythe.” The students fought to keep from smiling, forcing what disciplined composure that they could.

“However,” said Jacob quickly, “there is still one task left to fulfill.” He raised his voice. “Now, show me that you are worthy to represent our village beyond these walls. Show me that your determination can be reflected in your talents!”

Every student in the arena bowed in unison, then rose and stomped the ground together as they took the starting stance.

"This is your final test!" Jacob finished. "Begin!"

As though they were performers, waiting for a show to start, the lines of young men and women started the intricate routine. As Jacob looked around, he saw the most encouraging thing that a leader could ever hope to see in their followers: confidence. There was a spark of determination that spanned throughout these kids that Jacob had never seen in such numbers before. In fact, the older classes seemed the least confident of the students in front of him. It all, he knew, was the result of the boys at the front. Soekka and Sprenger led the arena. Jacob could see the eyes of their classmates occasionally follow the boys' movements from behind, as though being guided or perhaps inspired. When a member of the group was out of sync at any point, it always seemed to be one of the older students. Most of whom had a determined focus to perform what they had practiced for years already. Almost none of them had the smooth confidence of the youngest class, who moved together in fluid harmony.

Half the time, half the training, double the confidence, Jacob thought cheerfully to himself.

Though he knew it to be unorthodox, Jacob gazed around at the students with a beaming smile. They were practically flawless in their timing, their accuracy, and their focus.

This generation, Jacob concluded, *will save this village.*

With a large thud and cloud of dust, every student, younger and older, slammed their palms to the ground and bowed their heads, finishing their routine. They silently waited, with only the sound of their heavy breathing being heard in the training grounds. No one moved, no one spoke. They all waited for Jacob.

Jacob, however, continued to draw out the silence. He wanted everyone there to contemplate what they had just seen. He wanted everyone to have the same realization that he had. To feel the gravity of what they had witnessed right before their eyes. These students, against all odds, against all doubt, just raised the standard of the scythe world. Not only did they learn and perform under strenuous circumstances, but they flourished under it; and they did it by working together. They all used their comrades of Durado to support one another and see each other succeed.

That is what it meant to be a scythe village. *That* is what it meant to be a scythe. And *that* is what so many had forgotten.

"My dear students," Jacob finally whispered slowly. "I struggle to offer you praise. It would seem that any I give shall fall short of what is deserved." Random observers slowly nodded their heads in agreement, but the students remained seeded in the final position. "I truly admire you for what you have accomplished and I hope that your own prowess is not lost to you." Jacob raised his voice. "You have just been tested in the skill-sets of our village. You have been pressured and you have been graded. In the morning, your masters will deliver you news of our decisions. Keep in mind that, win or lose, triumph or fail, there are strengths and weaknesses in scythe that even tests cannot show. I want you all to consider which of those traits you might possess." Jacob Spred his arms, billowing the black silk sleeves of his robe. "Now, I bid you to rise and take pride in your accomplishments today. Well done all!"

The small crowd began cheering excitedly as all of the students rose to their feet, many with a broad smile on their face.

-<>-

Jacob fell back into his high-backed chair with little grace and pulled his pipe out of his top drawer. He made sure the bowl was generously filled before lighting it and taking a deep pull. He let it linger for a moment before he released it and sat in his fresh cloud of smoke.

A light knock echoed on his door and Jacob sighed at the briefness of his break.

Errand stuck his blond head through the door. “My Lord,” he said. “The elders have arrived as you requested.”

“Scnd them in,” he grumbled.

Errand opened the door fully and stepped aside as Jaydon and Bakkon entered the office. The two of them came up and stood at the head of Jacob’s desk, neither showing any expression that Jacob could read; Jacob, too, made sure there was nothing that touched his face.

“What an exciting day that was,” Jaydon said flatly when the door closed behind them. “Many more exciting things are soon to come I expect.” Jacob said nothing in reply. He only stared at them through his cloud of smoke.

“You seem to be contemplating something,” Bakkon stated softly.

“I think you know quite well what I’m contemplating,” Jacob said in a gruff whisper back.

“Your family always seems to be contemplating something,” Jaydon pointed out. “We can’t be expected to always know what it is.”

Jacob continued to keep his voice soft and calm to prove that it would take more than these men to break his composure. “My family,” he said, “realizes the benefits of foresight. We have the gift of anticipation. We consider everything to the greatest detail that we can contemplate; this way we can predict outcomes."

"And no one can argue that there are any whom do it better," Jaydon said with unlikely sincerity.

"Then why," Jacob said, sharpening his tone, "did you two feel the need to tamper?"

Neither faltered slightly, not that Jacob expected them too. In fact, Jacob could swear that they seemed to be holding back smirks. The thought only made him more angry.

"We did nothing more than reinforce your theory," Bakkon said stoically.

"You," Jacob growled back, "risked everything falling apart. And do not for a second think that it's over, because it's not. Something like this can start as little more than a spark before it jumps to flame."

Jaydon tilted his head curiously. "If such a small thing would ruin your schemes, then I can't help but wonder about the delicacy of it all from the start."

"Indeed," Bakkon agreed. "You claim that they care for each other and push one another beyond an expected level, and we simply tested it. Some of us require tests to acknowledge such bold and unlikely claims."

"That is what we did," Jaydon continued for him as Jacob released yet another large cloud of smoke. "We tested your claims. You proved correct. Their skill is undeniable. I could not help but notice, however, that it was not Sprenger that rose to the occasion." He shrugged skeptically. "Perhaps our faith is placed on the wrong child."

Jacob straightened in his seat, then leaned forward and laced his fingers in front of his mouth and allowed his pipe to hang from the corner of his lips. He glared through the smoke at them. "I warn you now," he whispered. "Those boys' relationship is an intricate and fragile thing that has been constructed by deceit and secrets. If you continue to test it haphazardly, it will begin to fray." He glared even more fiercely. "What you did this afternoon could have sparked resentment and rage between the two. Should you tamper without consulting myself first, I will take it as a personal slight and challenge." He let his words hang in the air with his plume of smoke.

"Perhaps," Jaydon said, "you no longer want our input or our assistance?" He said it as though this was a threat in itself.

"Perhaps," Jacob remarked back, "you two are beginning to have doubts."

Their silence was answer enough. The three old men just stood there in silent smoke for a moment, before Jaydon and Bakkon turned and headed for the door.

"Let us know," Bakkon said softly, "should there be any progress in this plan that has moved so slowly for so long."

Without another word the two exited the office and left Jacob alone in his cloud of smoke, a glare still visible in the thick air.

Chapter 33

Recover and Celebrate

Sprenger looked over the village as the sun had just begun to cast deep colors and shadows throughout the rooftops and streets. The view from his room in the Healer's Quarters was a decent one, since it was on one of the higher floors, but his scenery was little more than the back of the Rithhold and a few near homes. Despite his restlessness, the healers insisted that he stay so that they can make sure his head injury was not worse than it appeared. They dressed Sprenger in soft sleepwear and told him they would send his clothes to be cleaned, but Sprenger had the feeling they only did it to keep him from running away. In addition to hitting his head, Sprenger also had scrapes on his cheek and a cut above his eye from when he hit the ground, and he had to endure the horrible experience of the healers scrubbing both injuries clean. The healer he had scrubbed with such gusto, that Sprenger was certain he was doing more damage than Soekka ever could. When the ordeal was over, they placed coverings on his cheek and wrapped one around his head for the cut above his eye.

Bored and confined to his small room with a single cot and chamber pot, Sprenger's mind wondered to his classmates and how they were celebrating the exams. He leaned on the windowsill and looked out the open window, lost in thought about the day's proceedings.

For so long he had been in intense training, been pushing himself and others, and now it all came to a tranquil halt. It was over in the blink of an eye. The majority of students were now downstairs relaxing in the Simmering Pools. A few of them were being treated for a small array of injuries that were accumulated during the tests. Kimimaro and Sprenger were among them, and Sprenger had been taken to this room and cleaned up despite his objections, while Kimimaro had bitten off the tip of his tongue when Tenni hit him in the jaw and was hardly able to object even if he wanted to. Sprenger's cheek hurt the most of everything, and the constant throbbing gave him uninterrupted reminders of what happened.

Sprenger replayed his fight with Soekka over and over again in his mind. He tried to reimagine what he could have done differently to have stopped Soekka. Every time he came up with a new approach, he came up short. No matter how Sprenger reconsidered his actions, he couldn't justify a win. He made very few mistakes, and even managed to surprise Soekka on a few occasions, but still he came up short. Soekka performed a move that could not have been stopped, and proved that he had skill left to reveal. Sprenger was somewhat upset that they ended up having to fight each other, as he would have much preferred being able to watch and cheer Soekka on from the sides. Now there had to be a winner between them and that is a cruel fate when one wants their friend to win just as badly as they wish it for themselves.

Sprenger continued to ponder all of it while gazing out over the village, unable to decide how he truly felt about it all.

Suddenly, Sprenger's tranquil thoughts were interrupted as someone unexpectedly dropped onto the sill of his open window. Sprenger went tumbling back in surprise and fell onto the small bed behind him.

"I hear you didn't disappoint in the exams," Juriah said as he crouched in the open window, shadowed by the sunset.

Sprenger was still in shock of his sudden appearance and hadn't really heard what he said.

"Where did you come from?" Sprenger gasped. He walked up to the window and pushed past Juriah to look up and around the outside wall of the Healer's Quarters, but nothing seemed a plausible route to get to his window. "How did you get out there?"

Juriah casually sat down in the sill and leaned against the frame of the window. "I also heard," he said, ignoring Sprenger's questions, "that you lost your fight."

"Honestly," Sprenger pressed, still looking around the window for any way to get to it, "how could *this* be any easier than just using the stairs?"

"But I guess it's the Routine that makes the biggest difference," Juriah continued. "That," he said raising a finger, "that I hear was quite a sight."

"How did you even know which window was mine?" Sprenger wasn't listcning to Juriah in turn.

"I hope the routine was enough to salvage your embarrassing loss in the sparring ring," Juriah continued indifferently. "After all, you'll need to be able to leave the village if you plan to be a Nymphigori." Sprenger pulled his head back through the window, now listening to what Juriah was saying. Juriah smirked at him, glad to have gotten his attention. "You didn't forget about my offer now did you?"

"You said that I should make sure my routine is perfect," Sprenger said quickly, "and that you would tell me more if I passed the exams."

"Indeed I did," Juriah said with a nod, "and you seem to have done both those things. So now I have no qualms in offering the opportunity whole-heartedly to become a Nymphigori of the Pantrores." He shrugged. "Unless you're not interested, of course."

"Of course I am," Sprenger blurted quickly.

"Good," Juriah said contently, closing his eyes and making himself more comfortable in the window.

“So what do I have to do?” Sprenger pressed impatiently.

“I already told you,” Juriah sighed. “Make sure the routine is perfect.”

“Well I’ve done that, so now how do I use it?”

“You will have to present yourself to the Pantrores,” Juriah lazily explained. “If one of them chooses to test you, then you will perform the routine. The Pantrore will move with you, performing their side of the bond, but any imperfections with your routine will throw you out of sync with them and they will stop.”

“My routine *is* flawless,” Sprenger assured him.

Juriah snorted. “That’s assuming that you even get chosen to begin with.”

“So what do I have to do to get chosen?”

“Absolutely nothing,” Juriah said flatly. “Either they will choose you or they won’t. There is no telling which it will be.”

Sprenger hesitated a moment with his next question, not sure if it was worth asking or not. “So,” he began slowly, “why did *you* choose me?”

Juriah opened his eyes halfway and stared at Sprenger. “Your mother was my fellow Nymphigori, and one of the few people I would be willing to claim as a friend in this damn village. I owe her a debt and I’m fulfilling it by giving you an opportunity to succeed her as a Nymphigori. If you are chosen, then I have also promised to teach you myself.” He closed his eyes again and shrugged. “If you are not chosen, then there is nothing more I can do.”

“Thank you,” Sprenger said softly. Juriah nodded, but it wasn’t necessarily to him that Sprenger was speaking. “So when do we try?” Sprenger said with more gusto.

Juriah opened his eyes and smirked at him. "You will be given the news of passing the exams tomorrow morning, then you will be given the rest of the afternoon off to celebrate. If you truly wish to be tested again, I will meet you at the front gates at midday."

Sprenger tightened his fists. "I'll be there."

-<>-

Tenni pushed aside the doors of the Healer's Quarters and walked out into the cool evening air. It felt very refreshing after having sat in the simmering pools for the last few hours. The water had felt very nice, but the steamy air was too thick for her liking.

She began to walk to the Manor, but then noticed someone walking towards her from the Rithhold. She smiled when she realized it was Master Kanto.

"Perfect," he said as he got closer, "just the student I was looking for."

She gave a small bow when he stopped in front of her. "I was just headed home after soaking in the simmering pools with the others."

"Good," Kanto said plainly. "I imagine there are a lot of aching students in there."

She nodded. "Most everyone, except Sprenger. He had to get his cheek and eye cleaned up."

"Other than that, how was he?" Kanto asked. "He didn't seem upset, did he?"

Tenni gave him a strange look. "Not from what I could tell. I don't think he was particularly happy about having to fight Soekka though."

"None of us were happy about that," Kanto mumbled.

"What?" Tenni asked confused.

"Never mind," Kanto said grouchily. He shook the thought away. "But on a better note, I wanted to congratulate you on *your* match. Don't think that just because Soekka and Sprenger stole the show that people didn't notice your impressive win as well."

Tenni shrugged modestly. "I told you on the first day that I was a fair sparrer. I actually prefer hand to hand fighting over most other types, but it's no good if my opponent has a weapon."

"I can tell you prefer it," Kanto said kindly, though his face remained expressionless. "I remember the forest and the bandits, and then today you reminded me again." He raised a finger. "Don't be too hasty to think that hand to hand can't be as dangerous as weaponed combat." He put his hands behind his back. "You simply need the proper equipment. That being said, I have a gift to congratulate you on an exam well done." He brought his hands back around and was now holding a leather glove in each hand."

Tenni was at a loss for words. She slowly reached out and took the gloves from Kanto. They were made of a very fine leather and beautifully stitched. She looked up at Kanto, not sure what to say. "Master Kanto, thank you so much."

He nodded, expressionlessly. "You're welcome," he said kindly. "I'm giving these to you for a very specific reason. Put them on."

Tenni gladly did so and loved the way they fit on her hands. They were the perfect thickness of leather that allowed her quite a bit of movement still. The only thing that felt strange on them was the line above the knuckles. There, the gloves were stiff and hard.

"The knuckles feel different, don't they?" Kanto asked. Tenni nodded. "That's because there are some small metal plates that were sewn over each knuckle inside the leather. This way, your hands can do more damage but take less."

Again Tenni was at a loss of words, so she gave up on them. Instead, she threw herself at Kanto and gave him a tight hug.

Kanto seemed apprehensive of it at first but then gradually relaxed and patted her on the back. "I hope they serve you well," he said softly.

Finally, Tenni released Master Kanto, then felt a bit abashed for her outburst. "Thank you," she finally said with another small bow.

Kanto nodded, seeming a bit amused, if anything. Then he turned back the way he came and gestured for Tenni to join him. "And how are you planning to celebrate the end of the exams?"

Tenni shrugged. "Nothing really," she admitted. "My parents aren't very fond of the idea of me being a scythe, so I doubt they'll have anything planned."

"I had hoped to take you lot for another meal," Kanto said. "It would seem Sprenger is not going to leave the healer's tonight, and I have not seen Soekka."

"I don't think he stayed," Tenni said. "The healer's wouldn't let him go with Sprenger while they tended his wounds and he wasn't in the simmering pots. I think he just went home. He's never been one to do much with our class without Sprenger there."

"Yes," Kanto nodded stoically, "I've deduced that. Soekka likes to remain focused, while Sprenger is almost his opposite in that respect. It's why the two of them are able to motivate one another to be better. They make up for the othcr's shortcomings."

"Those two never had many shortcomings in Cerri's class," Tenni said, trying not to sound bitter about it.

Kanto gave her a suspicious sidelong glance as they walked around the Rithhold. "They are prodigies," he said, "everyone knows that. But," he said to quell what Tenni was thinking, "that does not mean the rest of you aren't just as impressive. The best tend to overshadow the rest, as is the way of the world. I hope, however, you do not let your own accomplishments go unnoticed. You have done just a splendidly as the boys. You defeated an older opponent and did so with impressive display of skill. Even more impressively, you passed the Exerptus Exams after only a few months of training under a master. Those sorts of victories should not be lost on you."

Tenni could feel herself blushing a bit for some reason. She had never thought of it that way before and now felt foolish for always comparing herself to the boys.

"In fact," Kanto said, without any change to his demeanor, "I insist you allow me to treat you to a meal as a reward for such an impressive display today. Just because the boys are otherwise unavailable, does not mean we do not have cause to celebrate."

Tenni agreed gratefully and continued on with Kanto out of the fence surrounding the Rithhold and the Healer's Quarters. As they rounded a roothome and headed for a place to eat, something caught Tenni's eye.

Visible between gaps of several barky buildings, Tenni could make out the figure of Caymen. It was his quick movements that caught Tenni's eye more than anything. Caymen was practicing fighting forms in the fading sunlight of what appeared to be a garden.

Tenni stopped walking so that she could watch. Caymen's shoulder-length black hair would twirl in every direction as he spun this way and that. Tenni was in a bit of shock to see him training right after the exams. Surely there was nothing more to practice and no master would ask this of their student.

Then Tenni noticed the person standing next to Caymen. She was too far away to make out most of his features, but she knew who it was when she saw the long, sleek black hair and heavy silk robes. It was Caymen's father. Tenni, not normally very fond of Caymen, suddenly felt a pang of sympathy for him.

"Caddmon and his family are very strict," Kanto said from behind Tenni, apparently noticing that she had stopped walking and seeing what she was looking at. "Some of us were a bit surprised he even allowed Caymen to train under a master instead of just doing it himself."

Tenni watched Caymen for a bit longer but Kanto started to walk away yet again, and she knew this was her sign that they should not stare.

"Why would Caymen's father want him to train right after the exams?" Tenni asked when she finally caught up to Kanto.

Kanto's voice remained as unchanged as ever. "It is possible that Caddmon is not happy with his son's performance today. Much like many of you, he compares Caymen to Sprenger and Soekka. When his son fails to match the boys, he takes it as a personal insult that his son is not doing well enough."

Again, Tenni felt surprising bad for Caymen. He was never friendly with anyone in their class, and had a particular dislike of Soekka and Sprenger, but now Tenni could see why. The boys never had to try hard to be the best. They spend much of the classes goofing around until Master Cerri came over. Even without constant focus, they would set new records for everything they tried. Caymen hated when that happened.

"Shouldn't Master Kobei be bothered by Caymen over-training," Tenni asked.

"He likely is," said Kanto. "It is Durado law, however, that a parent always has the right to claim their children for training. They do not have to subject them to a master if they do not wish to. Much like what happened with your classmate, Gerrett."

"Why wouldn't you want to learn under a master?"

"Many old families, like Caymen's family, have unique fighting styles and techniques that are passed down through generations. Often, they want to keep these techniques within strict members of their bloodlines. A sort of family right, if you will." Kanto turned around another root with particularly large amounts of flowers and ferns adorning its sides and Tenni turned to follow. "Masters," Kanto continued explaining, "have their own styles of fighting, as I'm sure you've noticed. If a family does not want a mixing of techniques, they will request their child not to be taught by a master."

"But Caymen has both," Tenni said softly.

"It would appear so," Kanto agreed. "Do not worry too much for your classmate," Kanto assured as he stopped outside a large roothome with smells of cooked goods pouring out its open windows. "Having two teachers can also be quite beneficial. It's not easy," he admitted quickly, "but being a scythe rarely is."

Tenni smirked at him and nodded her understanding.

"Now," Kanto said in the fading red light of the sunset, "let us focus on your accomplishments and indulge in a large meal." He seemed like he was going to smile at her, but his stern face simply wouldn't allow it. Instead, he opened the door of the foodhouse and gestured Tenni inside.

Chapter 34

The Forest Nymphigori

The next day in Durado was some of the most exciting that the village had seen for years. Jacob sent word to all of the families of students that competed in the Exerptus Exams to let them know the results. Whether to their surprise or not, the entirety of Cerri's most recent class had passed with high marks. Most of the older students had passed as well, with the exception of Kimimaro and two others from older classes.

With such surprising news, the village was in a complete buzz about the news. Not only had people doubted that Cerri's class would pass, but they thought it was an insult that Durado would lower its standards of junettin. When they found out that Cerri's class not only passed, but outperformed the older students, it became the only topic on people's lips as they bustled in and out of roothomes.

Granny Karla had come up to Sprenger's room in the Healer's Quarters with Soekka, and gave him the scroll with Jacob's congratulations. Soekka was beaming as he waited for Sprenger to read the scroll, but then revealed that he was more excited about the fact that Kimimaro didn't pass. Sprenger told him about Kimimaro's tongue being bitten off when Tenni punched him, and they laughed all the harder for it.

Granny Karla, who did not normally permit mocking or boasting, seemed to pretend she had gone momentarily deaf during their discussion. Once they had calmed, she offered to take them out for a treat to celebrate and they began to discuss what they wanted to do.

Then, with guilty dread, Sprenger remembered he was going to try and meet Juriah and go to the

Shattered Hill. He hadn't even thought about how he was going to explain it to either Karla or Soekka. He doubted Karla would allow him to go, and he didn't want to upset Soekka again now that he had finally returned to his old self.

He thought for a bit, then hesitantly told them he forgot that Master Kanto asked to speak with him today after he was out of the healers. His mind started to race to fill any gaps in this story that Granny Karla might find, but she didn't seem to think much of it and moved up their plans so that Sprenger could leave them by mid-day.

Soekka, on the other hand, seemed not to believe this ruse. He didn't say anything, but eyed Sprenger suspiciously every time it came up. When Sprenger finally left them, Soekka didn't say anything in farewell.

Sprenger's next task was to leave the village in broad daylight somehow but found that Juriah was waiting for him at the front gates. He was leaning next to the giant doors with his eyes closed, as though he were sleeping in the sunlight. When Sprenger ran up to him, he neither acted surprised nor impressed. He simply gave Sprenger a satisfied nod and yelled rudely up to the guards to open the gates.

Within moments, Sprenger was racing through the canopy, back to the Shattered Hill. He almost could not recall the journey this time. His mind was too distracted by what was to come.

Now, standing in the bright sunlight, surrounded by the wall of rockfaces, Sprenger took a deep breath. The tall grass of the glade brushed against Sprenger's pant legs. Compared to the bustling village, the Shattered Hill was silent and calm. The only sound was the faint trickle of water between the rocks as it flowed into the shallow pond behind him.

Konn lay nobly out in the grass in front of Sprenger. The massive Pantrore was even more magnificent in the daylight. His glistening black top was peppered with greying hairs, but his shimmering white underside was pristine. Even while laying down, Konn looked down on Sprenger with dinner platter-sized eyes from a towering height. Right in front of him lay Satra and Setdo. The two smaller Pantrores had very different expressions to them. Satra's brow and snout were wrinkled with a half-hearted snarl as she watched Sprenger from across the grass. Sedto, in comparison, seemed rather curious about Sprenger's presence before them. The three beasts just stared at Sprenger silently as he gradually approached them, then stopped apprehensively.

Sprenger looked behind him at Juriah, who sat cross-legged on a fallen boulder. "Nothing is happening," Sprenger whispered to him.

"They're just as unsure about this as you are," he said back. "Move closer."

Sprenger took a deep breath and took several steps closer to the three cats. Juriah told him that they would judge him, so Sprenger stood tall and proud. If they could truly tell what kind of person he was, he wanted them to see that he wasn't scared, that he was strong. Though, as time passed without any movement, Sprenger caught himself doubting that very thought.

Sprenger's breath caught in his chest. Slowly, Konn rose from the grass. Sprenger stood as calmly as he could and watched as the massive creature walked towards him. Sprenger became more and more nervous as Konn came closer, but still Sprenger held his ground.

As if Sprenger wasn't even there, Konn walked right over him. His giant paws landed to each side of

Sprenger before lifting away and being replaced by the back set. Even standing at his full height, Sprenger's hair didn't come close to Konn's white underside as it passed overhead, and Sprenger just gawked as the giant cat stepped over him gracefully.

Sprenger gave an inconspicuous sigh of relief as Konn's giant tail brushed past him, and he continued to look forward at Setdo and Satra. After a few moments, Sprenger heard Konn drop to the ground behind him and he assumed he went to lay behind Juriah as he had last time.

Then, following the cue from Konn, both twins rose together, but only Satra began to move forward. Sprenger swallowed back the nervous lump in his throat. He was oddly more afraid of Satra than he was of Konn, who had yet to show the same aggression Satra had. Her eyes were intimidating to say the least; they were the eyes of a true hunter and they watched Sprenger like prey.

Without taking her killer eyes off him, Satra walked straight past Sprenger and joined Konn behind Juriah.

Now it was just down to Setdo, but unlike Satra's eyes, Setdo's were curious. He began walking towards Sprenger, staring into him deeply. He sniffed the air chuffed softly a few times, though Sprenger wasn't sure if that was good or not.

Sprenger held his breath. If Setdo walked past him then that was that and Sprenger was not meant to be a Nymphigori. The thought was making him nervously impatient with it all and a knot tightened in his stomach.

Like Konn, Setdo headed straight for Sprenger, but before he reached him, Setdo stopped.

"That's it," Juriah yelled from behind. "He's chosen you! Now show your worth as a scythe!"

Sprenger took the beginning stance for the Exerptus Routine, and as he did so, Setdo lowered his head and watched for Sprenger to begin.

One step after another, Sprenger performed the routine, and with every step, Setdo had one to match. It became an intricate dance between the two of them, and Sprenger became immersed in the ancient power that was now brewing between them. Fluently, Sprenger and Setdo replicated a tradition that was older than both of them combined, older than anything left in this world, yet here it was; as unchanged as the first time it was performed.

Sprenger slapped his palm to the ground in the final step and froze as he realized Setdo's eyes were inches from his face. Sprenger could feel every hot breath as Setdo exhaled, and the two just crouched there, looking into each other's eyes.

Slowly, Sprenger reached forward and placed a hand on Setdo's nose. Everything around them began to buzz and vibrate as Setdo emitted a deep hum. The feeling swept up Sprenger's arm and he felt tears beginning to form in the corner of his eyes.

This moment was more exhilarating than any Sprenger had ever felt before. He couldn't hold back a broad smile as he looked into Setdo's big eyes. He could feel their new connection, their new bond. Sedto had chosen Sprenger.

I'm like you now, mom, Sprenger thought as a tear rolled down his cheek, *I'm a Nymphigori.*

-<>-

Jacob leaned back in his high-topped chair and began tugging on his pointed beard to contemplate what he had just heard. He hadn't quite decided if the news was good or not.

Kanto, on the other hand, did not look happy about it in the least. The man didn't let his disapproval touch his face, but Jacob had enough experience with scythe; he wasn't fooled by Kanto's composed expression. He stood mute in front of Jacob's desk waiting for an answer.

Jacob looked over at Juriah, who was leaning cross-armed up against the wall to Jacob's right. His eyes were closed, making him appear as though he was possibly asleep, though Jacob knew he wasn't. He often let people believe his guard was down, when in actuality, he was well aware of everything around him. If there was ever a man who never dropped his guard around anyone, it was Juriah.

"So he knows then," Jacob said softly, more to himself then anyone. He looked over at Juriah, remaining outwardly calm but roiling with irritation inside. "Why did you tell him what was required? Why now? Why not when he first discovered the Shattered Hill?"

Juriah's eyes snapped open and looked at him with that powerful, almost hateful, gaze. "I was not aware that he was training for the Exerptus Exam then. I thought I had another year or two. And I told him because it's his right to know, and my place to inform him."

Jacob noticed Kanto's fists tighten all the harder at his sides. "It was not your place," he snapped. "This cannot happen." His voice revealed his emotions to Jacob, even if his face didn't. "Sprenger cannot become a Nymphigori. Such a thing could cause everything to fall apart, not to mention that if another village found out, it would give them the right to declare war."

Jacob fully agreed with him. These events were too dangerous to be allowed to continue, especially with so much at risk. But he didn't say anything out loud yet. He had to wait until he had heard everything before he allowed himself to come to a decision. Jacob glanced at Juriah for his response.

"It will not cause everything to fall apart," Juriah corrected. "Quite to the contrary." Juriah reached inside of his leather vest and removed a small scroll of paper. He gave it a lazy toss. It landed with a thump in the middle of Jacob's desk.

It was a scripture. White paper was wrapped very delicately around twisted gold rods that formed two roses on both ends. It was something that should always be handled with care and respect, since inside was someone's final wishes in this world. Jacob knew all too well whose last wishes these were.

Kanto seemed to realize what it was and whom it came from as well, because he was staring at it as if it were a viper about to bite him.

Jacob grabbed the small scroll off his desk, and carefully unrolled it. It belonged to Sasha without a doubt. It was nearly identical to the one she had left him, though of course with a different message.

This one read:

Juriah-

I'm not sure if you understand what I did or not, but just know that I have no regrets about doing it. Please don't blame yourself or anyone else. My actions were mine alone.

You may not yet understand my intentions, but I hope you trust me enough to do your part. I have set a plan for my son, Sprenger, into motion. A plan that may be just what we need to save our village. One part includes you, Juriah, if you're willing.

We both know the scythe world will eventually fall back into chaos, and when it does, we will need Nymphigori on our side. Show him our secrets, and explain to him only what he needs to know about me. I ask that you train Sprenger, if he is chosen, to be a Nymphigori. It is his family right.

Train him to be strong like you Juriah, train him to be great.

Jacob gave a heavy sigh and began tugging on his beard again. This was not what he expected from her. She must have known the danger it put Sprenger in to become a Nymphigori, and yet she still thought it worth it. There it was, written in one of her scriptures, and so Jacob intended to respect it. After all, she had been right so far. Perhaps she truly did know what she was doing.

Jacob handed the scripture to Kanto, who was hesitant to take it. He watched silently as Kanto read the scroll for himself. Again, nothing showed on Kanto's face, but there was a fire burning in his eyes that no man could be trained to hide.

Very gently, Kanto rolled the small scroll up and placed it back on Jacob's desk. His hand lingered on it for a moment before he completely let it go.

"Fine," Kanto said with surprising composure. "But even if this were to happen, how is Sprenger to continue his training as a scythe while also training as a Nymphigori?"

Jacob looked over a Juriah. "I would also like to know the answer to that question. It is not likely that even Sasha could have predicted his advancement to the Exerptus Exam so early in training."

"I have no interest in basics," Juriah grumbled, indifferently. "My only task is to train him as a Nymphigori. I will work on his skills as I see fit as time goes on, but for now I will leave training him as scythe up to you."

"I agree with that," Jacob nodded, seeing the fair compromise he was not anticipating from Juriah. "It is, after all, your right to claim Sprenger as your student, Kanto. Perhaps the two of you can alternate days in which to train Sprenger. It won't be easy, but I think Sprenger will be able to do it."

Kanto slowly nodded his agreement, however reluctant it may have been.

"It certainly won't be easy," Juriah added. "In most cases, Nymphigori are already trained scythe, so they already possess the basic skills necessary to fight with a Feral Beast. In Sprenger's case, however, he will have to learn everything at once, which may prove to be overwhelming."

"Sprenger is stronger than any of us know," Jacob said softly. "Just look at what he did with the Exerptus Exam. He has a knack for rising to the occasion. We just need to watch and instruct where needed. He'll do the rest."

Kanto seemed about ready to say something, but he was interrupted by an insistent knock at the door, shortly followed by a man entering Jacob's office. It was Parken, Jacob's guard and informant.

The tall man quickly dropped to a knee beside Kanto. "Pardon the interruption, my lord, but we have the information you requested about Tranis."

Jacob sat upright in his chair. "What did you find?"

Parken rose to his feet. "Tranis and his team once had an assignment from Scythrith Danko in the wars to learn what they could about enemy Nymphigori. It was considered high-ranking espionage and all information gathered was strictly concealed."

Jacob felt a chill run up his spine.

Juriah pushed himself off the wall and stared at Parken intently.

Kanto moved around him so that he could look at him more directly. "What kind of information?" Kanto asked seriously.

Parken eyed each of them curiously. He had no idea what horrible timing his announcement had. It wasn't his fault, of course, but this was possibly the worst news they could have received right now.

"As we all very well know," Parken began, "Tranis and his squad were second-rate scythe to say the least. They did, however, have admirable talents in evasion and stealth."

"That's because they were well-practiced at avoiding fights that they knew they'd lose," Juriah mumbled.

"Exactly," Parken agreed, "so they were the perfect squad for infiltration and information gathering. Their main purpose was to learn everything they could about enemy Nymphigori, but the wars ended before their information could be used, and it was discarded after the peace treaty."

"What possible purpose would that serve Demaedura?" Kanto asked Jacob, but when Jacob did not answer, his gaze shifted to Juriah.

Juriah wasn't looking anywhere in particular, just contemplating the situation. "Demaedura has been hunting Nymphigori for the past few years while I hunt him. It is nearly impossibly to infiltrate his network of spies without alarms going off everywhere and every time I got close, I would end up fighting off Adimortis. The last I knew, he wants his war to be as bloody as the last. To do that, he wants Feral Beasts in the fighting. He would need to know how to recruit them, or how to kill them if he couldn't."

Parken's brow furrowed with confusion. "But there are no Nymphigori. They were all killed." He bowed his head respectfully to Juriah. "With the exception of you, Lord Hessiet."

The room fell silent for a moment.

"Thank you, Parken, that will be all," Jacob calmly said to his guard.

Parken gave a bow of his head once more then left the room.

Once they were sure he had left, Kanto turned back to Juriah. "What kind of information would Demaedura need for such a goal?"

Juriah crossed his arms. "Demaedura knows as well as any of us how possible it can be to hide a Feral Beast and their Nymphigori. Just like we have, other villages probably still have Nymphigori, or at least a Feral Beast. The secrets to becoming a Nymphigori are heavily guarded, usually within families. Feral Beasts will not accept a scythe as their Nymphigori unless they prove themselves first, and every beast requires a different kind of proof.

"A Pantrore, for example, requires a scythe to show their worth by performing the Exerptus Routine flawlessly. In fact, I'd be willing to bet that's the reason it is taught in our village in the first place."

"So Demaedura can simply learn these secrets and become a Nymphigori?" Kanto asked.

"Demaedura can never become a Nymphigori," Juriah said bluntly. "Beasts consider who the person is as well. Demaedura's heart is too black and his mind too broken, but he has plenty of vassals already under his command that he can send to attempt a bond. Demaedura must first find the Feral Beasts, or recruit their Nymphigori. A beast will not choose another if it is already a companion to a Nymphigori. We all know how good he is at recruiting."

"So Demaedura could come after Sprenger?" Kanto said alarmed, and rightly so in Jacob's mind. Juriah's dark stare was answer enough. "Lord Scythrith, we must stop this now then."

"There is very little chance that anyone but us knows about Sprenger," Jacob reassured him calmly. "But it still raises my concern. I doubt Sasha planned for something like this. We cannot hope to train him to fight Demaedura and his Adimortis."

"I can," Juriah said flatly. Jacob looked over at him, his gaze dead serious.

"No," Kanto said quickly, "his training is my responsibility. I will continue teaching him as a scythe is meant to be taught, and that will be enough."

Clearly talking about this had gotten to Kanto. He had lost his composure.

Juriah seemed unfazed by it all. He looked away from both of them as if he were no longer interested. "For now," he said plainly, and began walking to the open window behind Jacob. He hopped up on the sill and crouched there like a gargoyle overlooking the village. He looked over his shoulder at them with that hawk-like gaze. "But when the time comes that your methods are no longer adequate, then I will expect you to turn his training over to me." With that, Juriah dropped from the sill out of sight.

Kanto's fists looked as though they would start bleeding, he was squeezing them so tight.

Jacob leaned back in his chair with a heavy sigh and began rubbing his temples with his index fingers. "I really wish he would just use the door."

Chapter 35

Mission II: Escort

There he was, pushing his way through the crowd of mingling villagers. Kanto rolled his eyes as he stood cross-armed just off the main road. Tenni and Soekka had been on time, Sprenger should have been too. He wasn't that late, but still, late is late.

"You're late." Kanto looked down at the panting boy, who gave him a quick bow. He started to explain something about the people in the merchant's market, but Kanto raised a hand to cease his excuse. "You will do extra uprights for your lateness, but not until after the mission is complete."

Sprenger threw his head back with a large groan of protest and seemed ready to complain. Luckily for him, he saw Kanto raise a challenging eyebrow at him and stayed quiet.

Kanto watched him as he went over to stand between Tenni and Soekka. This was the squad's first official contract out of the village. It had been less than a week since they were delivered news of their success at the exams, and they had been nothing but eager since.

Sprenger and Soekka whispered something to one another and began laughing. Tenni swung her arm across Sprenger's face, knocking him on his back and causing Soekka to laugh all the harder.

Sometimes Kanto found it hard to continue believing in a plan that so much had happened for already. So much planning and so much hope was placed in the boy now lying on his back in the dirt. Kanto caught himself having to use the memory of the Exerptus Routine as reassurance at times like this.

Kanto shook his head, more inwardly than visibly. He must trust his Scythrith's decision and hope their faith had not been misplaced. Sprenger slowly rose, rubbing his reddened cheek while glaring at Tenni.

"Alright, enough," Kanto growled. All three stood more alert and upright. They had delayed long enough. It was time to begin. Kanto hated the smell of manure and the stables reeked of it. He wanted them to be on their way. "Since this is a low-ranking mission, we will not take four steeds. Our needs are low priority to other scythe on more important missions." That was not necessarily a lie, but it certainly wasn't all true either. Luckily, they didn't object. They certainly didn't look happy, but they kept quiet about it. "We will need to pair up on two steeds. Sprenger, you ride with me. Tenni and Soekka, you ride together." Now the objections burst forth like a torrent. "The next person to complain will join Sprenger in uprights," Kanto snapped. The group immediately fell silent with deep scowls. Kanto expected as much. That was, after all, the whole point. This squad would learn to work together, eventually. They needed to if they hoped to be successful after their training.

They had already shown signs of great teamwork with the bandits in the woods, but Kanto needed to push it even further. They couldn't wait for life or death situations to call on teamwork. Soekka and Sprenger were inseparable, which would no longer suffice in a quad of three.

"Come." Kanto motioned with his hand and headed towards the large, open roothome behind them. Unlike the other roothomes of the village, this one was more of a giant stump. The remnant of an ancient giant that left behind a brim of its former trunk. "Should you ever need to travel a large distance to complete a mission, which you most certainly will, then you bring the mission details here." They walked through the opening that was the main entrance. Inside, the ground was a loose mixture of straw and mud but the top was open to the air. Bark surrounded them on all sides and encircled the many small paddocks within. From each side, black steeds with large white spots peered curiously over their stall walls or paddock doors, snorting for a treat or scratch. At the opposite end of the large stable, under a shaded overhang, sat a young woman at a table covered with papers and horseshoes. She had her large mass of curly red hair pulled back out of her face, giving full view of her freckled features.

Kanto gestured with a small nod towards the young woman. "To procure steeds, you will need to present your mission statement to the stable master. They make the final decision on whether or not you truly need steeds to complete your mission in a timely manner."

Tenni pulled her braid over her shoulder and began stroking it. "I've never ridden a steed before," she said a skeptically.

The red haired woman looked up at hearing Tenni and gave her a warm smile. "Don't worry, these steeds are trained for inexperienced riders. They will do most of the work for you, and they can even recognize several voice commands. These steeds will even traverse the treacherous roots of our beloved forest without much guidance. You'll be fine."

She turned to Kanto and held out her hand without a word.

Understanding her meaning, Kanto pulled their mission statement from his vest and handed it to her. "We would appreciate two steeds, if you'd please." Kanto hoped she would not question why he was not asking for four and spoil his bluff. Luckily, she didn't.

She handed him back his mission statements after looking it over. "Very well. Give me a moment, please." She went over to an empty stall that had dozens of saddles of every design and size draped over the stall walls and benches.

After a few moments of examining the styles for what she was looking for, she pulled two odd-looking ones from the wall.

Holding each under an arm she rejoined them. "These saddles will be the most comfortable for pairs riding. I'll retrieve your steeds, then show you how to saddle them if you'd like?"

"I would appreciate it." Kanto replied, thankful not to have to give the lesson himself.

The woman disappeared into one of the large paddocks before returning leading two black and white spotted horses by the reigns. The only difference between the two horses was the configuration of their spots. Otherwise, they were just as indiscernible from one another as the dozens of other horses around the stable.

The stable master retrieved one of the saddles and began explaining how to go about saddling the anxious steeds.

Kanto paid her little attention. He watched his young squad standing in front of him. Sprenger was standing between Soekka and Tenni, as he always did. He never had any care about him who he was around.

Perhaps it wasn't all for not. Perhaps Jacob was right and they have yet to see what Sprenger was capable of. Kanto hoped, for all their sakes, that Jacob was right. That Sasha was right.

Kanto stared down at Sprenger. He couldn't see his face from behind, but he knew Sprenger was smiling. He was always smiling when learning something new, as if the thought of something new excited him. His attention was often short-lived, but it always began with an admirable eagerness.

Kanto allowed a small smile to come to his mouth, before pushing it back again. Kanto stared down at his short, spiky brown hair. *He has her hair.*

"That," the stable master finished, "is all there is to saddling a steed." She turned her attention to Kanto. "Will that be enough, or are there other things you would like me to explain before you're off?"

Kanto gave an uninterested wave of his hand. "Just the basics will do for now. They'll figure the rest out as we go."

"Alrighty," she replied with a giddy smile. Returning her attention back to the young ones, she began explaining how to encourage the steed to stop and go, and how fast they would like it to travel.

Kanto stared back down at Sprenger. He always stood between Soekka and Tenni, since they would not stand by each other if given the choice. Sprenger, on the other hand, never seemed to care in the least. He was not like everyone else; he loved being around almost everyone. Nowadays, scythe looked out for themselves and cared about few others, which has separated them in all ranks. Their separation was going to be the village's downfall. They didn't used to be that way, but now, that was just the way it was.

Kanto knew that he was just as guilty as everyone else for allowing their village to become like this, but he also understood the difficulty of allowing yourself to become close to someone when, in all likelihood, they would be taken from you.

Perhaps it was too late for the scythe of Kanto's time, but he would do his part in this plan. He would help it in any way he could. It was with this generation that the village would start anew. And it all depended on that boy.

Apparently losing interest in the stable master's lecture, Sprenger was blowing puffs of air at passing flies.

Kanto gave an inward sigh. *Then again, maybe our hopes are not but a dream that Sprenger will be crushed under.*

"As long as you keep these things in mind, you'll have little to no trouble with your steeds," the stable master concluded.

"Thank you, that will suffice," Kanto said, anxious to be off.

The red haired woman quickly saddled the remaining horse and wished them luck on their mission. Kanto gave her his thanks and grabbed the reins of the closest steed, and instructed Soekka to bring the other.

Outside the stable, Kanto took a deep breath of fresh air. It was rapture to fill his nose with clean air after standing in the stables.

The group made their way through the bustling village to the gates, pulling both horses along by their halters. Once they reached the massive doors to the village, they opened with deep moan. The group moved through and waited as the doors boomed shut behind them.

Kanto mounted his horse and pulled Sprenger up behind him. Soekka, obviously begrudgingly, did likewise with Tenni.

Once everyone was settled, Kanto held out an arm, pointing their direction through the trees. "We'll ride east once we leave the forest, to the city of Hellnate. Once there, we will meet up with Prince Preamp and his battalion." Kanto shifted his arm to straight ahead of them. "Then we escort the lot of them back to the Kingscity of Billingdor."

"If he had a battalion with him," Soekka grumbled, "then why does the prince need us?"

"Because some of his soldiers were robbed in the night by a rogue scythe on their way to Hellnate a week ago. One of the guards was killed during the attack. His soldiers were next to useless when it came to defending their comrade's coins from the stealth of a trained scythe. The prince worries that his own life could be at stake and knows that he needs scythe to defend against scythe." Kanto had forgotten that this would be this lot's first time seeing the world and its people outside Durado. He realized he had much to explain to them before they arrived at their destination, but much of it they were going to have to learn on their own.

His horse snorted in anticipation when Kanto urged him forward. Soekka seemed to have forgotten how to tell his horse to move, but his steed noticed its companion walking away, and followed of its own accord. Tenni must have said something, because Kanto saw Soekka give her a vicious glare over his shoulder.

Kanto sent the horses at a brisk walk down the road that would lead them into the looming forest and onto the paths that would lead them out. He kept his squad distracted by quizzing them on formations and scenarios. When he failed to stump them with continuous questions, Kanto moved on to explain what they might expect on a mission such as this, and began setting rules to avoid any complications.

"Leave the guards alone on this mission," Kanto said sternly. "They will guard their prince in the manner they see fit, and it is not our place to question it, no matter our views. They will resent our being there. We are the proof that their prince does not trust in his own guards' ability to protect him. Ignore them, many did not choose to be soldiers, so in all likelihood, some will not be friendly towards you. Most will avoid you completely.

"Remember, we are scythe. We are not subject to this prince or his father. Our loyalties lie with our Scythrith and our village only. That being said, this is still a member of the royal family and should still be treated with the same respect as anyone else of rank. Is all that understood?" All three students nodded affirmatively.

Sprenger poked his spiky head out from behind Kanto's shoulder. "What do you mean 'most didn't choose to be soldiers'? How else could they become soldiers if they didn't choose it? Why didn't they be something else?"

"Yeah," Soekka agreed, "what do they have to be unhappy about?"

This was one topic Kanto knew he was going to have to explain, especially when he asked Jacob the exact same question before his first escort. He would answer the same as Jacob did then. "In any scythe village, strong, able-bodied men and women are expected to be scythe. Often, it is a profession passed down through families, much like any other profession. Should one not wish to be a scythe, they are not looked down upon, but are expected to benefit the village in other ways instead.

"In the cities we will be visiting on this mission, you will see a myriad of beggars on the streets. They rely on others around them to survive, and do not give benefit whatsoever to the cities that hold them. We ask that everyone does something to help, or have a very good reason not to in scythe villages. In Durado, work is found for those that don't have it, and if they refuse it then they are no longer permitted to call Durado their home, and they are banished. A rare event, but possible."

All three young ones continued to stare attentively, including Sprenger from behind Kanto's shoulder.

"We are given every reason to want to be scythe," Kanto continued to explain. "We can achieve no higher honor than to give our lives for our village's protection. We are symbols of respect that is recognized from each corner of the world, and we live comfortably for our commitments to our villages. It is a difficult but rewarding life, and one that many dream of."

Soekka's brow furrowed. "What does all that have to do with soldiers?"

"I want you to understand some of the differences between a scythe village and a city," Kanto answered. "Soldiers, for example, are recruited to serve in an army, often times against their will."

"What good is a fighter that doesn't want to fight?" Tenni asked.

"By himself, not much good," Kanto admitted, "but the purpose of recruitment is to draw large numbers. A king's strategy for maintaining power is not to create the most skilled fighters, as we do. A king is able to call upon a massive force of men that require little training, and simply wash away his enemies in a flood of men and steel.

"That is why many guards on this mission will appear undisciplined or uninterested, because many were pulled from their lives to serve their king's wishes." Surprisingly, none of them interjected more questions, but rather stared ahead in thought. *A rare sight for this lot.*

For the rest of the day, they kept the steeds at a brisk pace. They wove down the small path that led through the forest. Intricate roots surrounded them at every turn, but this was one of the few paths that led out of the forest without much effort. The horses carried on without complaint, clearly having taken this very same route many times in the past. After a hours of riding and complaining about their bums, the group emerged from the shade of their ancient forest, into the open meadows of the Southern Kingdom.

They stopped here, to give everyone a break from riding, Kanto was quick to carry on. Kanto led them across the rolling hills and up onto a dirt road with deep trenches carved into it by countless wagon wheels. The students all looked around curiously, especially when other travelers would pass them on the road. They all asked questions about the kingdom as they came to mind, but none more so than Tenni. She seemed to have a clear idea the differences in culture, and seemed to want to know how best to not offend people here.

By late afternoon, they arrived at the gaping portcullis of Hellnate; a sight Kanto was all too familiar with. The majority of times Kanto had seen this city in the past, he was spilling blood on its streets in order to protect Durado's borders. More than once, enemy scythe were hidden in its streets or threatening valuable allies within the Southern Kingdom. It wasn't until recent years that their missions the city became more peaceful. He forced the lingering memories from his head and made himself focus on the mission at hand.

They were stopped for only a moment by guards before Kanto announced who they were and demanded to be taken to the Prince Preamp. The guards, though not welcoming, wasted little time discussing it under Kanto's burning gaze, and led them up the main road of the city.

-<>-

"These are some new mission requests I have just finished sorting," Errand said as he plopped the stack of envelopes in front of Jacob.

The weathered scythe leaned back in his chair with a heavy sigh. "Thank you, Errand." Jacob slid the pile to the side of his desk before looking back up with his wise eyes. "You may speak your mind with me lad."

Errand flinched slightly with surprise. "Pardon me, my lord?"

"I know when something is tormenting your mind." Jacob gave him a soft smile. "If it would make you feel better, you may share it with me."

Errand released a heavy breath from his nose. "It's about Sprenger, actually, my lord."

Jacob made sure to keep his expression warm. "Very good, then. I rather enjoy talking about Sprenger." Jacob had expected as much. He hated to think he would have to start defending his decisions already, but Errand was harmless enough, just fraught with curiosity. Jacob kept his voice gentle so as not to show any sign of displeasure with Errand's honesty. "The boy has a way of commanding our full attention, even when he's not here. Come now, what mischievous thoughts has he given you now?" Though, he already knew the answer.

Errand remained silent for a moment before answering. "It's just the mission, my lord, I wonder if we shouldn't have sent him away from the village so soon." His voice gradually became more urgent as he spoke. "What if something were to happen to him? Demaedura could be somewhere out there. He hasn't been trained enough yet. He just," Errand stopped himself, and released another slow breath through his nose. He calmed his voice again. "It's just that so much depends on him."

Jacob understood. He was overcoming the same apprehension himself. He gave a few modest nods of his head. "I see." Jacob pulled his pipe from his left drawer and quickly lit it with a stick and the candle on his desk. After taking a few puffs, he continued. "You're right, much does depend on him, but that does not make him any less of an aspiring scythe. Would you like to be the one to tell him he must stay home while everyone else is away on missions and completing contracts?" Jacob leaned back and smirked to himself before he released another puff of smoke. "Imagine the tantrum that would ensue."

"I understand that, my lord," Errand pleaded, "but we lost so much already for it to be wasted now on such unimportant missions."

If there was anyone who understood the truth of that, it was Jacob, but he did not say so aloud. "Believe me, my boy, you do not bear this worry alone." Jacob stood, and moved to look out the window behind his desk overlooking the village. He watched the many people wander in and out of moss and plant-covered buildings. He watched children hop from one stone to another on the footpaths. Overhead, the shadows of occasionally passing patrol scythe darted over them all like a passing bird. "This plan was set into motion nearly a decade ago, and it is only now coming to a boil." Errand came and stood next to him. He too, looked over the village, but Jacob could sense he was not actually watching. "There will always be dangers out there that threaten Sprenger, but we must believe in his strength to overcome them. I believe Sprenger will be a great scythe someday, maybe even Scythrith, but not if we lock him behind our walls."

The two gazed silently out over the bustling village of Durado for a time before Errand spoke. "I'm sorry, my lord. My doubts were misplaced. For that, I apologize."

Jacob laid a strong hand on Errand's shoulder. "You have nothing to be sorry for. It's that caring for Sprenger that is key to his future." Jacob let out a heavy cloud of smoke. "We must trust in my daughter's plan. If we ever lose hope, it will all have been for not."

Chapter 36

The Difference of Cultures

Sprenger stared into the small, secluded campfire, allowing his mind to wander while he listened to it crackle and hiss calmly. There was certainly plenty for Sprenger to contemplate after their long day on the road to Billingdor. It had been an interesting day of traveling with the prince and his guards, and one that everyone was glad to be done with. Once darkness had begun to fall, the entire company stopped to make camp off the side of the road. The princes' many servants and guards pitched a grand tent for the royals before pitching their own smaller versions and starting fires throughout the camp.

Like the soldiers, Master Kanto had his squad set up on the outskirts of the soldiers' camp. For much of the evening, shouting and laughing could be heard echoing from around the campfires of the camp.

Sprenger was alone at their fire for the moment. Tenni and Soekka were on their own patrols around the periphery of the camp. By request of the general, Master Kanto was standing guard at the crown prince's tent himself. Sprenger had just finished his patrol and sent Soekka off to start his rotation.

Each time one of the young scythe returned, they had a new story of what they could see or hear in the camp. Often, their squad was the center of many drunk conversations between soldiers, and very few were friendly. After everything that had happened on the road, none of the students were surprised to hear what they were saying. The day had been an obvious indicator of the soldier's opinion of scythe.

After retrieving the prince and his battalion from Hellenate, all four members of Kanto's squad took up positions around his open-topped cart. Apparently not willing to spend long days in a carriage, the prince preffered a more comfortable means of transport. The first thing that was apparent to Sprenger, was that, in addition to the plush seats in the cart, it was practically overflowing with. It had a small cloth overhang to provide him shade from the heavy heat of the day, but never seemed to provide shade in quite the right area that the prince was sitting. Something he commonly complained about.

Kanto was at the front of the cart, walking with the general, who rode a brilliant black horse. He was a young man, barely into his twenties, but he held a professionalism that wasn't seen anywhere else in the army. Soekka was to the prince's right and Tenni to the back. Sprenger walked along the cart's left and was getting impatient with the pace they were moving at. Their steeds were with the rest of the cavalry somewhere to the rear, and all of them were forced to walk, along with the majority of soldiers accompanying the prince.

Sprenger looked over to the prince again, and once more couldn't believe the sight. Sprenger had a noble man pictured in his head before the mission was underway, but his perception couldn't be farther from the reality. In the cart sat a boy that was even younger than the students. He had glossy brown hair that looked to have been washed and brushed everyday of his life, and did not have a single hair out of place. He was thin but still had a little babyfat in his cheeks, making him appear even younger. His nose was small and round, though it was commonly wrinkled with displeasure at various things.

The prince was restless in the cart throughout the trip and would through himself back into his pillows and fidgeted with a gold dagger that had an intricate design running up its pommel. Sprenger doubted that it was for actual combat, but the prince would occasionally stab and imaginary foe in the air in front of him from time to time. He was wearing a thick bright green jacket with a frilly white shirt protruding around the collar, and bright green pants to match the top. Such an outfit was clearly not meant for the warm weather, and the prince's bright red cheeks confirmed it.

The prince dropped his dagger into his lap with a moan. "How much longer is it going to take?" he complained up to the general in front of them. "I'm going to die if we don't get there soon."

"We will not be back to the city until tomorrow, Preamp," the young general called back to him from his horse. "You will be fine until then."

"Will not," the prince whined. "It's so hot out here."

Sprenger rolled his eyes. *What a brat.*

The prince sat up and looked from Soekka to Sprenger. "One of you two get me some water."

Sprenger and Soekka gave each other a look from across the cart. Neither of them had enough water to share with someone else. Their water was in small leather pouches across their backs and were meant to only be drank by one person, not to mention they were specifically told not to speak with the prince or any of the guards. What was worse, Sprenger knew the prince had water earlier, but poured it out because it didn't have molasses in it. The general warned him he wasn't going to give him more after that.

Again, the prince looked insistently at Sprenger and Soekka for their waterskins. When he realized he was being ignored, the prince glared at Sprenger. "Are you deaf?"

"I wish I was right now," Sprenger grumbled without looking up at the prince.

The prince clamored over a large pillow and stood in the cart. "What did you say to me?"

"I don't have water for you," Sprenger snapped at him, irritably.

The prince attempted to stand taller and puff out his chest. "Do you know who I am, scythe?" He put his fists on his hips. "I am Prince Preamp, son of the King Pryon, and I commanded you to give me water."

The cart hit a rock in the road and the prince went toppling over into his pile of pillows. Sprenger, Soekka, and even Tenni from behind tried desperately to keep from laughing, but not with complete success.

When the prince managed to sit up again, his face was even more red with embarrassment. "How dare you laugh at me!" He yelled at Sprenger, who had to look away to keep from laughing again. "You stupid scythe think you're so amazing," he said as he began to fix his pillows. "You're lucky my father lets you hide in our forest. When I'm king, I'll make sure you remember who rules the lands."

"Your forest?" Sprenger challenged.

"Preamp!" the general yelled over his shoulder. "That's enough! Show respect to our allies."

The prince crossed his arms defiantly. "I didn't hire them," he grumbled.

"No, I did." The general glared over his shoulder. "And you will give them respect or I'll be sure to tell father what a brat you're being to our neighboring scythe."

"You always tell father." Preamp lowered his voice. "It's the only power you have."

"What did you say?" The general asked, challengingly.

"Nothing," the prince moaned.

This was not the first time the general had made threats like this, and was the only one who spoke to Prince Preamp as though they were equals. Despite him introducing himself as General Brandon, Sprenger could not help but sense the two were brothers somehow.

Kanto looked over his shoulder as well after the general quelled Prince Preamp. "Sprenger, you be quiet too," he said sternly.

"What did I do?" Sprenger objected. Kanto gave him a look of warning instead of answering so Sprenger fell silent.

The prince sank back into his pillows with his arms crossed like a defiant child. "When I'm king I'll get rid of you annoying scythe," he grumbled so the general wouldn't hear.

I'd love to see you try, Sprenger thought with a silent scowl.

Now that the day was over, Sprenger just stared into the flames of their solitary fire, thinking about what he had learned of kingdoms and their ruleers. After several aggravating hours on the road, he wished he could just go to bed, but he, Sockka, and Tenni would have to be up all night patrolling around the camp. Two always walked around the camp while one took a break, and Sprenger was on his break now. Kanto was personally guarding the prince and general's tent himself and said he would not see them again until morning. Sprenger could have started to sleep, but he didn't want to be groggy, so he forced himself to stay awake for at least one more rotation.

He pushed the annoying prince from his mind as he watched the embers sputter and hiss and thought about Setdo instead. It had been over a week since he became a Nymphigori, and now he was away on a mission instead of training. Somehow, Master

Kanto was already aware of what Sprenger had done, and began planning out a new training schedule for him. They decided that Juriah could train him on a few afternoons, but not every day. Kanto's training still took priority.

Though Sprenger began to think of training, his mind gradually shifted to his mother, and he tried once more to visualize her face in the flames. Nothing formed but a smile in the embers. He wondered if she would have trained him herself if she were still alive.

A twig snapped to Sprenger's left and he sat up to see a rabbit dart away. He lowered his head back down and stared into the flames again. At one point, Sprenger was hardly concerned with anything roaming around out here, but then he remembered how Demaedura, Phenex, and Tranis all appeared out of nowhere when he wasn't worried before. None of them had been captured or killed after the attack on the village. That thought put Sprenger somewhat on edge. He hoped the lot of them had left Durado's forest, but not knowing for sure was an eerie feeling.

Sprenger wrapped his arms around his knees and rested his chin on his arms. He wasn't entirely sure he'd be willing to protect the prince should scythe like that show up. He had to complete the contract, he knew, but the idea didn't appeal to him. Scythe weren't allowed to abandon a mission, once they accepted. If scythe were known to leave in dangerous situations, no one would hire them. For that reason, younger scythe were only allowed on missions that weren't likely to be dangerous. Only elite scythe were sent into violent situations, and sometimes they did not return.

That brat is certainly not worth dying for, Sprenger thought as he threw a twig into the embers and watched it ignite.

Chapter 37

Ancient Alliances

As the dry season reached its peak in the Southern Kingdom and the Ancient Forest, the days remained sunny and beautiful without a cloud on the horizon. Under the shade of the giant trees and massive leaves, the forest remained cool and refreshing, but the same could not be said for the village. Durado's normally green architecture was becoming brown in unshaded areas and flowers were starting to wilt. Areas of green grass were becoming fewer as they dried out under the sun's endless rays. The villagers that had not already donned their silk apparel, quickly did so, and shops that provided shaded areas became more desirable than those that did not.

As time went on, fewer people continued to discuss the inspiring performance of Cerri's class at the Exerptus Exams and the most common reason it was brought up was the arguments that stemmed from the many bets that were placed on the students by various villagers. The students received the occasional praise from unknown villagers as thanks for their winnings, which none of them seemed to know how best to respond to.

Master Kanto told their squad that scythe should not gamble, especially when it came to affairs of other scythe. It was considered very poor form when scythe were found betting on one another's lives.

Once they had returned from their tedious escort mission in the Southern Kingdom, their training greatly intensified. Kanto's trained proved to be the most difficult thing Sprenger had ever endured, and for the first time in his young life, he found the processes of becoming a scythe to be very humbling. Kanto was tediously meticulous when it came to technique and basics. He challenged them to tedious workouts that showed the students just how much endurance they truly lacked.

Today, however, it was not Master Kanto with whom Sprenger was training.

Sprenger hit the ground so hard that it knocked the wind out of him for what was probably the third time that morning. It was several agonizing moments before he could draw air back into his lungs and he was able to sit up. As he pushed himself upright, he looked over at the stump he had been aiming for. His blade wasn't in it.

Damn, I missed again, he thought with a groan.

"Again," Juriah called from his rock in the center of the glade of the Shattered Hill. Konn lay behind him, watching curiously. "You lost your balance when you began to throw. You must be able to do both to fight from Setdo's back."

Sprenger took a calming breath and rose to his feet once more. Setdo came over and gave Sprenger a worried nudge, and Sprenger put a reassuring hand on his nose. "I'm okay," he assured Sedto. "We may want to take this one slower, though."

"Again," Juriah repeated impatiently.

Sprenger had been alternating his time between Kanto and Juriah's training for a couple weeks now, and it didn't take long to notice the differences between the two teachers. In fact, there were more differences than similarities between them.

Kanto would only ever work on one thing at a time and demand total focus to that one task, almost tediously. Juriah, however, would often be training one thing and talking about something entirely unrelated. Now it became a habit for Sprenger to have a casual conversation while training to take his mind off whatever drill they were tasked with. When Kanto made the group do uprights for long periods of time, Sprenger would try to talk to Soekka and Tenni about anything that came to mind, just to distract him from the pain in his arms and shoulders and the blood rushing to his head, but Sprenger never made it very far into conversation before Kanto demanded his silence and focus.

Kanto also seemed fond of repetition to work out problems, refusing to allow the next steps of technique until what he saw was perfect. He emphasized control of everything they were doing and constantly reminded them that advancing would be pointless if their foundation was not sturdy. Juriah, on the other hand, would find ways of punishing Sprenger for flaws in his technique. When they would spar, Juriah looked for weaknesses in Sprenger's defense, and would strike him again and again until Sprenger finally learned to stop it. While Kanto's methods were tedious, Juriah's were far more brutal, and Sprenger wasn't sure who he preferred at times.

Though not surprisingly, there were similar differences in both scythe's personalities. Kanto was strict but understanding and patient. Juriah was the farthest from patient that Sprenger had ever encountered. He was quick to temper and seemed to always be irritated about something, though Sprenger learned to take this in stride. Despite his gruffness, Juriah had a humor to him that Sprenger could not help but enjoy. He was blunt and very vocal about his thoughts, and would even joke with Sprenger during training with his own form of dark humor. Master Kanto, as if his polar opposite, had no sense of humor that Sprenger had ever detected. His face was unreadable and his emotions were always hidden. The most Sprenger had noticed was that he would stay quiet when the students were joking about something, as though he was silently enjoying the humor in his own, stoic way.

Sprenger was beginning to feel the fatigue of all the additional training, though. He would often spend his days off sleeping or just relaxing with Soekka in the sun. These sorts of days used to be spent training on their own or doing some sort of challenge to try and best the other. Since being trained by Kanto, however, neither of the boys wanted to waste what energy they had left on anything but training.

It took longer for Sprenger to build up the courage to tell Soekka and Karla what he had done after the exams, and both were resentfully silent for a time after. Now, Soekka seemed to be getting better about the whole situation. There was a time that Sprenger wondered if Soekka resented him, but gradually Soekka returned to his old self. He still didn't like to talk about Sprenger's Nymphigori training, but he was becoming more sympathetic about Sprenger missing Kanto's lessons to train with Juriah. Soekka would even come home and show Sprenger what they had worked on so that Sprenger wasn't so lost when he rejoined them for training.

After hopping up and crouching on Sedto's back once more, he attempted throwing a blade at the target yet again. This time, Sprenger heard his blade hit the dead wood before he hit the ground. The fall still hurt, but at least he had hit the stump this time.

"I suppose that's as good as it's going to get today," Juriah said flatly.

"Finally," Sprenger grumbled under his breath as he pushed himself up. Setdo gave him a very course lick to the back of his neck and Sprenger rubbed the soft fur under his jaw before Setdo went to lay on Konn's back leg.

Sprenger was becoming addicted to being around Sedto. Whenever he wasn't around him, he wanted to be. It felt good to see his companion beast running up to him when he would drop down into the glade, and any dread that Sprenger felt that day would melt away with Sedto's touch.

Juriah hopped off his rock and walked towards Sprenger. Even though Sprenger was glad to be done with this exercise, he knew that it was still far too early to be done for the day and could only imagine and dread what Juriah had planned for him next. He used his knee to push himself up from the grass.

"We will practice that more next time," Juriah said. "Hopefully you will be able to stay on Setdo's back *and* hit the stump after one more day of practicing it." Juriah strode straight past Sprenger to the stump where Sprenger had just imbedded his blade. With a sharp yank, Juriah pulled the blade free and tossed it over to Sprenger. "Now we are going to work on your sparring."

Kanto also stopped for breaks, Sprenger noted, which Juriah only did when the need was too pressing to ignore. The only time they stopped for breaks was to eat and when Sprenger could barely stand. Sprenger also could not help but notice that Juriah never missed a meal, even if Sprenger wasn't allowed to stop.

Sprenger pushed his blade back up his sleeve. "But I sparred when I was with Master Kanto this week."

Juriah gave a humorless snort. "I hardly consider that sparring. You require a much greater physique to be a Nymphigori, and occasionally knocking fists with your friends will not achieve it."

Sprenger scowled. He already knew how to spar. Not only did he do it in Kanto's lessons, but with Soekka for fun too. "I'm already good at sparring,"

Sprenger protested, then remembered Kanto's first lesson to them the day they were assigned masters. He wished he hadn't said that to Juriah now.

He nervously waited for Juriah's response, regretting his protest. Kanto would have been upset if Sprenger objected to a workout and would often add more to it as a punishment. Juriah, however, seemed not to mind and simply threw his vest to the side along with his sword and shirt. "Then this should be a quick lesson."

Though Sprenger was confident in his abilities, he couldn't help but be a bit nervous. Juriah was an intimidating sight, especially compared to Soekka. At least Soekka had a similar build to Sprenger, so he never was intimidated by him, but Juriah was a completely different matter.

Juriah was a fully developed scythe. There was no muscle on his body that was undefined. There were scars apparent in several different places to show the intensity of fights in his past. Sprenger began to feel inadequate by comparison when he pulled off his own shirt.

Juriah just stood across the way, waiting for Sprenger to be ready. Sprenger stretched his back. This could be his first chance to show Juriah how much he learned since they first met in the forest. Juriah hadn't seen Sprenger and Soekka fight in the exams, but Sprenger knew that he had impressed everyone there. He wanted to show Juriah that he wasn't as inexperienced as Juriah seemed to think he was.

Without warning, Juriah sprinted at him. There was no time before he had cleared the distance between them and Sprenger wasn't ready for him. Sprenger flinched at the sudden assault and threw his arms up in front of his face to stop the blow he was sure was coming.

"How can you see me if you cover your eyes?" Juriah shouted, then Sprenger felt a fist burying itself into his stomach. The blow pushed everything out of Sprenger. Luckily, he hadn't eaten in a while.

Juriah wasn't finished; as Sprenger crumpled under the hit to his stomach, Juriah swung his leg around to kick Sprenger, who barely got his arms up in time to block. The impact was still too great, and it sent Sprenger tumbling backwards across the grass.

Sprenger was desperate to regain his bearings and stay on his feet, but Juriah would not allow it, and Juriah was over him as soon as Sprenger stopped rolling. Sprenger tried to get his feet underneath him, but before Sprenger even realized what was happening, Juriah brought a powerful knee into Sprenger's stomach. Sprenger's gasp of pain was quickly ended by Juriah's fist hitting him across the face. Sprenger was once again tumbling across the grass, only this time Juriah did not follow.

Sprenger desperately tried to suck air back into his lungs, hoping desperately that they were done this time and he could recover. He could taste blood in his mouth, and pain in his stomach. Sprenger just lay where he was in the grass, worried that if he stood, Juriah would attack again. He wasn't sure how long Juriah would allow him to rest, so he took advantage of every moment before he rolled over and slowly began to push himself upright.

Juriah was just watching him with that hawk-like stare. "If you flinch, your enemies will not waste the opportunity to attack your opening." Slowly, Juriah walked over to him.

Juriah reached out with his index finger and gave Sprenger a sharp poke on his forehead. "Still think you're good at sparring?" Juriah said with a smirk. Sprenger didn't want to answer. Still smirking, Juriah walked back to where he stood before.

Sprenger took deep, filling breaths and wiped the blood from the corner of his mouth. When he was ready, Sprenger took a strong stance and waited for Juriah's next move.

Again, Juriah sprinted at him, but Sprenger forced himself to stay put this time. Juriah swung at his face but Sprenger blocked it with his arm. He saw Juriah's knee beginning to rise, so he held both hands down to stop it before it got to his stomach.

Sprenger swung for Juriah's face, but his fist landed in Juriah's palm. His vice-grip closed around Sprenger's fist. With a sharp pull to his arm, Juriah sent Sprenger flying, but Sprenger adjusted and managed to land on his feet.

Sprenger sprinted for Juriah now. He swung his leg as fast as he could. It slammed into Juriah's forearm before it could reach his face.

Juriah pushed forward with a series of quick jabs. Sprenger knocked most of them away, but some still landed. He forced himself to keep going after Juriah landed a hit, knocking away as many of his hits as he could.

The two of them continued at this rate for several agonizing minutes. Sprenger's whole body was protesting it after a very short time. Everything was burning, and there seemed to be no end to Juriah's assaults. After a short while, it took all his effort to make simple moves, and they were quickly becoming inadequate for this fight.

A sharp kick to his chest knocked Sprenger onto his back and ended it. "I will admit you did better than I expected you would," Juriah said as Sprenger just stared up at the sky while trying to catch his breath. “Granted, that’s not saying much.”

Thanks, Sprenger thought, but didn’t have the energy to say it. Sprenger was breathing so heavily that he wondered if he was ever going to be able to catch his breath. He couldn’t make any part of his body move. Everything hurt. He just lay on his back for a time, looking up at the sky and listening to his own heaves.

Eventually, his battered limbs started to respond to his pleas for movement, so Sprenger sat up and looked at Juriah, who was crouching and staring back at him. He was covered in a thin sheen of sweat but showed no other signs of their quarrel.

He smirked at Sprenger. “You attempted to stop my attacks completely, but when you’re fighting an opponent that far outmatches you, it would benefit you to avoid their attacks altogether.” Sprenger nodded his understanding. It made sense; all of Juriah's attacks were so forceful that Sprenger’s defenses were useless. “But,” Juriah continued, “you can’t see their attacks coming if you cover your eyes. Keep your eyes on me at all times this time.”

“*This* time?” Sprenger sank forward past his knees. “You mean we’re not done?” he whined.

Juriah just smirked. “I’ll give you a moment before we start again.”

How kind of you, Sprenger thought bitterly.

Sprenger sat there for a while and enjoyed the sun. He realized that he was covered in sweat, and grass was clinging to him in various places where he had been sent tumbling across the ground. Juriah continued to crouch and closed his eyes as he waited, something Sprenger noticed he did often. Sprenger wasn’t sure how long Juriah would give him but in a short time, he got his answer.

"That's long enough," the Hessiet said before he stood. "Again."

Sprenger sighed but stood anyways. Sitting had felt so good that standing was almost like forcing himself out of bed after a wonderful dream.

Once he was on his feet, the fatigue lessened and Sprenger mentally prepared himself for what was about to come.

This time, however, he didn't wait for Juriah. They ran at each other at the same time. Sprenger ducked Juriah's leg as he spun past, planting himself behind him. Sprenger began every series of punches and kicks that he could think of, but nothing got through.

Despite being unable to actually hit Juriah, Sprenger's constant assaults were enough to keep Juriah from attacking him back. It took no visible effort for Juriah to stop or avoid Sprenger's attacks, but Sprenger made sure that there was no time between them to counter. Or, at least, none that Juriah felt inclined to take advantage of. After a time, it became clear that Juriah was toying with him. Just when Sprenger thought he understood the Hessiet's fighting style, Juriah would alter something and Sprenger had to readjust his methods.

Sprenger took a heavy swing at Juriah, but instead of stopping it, Juriah moved around it. In an instant, he was behind Sprenger.

Out of instinct, Sprenger ducked. He could feel Juriah's arm swing over his head. Sprenger tried to take advantage of the opening, and quickly spun around with his own punch.

Again, it landed in Juriah's palm with a smack.

The two of them just stood there for a moment with Sprenger's hand locked in Juriah's grip. Sprenger tried to catch his breath but none he took seemed to be enough to fill his lungs. The two stared at each other for a moment.

Finally, Juriah dropped Sprenger's hand and straightened his posture. "That's enough for today."

Sprenger allowed his shoulders to slump over. "I'm going to be sore tomorrow," he whined.

Juriah went over and tossed Sprenger's shirt to him. "Probably," he said with a nod. "At least you have tomorrow free to recover."

Sprenger snorted in reply. Recovering was not how he had hoped to spend his day off.

They gathered their things and said goodbye to Konn and Setdo. Satra was relaxing by the water and never cared about greetings or farewells, and Sprenger never cared to push his luck with her.

The climb out of the Shattered Hill was slow and more strenuous than usual. Sprenger's arms were barely willing to pull him up onto rocks, but on the way down it was his legs that nearly gave out more than once. Juriah hopped effortlessly from one boulder to another, but Sprenger took each step as though he was an old man that worried about falling. Juriah stood at the bottom and mocked him loudly until Sprenger finally moved faster and finished his descent.

It didn't require discussion for both of them to decide that moving in the canopy wasn't the best idea for Sprenger today. Instead, they just casually walked through the forest in silence.

Sprenger looked up at the towering trees around them as they walked around their impeding roots. They really were magnificent and Sprenger had a new appreciation for them after seeing the open land of Southern Kingdom. Some were probably so tall that only birds would have ever seen their tops.

Suddenly, Sprenger walked straight into Juriah's back. For a moment, Sprenger thought he had walked into a tree. Rubbing his forehead where it had knocked against Juriah's sword, Sprenger looked around Juriah and was very surprised at what he saw.

Soekka was standing in the middle of the path. *What is he doing out here?* Soekka shouldn't have been allowed to leave the village without an escort. Training must've just ended with Kanto, but Sprenger would've thought Soekka would go home, not come here.

Sprenger moved around Juriah, who was clearly waiting for an explanation as well. He wouldn't ask for it, but Sprenger knew he expected one.

"What are you doing out here, Soekka?" Sprenger asked as he continued rubbing his forehead, assuming the reason was harmless. He felt a lump forming on his brow and silently pouted that another spot was going to be sore tomorrow. *I hate having bruises on my face,* Sprenger brooded inwardly as he waited to hear Soekka's reason.

"I need to talk to you," Soekka said in a very serious tone.

Sprenger ceased comforting his new injury. "Why didn't you just wait for me to get home?"

Soekka's gaze hardened. "Not you," he glared at Juriah. "Him."

Sprenger gave Soekka a nervous look, then peered over his shoulder at Juriah. The Hessiet watched Soekka with a hateful stare. A horrible span of silence filled the forest around them. Then, without a word, Juriah took slow steps past Sprenger, towards Soekka. Sprenger stayed where he was. His gut wrenched as he sensed something dreadful about to happen but he didn't know what he should do.

Soekka readied himself defiantly as Juriah neared, but then seemed surprised when the Hessiet didn't stop. Instead, Juriah walked right past Soekka, as if he wasn't even there. "Go away," was all he said as he passed, not even looked at Soekka as he did so.

Soekka clearly did not intend to do anything of the sort. He turned on Juriah sharply. "I want to know-"

"I know exactly what it is you want to know," Juriah interrupted irritably. He stopped walking but didn't turn around. "Go away," he repeated, even more sternly this time.

Soekka's fists were clenched at his sides, as if to give him confidence. He took a quick breath and continued to speak to Juriah's back. "Durado hid our Feral Beasts because we feared being without them," he said matter-of-factly. Juriah turned halfway to look at Soekka as he continued to talk. "Yours were hidden in the Shattered Hill, and I want to know where my parents' were hidden."

Sprenger couldn't believe it. Soekka still hadn't let that idea go since Cerri had mentioned it before the Exerptus Exam. *Has he really been thinking about that this whole time?*

Juriah stared at Soekka for a moment. "They're gone. Let them go."

"I know they're not gone!" Soekka screamed at Juriah, suddenly unable to stay composed. "I can't say how I know, but I feel it in my heart. I sense the holes in everyone's stories of their disappearance. You know where they are. Tell me!"

Juriah's expression didn't change as he glared back at Soekka. "No," he said flatly. "They cannot be controlled."

Sprenger was dumbfounded. *What?!* Had Soekka been right? The Pysliths were still alive somewhere and Soekka had figured it out. Sprenger, too, wanted to start asking questions, but held his tongue. He didn't know what to do. Should he encourage Soekka or should they listen to Juriah?

Juriah turned again and started away. "There will never be a Nymphigori to the Pysliths again. I will personally make sure of it."

"No!" Soekka shouted desperately. He started to reach for Juriah in attempt to turn him around, but Juriah shot him a deadly glare over his shoulder. Soekka froze, realizing how dangerous of a situation he was toying with. Juriah's glare was as clear a warning as any he could have given: be careful. Confident that he had made his point Juriah sprinted up the closest tree and disappeared into the canopy.

Soekka fell to his knees shaking. Sprenger rushed over to him. Soekka's fists were clenching so tight that Sprenger could see his knuckles turning white.

Sprenger placed a hand on his shoulder and knelt down next to him. He had absolutely no idea what to say. Normally it was Soekka who was comforting or calming Sprenger.

The two of them just knelt there as Soekka shook in frustration.

"What did you hope to accomplish with that?" Sprenger whispered.

"I don't know," Soekka said through near sobs. "Cerri said the Pysliths might still be alive and that Juriah was the only one that would know." He shook his head. "I tried to forget about it, I really did, but I just had to know." He took a deep breath. "Now I know that they're out there somewhere, but it seems I'm no closer than when I started."

Sprenger felt so sorry for Soekka. He knew exactly what he was feeling. Sprenger felt the same building frustration the night he snuck away to the Shattered Hill. Sprenger remembered how he felt when no one would help him answer his questions. He hesitated for a moment. Sprenger wanted to say something, but wasn't entirely sure if he should. "If they are out there," he began slowly, "then I'll help you find them."

-<>-

Jacob looked up from the report he was reading as Errand burst into the office.

"Lord Scythrith," he said frantically, "we figured something out." He stopped in front of Jacob's desk. "We know why Demaedura went to such lengths to break Tranis out."

Jacob leaned forward in anticipation. "What did you find?" he asked calmly.

Errand was holding a small stack of papers, and held them out to Jacob, who took them and began looking through them.

"Tranis and his team were assigned to acquire as much information about enemy Nymphigori, as we well know," Errand explained while Jacob read, "but it goes much deeper than that. Tranis kept a personal log of everything that he learned. We discarded his reports but he still has his log. If Demaedura were to get that log, then he would know every secret to every Nymphigori, or at least enough for him to pursue them."

Jacob gave an understanding nod. "Juriah already warned us that would happen."

"But that's not what we should be concerned about." Errand leaned in closer. "Tranis's neighbor in the cell next to him heard about the main reason why Demaedura has returned. It's because Juriah didn't kill the Pysliths. They're still alive, and somehow Tranis knows where they are." Errand's eyes became more intense. "Lord Scythrith, if Tranis tells

Demaedura where they are, then he will also know how to control them."

That certainly was concerning news. Jacob slowly began tugging on his pointed beard as he thought about it. "Juriah assured us that the Pysliths were taken care of. Why would he lie about such a thing?"

"Because he's Juriah! He's not one to be trusted!" Errand was becoming frantic. Jacob didn't really blame him, they were discussing very frightening things. Even still, Errand should at least try to keep his emotions under control. He was a scythe, after all.

"Calm down, my boy. I'm sure there are reasons that we do not know of." Jacob dearly hoped what he was saying was true though he knew perfectly well that this would not be the first time that Juriah had manipulated important truths to fit his own agenda. "Let us keep a rational mind about all this, shall we?" Errand took a breath and nodded his agreement. "Good then. Now, assuming that what you heard is true, we have a very serious decision to make."

Errand's expression became unsure. He wasn't a very skilled scythe when it came to his emotions nor hiding them on his face. "Lord Scythrith, I don't think we could kill the Pysliths if we wanted to. If Juriah couldn't-"

"I'm not suggesting we kill them," Jacob said calmly to quell Errand's protest. "I'm suggesting we re-forge that ancient alliance."

Errand turned ashen. "You don't mean."

"I do," Jacob said with a nod. "We need another Nymphigori."

Chapter 38

Negotiations

The sun was beginning to set over the vast white wall that surrounded the village. Jacob loved looking at Durado while the sun set. It was a sight that could brighten the darkest of moods he was in, even if just by a small amount. He was in dire need of its calming affects at the moment. The quiet office around him was about to become a raging battlefield, but hopefully not literally. The possibility still existed though.

Errand was standing silently against the wall next to the window, waiting to hear how this would play out. The poor boy was probably nervous, because he kept tapping his finger on his hip.

Jacob noticed the door beginning to move in the reflection of the window. Parken slowly opened the door and slid halfway through.

"Lord Scythrith," he said politely, "Lady Karla has arrived."

Jacob sat back down behind his desk. "Thank you Parken, you may let her in."

Parken opened the door completely and ushered the patiently waiting Karla through. She gave him a polite nod as she passed him, though she almost had to strain her neck to look up at the man, who stood considerably taller than her. Once she was through, Parken gently closed the door behind her.

Jacob gave her a warm smile. "Thank you for seeing me on such short notice, Karla."

She returned his pleasant smile. "Oh Jacob, don't be silly." She casually walked over to one of the small wooden chairs by the fireplace and brought it over to Jacob's desk. "I've always enjoyed our conversations." She very gracefully lowered herself into the chair, and began smoothing out her grey cloak over her lap. "Besides, I have very little to do in retirement, especially now that Sprenger just eats and sleeps when he gets home."

"How is everything going with his duo-training?"

"Fine, I suppose. It has certainly been wearing him out lately." She gave a dismissive wave of her hand. "But you know Sprenger. If he had any energy left when he came home, then he would just burn it away training with Soekka anyways. Even tonight, Sprenger came home covered in bruises, but still wanted to let Peter out."

Jacob raised a curious eyebrow at her.

"Oh," she said with a shake of her head, seeming to realize he didn't know what she was talking about. "The boys play this game where they chase my cat all around the village. They keep track of who catches him the most. They've done it for years. Even Peter seems to enjoy it."

Jacob chuckled softly. "Ah, I think I've seen them running around haphazardly before, but could never understand why."

"It's an ongoing contest with those two. They've kept a strict count of the score for years. Though I don't know the exact numbers, I know Soekka is ahead."

Jacob smiled at that. "No wonder that Sprenger was eager to begin another game; he was never one to slow down when he was behind."

"That is usually true, however, Soekka finds satisfaction in winning. Sprenger knows this, and I've noticed that Sprenger suggests a new match when Soekka is in a poor mood. I don't know for sure of course, but I think Sprenger lets Soekka win to make him happy, but attempts to move ahead when the opportunity presents itself." Karla crossed her legs.

"So," Karla went on, "to what do I owe the pleasure of this audience? I assume I will not be happy about it?"

The question caught Jacob by surprise. "What would make you say that?"

Karla looked over at Errand. "Him."

Errand darted a startled look from Karla to Jacob.

"He has looked nervous from the moment I arrived." She gave Errand an amused look. "Honestly my boy, you really should work on keeping your emotions under your skin."

Errand dipped in a small nervous bow. "Yes ma'am."

Karla gave a dismissive wave of her hand. "That was not an order. Simply a suggestion. Who was your teacher?"

"Master Grailic, ma'am."

"Ah," Karla said with amused realization, "that would explain it."

Jacob chuckled softly. "You are an amazingly cunning woman, my dear."

Karla gave him a very sly look. "Oh I can gather more than that. I can assume that he's nervous because you plan on telling me something that he expects will make me angry, and from that short list of things, there are even fewer still that you would have reason to discuss in this office.

"I can think of only one topic you two would talk about that you know would make me angry, and that would be my boys. So let's hear it. But I cannot promise to remain calm if this involves distressing news about either Sprenger or Soekka."

Well she certainly removed the issue of beating around the bush, but Jacob still had other things to ask her before he revealed their latest plan. "Karla, I'm afraid I must bother you for any information that you have about the Pysliths."

She examined him for a moment, clearly aware that he wasn't to the topic of true interest yet. "Little to nothing I'm afraid. I never married, so my family's secrets were not passed to me since I would not be able to pass them on to my own children. When my sister married, she was taught, along with her new husband, how to control the Pysliths, and they in turn taught it to my nephew when he married. When my nephew and is wife died, they took the secrets with them to the grave."

Jacob thought as much, but he just wanted to be sure.

"And why," Karla said curiously, "would any of this be important to you? Last I was told, the Pysliths were destroyed."

Jacob gave a heavy sigh. "That may not be the case, I'm afraid."

Karla's expression became more serious. "Then it needs to become the case." The way she said it reminded Jacob of a time when this woman commanded legions of scythe. "If the Pysliths are not gone, then we need to eradicate them immediately. Demaedura has returned, Jacob. They must not be left unattended."

Jacob straightened in surprise. "How do you know about Demaedura and the Pysliths?"

"That was his intent when he left the village all those years ago. It makes sense that it is still his intent," she snapped, seeming impatient with having to explain something so obvious.

Errand gently pushed himself off the wall. "We have concerns that Demaedura needed Tranis because he knows how to control the Pysliths as a Nymphigori."

Karla dismissed the idea with a flick of her hand again. "Demaedura already knows how to control them. He simply needs Tranis to show him where they are if anything."

Errand looked startled. "How could he possibly know how to control them without Tranis's help?"

Karla looked away from him and stared off into nowhere in particular. "Because my nephew and his wife told him before they died. I'm sure they did it to prove their loyalty when he asked. Whatever the case may be, Demaedura knows all the secrets that my family has guarded so closely since Nymphigori first came to be." She gave Jacob a sharp look. "And that is precisely why the Pysliths need to be destroyed before Demaedura finds them."

Jacob silently took a bracing breath. If she wasn't already upset, she was going to be. "Karla, there may be another way to stop Demaedura from acquiring the Pysliths. And since we all know that they are not so easily defeated, perhaps it would be wiser to ally with them once again."

Karla stared curiously for a moment. "Impossible." She finally said. "The only way to do that would be to win the over the male. For all we know, Sassor died years ago and a new male has taken his place. If that's the case, then we have no idea the requirements for creating a bond with it."

Here it comes. Jacob leaned forward. "What if Sassor was still alive? Could we assume he would recognize the scent of kin of his former Nymphigori?"

Karla's eyes went wide with realization. "No," she whispered softly. "No. you can't be serious."

"Karla, you have to understand that we have extremely limited options here. Our only chance is if Sassor is still alive, and he accepts Soekka to replace his parents."

Karla stood abruptly. She looked at Jacob as though she was resisting the impulse to dive over the desk and strangle him. Jacob dearly hoped she continued resisting that impulse.

"How much are you willing to risk, Jacob?" she spoke with great control, despite how difficult it must have been for her. "It wasn't enough for you to risk Sprenger's safety, as well as open war, but now you want to risk Soekka too? When will you stop before you risk everything that we've worked for?"

"If we stand idly by, and we allow Demaedura the opportunity to acquire Feral Beasts, then everything we have fought for, sacrificed, and lost, will all have been for nothing. If he gains control of the Pysliths then he will no doubt unleash them on Durado." Karla looked away from him, but Jacob did not lighten his stare. He was charged with protecting Durado, and this was the only way he could see fit. Karla must be willing to see that too. "Do not think that I have done this light heartedly, Karla. I know full well what I'm asking of these boys, and believe me when I say that I would not be doing it if I thought that there was any other way."

Karla was silent for a moment. When she finally spoke, Jacob could tell that she was either holding back great anger or great pain, or some combination of the two.

"It's very unlikely Sassor is still alive, and even if he was, then it's even more unlikely that Soekka will be able to win him over. He could be killed."

Jacob softened his voice. This woman was on the brink of breaking down thinking about what could happen to the boys she raised since they were toddlers. "But there is still a chance, however small it may be. We must still try if there is to be any hope."

Karla still wouldn't look at him, but then she finally gave a slow nod of her head to show her reluctant agreement.

-<>-

Kanto stepped past Parken into Jacob's office. A fire was lit in the fireplace, casting flickering shadows throughout the room. Jacob sat behind his wooden desk in his high-backed chair. Lady Karla was sitting politely in a wooden chair to the side of Jacob's desk. Jacob's assistant Errand was there too, leaning up against the wall next to Jacob.

Not the group of people Kanto expected to see after he was summoned by Jacob.

Kanto strode up to Jacob's desk and gave a bow from his waist. "You summoned me Lord Scythrith?"

"Kanto," Jacob said politely. "Thank you for seeing me. How is your squad fairing?"

Kanto knew that this wasn't the real reason why Jacob summoned him, but he answered anyway. "They continue to surpass our expectations. I'm constantly having trouble thinking of exercises they find difficult and that remain difficult for them. Even now, Sprenger manages to keep up with my training. I suspect with help from Soekka."

Jacob smiled at that. "That is very encouraging to hear. In fact, that's exactly what I was hoping to hear."

"Why is that?" Kanto asked, not unkindly.

Jacob leaned back and rested an elbow on each arm of his chair and laced his fingers over his chin. "We have a situation, I'm afraid. Do you remember Sassor, Kanto?"

Kanto looked over at Lady Karla, who refused to meet his gaze. "How could any of us forget?"

Kanto had led squads in those days, when Demaedura's treachery was discovered, and that he had swayed several followers to his cause. Kanto had been charged with the task of snuffing out those followers. Demaedura himself was left for Juriah.

Kanto remembered when he was told that Soekka's parents were discovered to be loyal to Demaedura, and when Kanto and his squads confronted them, they unleashed their Feral Beasts on the village.

Kanto looked back to Jacob. "What of him?"

"There's a possibility that he may still be alive," Jacob explained calmly. "What's worse, if we are indeed correct about this, then it means Demaedura is attempting to take control of him and the Pysliths."

Kanto wasn't really surprised by this. Even with the largest Pysliths battling with Juriah elsewhere, Sasha and her Beast were hardly enough to protect the village from the remaining Pysliths. They were difficult creatures to kill, and their numbers were greater than anyone had initially thought.

Kanto looked back at Karla. "How is it possible for Demaedura to bond with Sassor? I thought that once he was bonded to your nephew and his wife that he could be bonded to no one else?"

Karla nodded slightly. "That is for the most part true. Sassor is not likely to bond with someone outside my nephew's family, but it is still possible. Remember, Sassor is not like Sasha and Juriah's beasts, who only bond to one person in their lives. Sassor can take any number of Nymphigori over his life, but once a bond is made, he is unlikely to deviate far from it."

"Meaning a family member?" Kanto clarified.

Karla nodded again.

"Then wouldn't you be able to bond with him?" he asked her.

"I'm not an immediate family member. Besides I'm too old for such a bold endeavor."

"We need Soekka to do it," Jacob finally said to end the questioning.

Kanto had figured as much. "You think that if Sassor is alive, he will accept Soekka as his Nymphigori?"

Jacob nodded behind his laced fingers. "That is our hope."

Kanto raised a curious eyebrow at him. "And how are we planning to train him to control them? I for one don't know a single thing about Pysliths and their Nymphigori."

Jacob dismissed the question with a wave of his hand. "That isn't our concern at the moment. Right now our only objective is keeping the Pysliths out of Demaedura's hands. The issues of their bond can be sorted once that is no longer a threat to this village."

Kanto nodded his understanding.

"I'm surprised at you Kanto," Karla said with a professional indifference.

Kanto gave her a curious look. "In what way?"

"You were so upset when similar news was given about Sprenger, but with Soekka, you didn't so much as flinch. Do you not have the same concern for Soekka as you did for Sprenger?"

"You misunderstand me, Lady Karla. My concern was for the repercussions to come once another village discovers we have a Nymphigori. As far as I'm concerned, that die has already been cast. We are probably no more likely to be discovered with two Nymphigori as we were with one."

Errand, who Kanto had forgotten was even there, pushed off his place on the wall and raised a finger to Kanto. "Technically, Juriah is also a Nymphigori. So we really have three Nymph–i– gor," he slowly fell silent under Kanto's annoyed glare, and slipped back to his original spot on the wall.

"Speaking of Juriah," Kanto continued, "I assumed he is yet to be informed of this plan?"

"I've already summoned him to meet us here," Jacob assured him.

"Do you really believe Juriah will lead us to the Pysliths?" Karla asked Jacob. "After all, the Pysliths once again being free in the world is probably the last thing he wants."

Jacob leaned back in his chair and began tugging on his pointed beard. "It will certainly take some convincing, but I hope that he will see that there is no other way."

Errand crossed his arms. "Do any of us truly believe that Juriah is the understanding type in the least?" He shook his head, seemingly to himself. "I know exactly what he'll say."

"Do you, now?" Juriah asked from the windowsill. All heads turned to him as he hopped to the floor. Kanto could swear he heard Errand squeal slightly when he saw Juriah staring at him, but he could have imagined it. Errand quickly moved to the other side of Jacob's desk to put distance between him and Juriah, probably to put Jacob between them as well.

Smart move, Kanto thought to himself.

Juriah sent an annoyed glare around the room at them all. "What's all this then?"

Jacob pushed himself up from his chair and stood to face Juriah directly. "Something critical has happened, Juriah."

Juriah took another look around the room at them all and smirked. "I can see that." He looked back at Jacob. "I can't imagine what critical thing could have happened that would require a pawn," he gestured to Kanto, "a coward," then gestured to

Errand, who looked away ashamed, "and two antique scythe."

Jacob glared but it was Karla who spoke first. She sat calmly in her chair with her hands folded in her lap. "You should respect your elders," she said as though she was reminding a child to mind his manners.

"No, we should bury them," Juriah scoffed.

"Juriah, this is serious," Jacob growled.

"Then I suggest you spit it out before you die of old age," Juriah said, almost tauntingly.

Jacob took a calming breath. Kanto followed his teacher's example, realizing he was clenching his teeth, and took a deep breath through his nose as well.

Jacob started again, this time in a calmer voice. "We have strong reason to believe that the Pysliths are alive and well. Is this true?"

Juriah gave an uninterested shrug. "It's a possibility, I suppose."

Karla pointed a bony finger at him. "You told us that they were destroyed."

Juriah crossed his arms defiantly, "I said that they were taken care of, and they were. It's not likely that there are any still alive, but the possibility still exists."

"*How* is that possible?" Kanto asked.

"I trapped all of them, including Sassor, in a cave in the mountains. Konn caused a rockslide over the entrance, and that was that. I imagine the larger ones, such as Sassor, fed off some of the smaller ones for a time, but eventually they would have run out of food and starved. However, it wouldn't surprise me if some of them found a way out. Sassor certainly wouldn't fit anywhere except through the entrance, but the smaller ones maybe found a way through holes in the rockslide."

Karla shook her head. "Trapping them wouldn't be enough. These beasts do not need to eat a lot very often. They can survive a great deal of time on nothing more than each other."

The thought of something eating its own kind made Kanto's stomach lurch. Either that, or it was the thought that the Pysliths still lived in the world.

Jacob gave a gruff sigh. "There we have it then. It's possible that more beasts of old still survive in our lands. This must be pursued and quickly. Demaedura may have already found them, and we must act-"

Juriah gave an amused snort, cutting off Jacob's sentence. "Is that what this is about? I already told you that Demaedura cannot become a Nymphigori. Besides, he doesn't know where they are."

Jacob and Errand exchanged a look for a moment, before Jacob turned back to Juriah. "Tranis claims to know where you trapped Sassor," Jacob explained. "That's why Demaedura sent the Adimortis to break him out. Not to mention, Demaedura learned all he needed to know about the Pysliths from Sortan and his wife."

Juriah's expression turned dark. "I'm well aware of that. If it weren't for that damn family, Demaedura's power wouldn't have grown so quickly. Because of them, I couldn't even kill him as a Hessiet *and* Nymphigori." He gave a small shrug as his thoughts shifted elsewhere. "As for Tranis, the man is scum. He would have told any number of lies to escape prison."

Jacob waved away the comment. "Even so, I'm not willing to risk it. We need to take care of this now. Juriah, you will lead Kanto and his team to where you trapped Sassor, while we continue to comb the forest for any sign of Demaedura."

"Oh, I hardly think so," Juriah said hotly. "I can't take Konn with me so I have very little chance of killing Sassor, if he is alive. You can look for them on your own. Even if you think you could kill him, I refuse to let Pysliths be free in the world again." He started walking towards the window. "I'll have no part in it."

"I don't want to kill him." Jacob said flatly.

Juriah stopped but didn't turn around. "What?" He asked in a low voice.

Kanto could feel the energy of the room shift. Juriah was indifferent until this moment, but now he could sense a change to the Hessiet's mood.

"I don't want to kill him," Jacob repeated. "I want to ally with him again."

Juriah spun around on his heels. "Are you crazy?" he snapped. "And who, dare I ask, will become Sassor's Nymphigori?"

Everyone in the room braced themselves for Jacob's answer. This was the moment they had all been building up to.

Jacob's voice somehow remained calm. "We're going to ask Soekka to claim his family right."

Something in Juriah began to boil. If his heated gaze could start fires, the whole room would be ablaze. Kanto made sure his blade was ready in his sleeve, should he need it.

Juriah's fists were clenched tightly at his sides. His eyes did not leave Jacob's. "You idiots," was all he said at first. No one saw fit to respond to him. Juriah and Jacob just stood staring at one another for a time, as if they were seeing if the other would back down. When neither did, Juriah continued. "How many times are you going to make the same mistake before you learn?"

"Why do you blame Soekka for his parents' mistakes?" Jacob asked gently.

“Lust for power is a trait that can be passed along just like any other. Today, the brat tried to make me do the exact same thing you are now.”

Everyone in the room exchanged looks of surprise.

Soekka should have no idea about any of this, Kanto thought to himself.

“That explains a lot.” Karla grumbled. When everyone gave her a questioning look, she explained. “Soekka has been very upset lately, ever since he learned about his parents. Then, when Sprenger discovered the Pantrores were alive, Soekka became fixated on the idea that the Pysliths were alive as well. Today, Soekka and Sprenger came home very upset.” She shot Juriah scowl. “I assume because of whatever you said to him.”

Juriah paid her no attention. “My point is that he is already looking for strength that he does not currently possess, which is something that leads scythe down dark paths. He cannot be trusted with Sassor.”

Jacob kept his voice calm. “He’s just a boy who wants to find some connection to his family that he lost at such a young age. I believe a similar want drove Sprenger to the Shattered Hill.”

“That’s different,” Juriah grumbled, clearly having no better rebuttal.

“Why?” Kanto pressed.

“Because Sprenger’s family does not have a history of trying to destroy the village!” Juriah barked. His glare became deadly and his hands clenching into fists. Kanto gently gripped the blade in his sleeve. “None of you understand what it took to stop Sortan and his wife with Sassor. They were by far the greatest vassals Demaedura had ever acquired. I will not endure another battle like that one.”

Jacob took his seat. "That is why it is so important that we keep Sassor under our control and not Demaedura's."

"It's not Sassor I'm worried about," Juriah growled, "it's that brat having him."

Jacob sat back calmly in his chair. "Which is precisely why I'm putting them both under your care, Juriah."

"What?" Juriah said, clearly caught off guard. He was echoed by everyone else in the room.

Jacob took on a content and enticing tone. "It's working with Sprenger famously. I see no reason why Soekka would be any different. Juriah will be their watcher when they are Nymphigori, and Kanto will be their teacher when they are scythe." He gave Juriah a coy look. "That way if Soekka does indeed have disturbing intentions, you will be the first to know about it."

Juriah didn't say anything for a while. He just stared intently at Jacob, who didn't flinch away from his gaze in the least.

"You still haven't explained the plan should the worst happen," Juriah finally said.

Jacob raised and eyebrow. "You mean if Soekka is killed?"

"I couldn't give a damn," Juriah growled. "I mean if Sassor denies him and then is free in this world again."

Kanto glared at Juriah. Such a disregard for life was what Kanto hated the most in Juriah.

Jacob stared curiously at Juriah, as if the question was simple, though Kanto knew he was pondering the answer himself. "Should that happen," he began, "then I will inform the Council of Sassor's survival and they will go to all lengths to destroy him. You will not need to lift a finger."

Errand shot off the wall. "My lord! The Council is the last people that we want knowing about this and investigating our village."

"I agree," Kanto said quickly, "that would put Sprenger in danger as well. We cannot forget that this village has other secrets that could bring us to war."

"I will protect Sprenger from the Council," Juriah said to Kanto, speaking to him for the first time. "The Council would not dare cross me again."

"You all forget that that is not our worst case," Jacob said from behind laced fingers.

Karla nodded in her chair. "He's right. The Council is there to keep peace and would avoid another war if they could. We have defied them, lied to them and schemed around them since the end of the last Great War, and here we remain. The Council should worry us, but far worse could happen to this village. I hope I don't have to remind you that Demaedura's goal is the destruction of this village entirely. He does not care how, and there is little doubt he cares about anything less than total havoc on Durado. *He* is our worst case scenario. *He* is what we should be going to any and all lengths to deter, not the Council."

She's right, Kanto thought reluctantly. Errand seemed to agree as well, for he returned to his spot on the wall without another word.

"Very well," Juriah finally said. He raised a finger, "but if that brat makes one wrong move under my watch, I will not hesitate to-"

Jacob held up a hand to stop him. "I understand."

Juriah gave a slight nod. "Then get him ready. If Demaedura truly knows where Sassor is than he already has a good head start. We leave for the mountains as soon as possible. I will take Soekka there myself and we will see where it goes from there."

Jacob shot Kanto a look that instructed him to say something quickly. "My entire squad will be going, including myself," Kant said sternly to the Hessiet.

Juriah turned to him. "You must be joking."

Kanto, as Jacob did, remained sturdy under Juriah's gaze. "Not at all. Soekka is not yet a Nymphigori, and very well may not be. He is under my care until then. We will do this as a team, and we will remain a team when it is done. Besides, the extra help may come in handy. I know Soekka will want Sprenger there, and we know Sprenger will want to go. Is there anyone in this room that doubts he will stay put if we tell him to?"

Juriah snorted disapprovingly. "Oh, sure, let's get all of them eaten." He threw his hands up in the air. "Why not?" Juriah hopped up on the windowsill before dropping out of sight.

Errand waited a moment to make sure he was gone, and then looked at Jacob. "Why do I get the sudden feeling that this is a bad idea?"

Karla was rubbing her temples in the chair next to Jacob. "Because we just entrusted our most promising hopes for the village to a madman."

Chapter 39

A Dangerous Mission

Jacob's early morning summon had caught everyone off guard, it seemed. Tenni didn't even have time to braid her hair before Kanto told her to come with him to get the boys. Sprenger had considered hiding or perhaps playing ill when Granny Karla had told him Kanto was waiting for them downstairs. Apparently, Sprenger was too slow to respond, and when he had almost fallen back asleep, Kanto himself came up and forced Sprenger out of bed by flipping him and his mattress onto the floor.

Sprenger and Soekka were rushed to dress and follow Kanto with Tenni through the dark village to the Rithhold. It was either very early, or very late. Sprenger couldn't tell which. Either way, the sun was nowhere on the horizon and the birds hadn't even started chirping yet.

Kanto told them they were assigned an important mission, which all of them suddenly became excited about: if something could not wait until dawn then it was something serious and critical. All of them rubbed sleep from their eyes, but followed without complaint of the hour, and arrived in Jacob's office with eager curiosity.

For the next several minutes, Sprenger couldn't believe what he was hearing. Jacob explained to them about the prison escape and how it may have been more dangerous than they originally anticipated. Sprenger could see Soekka's eyes get wider with anticipation as Jacob explained everything.

He told them that this prisoner still poses a great threat to our village. Demaedura, a rough-scythe of Durado, has been wanted and hunted for years by dura-scythe, and has returned to threaten them once more. It all became so overwhelming, the students stared slack-jawed at their Scythrith as he spoke.

As Sprenger stepped out the front entrance of the Rithhold with Soekka close behind him. There were no words between the two of them, just shock. Master Kanto and Tenni were still in Jacob's office; Jacob had asked to speak with them alone for some reason.

Sprenger turned around to face Soekka, whose eyes were wide with disbelief. When Jacob explained to them about Sassor, Demaedura, Tranis and everything that needed to be done, Soekka almost collapsed in surprise.

Sprenger smiled at Soekka, unsure what to say, but Soekka gave him a similar look. They both knew the other's excitement and didn't need to put words to it. Not that they could, apparently.

Finally, Sprenger broke the silence. "Kanto told us to go collect our things for a long mission and then meet them at the gate. I guess we should go pack." Sprenger couldn't stop smiling as he said all of it.

"And tell Granny Karla," Soekka grumbled jokingly as he, too, tried to contain his excitement. "I wonder how she'll take it."

Sprenger shrugged. "Either she'll be angry or she'll be overly worried. Either way-"

"It'll be bad," the boys said together, then started laughing.

They started off down the road. "I'm betting it'll be 'overly worried'," Soekka said as he put his hands in his pockets. "She worries about basic missions; this one will probably give her a fit."

It was nice to finally see Soekka back to his old self. Sprenger felt like it had been such a long time since Soekka had been truly happy. *Not since we found out about our parents,* Sprenger realized. They spent the rest of the dark walk home talking about what they thought the Pysliths would be like.

"Do you think Granny Karla was being serious when she told us that the Pysliths could grow to be the size of a river?" Sprenger asked Soekka.

Soekka casually shrugged his shoulders as if he wasn't actually that interested in the Pysliths anymore. "I don't know, but I doubt it. There would be no way to hide a river."

"I guess that's true," Sprenger admitted.

"Then again," Soekka added, "you said Konn was the biggest thing you had ever seen. 'As big as a house', you said."

"Bigger," Sprenger corrected under his breath, but Soekka didn't notice.

"If that's true then I guess there's no way of knowing what we are going to find in the mountains."

Sprenger understood the truth of that. With everything that had happened in the last few months, Sprenger would believe anything at the moment.

Soekka kept a cool head the entire way back to the house, even though Sprenger knew he was a boiling cocktail of emotions. It was always a curious thing to Sprenger, how Soekka managed to keep his cool in most situations. Sprenger always tried, but to little avail.

Peter greeted them at the front of the house by weaving in and out of their legs; his way of telling them that he wanted to go back inside. Peter was the first one through the door when Soekka opened it and the boys slowly made their way in after him. As Sprenger followed Soekka in, he was surprised to see both of their bags at the foot of the stairs, and both appeared to be packed.

Granny Karla came around the corner of the kitchen and gave them a warm smile. "Everything is ready for your journey into the mountains. I put your wool cloaks on the hooks in the stairwell, and trust me, you'll need them. The mountains are much colder than the forest, and it doesn't take long to notice. So, now, you should have enough time for some breakfast before you go." She ushered them to follow her into the kitchen with a wave of her hand. "Come on, quickly."

"She knows everything," Soekka exclaimed under his breath. "How does she always know everything?"

Sprenger could only shrug in response. It seemed as if Granny Karla was always a step ahead of them with everything they did.

In the kitchen, Sprenger could smell the fresh rolls before he saw them sitting in the middle of the table next to a jar of jam. Granny Karla had already returned to cleaning the dishes in the wash bucket when the boys came into the kitchen.

She looked over her shoulder at them. "Eat quickly and then get a move on. Kanto will probably want to leave as soon as possible."

Sprenger eagerly took his seat and grabbed the closest roll, along with the jar of red jam. Soekka was slower to sit down. He was still looking perplexed by Granny Karla, but he didn't say anything. He just eyed her suspiciously before finally grabbing a roll and snatching the jam away from Sprenger.

Granny Karla finished the dishes while they ate, then came and took her seat across from them and patiently waited without a word as they finished. *She is a very odd woman sometimes*, Sprenger thought to himself as she stared quietly at them with her loving old eyes.

As Sprenger finished his roll, Granny Karla snatched the lot of them away before Sprenger could grab another.

"That's enough," she said quickly. "Off you go then." She dropped the rolls into a basket and put the plate in the bucket to be cleaned. She turned on her heels. "Come on boys, I'll help you get ready."

She handed each of them their packs, which were surprisingly heavier than usual, and rolled their cloaks up into tight bundles and helped strap them onto the top of their packs.

She stepped back a moment as if to admire them. "There, I think you're ready." She opened her arms wide. Sprenger and Soekka went up and gave her a tight hug together. "I love you," she whispered in their ears, "and be safe." She released them from the hug, and then raised a bony finger to them. "And don't get eaten," she said sternly.

"How did you-" Sprenger began, but Granny Karla gave them a quick push for the door.

"Now hurry," she said with one final shove out the door.

She could be a very *odd woman sometimes*, Sprenger thought as they were pushed back onto the street once again.

Sprenger and Soekka shared confused looks as the door shut behind them.

"Well," Sprenger said eagerly, "that was easy."

Soekka didn't seem to know what to say or even how to feel. His expression alternated between shocked and amused, but just ended up smiling with Sprenger as they tightened their packs over their shoulders.

While they were getting ready and eating, the sun's first light started to fill the distant horizon behind the trees. The boys made their way to the gates, saying good morning to people as they slowly began to emerge from their homes and shops. Many wished them luck on their mission, though none had any idea what it was. They just simply knew a departing scythe when they saw one. Sprenger wondered what people would do if they really knew the intentions of today's mission, if they would still wish them luck or not.

Kanto and Tenni were already waiting for them at the front gate. Kanto stood as expressionless as ever, staring intently at everything around him. Tenni had managed to fix her braid since being summoned to Jacob's office. She was savoring a breakfast sausage, a rare treat for someone of her family's stature. *Working at the Manor must have its benefits.*

Both boys gave Kanto a respectful bow, which he returned with a nod. "Good we're all here, and hopefully you've brought everything you need. If all goes well, we will be gone for a few days. If not, then it may take quite a bit longer." Kanto crossed his arms and lowered his voice so that no surrounding ears could hear. It was almost difficult for Sprenger to hear him over the growing crowds behind them. "Now, as for the mission itself, it must be completely understood that this is bigger than anything we've done before. This is no escort or some other low-ranking mission, this mission may have our entire village's safety on the line. And as with many missions of its importance, it will also be incredibly dangerous, so keep your wits about you. It is also important that you do not talk about this mission to anyone without permission. This is what it means to be a scythe. The more important mission, the more secretive it often is. Is that all understood?"

"Yes, Master Kanto," the group said together.

"Good," Kanto said with a nod. "Now once Lord Juriah arrives, we can be off."

"Wait," Tenni said suddenly, "Lord Juriah is coming with us?"

Kanto scowled slightly. “Only Lord Juriah knows where the Pysliths are hidden. He will have to lead us there personally.”

“Is,” Tenni hushed her voice, “is that safe?”

“Not much about this mission is safe,” Kanto pointed out.

Not seeming to be comforted by Kanto’s answer, Tenni pulled her braid over her shoulder and stroked it gently.

“You don’t need to worry, Tenni,” Sprenger reassured. “He’s really not that bad.” Sprenger had forgotten what other people thought of Juriah. Most saw him as nothing more than the Reaper of Durado, a weapon of the village. Few knew him as Sprenger did.

“So where is he?” Soekka asked.

No one had a response.

As they waited, the three students talked about how they explained the mission to Granny Karla and Tenni’s parents. Tenni seemed just as baffled as the boys when they explained Granny Karla’s uncanny preparations. Tenni, on the other hand, didn’t even get the chance to tell her parents. They were busy so Tenni told others who promised to pass on the message. Sprenger wondered what it was that Tenni’s parents did in the Manor that would keep them so busy.

The conversation was cut short, when, all of a sudden, the buzzing noise of the crowds around them began to wane. It was slow at first, Sprenger hardly noticed it, but as it progressed, it became unmistakable.

“Finally,” Kanto sighed.

Sprenger turned around and, sure enough, Juriah was making his way up the road towards them. The only thing different about him from his typical apparel, was the pack that he had on his back. People quickly moved out of his way, watched him carefully, and conversations hushed as he passed them. Several scythe gave a deep bow as he passed, but Juriah didn't even glance in their direction.

As Juriah came up to them, he took in Tenni, Soekka, and Master Kanto for a moment. "Oh, good," he said with obvious discontent. "I'm so glad you could all make it."

Kanto gave a slight nod. "Juriah." He still managed to sound respectful despite what Sprenger knew to be his true feelings.

Soekka and Tenni scrambled to Kanto's side and began a deep bow. Juriah strode past them uninterested in their courtesies.

"Let's get on with it then," he said impatiently. "I hope you all brought something warm. You'll need it." Without slowing a step, he headed through the massive gates.

Soekka and Tenni gave Sprenger a concerned look, which Sprenger responded to with a small shrug, not knowing how else to reply.

Kanto ushered them to follow Juriah while he took the rear of the group. There was a short moment where everyone had to quicken their pace to cover the distance Juriah had already put between them as he headed through the gates and around to the side of Durado's wall.

Juriah led the four of them completely around the village to the back of Durado. With the sun being so low in the sky, the shadow of the wall made the air quite chilly. Sprenger and Soekka pulled their hands into their sleeves to help keep them warm. Tenni crossed her arms since her sleeves we too short to pull over her hands, but the gloves Kanto had given her seemed to be more than enough to keep her hands warm.

"Should we put on our cloaks now?" Tenni asked quietly.

Kanto gave her an unsure look. "I wouldn't recommend it yet. You will warm up quickly as we make our way through the forest. You will probably need them when we move into the mountains."

"I've always wanted to go into the mountains," she whispered back to the boys with a bit of excitement.

"Why are you talking so quietly?" Sprenger asked.

Tenni look ahead at Juriah, then back to Sprenger. "I'm not," she snapped, but again was whispering.

Sprenger smiled, realizing she was nervous around Juriah.

"Tenni, relax. You don't have to be-" Sprenger walked right into Juriah as he stopped suddenly. Annoyed, Sprenger punched Juriah on the back of the shoulder. "Don't do that!" he complained. At least this time Juriah was wearing a pack over his sword.

Juriah gave him an amused smile over his shoulder. "Pay more attention then."

Kanto came up to stand by Juriah. "Why are we stopping?"

"There is no trail through the forest to where we are going. We need to move through the canopy." Juriah's tone was an accusing one.

Kanto's stare hardened. "Everyone in my squad is capable of at least a moderate pace in the canopy. They're not used to carrying packs, but I believe they will be fine."

"Good," Juriah said flatly, "it would be a shame if we have to leave someone behind." Juriah ran at the tree directly in front of him, jumped up and grabbed a branch, twirled around it and landed in a crouch on top of it. He hopped from one branch to another, gradually making his way into the forest. The rest of them quickly headed for trees of their own, and followed.

It was much more difficult to move through the trees with all of their supplies on their backs, but it wasn't long before the trees became immensely larger and their branches became much easier to move across. Juriah kept a swift pace, but no one seemed to have trouble keeping up.

After a long while, Sprenger's legs were beginning to burn, and it was becoming more and more difficult to keep pace with Juriah. Soekka stopped on a large branch just ahead, so Sprenger stopped next to him and Tenni likewise came up next to Sprenger when she saw the opportunity to rest. They all had beads of sweat on their foreheads and were breathing heavily.

Juriah didn't notice them stop and kept moving forward, but Kanto dropped from a higher branch to the one all three of them were sharing.

"Don't stop," he pressed. "It will only make it more difficult to start again." He pointed in Juriah's direction. "The trees break just ahead. We will rest shortly, I promise."

Soekka took a deep breath and continued on to the largest branch closest ahead of them. Sprenger followed with Tenni close behind. Kanto moved higher up in the canopy to oversee all of them. Juriah was waiting crossed-armed on a branch a good distance ahead, but when he decided they were close enough, he took off again.

Gradually, the trees began to thin and their branches began to narrow. As they did, moving from one to the next became too dangerous to continue. One by one, each of them dropped to the ground, ending with Kanto. It felt good to walk again and to have the steadiness of the ground underneath them. Everything from Sprenger's waist down was still burning, making his steps slow and shallow. The only thing he could hear around them was everyone's heavy breathing.

A branch cracked to their right and Sprenger turned to see a scythe standing among the leaves, looking down on them. *A patrol scythe.* Sprenger, Soekka, and Tenni looked up at him nervously, but Kanto began pushing them forward.

"Don't worry about him, he's just making sure we're scythe of Durado," Kanto assured them.

"Which we are," Juriah grumbled angrily. "Which means he can be on his way!" he yelled up to the patrol scythe, who gave a frantic bow of respect and began hopping from one branch to the next and out of sight.

Juriah led them out into the open, where the sun had risen to the top of the sky. They had been in the canopy for hours.

"Shall we take a break then?" Juriah asked as he dropped his pack on the ground.

Sprenger, Soekka, and Tenni's only response was to plop to the ground with heavy groans.

Juriah raised an eyebrow at them. "I'll take that as a 'yes'."

Sprenger took off his pack and flopped onto his back. "You know, I'm going to be really mad if we go through all of this just to get eaten." Sprenger jerked as Tenni hit his exposed stomach.

"Don't say that!" she snapped. "I'm already nervous enough."

Sprenger curled up into a ball with a moan, babying his stomach.

Soekka chuckled at him. "I hope we don't get eaten either."

Kanto crouched behind Soekka. “Everyone just focus on the task at hand. We can handle anything that we’re faced with if we just keep our focus.”

Juriah snorted as he chewed a mouthful of jerky. “Optimism will do you little good when you’re being passed through Sassor’s gut.”

Kanto gave him an annoyed glare. “Why don’t you just tell us where we’re going?”

Juriah flicked his thumb lazily over his shoulder to nowhere in particular. “That way.”

Sprenger sat up. “How far?”

“We will make it to the mountains this evening then camp. It’s about another day’s hike from there.”

“Our classmate told us that your fight with Demaedura took you all the way to the mountains,” Soekka said. He then began digging through his pack and took out rolls wrapped in a cloth. “If the Pysliths were trapped in the mountains, does that mean my parents were with you when you fought Demaedura up there?” He tossed Sprenger a roll and bit into his own, awaiting Juriah’s answer.

Juriah and Kanto exchanged a very brief look for a moment that caught Sprenger’s attention. “They were there,” Juriah said flatly, and took another bite of jerky.

“What were *they* doing up there?” Soekka pressed.

“Fighting,” Juriah growled. His brow began to furrow, but Soekka didn’t seem to be taking the hint to stop his questioning.

Sprenger watched Juriah carefully. *Something about this conversation is making Juriah mad.*

“Well yah, but who were they fighting?” Soekka continued. “I’ve been curious lately if they fought Demaedura himself or if there were more of his followers involved in the fight.” Sprenger could sense

Soekka's pride welling up. Now that he knew his parents actually did die fighting, Sprenger was sure that he was imagining every elaborate and possible way that it happened.

Kanto sat in front of them, partially blocking Juriah from view. Sprenger stopped chewing. Something was happening that Soekka wasn't realizing.

"That was a very tragic and chaotic night in Durado," Kanto began. "Demaedura's treachery was just discovered and his followers were rioting in the village. Your parents were two of many that were lost that night, but there was simply too much happening for us to know the details."

Soekka nodded solemnly, seeming satisfied with the answer for the moment.

Sprenger, on the other hand, wasn't. *There has to be far more to it than that.* Sprenger couldn't figure out why, but he could tell that Kanto and Juriah were deliberately leaving something out; Juriah especially.

Sprenger decided not to push it at the moment. There were far more demanding things at hand today, but he certainly was not ready to let this go.

They spent the next few minutes talking about trivial things. Somehow they landed on the topic of Setdo, and how Soekka was looking forward to seeing him finally, assuming they got to train together. Tenni also wanted to see Setdo, so Sprenger, with Juriah's consent, agreed to introduce them both aftcr the mission.

Eventually, Kanto and Juriah decided that they had rested enough and instructed them to get ready to leave. Juriah stood cross-armed waiting for everyone to pack up. When Soekka threw his pack over his shoulder, Juriah turned and started towards the mountains. Sprenger ran up next to him.

"So why couldn't we bring Konn and Setdo?" he asked Juriah.

Juriah gave him an almost amused look. "Because they're not supposed to exist, remember? It will be difficult enough getting Pysliths back to the Shattered Hill without being noticed by anyone, but Konn would certainly draw attention going back and forth. If this mission fails, then exposing Konn and Setdo would have no benefit, and could lead to their deaths."

Sprenger looked around at the open fields surrounding them, then the forest behind. "You really think someone will see us out here? I'd feel better with Sedto around if the Pysliths aren't friendly. The fact that Demaedura could be out here somewhere doesn't make me feel better either." Sprenger put his hands behind his head. "But then again, he's probably more scared of you then he is of Konn."

Juriah smirked at him. "Can you blame him? Once you get better at sparring, he'll have to worry about you coming after him too."

Sprenger gave him a haughty smile. "You know it. I wouldn't mind a rematch with Phenex either."

Juriah snorted a small laugh. "The day you lay a scratch on Phenex is the day I have nothing more to teach you. You'd practically be a Hessiet."

"Is that a challenge?"

Juriah raised his eyebrows in amusement. "Sure, why not? If you can give Phenex a scar on his face like the one I gave him, then I'll introduce you as my equal, a Hessiet, from that point on."

"Deal," Sprenger said boldly. He liked the sound of that a lot. *Sprenger of the Hessiets.* "Who knows," he shrugged, "you may be calling me a Hessiet before this mission is over."

Juriah smiled and poked Sprenger's forehead with his middle finger. "Don't get too carried away. We still have a lot to get done before that day comes."

Sprenger shrugged again. "We'll see I guess."

-<>-

Tranis squirmed in Phenex's grip, desperately yanking at Phenex's black sleeve to free his throat. Phenex just squeezed harder. He wanted so badly to just crush his throat and be done with this man forever, but luckily for Tranis, they still needed him.

Phenex threw him into the snow in frustration. "This search has been going on too long!" he barked. "Do you know where they are or don't you?"

Tranis took deep breaths as he sat in the snow rubbing his throat. "I-don't-know-exactly-where-they are," he said between breaths. "I last saw them in the summer, when there was very little snow on the mountains. Everything looks different now. The rainy season is about to set in and there's more snow up here than there was before." Phenex stepped towards him. "I'm trying to remember as best I can. It's not my fault." He quickly pleaded.

Phenex gripped the cold chain in his hand all the tighter. When this was all over, Phenex would truly enjoy killing this man. "Fine." Phenex moved closer to Tranis, who cowered in his shadow. "But your time is running out."

Chapter 40

Consultation

Jacob was bent over his desk, writing a lengthy letter with Errand patiently waiting by his side to receive it from him.

Parken opened the door. “Lord Scythrith, Elder Jaydon and Elder Bakkon are here to see you.”

Without waiting to be ushered in, two men strode into the office and stood in front of Jacob’s desk.

Jaydon gave Errand an insisting look out the corner of his eyes.

Jacob held the letter he was writing out to Errand without looking at him. The young man took it with a bow and said, “I will leave you then, Lord Scythrith.” He turned to Elder Jaydon and Elder Bakkon and gave them a deep bow. “My Lord Elders.” They nodded politely in return. With that, Errand left the office and closed the door behind him.

Jacob smiled at the two men in front of him. “To what do I owe this rare visit?”

“You know quite well why we’re here Jacob,” Bakkon said in his gruff voice.

Jacob smiled, leaned back in his chair, and began tugging his beard. “I’m quite sure I have no idea to what you’re referring.”

Jaydon gave him an annoyed look. “Your daughter’s plans have taken quite a few big leaps lately, and we thought it may be time to discuss them with you.”

Jacob gave them a mockingly confused look. “Plans? What plans?”

Unamused, Bakkon opened his mouth to speak, but Jacob cut him off. “Oh,” he said as though he just had a sudden realization, “you must be referring to the plans for our village's future that you two wanted no part in because they seemed 'farfetched' and 'risky'. Are those the plans you're talking about?"

"You are correct that we wanted nothing to do with your family schemes," Jaydon said, "and yet you still send us updates with every step that is taken."

"And I trust those 'updates' are properly destroyed?" Jacob said a bit more seriously.

"Of course," Bakkon said, "such things cannot ever be discovered in writing. Have more trust in us. We are, after all, your advisors and comrades, Jacob."

"And that is exactly why I send them to you. Granted, this has all been so well laid out for us that your input has not been necessary."

"We agreed with you up until recently," Bakkon said. "Now it seems things have taken a course that no one could have foreseen."

"Indeed," Jaydon added, "and so we have agreed that it is our duty to help in every way possible with these recent developments with Soekka, son of Sortan. There is no doubt that it will take all of us to pull something like this off."

"I honestly wasn't sure what you two would do when you found out," Jacob said truthfully. "I considered not telling you at all."

"Why?" Bakkon said surprised. "Do you not trust us as old friends? Have we not kept your secrets thus far? What reason would you have to lie to us?"

"Not lie," Jacob defended, "omit." Both mcn gave him a look that they were uninterested in being toyed with. "And I considered omitting this, because you are Durado's council members. You have already risked enough as such, and this is an act of war by the Council's standards."

"You are right," Jaydon admitted, "but everyone in this room knows that there are greater threats growing in this world that the Council refuses to acknowledge. Don't think us so shallow as to put the safety of our home at risk because the rotting old scythe of other villages expect us to."

Jacob smiled. "Which is why I *did* inform you." Jacob stood and gestured to the chairs around the dark fireplace. "Please sit and I will inform you, in detail, of everything that you wish."

The three old men moved over to the chairs, and each of them proceeded to take out a pipe and fill it with tobacco. After they passed around a large match, and took a few deep pulls from their pipes, Jaydon leaned forward and said, "Now tell us, how do you expect to keep another Nymphigori secret?"

Jacob took a heavy pull from his pipe before he answered. "If Kanto and Juriah are successful in retrieving Sassor, I have instructed them to take him to the Shattered Hill. There, the Pysliths and Pantrores can remain hidden while Juriah trains Soekka and Sprenger."

"And you trust everyone involved to keep this to themselves?" Bakkon asked, slightly belittling. Bakkon was not a trusting man and always disagreed with involving more people in schemes than was necessary. Jacob understood his cautions, but had more trust than the elder.

"The only person that didn't already know of the goings on here was Kanto's third squad member, Tenni," Jacob explained. "Before they departed, I spoke with her and explained the basics and asked for her cooperation and secrecy. It was no accident that I selected her to be the third member of Kanto's squad. We knew that she would someday have to take on a great deal of responsibility."

"We knew she would be privy to the original plan and play a strong role in it, but all this business with Nymphigori and Feral Beasts was not in our original intentions. What all did you tell her about our current situation?" Bakkon pressed.

"Near nothing," Jacob assured him, "besides Durado's hidden beasts, and that her squad is selectively special. She is not a dull girl, and took it all with great maturity. I think she will prove to be an invaluable friend to those boys in hard times. I would make a point that friends are one of the more critical aspects to all of this. If the boys start to feel isolated by their roles and abilities, then we may end up with a similar situation as before."

Bakkon nodded his approval, seeming to be satisfied with all of Jacob's answers.

"I'm curious, though," Jaydon said. "How will Juriah possibly be able to train Soekka? Despite what *he* may think, he does not know everything in this world. There must be secrets to the Pysliths that can only be taught by their trained Nymphigori. Having a connection with beasts is not enough. One must also understand how to control them. Lack of control can be a deadly mistake when it comes to Feral Beasts, Pysliths especially."

"You're exactly right," Jacob said with a coy smile.

"Once again," Bakkon said to Jaydon, "Jacob seems to have more to his plan than meets the eye."

"Indeed," Jaydon agreed curiously.

"As we can all easily imaginc," Jacob began, "Juriah was not eager for this mission to be carried out, and there was little that could be said to him to change his perspective. In fact, I doubt Juriah has any intention of actually seeing this mission through. I sent Kanto with him to ensure all that could be done, would be. I assigned Soekka to train under Juriah simply to give Juriah and ourselves an ease of mind.

The Pysliths will be right under his nose, and I think we can all agree that there is no one more skilled at killing Pysliths than Juriah. If Soekka loses control, Juriah will be the first one there to counter it.

"Soekka's training, on the other hand, will hardly be that of a trained Nymphigori, but that isn't necessarily a bad thing." Both men raised their bushy eyebrows curiously at Jacob. "We must keep in mind that there is no real reason for Soekka to become a recognized Nymphigori. That was never the intention of this mission. We did not send him out to become one, we sent him out to prevent Demaedura from acquiring one. Soekka will simply serve as a caretaker and guard to the Pysliths while Juriah serves as a guard for him."

Jaydon chuckled. "Seems your family's genius has not dwindled with time. Let us hope that this plan is as well laid out as you make it seem."

Jacob became a bit more serious. "But I must confide in you the worries that I have now." Jacob may have confidence in his plan, but that didn't mean that there weren't any doubts.

Bakkon nodded. "Please do."

Jacob took another pull of his pipe before he spoke. There was a certain way he wanted to explain his concerns, in hopes that elders would share in them. "Manipulating people, as I am with Soekka," Jacob began, "can have grave results, should they realize their role. Especially someone so gifted and driven as Soekka. Though I did not lead him astray, I also did not correct him when I saw the hope in his eyes of becoming as reputable as his parents. I fear Soekka may resent his limited potential as a Nymphigori."

"What reason would you have to think that Soekka would grow resentful?" Bakkon asked. "I would think him to be satisfied with any role involving his family's Feral Beasts. It is more than he should ever have had hoped to acquire."

"Because," Jacob said gravely, "you do not know his relationship with Sprenger as I do. Those boys thrive in competition with one another, and always have. Their rivalry has been healthy to this point and has led to little discord between the two. However, Kanto has been informing me of a change he had been seeing in Soekka since Sprenger became a Nymphigori. Kanto believes that Soekka could not handle being surpassed by Sprenger in a way that he could not match. The boys have been equals their entire lives. Sprenger acquiring a Feral Beast and a highly renowned teacher was enough to frustrate Soekka."

"Ah," Jaydon interjected, "and you fear that this resentment may grow again if Sprenger's Nymphigori training continues to advance while Soekka's remains at a standstill."

Jacob nodded. "Indeed. I would hope Soekka to be better than that but-"

"Why?" Bakkon interrupted. "Why would you hope for such a thing when you know in your heart it will not likely come to be?"

This is what made Bakkon invaluable as a consult. *He will never hesitate to say what is feared,* Jacob reminded himself.

"This," Bakkon continued, "should rightly be our new top concern. Though I too hope it is not so, we all know that his father was a power–mongering man. We must proceed, from now forth, as though Soekka is as well. Kanto and Juriah both must supervise Soekka at all times and monitor him for any changes. If we allow his frustrations to grow too far, then there's no telling what could happen. I am willing to entertain the idea of maintaining an alliance with the Pysliths, but there will need to be certain conventions in place this time around. We must leave no room for error."

"I must agree," Jaydon added. "If we let our guard down with this, we will later come to regret it. Soekka must be watched closely, and suppressed if need be. The Pysliths, too, will have to be controlled. We must not let them breed. Keep the ones that are still alive, aye, but they are a species that is too dangerous to be allowed to grow without a trained Nymphigori. Their true threat was never even known until it was too late, and that was their overwhelming numbers. Last time, we put too much faith in our Nymphigori and it gave them a chance to surprise us. This time, we must maintain the control and know exactly what's going on at all times."

Jacob feared this would be the consensus, but he supposed he knew it all along. *I simply needed it said to me.* Jacob blew out a large cloud of smoke and allowed it to waft over him. "Thank you both for your words. If you both think this best, then I too agree." *I am sorry I did this to you Soekka.*

Chapter 41

Fair Warning

Sprenger grouchily followed Juriah through the trees and the snow. He would only take his hands out of his wool cloak long enough to brush away snow left on his shoulders by low-hanging branches, then he would quickly return them to where it was warm.

Sprenger was already tired of the cold. He had been cold since they entered the mountains last night, and it had only gotten colder since then. Everyone else was probably settled around a fire by now. *Not fair.*

Juriah pulled him aside before they were even finished setting up camp. He said that even a mission isn't an excuse to stop training. He couldn't tell if Juriah was joking at first, but he quickly snuffed out any doubt as he started to drag Sprenger through the snow. Soekka and Tenni didn't have to train while they were on a mission. *Not fair.*

Juriah pushed a particularly large branch out of the way as he walked past. When he released it, it recoiled with a vicious snap. Had Sprenger not ducked, it would have hit him across the nose. Sprenger was used to it by now, though. This was what happened with every branch that reached across their path. Sprenger wasn't sure if Juriah was making sure he was staying alert, or if he simply didn't care.

Finally, Juriah stopped so Sprenger went up and stood next to him. They were standing in front of a very large sheet of ice.

"A pond?" Sprenger asked.

Juriah shrugged. "A marsh or something to that nature in the summer."

Sprenger bent forward and wiped the snow from the smooth surface and admired the glossy layer beneath. "So why are we here?"

Juriah pulled his thick black wool cloak over his head and hung it on a dry branch to his right. "We're going to spar on it."

"We're going out on it?" Sprenger looked out at the pond.

"Yep," Juriah answered bluntly. "You'll learn to keep your balance out there fairly quickly, or you won't remain on your feet."

Sprenger leaned over the ice and stared at his cloudy reflection. "How do we know if it's safe?"

"Test it," Juriah said flatly.

A sharp kick hit Sprenger's bottom and sent him sprawling out onto the ice. When he stopped sliding, Sprenger froze spread eagle on the glassy surface. He didn't want to move. The thought of falling through made him too nervous.

Juriah casually walked past him. "Seems fine to me."

Sprenger slowly and cautiously stood. "That wasn't funny," he grumbled.

Juriah gave him a coy smile. "That depends on which side of the kick you were on." He walked out to the center of the ice. "You're going to want to take your winter cloak off."

That idea didn't appeal to Sprenger in the least. He grumbled to himself before pulling the cloak over his head. His body instantly tensed at the exposure to the air. He had a shirt on underneath, but it was hardly helping to keep him warm. Sprenger hung his cloak over Juriah's on the broken branch and stepped back out onto the ice.

It was an odd feeling being on the ice; for the first few steps, Sprenger nearly lost his footing each time. Juriah was watching quietly, allowing Sprenger to get a feel for it before whatever attack he had planned.

Slowly, Sprenger walked up and stood in front of Juriah. Juriah took a fighting stance and Sprenger mirrored him, but slowly.

Juriah came at him, slower than usual but his hits still had the same impact. Every time Sprenger blocked a hit, it sent him sliding backwards a bit until he felt his back foot hit snow. Now Sprenger had nowhere to go, and Juriah still pushed forward.

Juriah kicked at him, Sprenger pushed off the snow and slid under his leg, but nearly fell before catching himself. Even Juriah faltered a bit after his kick sent him twirling around.

There was a slight pause while they reoriented themselves, but Sprenger took advantage of it and attacked Juriah. Sprenger couldn't seem to push him back as effectively, but Juriah was definitely sliding backwards from Sprenger's hits, albeit slowly. Sprenger tried jumping slightly to knee Juriah in the side but his foot slipped out from under him and he hit the ice hard.

Sprenger gritted his teeth as his arm and hip were shot with pain. Juriah stood over him and waited for a while before reaching out his hand to help him up.

Sprenger allowed Juriah to pull him to his feet and took a deep breath before taking a fighting stance again. Juriah gave him a slight nod and likewise took a stance.

This time Sprenger decided to stay defensive, and to keep his feet on the ground. Sprenger didn't allow Juriah to push him back this time by weaving all around him in the center of the pond. By using the ice, Sprenger could glide through Juriah's attacks for a long while until Juriah would eventually catch him off guard, and send him sliding into a snowbank.

Sprenger stood and brushed snow off his shirt. *This is so not fair.*

-<>-

Soekka watched from across the fire as Sprenger rubbed his lower back in discomfort. Whatever he and Juriah had done that morning had certainly taken its toll on Sprenger. Soekka could only imagine what kinds of ruthless training Juriah made him endure. It was becoming a worry that Juriah would kill Sprenger in training before he even had the chance to use what he learned. *I guess I'll have to endure similar training if Sassor is still alive,* Soekka reminded himself.

Soekka had thought of little else since Lord Scythrith had explained the situation.

With all of them standing attentively in front of his desk, Jacob leaned had leaned forward in his chair. "I am giving your squad a high-ranking mission." All three students shifted slightly, but tried their best not to react or seem surprised when he told them. Only Sprenger allowed a childish grin to hit his face. "Before I explain the details, you must understand that this mission may sound absurd, but I assure you the situation is quite pressing and real. What I am about to tell you, you may not believe, but I ask that you keep your minds open and listen to all I have to say. Everything follows, believable or not, may never be repeated." His wise gaze fell on Soekka. "Can you all do that?"

"Yes, Lord Scythrith," they all said together.

As Lord Jacob explained the finer details, Soekka became more and more anxious. As he began to realize the intent of this mission, Soekka could feel tears welling up inside him, despite his best efforts to conceal them. He made sure to keep what composure he could, but the task was proving difficult.

Soekka pulled his cloak tighter around his neck, as a breeze blew over him from under the cover of their tree. Kanto had found the largest pine tree he could. Underneath, the ground was frozen, but clear of snow. They built a small fire and dug the surrounding snow out even more to block the wind. The pine's branches were high enough above them to prevent the flames being a threat to the tree, but low enough to keep some of the heat trapped underneath. It was an odd experience for Soekka, he had never seen trees like these before. They had long green needles instead of leaves. He admired the height and thickness of the tree from under its coverage. It was nothing like the trees that surrounded the village. These had branches fanning out from all around the tree, giving no room for someone to move through them. The trees around Durado were far bigger, but they had fewer, larger branches on them, making them much easier to move around in.

A smell wafted over Soekka that brought his attention back to the group.

Juriah was crouching next to the fire, twirling a sweetbar over the flames, and the sugar on the dessert was beginning to glisten into a glaze. All Soekka could think about was that smell; it filled their entire make-shift shelter. Soekka wasn't sure if that was such a good idea, considering the circumstances. Master Kanto had not made anything over the fire precisely to avoid drawing unwanted attention, should they not be alone on the mountain. It was a shame. Soekka could really use some hot soup after walking through the snow.

Juriah stood, or at least as much as he could under the branches, and admired his snack for a moment. He then went and sat next to Sprenger, who had shifted to rubbing his shoulder instead. Juriah grabbed the sweet bar at the bottom corners and snapped it up the middle, as they were made to do easily, and handed one half to Sprenger, who accepted it with a lustful stare.

"There," Juriah said, "that will help warm you up."

Juriah confused Soekka. He was likely the most unpredictable man Soekka had ever met. *That's probably one of the reasons that people avoided him.*

Needles fell around them as Kanto pushed his way through the branches. "I could smell that outside." He growled at Juriah, who seemed to not really be listening. Sprenger, on the other hand, stopped mid chew and slowly lowered his half of the sweetbar into his lap, as if that would be enough to fool Kanto.

"What if Demaedura has scythe nearby?" Kanto challenged.

Juriah closed his eyes and took a bite of his half. "Good," he said plainly. "I much prefer when my enemies come to me."

Kanto's face remained calm, but there was clear agitation in his voice. "I personally have no desire to fight the Adimortis up here, Juriah."

Juriah, still with his eyes closed, shook a finger at Kanto. "That's because you seem to lose your fights with the Adimortis."

Tenni, Sprenger, and Soekka all watched Kanto quietly, waiting to see how he'd react. There was a moment of stern tension around the fire and the students made sure to stay out of it.

Luckily, Soekka heard him release a quiet breath from his nose. Without another word, he sat on the ground to the other side of Tenni.

Seeming to be in the clear, Sprenger resumed eating his sugary snack.

"Make sure you are ready to leave shortly," Kanto announced. "We will leave our effects here and only take what we need. Packs and food can remain behind and we will retrieve them when we return tomorrow. Be prepared to defend yourselves if the situation calls for it, but dress warm."

Soekka was becoming anxious to be off. In a short while, he would be a Nymphigori like his parents were. He wished he knew more about what that meant, but he had little to go off of. His mind was formulating all sorts of various images, but Soekka was well aware that he had no idea what image was truly representative of what he would become.

Something must have reflected on his face, because Tenni looked at him. "You seem nervous."

Soekka nodded slightly. "But also excited," he admitted.

"Soekka," Kanto said, "I understand how you're feeling, but you must keep an open mind. You may not find what you hope to find. We are taking a long shot with this mission and need to be prepared for anything."

"Yes, Master Kanto," Soekka said humbly.

Sprenger sucked the remaining glaze off the tips of his fingers. "I bet at least some of them are alive, based on what the Old Man told us about how long they could go without much food. If he thinks that there's enough of a chance to send us off so quick, then there must be something to find."

"I agree," Tenni added encouragingly.

Juriah opened his eyes and looked over at Soekka. "It matters not if *some* of the Pysliths survived. Sassor himself is the only one that matters. This whole mission will be pointless if Sassor is not among the living. He is your link to controlling the others. Until, or even if, we find Sassor and he accepts you as his

Nymphigori, we will have to worry about being attacked by the lesser Pysliths. Do not waste your time on anything but Sassor; he's the only one that will recognize you. You will be just as foreign to the others as we are."

"How will I know which one is Sassor?" Soekka asked.

Juriah closed his eyes again. "You'll know."

Chapter 42

Mountain Springs

It didn't take long for Sprenger to miss the warm cover of their tree. His shoes hadn't even finished drying from when he went out to train with Juriah that morning, and now fresh snow was melting into them. Sprenger tried to keep step in Juriah's footprints in the deep snow as much as possible, in the hope of keeping his toes somewhat warm, but it was a difficult task without looking foolish.

At least it was sunny today, unlike when they first entered the mountains. In fact, the sunlight gave everything a new bright, reflective look. Snow piles on branches of trees shimmered with countless sparkles, while the ground seemed to be one giant sheet of reflected light. The air was still cold, but the sunshine added warmth that quickly disappeared in the shadow of looming evergreens.

They hadn't been hiking for long, and they made slow progress in the calf-high snow, but they could feel the mountains get steeper as they trudged along. Juriah would periodically stop and look around before moving on, giving no indication if he saw whatever it was he was looking for. Since Juriah was the only one that knew where they were going, no of them bothered to help look for possible routes. They all followed in a quiet line behind him and stopped whenever he did.

They continued on for a couple hours, and from time to time, Sprenger could have sworn that he smelled something, but then it would disappear as a light breeze swept the mountainsides. It was a faint smell, but as they continued, it was becoming more and more distinct. Sprenger almost recognized it, but he couldn't think of where he had smelled it before.

"Do you smell that?" Soekka asked from behind. "It smells like the simmering pots in the Healer's Quarters."

Soekka was right. It was the exact same smell of foul eggs that the simmering pots had.

"Where's it coming from?" Sprenger asked Juriah ahead of him.

"These mountains are full of hot springs. One of which is fed to the Healer's Quarters for the simmering pots. We need to find the one near the cliffs up ahead. That is where," Juriah hesitated for a moment, "where the Pysliths became trapped in a cave." Juriah had stopped himself from saying something else, but Sprenger knew he would deny it if asked, so he left it alone for the time being. "We are almost there."

Though he knew Juriah couldn't see him, Sprenger couldn't help but glare suspiciously at the back of Juriah's head.

"Be cautious guys," Kanto warned from behind Tenni. "Keep an eye on your surroundings. Remember, we are not the only one's interested in finding this place."

Everyone fell silent, and it was then that a sudden dread gripped Sprenger. He joked about the danger before, but now it seemed all too real. He readied the blade in his sleeve. The feel of the pommel gave him some sense of comfort, but the eeriness of the situation was still present. Nothing moved around them. The stillness almost made Sprenger even more nervous.

As they approached a wall of towering cliffs, something began to change in the surrounding trees. Broken branches weren't an odd thing to see on trees, but now it appeared that there wasn't a single tree that was fully intact. Almost all were clearly missing limbs, some as thick as Sprenger's waist, while other trees were toppled or broken completely in half. The farther ahead Sprenger looked, the greater the amount of damage was done. Broken trees were visible under layers of snow, and bare logs were all that was left of others.

Sprenger looked back. Soekka and Tenni had noticed it too. Even Master Kanto was looking around curiously.

"What happened here?" Tenni whispered.

As Sprenger looked around, something caught his eye. On one particularly barren tree was something glinting in the sunlight. Sprenger had to strain his eyes with the bright snow to see it, but once he realized what it was, there was no mistake. Imbedded in the dead wood, was a scythe's blade. Sprenger began looking for other dead trees that were not covered in snow, and sure enough, several of them were stuck with throwing blades or sparring blades. Most had rusted throughout the metal, while others were only handles sticking out of snow.

Before Sprenger could ask, Juriah confirmed his suspicions. "This is where the battle against Demaedura and some of his followers took place, aside from the fighting in the village. Our fight led us over a great distance, but this is where Demaedura tried to make his last stand." Juriah motioned with his arm. "What you see around you is the resulting devastation that the Feral Beasts were capable of."

Sprenger wasn't surprised, and had the rest of them seen Konn, they wouldn't be surprised either.

Everyone moved quietly onward. The hike gradually became steeper as they neared the approaching cliffs. Had the sun not been to their backs, the looming cliffs would have robbed them of any sunlight and warmth.

"Over here," Juriah grumbled.

He led them to the left, where the smell of the water was most potent, and Sprenger began to make out the slight sound of running water. Sprenger saw the steam before he saw the stream. The water was a yellowish color in most areas and almost purple in others due to the rocks underneath. The snow on the bank was melted into overhanging icicles dripping into the warm water below. The stream itself was only about two feet across and no more than a foot deep.

Juriah stopped close to the bank. “This stream comes from a spring in the cave we are looking for.” He looked upstream. “It’s right up there.”

Juriah began to take a step forward when there was a sudden uproar of water. A purple serpent burst forth from the stream at Juriah, who barely pulled back in time to avoid the snake biting into his shoulder. Juriah faltered backwards, reaching behind him for his sword.

Without hesitation, the snake whipped around and struck at Sprenger, but recoiled with a hiss as a blade imbedded into its side. The snake let out a screeching hiss as its body clenched and coiled around the blade.

Juriah lunged forward and lopped off the snake’s head with his sword. The head fell into the snow, but the body continued to thrash wildly.

Kanto came running up to Sprenger. “Get back,” he urged to Sprenger, who gladly withdrew to where Soekka and Tenni were standing wide-eyed and with blades at the ready.

The snake continued to thrash blindly in the snow, littering the white with drops of red blood. Near its middle, the serpent was as thick around as Sprenger’s leg. It was several feet long, but Sprenger couldn’t be sure exactly how long, since much of it was still in the water.

Kanto slammed his foot down on the snake's body, which continued to wriggle under his boot. He crouched down and pulled his blade free of the snake and readied it again.

"What's wrong?" he asked Juriah, who was staring intently down at the snake.

"This isn't possible," Juriah whispered.

Kanto stood. "What do you mean?"

Juriah replaced his sword on his back. "This Pyslith is no more than a few years old." Kanto gave him a curious look. Juriah's expression became more heated. "Not only are the Pysliths still alive, they're breeding."

Kanto worked his blade back into his sleeve. "So now we know that they're alive, but can we say if Sassor is alive? There must be a male in there if they're breeding."

Juriah nodded, and then looked upstream with a hateful glare. "He's in there alright, and it would appear he is very much alive."

Something caught Kanto's eye in the stream.

"Back!" he shouted.

He and Juriah leapt backwards away from the water. Juriah stood watching the stream with clenched fists and a furrowed brow, while Kanto once again readied his blade while holding out a protective arm in front of the three students. Each of them readied a blade behind Kanto.

"What did-" Sprenger began to ask but Kanto shushed him.

It wasn't long before Sprenger got his answer.

A purple nose began to rise from behind the bank, a forked tongue whipping wildly in and out of the front of its mouth. As it slowly rose out of the water, Sprenger raised his blade. This snake was even larger than the last and as thick as Sprenger's waist.

The giant serpent slowly slithered up onto the snowbank where the first snake was still blindly squirming in the snow. The larger snake seemed to examine the body for a moment before biting down on the bloody stump that once held a head. Inch by inch, the first snake disappeared inside the other.

Tenni covered her mouth with disgust.

Soon, all that could be seen of the first snake was the tip of its tail hanging from the corner of the larger snake's mouth. With one final gulp, that too disappeared.

Once finished, the giant snake turned back to the stream and disappeared behind the snowbank.

"That must be how they've stayed fed," Kanto said after relaxing a bit. "If any animal were to come near the water, a Pyslith would kill it and take it back into the cave."

Sprenger felt a bit queasy as he realized something. "You mean they-"

"Throw it up so the larger ones that can't escape can eat it," Juriah finished. "Yes," he answered with a nod.

"They're alive," Sprenger heard Soekka whisper under his breath. Sprenger looked over at him. He was staring wide-eyed at the stream. He looked over at Juriah. "Why don't the ones that *can* get out just leave then?" Soekka asked.

"They would never venture out on their own," Juriah answered. "They would never leave their breeding male. Besides, I'd bet that the snow would be enough to freeze them to death if they got too far from that stream."

Sprenger saw concern brush over Soekka. *He's not handling all of this as well as he should be,* Sprenger thought. Soekka must have realized something similar because he seemed to calm himself.

Sprenger knew what this moment meant to Soekka. He had experienced it himself, but Sprenger also knew that keeping a level head in times of excitement was a test that all scythe must pass.

"If they freeze," Soekka said to Juriah, who was still watching the stream, "then how do we get them off the mountain?"

"One thing at a time," Juriah grumbled, but Kanto gave him a look for a better answer. Reluctantly, Juriah added, "The bigger ones will have no problem getting down. Trust me when I say it takes far more than snow to kill *them.*" Juriah began walking towards the cliffs. "Stay away from the stream."

"Obviously," Sprenger grumbled to himself. He looked over at Tenni. She was watching the stream, still a bit shocked and then looked at Soekka as he walked past her. She gave Sprenger an apprehensive look. He returned it. All doubt of finding anything on this mission was gone now, and the two of them could sense one another's nervousness.

As Sprenger turned away, there was another burst of water from the stream and Tenni screamed. Everyone looked over as Tenni was knocked to her back, holding a Pyslith's head tightly in her hands, attempting to hold the mouth shut as it began to pull its body over her in the snow.

Sprenger began to move to help but then everyone flinched as a roar echoed across the snow, and Setdo came bounding over them from the trees. He leapt over to Tenni and grabbed a hold of the Pyslith just below its head and shook it violently with deep growling, which was only drowned out by Tenni's startled scream.

Once Sedto pulled the Pyslith completely off Tenni, she frantically crawled backwards in the snow to Sprenger, who helped her up.

"Setdo?" Sprenger said in shock. "What are-"

"What are *you* doing here?!" Juriah screamed as he pushed past all of them angrily, nearly knocking Soekka to the ground. Setdo stopped his vicious assault of the now limp Pyslith. The Pantrore crouched and put his ears back, apparently apprehensive of Juriah.

To everyone's surprise, Juriah began to beat on Setdo's forehead with his fist. "You stupid waste of fur, leaving the Hill, risking everything," he said between hits. Setdo just sat there and closed his eyes with each blow, still holding the limp Pyslith in his mouth. Sprenger doubted that the hits were doing any damage, considering Setdo's size, but he wanted to step in to stop Juriah all the same.

Apparently burning out his temper, Juriah stopped and let out a frustrated breath. "Your damn beast always leaves the Hill when he shouldn't." Juriah turned to Sprenger. "I was worried the idiot would start following you." He spun back around to Setdo. "But I didn't think you would come this far!" He struck Setdo on the head again, and again Setdo just sat there.

Juriah stormed away in frustration, so Sprenger grabbed Tenni's arm and pulled her with him. Soekka came up as well to look at Setdo. Setdo stood up excitedly, still holding the dead Pyslith in his mouth, but then dropped it as Sprenger got closer.

Sprenger went up and wrapped his arms around the giant cat's neck. "Hi Setdo," he whispered. "I don't care what Juriah says, I'm glad you're here." Sedto chuffed in reply.

Tenni and Soekka just stood there and gawked, much like Sprenger had when he first saw Setdo.

Tenni stepped forward nervously and bowed. "Thank you for saving me, Setdo."

Setdo just tilted his head and gave her a curious look.

"Wow," Soekka whispered. He started to say something else but Kanto interrupted him.

"Come this way," he called, seeming to have no interest in Setdo's appearance.

As the group approached the cliffs, the knot in Sprenger's stomach tightened even more as they followed Kanto, so he placed a hand on Setdo's warm side to reassure himself.

It wasn't hard to find what they were looking for. Sprenger examined the section of cliff that the stream led them to. It was evident that there had been an unnatural rockslide in the area. Boulders of every size were piled onto one another. Frozen dirt and ice filled in the gaps between them. Sprenger even saw the remnants of a few trees jammed in the rubble. Sprenger followed the path of the slide all the way to the ridge line high above them.

Seeing their obstacle posed a new question for Sprenger, but Soekka was quicker to say it aloud.

"How are we supposed to get through *that*?" Soekka asked doubtfully.

Juriah gave an uninterested shrug. "I don't know. I only agreed to bring you to your Feral Beasts. Aside from that you're on your own." Juriah walked away from the cliffs and leaned up against a tree that had been stripped bare.

"You must be joking," Soekka growled.

Juriah crossed his arms casually. "I suggest you start digging."

Sprenger slumped and slapped a hand to his forehead. He should have known Juriah would sabotage the mission somehow.

Kanto stepped out in front of them. "You knew about this and still you said nothing?" His voice didn't sound angry, in fact it didn't even sound surprised.

Juriah closed his eyes as he rested his head back on the tree. "As I told Jacob, this mission was a waste of time. Perhaps now he will take *your* word for it."

"You lied," Soekka said through clenched teeth.

Juriah didn't seem too worried about any of their reactions. "I told everyone that they were trapped under a landslide, so what did you all expect? A big door that would swing open when I turned the key in the lock? If something is strong enough to keep a Feral Beast *in,* then you should probably assume it's strong enough to keep you *out.*"

Sprenger added a scowl to the collection, and Setdo snorted angrily, though probably not because he knew what was going on but because everyone else looked upset.

This was a dirty trick. *A wet and cold dirty trick,* Sprenger reminded himself when he thought about all that they had to do to get here. Before anyone could rebuttal, Kanto pulled his pack over his shoulder, knelt to the ground, and began to take something out of it.

"Luckily," Kanto said calmly, "Lord Scythrith did take that into consideration, and he expected you to make this mission as difficult as possible. That, by the way, is why I'm here." He began producing fist-sized clay jars from his pack. Even Juriah looked at them curiously as Kanto laid them in the snow. The jars were completely sealed with clay and the sides were painted with starry patterns. From one end of each jar protruded coils of thin, braided rope. Kanto produced five jars in all, and gently placed them in the snow.

"Unless there are very large hammers in those small jars," Juriah said skeptically, "then I doubt they'll do you much good."

"What are they?" Tenni asked curiously.

"Lord Scythrith had them in a vault somewhere," Kanto explained. "He said they were a gift from some miners. A thank-you gift after a contract with them a while ago. For years, he has been saving them for a special occasion."

Sprenger agreed with Juriah's skepticism. "I still don't see how those will help."

Kanto shrugged. "I'm not completely sure either. Lord Scythrith said to put them as far under the rocks as we could, light the rope, and that's it." He threw his pack back over his shoulder. "Oh, and to stand back. There could be a violent eruption," he said with the same emotionless voice as he said everything else.

Juriah snorted, amused. "You plan on moving boulders with five clay balls and the word of a crazy old man?"

Kanto glared at Juriah. "Considering that 'crazy old man' is one of the wisest men I have ever met; yes, I will trust him."

Kanto scooped up the remaining jars and headed for the rockslide. He moved cautiously, watching the water for any sign of movement. The stream disappeared under several boulders, but even from where he was standing, Sprenger could see there were large spaces between the boulders for the smaller Pysliths to swim through.

Once Kanto decided that nothing was going to emerge suddenly from the water, he began examining the rockslide closely. He would periodically put his hand between boulders to see how far he could reach in, comparing the depth of different spaces. If he was pleased with the depth, he would put one of the clay jars in the crevice. Once all of the jars but one were in place, he gathered the ends of the thin ropes, which held surprising length in their coils. "I'll save one in case this doesn't work and we have to try again," he explained. He looked back at Juriah. "Before I do this, what can we expect inside?"

"Some damn big, angry, hungry monsters, you idiot," Juriah snapped bitterly.

Kanto rolled his eyes. "I meant numbers. How many were originally trapped?"

"Three mature females, and of course, Sassor," Juriah growled. "Not counting whatever spawn have accumulated over the years."

Soekka stepped up next to Sprenger, and looked all the way up the rockslide. "I guess there's more in there now."

Tenni was standing closer to the stream, watching it cautiously. She looked over at Kanto. "What should we do when the smaller ones come out, or if they won't let Soekka near Sassor?"

Kanto thought for a moment. "We will give everything a chance to leave the cave. If Sassor comes out, Soekka," he gave Soekka a serious look, "approach him but move slow. Sassor has to recognize you." Soekka nodded.

"And what if he doesn't come out?" Sprenger asked, dreading the answer.

"We go in," Kanto replied.

Everyone turned around when Juriah started chuckling behind them. "You lot think they're going to let you walk in there?" He let out an amused sigh. "They will come out alright, and they'll be hungry. They won't just be like the ones in the stream either," he shook his head. "No, no. There are possibly three, fully grown females in there, and they will be looking for a fight."

Kanto began thinking it over again before he spoke. "Our mission is Sassor. When we first open the entrance, we must hide and give everything a chance to move out. However, anything that becomes a threat we have to treat as such. If there are still fully grown Pysliths in there, then I will bait them away from the cave."

Juriah perked up a bit. "Ooo I like that idea."

Kanto ignored him. "I want you three to focus on getting to Sassor. Soekka, you know what you have to do. Tenni and Sprenger, you protect him and watch his back until something happens. Any questions?"

"Where do I fall into your plan?" Juriah asked.

"You've been playing your own game up to this point," Kanto said as he held up the ropes to the clay jars. "I expect you'll continue to do so, despite any plan I make."

Kanto pulled his flint from his pocket, and after a few tries, managed to light the ropes. They erupted in flame and sparks and began to burn down their individual paths.

Kanto watched them for a moment, then remembering Jacob's advice, moved back to where Sprenger, Soekka and Tenni stood, with Setdo settling in the snow behind them. Seeming to still not be sure, he ushered them back farther, next to the tree Juriah was leaning on.

Sprenger had never seen anything burn like those ropes. They shimmered and sparkled as they burnt, rather than with a normal flame. He looked over at Soekka, who was likewise watching them burn, but with far more eagerness.

Everyone watched with nervous anticipation as the ropes burnt away, until they disappeared into the crevices. For a moment there was nothing.

Suddenly, Sprenger was thrown back as the mountain echoed with a thunderous boom.

-<>-

Tranis trudged through the snow, trying desperately to find an area that looked familiar. It wasn't working. It had been so long since he was last up here and it would've been hard enough to remember without the snow changing how everything looked. Phenex was a few steps behind him, watching him with an expressionless, but still menacing stare.

Tranis flinched as the silence was broken around them, and a boom echoed through the mountains and across the snow. It came from somewhere to their left. *What was that?*

Phenex was looking in the same direction, probably wondering the same thing himself. After a moment of silence, Phenex began walking in the direction of the boom, as if it was more likely to show him what he was looking for than Tranis.

Tranis considered taking his chance and running, but he knew that he wouldn't make it past the length of chain of Phenex's flail. Fear got the best of him and he silently followed behind. Tranis knew very well that if Phenex found where Sassor was, he would no longer have much use for Tranis.

Chapter 43

To Battle a Pyslith...

Sprenger opened his eyes, but it was so bright that he had to close them again. There was a high-pitched whistle in his ears that remained even after he covered them with his hands. Something kept touching his face, but he couldn't tell what it was. He squinted his eyes open a crack, only to see a large black nose huffing over his face.

Setdo was standing over him, sniffing him curiously, and bumping Sprenger's face with his nose. Sprenger pushed him back and sat up in the snow. He shook his head in attempt to clear the persistent whistle in his ears, but with no luck. To his left, Soekka was just starting to push himself up from the snow as well. He was bleeding from a cut on his cheek but looked otherwise unharmed. Sprenger looked around. Tenni was on her knees, with one hand on her head, and the other searching for something in the snow. Apparently she had dropped her blade, but after a few moments she pulled it from under the snow and replaced it in on her waist. Behind him, Sprenger saw Kanto staggering to his feet.

Something was becoming audible through the whistling in Sprenger's ears. It was like someone was trying to talk but all Sprenger could hear was mumbling under the high-pitched whistle. Gradually, the whistle began to lighten and the talking became more understandable. Sprenger looked around for the source. No one was talking from what he could see. They were all still trying to gain their wits back as well. As the mumbling became clearer, Sprenger could pick up what the person was saying, and it became very clear who was talking now.

Sprenger turned around to where Juriah was leaning against the tree, but now he was kneeling in the snow and holding a hand to his head and squinting uncomfortably.

"Crazy, stupid, old man, stand back my ass," were a few things Sprenger could hear him saying, with heavy cursing woven between each statement.

Sprenger heard something fall in front of him. He quickly turned around, having remembered what just happened. Boulders were falling from the cliffs into a now very large hole at the center of what used to be the rockslide. Stones of several smaller sizes were scattered all around them, peppering the white snow along the base of the cliff.

Everyone seemed to regain their bearings at once, and stood quickly, remembering what was about to happen. Even Juriah became silent and cautiously drew his sword in anticipation as he rose to his feet in the snow.

Setdo nuzzled the back of Sprenger's elbow so Sprenger put his arm over his large head to assure him that he was fine.

Suddenly, Setdo's demeanor changed. He began growling at the entrance to the cliff, and Sprenger could feel his spiny hair beginning to rise under his hand. Everyone readied a blade. No one doubted what Setdo could sense approaching.

"Everyone hide," Kanto said softly.

Without taking their eyes off the entrance, everyone began stepping backwards. They hid behind a fallen tree and peered over the top. Juriah replaced his sword and joined them behind the log. Setdo crouched next to Sprenger at the end of the tree, where the last of its weathered roots remained. Even with his black top, Setdo was well-hidden lying in the dirty snow.

Soekka rose higher, to better peer over the log, but Kanto put a hand on his shoulder to stop him.

"Stay low," he whispered to Soekka.

"How long until we go in?" Soekka asked anxiously.

"We don't go in until we're sure the majority are out," Juriah answered. "We would not last long at all in there."

Soekka looked back to the entrance impatiently.

"Something moved!" Tenni whispered suddenly.

Everyone looked closer. At first, Sprenger couldn't see anything, but then he noticed the shadows shifting just beyond view. For a bit, there was no movement again, and everyone anxiously watched. Then something flickered for a brief moment just behind the shadows of the cave. It flickered again, then stopped. Gradually, it became larger and more frequent, and Sprenger realized what it was.

A huge forked tongue was examining the entrance to the cave, flicking up and down, smelling the air. Slowly, a giant purple snout began emerging from the shadows, the tongue darting in and out of the end.

Sprenger heard Tenni take in a small gasp.

"There's one of the females," Juriah grumbled.

As the Pyslith began slowly working its way out of the cave, Sprenger's gut began to clench. Its head was near the length of Sprenger's entire body, and as it moved farther from the cave, Sprenger could barely believe its girth. For several minutes, the Pyslith emerged from the cave, no end to its body seemed near, until finally the tail ended and the entire creature was visible before them.

It met fourty feet in length, easily, and had light purple scales that were reflective and smooth. Its underside was white, and only became visible when the creature lifted its head off the ground to examine something with its forked tongue. Its eyes were marble black and unblinking. It moved slowly back and forth in front of the entrance, curiously confirming its new freedom.

"It's beautiful," Soekka whispered to himself. He used the remnants of a small branch to support himself as he peered over the log.

The branch snapped under his weight, and the loud crack that accompanied it sent a cold prickle running up Sprenger's back. Soekka quickly dropped below the log and out of sight, along with everyone else.

The Pyslith ceased its examination of a large boulder and turned its head in their direction. It sent out its long black tongue to find their scent and began slithering their way.

"Idiot boy," Juriah snapped. "Everyone stay here, and stay hidden."

"Wait," Sprenger whispered, "what are you about to do?"

Juriah didn't answer, but rose to his full height, revealing himself from their hiding place. The Pyslith stopped and stared at him, smelling the air. It started pulling its body forward, near its head, and gradually began coiling up as it and Juriah stared at each other.

"What are you about to do?" Sprenger repeated.

Juriah pulled two blades from each of his sleeves. "We only came here for Sassor, and right now, our way is blocked. Their numbers won't be in our favor for much longer. I'll take care of her while we have the chance." He hopped over the log and began slowly walking towards the Pyslith.

Soekka's eyes widened. "No!" he pleaded, but as he began to rise, Kanto pushed him back down.

"Master Kanto, please!" Soekka begged. "Let me see if she recognizes me before we hurt her."

"Focus, Soekka," Kanto said sternly. "Don't let your emotions blur our goals. You heard what Lord Juriah said. Only Sassor will recognize you, if even him. We warned you that this would be dangerous and may require a fight. Let's see what Juriah does. He may need our help if others appear, and I expect you to be willing to do what is necessary if it comes to that."

Soekka took a breath and nodded, so Sprenger looked back over the log, along with everyone else.

Juriah was standing on a large boulder in front of the Pyslith, raising himself over the white sheets of snow around him.

"What's he doing?" Tenni whispered.

"He's staying out of the snow as much as possible," Kanto replied. "That way, he can move quickly if it strikes."

But that will only work once, Sprenger thought. *One strike will force him off that boulder and back into the snow. He'll need help.* Sprenger began to rise, but Kanto reached over Soekka and snatched his shirt, stopping him.

"You'll only get in his way," Kanto said, apparently knowing what Sprenger was thinking.

Juriah and the Pyslith just stared at one another for a moment. Then, without warning, Juriah threw one of his blades. It stuck in one of the female's giant black eyes. The Pyslith squirmed and let out a noise, the likes of which Sprenger had never heard before. It was an awful high-pitched shriek, coupled by discernible hisses. It began shaking its head in pain. As it opened its huge mouth to loose its horrible screech, its rows of long white fangs became visible all the way to the back of her mouth.

The female lunged from her coils, and headed full speed for Juriah, who crouched on the boulder, blade at the ready, and waited for her. As the female closed the distance, she raised her head off the ground, and when she was close enough, struck at Juriah with mouth agape.

Sprenger flinched as the Pyslith's head crashed over the top of the boulder, but Juriah spun to the side and landed in the snow. He jumped onto its neck and plunged his second blade behind the hinge of its jaw.

She screeched again and squirmed under Juriah, nearly shaking him loose, but he held onto his blade. He pulled the blade free to stab her again but flew forward as her tail wrapped around and slammed into his back like a giant whip.

Juriah was sent flying through the air, over all their heads, and landed in the snowbank behind where they were all hiding. He pushed himself up on all fours and shook the disorientation from his head. Juriah looked up as the Pyslith shrieked at him again.

She was squirming uncomfortably amongst her giant coils of body, attempting to remove the irritating blade in her eye, which was bleeding onto the snow below in small scarlet droplets.

Juriah pulled himself out of the snow and ran up next to Kanto.

"I can't tell if you're winning or not," Sprenger taunted.

"Shut it!" Juriah snapped back. He held his hand out to Kanto. "Give me that last clay jar." Without question, Kanto produced it from his pocket and handed it to Juriah, who used his blade to cut off the majority of the fuse. He held it out to Kanto impatiently. "Light it." Kanto pulled out his flint and managed to light it after the second try.

The sparks began falling from the fuse, as they had before, and Juriah hopped back over the log once again. He ran at the Pyslith with one hand holding the clay jar and the other gripping his blade.

The female ceased her squirming when she saw him approaching and lunged for him again. Juriah rolled over her snout and jammed his blade into the top of her head, using it as a handle to hold onto her as she thrashed. She raised her head far off the ground, forcing Juriah to release his blade, but he grabbed the crook of her mouth as he fell, and continued to hold on as she thrashed with irritation.

Sprenger was holding his breath through it all. He could see the fuse was nearly at its end in Juriah's hand. He almost yelled at Juriah to tell him to drop the jar but hesitated too long.

As the female began to shriek again, Juriah swung up and slammed the jar into the back of her mouth as she did. The female began thrashing violently once more, and when he saw the opportunity, Juriah released her mouth and slid down her neck until he jumped off her. She caught him midair with her giant tail and sent him violently tumbling through the snow once again.

The female cocked her head and struck at him while he lay in the snow but recoiled as her neck burst open with a boom. The snow all around her was instantly reddened with a shower of blood. Her head hit the ground as it was nearly completely severed, held onto her body by only a small chunk of muscle and skin. Her mouth was wide open, but nothing came out. She began convulsing violently, her body thrashed blindly, throwing blood in every direction.

Sprenger let out a long-held breath, as did Tenni. He looked over at Kanto, who watched intently, and then at Soekka, who was staring wide-eyed as if in shock. The only sound around them was the crunching of snow under the female as she squirmed around.

"He did it," Tenni whispered in disbelief.

Juriah slowly rose out of the snow to their right. He was breathing hard, and there was blood slowly moving down the side of his face. He just watched with a furrowed brow, as the female Pyslith squirmed in front of him.

"Alright," Kanto said, "remove your wool cloaks, and prepare yourselves." Kanto stood and hopped over the log but waited as the three of them pulled off their cloaks.

Sprenger folded his and hung it over a branch on the log tidily.

"Really?" Soekka scoffed. Sprenger noticed he had just thrown his behind them onto a snowy boulder.

"I don't want it to be wet for the way down," Sprenger defended.

"That's what you're worried about right now?" Tenni said in disbelief.

"Enough," Kanto snapped, irritated. "I can't think of a worse time for you lot to be bickering. Just be quiet and hurry!"

Even out here we get in trouble, Sprenger pouted.

The three of them hopped over the log and followed Kanto. Setdo joined Sprenger at his side as they all walked over to Juriah, who didn't take his eyes off the female as they approached him.

"What's next," Kanto asked Juriah when they came up next to him.

"The others will have heard that and be on their way," Juriah said seriously. "The numbers won't be in our favor for much longer." He finally looked away from the thrashing female and looked at Kanto. “Keep to your original plan. When the other two females appear, you draw them off and keep them distracted. We will stay out here and clear away any lesser Pysliths that come out. We’ll need that cave as empty as possible if Sassor doesn’t show and we have to go in after him.”

Kanto nodded his agreement.

Sprenger thought it incredibly strange that nothing was said about Juriah's recent success. Even a small amount of praise would seem earned. He wondered if this was something that was common amongst all scythe or if it was just these two.

A loud shrieking hiss echoed from the cave, pulling everyone’s apprehensive gaze over to the entrance. There was nothing there yet.

Kanto turned to face them. “This is about to get dangerous but focus and remember what you’ve learned. I have confidence in you lot.” He turned to Soekka. “Soekka, I know you feel conflicted right now, but remember that you hold no bond with these Pysliths yet. They are your opponents until you do.”

Soekka seemed to hesitate a moment, and Sprenger wondered if he would agree, but then he nodded. “I understand. I will do what I have to.”

“Good,” Kanto replied flatly.

Juriah pulled his sword from the sheath on his back. “Here they come.”

Everyone readied themselves with a blade as they watched the dark mouth of the cave start to move. Setdo crouched low by Sprenger, hunched his glossy black shoulders, raised the spiny hairs all over his body, and began growling.

Sprenger gulped into his dry throat.

Dozens of purple Pysliths of varying sizes began slithering out of the entrance of the cave, led by a second, equally massive female.

Chapter 44

Entering the Darkness

A swarm of Pysliths writhed and slithered over one another to get out of the mountain cave. They seemed eager to engulf themselves in the heat of the morning sun. At the center of their numbers was a second, fully-grown female Pyslith. Her girth was identical the first's; occluding the majority of the cave's black entrance. As she slowly examined the snow, dozens of forked tongues searched her surroundings, but most were drawn to the commotion the first female was causing in the clearing in front of them. She was still violently thrashing around with a nearly-severed head and her mouth opening and closing aimlessly.

The second female headed straight for her. With her huge forked-tongue, she examined the other female, and pulled back when she was almost hit by a convulsing coil.

Sprenger and the others stood at the ready. It seemed they hadn't been noticed yet with the dying female drawing all of the attention. The lesser Pysliths were exploring everything around them and leaving nothing unexamined. The largest any of them got was only about the size of the second Pyslith that appeared at the stream, but most were smaller than even that.

Sprenger looked over at Tenni and Soekka, who each gave him a ready nod. Kanto pulled six throwing blades out of his vest and held one between each knuckle. He carefully watched the new female without emotion, but Sprenger could sense the energy of the air about to change.

Kanto took a readied stance and leaned forward in preparation. "Ready?" he whispered.

"Go," Juriah said softly.

Kanto ran at the new female, and threw his first hand of blades at her head. They stuck in the side of her neck, just behind her head, and barely seemed to penetrate through her scales. They were far too small to really do any damage, but they were only meant to get her attention. She raised her head off the ground, arched her muscled purple neck, and shrieked intimidatingly. Kanto slid to a stop in the snow and threw his second hand of blades, which stuck into the underside of her jaw. She didn't flinch at the blades, but lunged for Kanto, who sprinted off, up the mountain. The female slithered hastily after him, crushing snow and trees alike, before the two of them disappeared over the ridge.

Sprenger realized he shouldn't have been watching Kanto. Instead, he should have been watching his surroundings. He turned just as a small Pyslith struck at him, but Setdo leapt onto it, tried biting it on its writhing neck, but missed. The two rolled in the snow as the Pyslith hissed in anger and began wrapping its purple body around him before it began squeezing Setdo in its coils.

Sprenger ran towards them to help, but stopped when the Pyslith shrieked in pain as Setdo's quill-like hair sprang to its ends, and stabbed through its scales. As it loosened its grip on him, Setdo jumped on its head and crunched down on its skull, killing it. Setdo dropped the still-squirming body and ran back to Sprenger's side.

Sprenger turned around to see Tenni and Soekka standing in front of two Pysliths that were holding themselves up to eye level, with mouths agape and hissing viciously.

Sprenger and Setdo ran for them. Setdo, again, jumped on top of the closest Pyslith and crushed its squirming body into the snow with his heavy paw.

Sprenger quickly moved up next to him and stabbed it through the top of the head while Setdo had it pinned down.

Tenni side-stepped the other Pyslith as it struck at her and brought her blade down on its body as it passed. It shrieked and quickly turned back on her, but Soekka stepped in front of her and jammed his blade under its jaw as it struck. He and Tenni removed their blades and jumped back as it struck at them again. Tenni backhanded it away, but it was quick to return to strike again. Setdo jumped on it from behind and sunk his teeth into its reflective purple scales. Its shrieks were short lived as Setdo began viciously thrashing his head from side to side, until the Pyslith was still and he was sure it was dead.

Sprenger heard snow crunching behind him and turned just as a large Pyslith struck at him. Sprenger flipped back and avoided it, but the Pyslith pursued him through the snow. Sprenger fended it off as best he could but his blade was doing little damage, and only seemed to aggravate it further when he tried slicing it defensively.

Their scales were thick and their bodies were pure muscle, and those were if Sprenger was able to make contact with his blade at all. The writhing, slender bodies were difficult to stab amidst all the movement, and there were rarely pauses between startling-fast strikes. As Sprenger knocked its head away with his foot, he was caught off guard by its tail coming around and slapping him in the side, sending him sliding across the snow. Sprenger glanced over to Soekka and Tenni for help, but they were busy with Pysliths of their own, and he could hear Setdo wrestling with one behind him. The Pyslith slithered through the snow after Sprenger, then rose to above Sprenger's head to strike.

The large Pyslith struck, but Juriah slid in front of Sprenger with his sword crossed in front of him protectively. He dug his toes into the snow as he absorbed the impact of the strike and the snake bit down on his sword. Juriah managed to stop it but was struggling to push back against its muscled neck. With a grunt, Juriah spun and pulled his sword free of its mouth, taking the top half of its head with it. The Pyslith began thrashing as the others had, spilling blood from the bottom half of its head.

Juriah wasted no time before running over to aid Tenni and Soekka, who were each fending off Pysliths with fading success. Before Sprenger could push himself up, Juriah had the attention of both Tenni and Soekka's Pysliths. Both of the students were standing back, with their blades raised, but Juriah showed no sign of requiring anyone's help as he taunted both snakes to focus on him.

Sprenger sat up in the snow and looked around. There were Pyslith bodies scattered everywhere in the clearing outside the cave. Some were still moving, but many were not. Juriah had left quite the trail of the serpents' bodies behind him while everyone else was dealing with only a handful.

There was a clank of fangs striking steel as Juriah used his thin sword to parry a strike from one of the Pysliths. Juriah smashed the other Pyslith's head under his foot as it struck at him and sliced the first up its white belly as it, too, struck again. As it fell away with exposed organs, Juriah released the other from under his foot, and decapitated it as it began rising from the snow.

There was a moment of silence that followed the limp body crunching into the snow beneath it. Gradually, everyone caught their breath after confirming no other Pysliths were near. Everyone was blood-soaked and panting heavily, even Setdo.

Everyone seemed to react at once when they heard snapping twigs and crunching bark behind them. As the group turned, Sprenger groaned. There were several Pysliths wrapped around trees, staring at them with black eyes from the forest. Their scales spiraled in indiscernible coils around the trunks of the trees, raising them completely off the ground. All of the snakes kept their necks poised to strike, as they silently watched the clearing and smelled the air with their tongues.

Juriah stepped forward. "They're trying to get out of the snow. They need to be in the sun to warm up and the snow is cooling them too quickly. I don't think they'll attack us, unless we get too close to the trees. This is our chance." He turned to Sprenger. "You lot need to get into that cave, now. I'll make sure nothing goes in after you." He looked over at Setdo. "You stay with me." Setdo growled softly, so Sprenger put a hand on his side.

Sprenger looked over at Tenni and Soekka. "You guys ready?"

Tenni and Soekka both nodded, though nervously.

"Then let's go," Sprenger said with fake confidence.

All of them ran for the cave, and when they got close, Juriah stopped. Seeing him do so, Setdo stopped too. Sprenger, Tenni, and Soekka slowed as they approached the entrance. Only Sprenger stopped to look over his shoulder at Juriah and Setdo, and they stared back until Sprenger turned away and followed Tenni and Soekka over the piles of rocks and boulders and into the cave. Sprenger suddenly felt exposed without Sedto and Juriah nearby, but it was a feeling he pushed from his mind so that he could focus.

They didn't make it far into the darkness before Tenni told them to wait. She knelt and pulled her small pack over her shoulder. "It's getting too dark," she whispered. "The entrance looks to be the only light." She pulled a round, palm-size glass bulb out of her pack. Inside, Sprenger could see it was full of wax and had a black wick. "Master Kanto gave me this after Lord Scythrith gave him the exploding jars." She pulled out her small flint and a thick matchstick and worked for a few minutes to light the stick. After she lit it, she lit the wick of the candle and held it up to Soekka as the jar began to glow. "Here," she said softly. "You need to lead the way." After a brief hesitation, Soekka took it gratefully.

When Soekka turned to start walking into the dark of the cave, Sprenger looked over at Tenni. "Glad one of us came prepared."

She smirked at him as she flipped her braid over her shoulder. "We all have a part to play in this."

The group slowly and cautiously moved forward into the humid darkness. The cave was warm, dripping water from the walls and ceiling, and reeked of the hot spring. Under their feet, they noticed a constant crunching and rustling, which, to their dismay, they found to be piles of old tube-like skins covering the cave floor.

Sprenger didn't complain, he much preferred the skin to the living ones right now, which all seemed to have moved outside. Though all of them were nervous of any shadows in the cave that Soekka couldn't immediate illuminate with the candle. Skins also made it difficult for there to be any silent movement in the cave, which only added to the anxiety that anything in here would quickly know where they were. Sprenger took some comfort in thinking that it might warn them if a Pyslith is slithering up to them, but it still didn't keep his heart from jumping every time his feet made any echoing noise.

All three students were tense as they moved deeper into the cave. No one spoke, even when one would stumble on a stalagmite or bump into the rocky siding. Then, gradually, the walls began to drift farther apart and the cave began to widen. The humidity became thicker, until it was nearly a fog of steam around them. The candle provided poor light in the larger area, and it didn't carry far through the steam in the cave.

Soekka slowed, so Tenni and Sprenger looked around him to see what got his attention. The cave's width was almost twice what it had been at the entrance; farther across than the three of them could reach if they stood at arm's length with one another. When Soekka stopped, Tenni and Sprenger went to either side of him and looked around. The fog had thinned as they stepped out into a large cavern. There was the reflection of the candle's light off water up ahead. In front of them, occupying the majority of the cavern floor, was a steaming pond that had small waves moving across it every few seconds. The pool extended all the way to the end of the cavern and nearly to each of its sides. It rippled slightly under the faint light of the candle, and Sprenger could faintly hear movement in different areas of the cave.

Soekka took a breath, and continued forward, towards the water's edge. He held out the light further and froze. At the edge of the water, near the back of the cavern, were five large Pysliths. They were larger than what could fit down the stream, and larger than most that had just been outside, with the exception of the two full-grown females. They were all tightly wrapped around stalagmites or coiled up near the side of the pond, watching the three of them with tongues simultaneously examining the air, but none moved.

Soekka looked away from them and held the candle out even farther. They were at the back of the cave, which left only one place for Sassor to be. Soekka stepped up to the edge of the water and held the candle out in front of him as far as he could reach over the water.

Tenni and Sprenger stepped back and watched patiently as Soekka stood confidently at the water's edge, holding the candle at arm's length, waiting for what he hoped was there.

Tenni stepped closer to Sprenger when the waves in the pond became larger and more violent as something stirred in the water. The waves began splashing up over the sides of the rocks and crashing into one another. The water even splashed over Soekka's feet, but he didn't move a bit.

The surface of the pond became rough as two massive figures began to rise from the dark water. Sprenger went wide-eyed as he looked up at the third mature female, and almost dwarfing her in size, was Sassor.

Chapter 45

What is Required

Sprenger could feel Tenni move closer to him as they stared up at the third mature female and Sassor, both of which were arching their necks to avoid the rocky ceiling of the cave as they stared down through the steam at Soekka's faint light. The female was the same as the two outside, though difficult to tell in the dark, Sprenger knew her to be a light purple with the exception of her white underside.

Sassor trumped her presence, however. He was much thicker in the body, and pure white throughout his girth. His black tongue, larger than most of the Pysliths outside, slowly moved in and out of his dripping, white snout.

Both Sassor and the female seemed to stare down at Soekka with intent curiosity, who remained where he was at the water's edge, holding the only source of light in the cave. There was only the sound of the waves churning calmly for a moment, as Soekka stared up at his parents' Feral Beasts.

Slowly, Sassor lowered his head to examine Soekka with his giant forked-tongue, causing another bout of waves to go crashing over everyone's feet. Soekka stood confidently as the water brushed his ankles and Sassor moved closer and closer. Sassor's tongue touched Soekka's arm when flicked out to examine the air, which caused them both to flinch back a bit, as if Sassor wasn't aware how close he was to Soekka.

Seeming taken aback by the unintended contact, Sassor recoiled slightly, but then moved forward again. He lowered his massive head to stare at Soekka directly, with a single eye, large enough to reflect all three of them on its glossy white surface. As his head got closer to the light, Sprenger noticed something different about it. His eyes were not the same as all of the others'. They were not marble black, but white and cloudy.

He's blind, Sprenger realized.

Tenni and Sprenger flinched as they heard movement to their right, and turned to see the other Pysliths moving towards them from the back of the cave. Soekka turned as well, distracted by the commotion, and likewise started preparing to defend himself from the smaller serpents.

Seeming to notice the change in Soekka's attention, Sassor raised his head again, and began smelling the air with his tongue. Everyone faltered back as he suddenly loosed a deep, shrieking hiss that forced the three of them to cover their ears. The cave echoed and vibrated with it. Sprenger could almost feel it pulsing through his entire body, just as strongly as he heard it. Luckily, for all of them, it was brief. The shriek ceased as quickly as it began, and everyone took a sigh of relief before uncovering their ears.

When Sprenger looked back up, the smaller Pysliths had stopped their advance around the water and were just watching them cautiously from their piles of coils.

Seeming to have accomplished what he wished, Sassor lowered his head back to Soekka, who continued to stand his ground, though with clearly shaken nerves. Sprenger watched Soekka nervously as he and Sassor regrouped. After a pause, Soekka took a deep breath and stepped up to Sassor's head as the giant serpent rested it on the wet rocky floor in front of him. There was no fear, no hesitation, only confidence as Soekka stared into Sassor's cloudy eyes. *Please be careful,* Sprenger wanted to say.

Slowly, Soekka lifted his free hand and reached out to Sassor's snout. There was a small pause before they touched, but then Soekka laid his hand on Sassor's white scales.

Suddenly, the water became chaotic as Sassor's body began bursting from the water, and Sprenger watched as Soekka, still with a hand on Sassor's snout, disappeared under mountains of giant white coils and water.

"No!" Sprenger yelled, but Soekka had already disappeared behind a wall of white scales that seemed to engulf the entire cave. Only a small bit of light from the candle showed through the top of Sassor's coils now.

Sprenger stepped towards him, but the purple female came whipping around Sassor and towered over them all as she gave Sprenger a fierce hiss of warning. She rose to a striking position, and revealed her large fangs, but didn't strike. She, and everything else, disappeared when the light from Soekka's candle vanished completely under Sassor's coils.

Tenni blindly grabbed Sprenger's arm. "Let's go," she yelled. When Sprenger tried to pull his arm free, she only tightened her grip. "There's nothing more we can do now." She yanked his arm again, and he reluctantly ran along with her.

Tenni ran back in the direction they had come and used her hand to follow the wall of the cave, all while pulling Sprenger along with her other hand. Soon, the light from the entrance was enough to lead them out. The two of them climbed over the fallen boulders of the entrance, and winced at the bright light of the day reflected off the snow.

As the two of them moved over the fallen rocks, they were met by Kanto and Juriah running up to them. Both were looking like they just escaped a battle. Juriah still had dried blood on the side of his face, and Kanto looked to be fairly scraped up as well.

Kanto took an anxious step towards them. “What is happening?” They could see his eyes darting from them to the cave, looking for Soekka.

Tenni and Sprenger took a moment to catch their breath, then Tenni spoke. “We found Sassor at the back of the cave. Soekka’s in there with him now.” Tenni shook her head. “Something was happening with him and Sassor and we had no choice but to leave.”

Tenni flinched when she looked over to her left. When Sprenger looked over, he jumped as well.

Sitting silently in a large pile of its own purple coils, black eyes staring directly at them, was the second female Pyslith. Her tongue slowly moved in and out of her snout as she eyed them hungrily. Kanto’s throwing blades were still visible in the side of her head but they seemed to not be causing any discomfort.

Juriah came over to them and looked over at the giant female as well. “We were attempting to fend her off for the last several minutes. Right after you lot went in, she returned and we could only annoy her enough to keep her from following you into the cave.” He turned back to look at them. “We heard Sassor’s call from inside, and when *she* heard it, she stopped her assault and has been like that ever since.”

“That’s what happened to us,” Sprenger exclaimed. “We were about to be attacked by a group of them in the cave, but Sassor stopped them.”

Tenni looked up to Kanto. “That’s a good sign, right?”

Kanto offered no indication of an answer on his face. “For all we know it is, but for all we know-”

"Soekka could be dead," Sprenger whispered solemnly, as he turned back to look into the black hole in the side of the mountain.

-<>-

Soekka had one spine-tingling chill after another run up his back as he stood his ground, surrounded by walls of muscular white coils. All around him, Soekka was encased in a room of white scales, reflective and smooth under his faint candlelight. Now, as though in private conversation, Sassor's massive head was the only thing within the white room with Soekka. Sassor was staring directly at him with huge blind eyes, and Soekka just stared back into them. Sassor's head was larger than Soekka's entire body, and his milky eyes the size of larger dinner platters.

The two just stared at each other in silence for what felt like hours. Soekka didn't know what to do. He tried to remember what Jacob and Juriah had told him about creating a bond with a Feral Beast. Something about there always being some kind of requirement. Unfortunately, he had no idea what it was for Sassor.

Soekka thought for a moment. *What all did Lord Scythrith tell us about the Feral Beasts? He said they were of great size and intelligence.* He contemplated that for a moment. *Great intelligence...*

"Can you understand me, great beast?" Soekka asked curiously.

Another chill ran up Soekka's spine as the air around him began vibrating as Sassor let out a deep humming noise that seemed to shake through all of his scales.

"Great beast, Sassor," Soekka began again. "My name is Soekka, son of Sortan."

The space around Soekka shook as Sassor began humming again.

"My parents were your Nymphigori. They died fighting by your side, or so I've been told." Sassor remained silent, so Soekka continued. "I ask to take my parent's place as your Nymphigori. Though," Soekka paused in hesitation, "I don't know what is required of me to do so. There is no one alive that knows. This may be the end of the Pyslith's bond with scythe, unless you accept me and help me to do what is necessary."

Sassor was silent and still. Soekka began to worry that his offer would not be taken, or that he didn't understand it as well as Soekka was hoping. Maybe he should not have admitted he didn't know what to do. Maybe he should have been more confident about it. Soekka's mind started to race on how to salvage the situation.

Then, Sassor's head began slowly moving towards him. Soekka stood his ground, though there was nowhere for him to go anyway. Sassor sent his giant tongue out and brushed it up Soekka's front. The tongue was smooth and slimy, and Soekka grimaced away from the forked end as it flicked up close to his face. After feeling where he was, Sassor moved his head closer until the front of his snout gently touched Soekka's chest.

Soekka's shirt fluttered as Sassor released a puff of air through his slit-nostrils.

Soekka just stood there, not sure what to do.

Sassor released another puff of air, this time pushing Soekka's silk shirt up and revealing his stomach until it fell back down.

"My shirt?" Soekka asked confused. Sassor hummed again. Soekka didn't understand, but he put down the candle on the stone ground and began taking off his shirt. As he did so, he felt his fingers become sticky. He tossed his shirt aside and heard it slop onto the wet ground with a clank from the blade in his sleeve. He knelt and retrieved the candle, then held it over his hand and saw that it was blood on his fingers that caused it to be sticky. Soekka paused. *My shirt was covered in Pyslith blood.* Worry suddenly swept through Soekka that Sassor knew he had killed Pysliths. *He could probably tell what kind of blood it was,* Soekka realized nervously.

Soekka felt a small sense of panic, but he slowly rose again, now bare-chested. There was silence, and Soekka wondered if he should say something about it.

He thought for a moment, then spoke. "I apologize for the blood but-" Soekka was going to continue to defend himself and explain how they were attacked, but Sassor began humming again.

What did I say? He thought confused. "Blood?" Soekka asked skeptically.

Sassor gave another deep rustling hum and air buzzed all around Soekka.

"The Pyslith blood?" Soekka added, but Sassor remained silent. He thought about it for another moment. "My blood?" Soekka asked hesitantly.

Sassor gave another excited hum, and then began using his tongue to examine Soekka's arm and followed it down to his hand. It was the hand that had Pyslith blood on it already, and Sassor shifted his massive head slightly to examine Soekka's other hand. When he discovered it clean, he hummed again.

Soekka raised his hand and examined his palm, not sure what to do. Sassor pulled his head back and began flipping his tongue up, slapping the end of his snout with it.

Soekka realized what he had to do, and nodded his understanding, then realizing the pointlessness of that, said it aloud.

Sassor gave a small hum of agreement, and then sat silently waiting.

Soekka knelt down, set the candle on the damp ground once more, and began rifling through his shirt for his blade. He pulled it free and stood again. He looked at his palm and thought about what he was about to do, then wondered if his parents had scars on their palms that he was too young to remember seeing.

Soekka released a ready breath. He held his blade down to his palm, and without hesitation, yanked it across his skin. He winced and clenched his hand shut, but slowly opened it to see blood beginning to pool in his palm and then drip to the cave floor.

Sassor began humming excitedly again as his tongue seemed to sense the new blood.

Soekka stepped forward, and reached his bloody palm out, ignoring the stinging feel of the separated skin.

Sassor's humming intensified as Soekka got closer.

There was only a brief hesitation when Soekka let out an anxious breath, then he laid his palm on the tip of Sassor's enormous smooth snout.

Everything around him, the air, the ground, and the coils surrounding him, began vibrating in Sassor's powerful and deep hum. Soekka stood there as the air and ground around him literally pulsed with energy and he felt Sassor's humming run up his arm and engulf his body. It was the strangest and most exhilarating sensation Soekka had ever felt.

Soekka just stood, wide-eyed, as he allowed the sensation to engulf him. A tear ran down Soekka's cheek. *I'm a Nymphigori.*

Chapter 46

The Nymphigori of Sassor

Soekka stood frozen to the spot with his hand on Sassor's giant white snout. He savored every second of it until the humming slowly began to fade away and everything seemed to calm. When it ceased all together, and everything fell still and quiet, Soekka huffed, exhilarated. He did it. Admittedly, with a great deal of help from Sassor, but he did it. He had bonded with Sassor and become a Nymphigori. He knew it, because he could feel it.

Soekka slowly removed his hand from Sassor's snout but cringed as the blood from his fresh wound stuck to Sassor's smooth scales. Left behind was a smear of red from Soekka's hand, and when he removed it, Sassor began smelling it repeatedly with his giant forked tongue.

Sassor, too, began to pull away and gradually uncoiled himself from around Soekka.

Fresh, humid air washed over them, and Soekka realized he was sweating. He looked around for his shirt, but Soekka seemed to have wiped it away when he was uncoiling his body.

I'll have to hope my cloak isn't too wet for the trip back down, Soekka thought as he glumly realized that he didn't need to remove his shirt after all. He felt rather foolish standing in the mountain cave, exposed like this.

He looked back up at Sassor, who was blindly staring ahead, and now being examined by the large female that hadn't left his side. She curiously brushed over him, and moved to his head, where she, too, began taking in the scent of Soekka's blood on Soekka's snout. Soekka noticed the other Pysliths beginning to slither over to Sassor as well, but they did not come to his head.

"I have a lot to tell you," Soekka said to Sassor, who looked in Soekka's general direction at the sound of his voice, "but right now, I fear others are looking for you. If you are willing, my teacher and team are here with me, and we will lead you to a safe place by the village. You will have to stay hidden, but you will be free of this cave."

Sassor, and even the female, hummed and hissed happily.

Then suddenly, Soekka jumped as Sassor lunged at him. The last thing Soekka saw was the pink inside of Sassor's mouth and black tongue as he was engulfed by the massive serpent.

-<>-

Everyone was standing around restlessly outside the mountain cave. It had been a while since Sprenger and Tenni had returned, and still there was no evidence of what was going on inside the dark tunnel.

Tenni was rifling through her small pack, making sure she knew where everything was, and if she was missing anything. Kanto was standing farther away from them, surveying the area for anything dangerous. He spent particular time watching the female that was still curled in giant coils off to the side of them, but she hadn't moved from that spot since she took her place there. Even still, Kanto seemed not to trust that she would remain inactive.

Juriah was wandering around, ridding the area of the small Pysliths, which continued to attack once they became warm enough to return to the snow. Of the dozens that emerged from the cave, there were hardly any left. Juriah insisted that if their numbers did not remain in check, then they might as well burn

Durado to the ground themselves. No one argued with him, not that he really gave them an opportunity to.

Sprenger was sitting on a boulder with Setdo curled up around him, just above where Tenni was organizing her things. The young Pantrore would occasionally pester Sprenger for some attention nudging him with his nose or bumping him with his head and chuffing, but was usually preoccupied watching anything that moved near them with intent eyes. Even with all the surrounding dangers, Sprenger felt safe laying against Setdo's stomach. His mind stopped focusing a while ago, and now he was contemplating what to tell Granny Karla if he didn't come back with Soekka. He had a nervous knot in his stomach, but this was different than normal. This was a knot of worry and dread that he had never really felt before. He also thought about how they would manage to stop such a massive creature if he turned on them. They discussed before that if Sassor didn't bond with Soekka, that he couldn't be allowed to be free. After seeing Sassor, Sprenger doubted even Konn would have an easy time with a fight like that.

Suddenly, Setdo's head turned and his ears perked, just as Sprenger sat upright. Tenni and Kanto turned around and looked into the cave. A low vibrating hum was echoing from inside the darkness. Sprenger could even feel the boulder he was sitting on start to vibrate. It lasted for a few minutes, then stopped. Nothing moved nor made a sound after it ceased.

"What was that?" Tenni whispered to Sprenger.

Sprenger didn't look at her. He just kept staring at the cave's entrance. "I don't know, but I hope it was a good thing."

Suddenly, Sprenger could hear something. The cave was booming as something inside moved towards them.

Setdo stood, with his spiny fur beginning to raise all over his body, as he turned to face the entrance of the cave. Sprenger and Tenni quickly jumped to their feet and ran over to Kanto. They all pulled a blade ready and waited.

They could hear something big moving and crashing its way up the cave, and Sprenger had a pretty good idea what it was. His suspicions were confirmed as Sassor's giant white head came smashing through the entrance, knocking down several boulders from the sides and roof.

Sprenger gawked as he saw Sassor for the first time in the light. He appeared even larger now, and his white scales shimmered all the brighter. There was one thing in particular that Sprenger was looking for but couldn't find, and that was Soekka.

Everyone was forced to abandon their positions and flee to a safer distance, as Sassor pulled himself entirely from the cave and began filling the open space with his massive girth. He lifted his head stories off the ground, then paused and licked the air with his giant black tongue. After a brief moment of examining the air, he blindly looked towards the area their squad was standing.

Everyone readied themselves nervously, even Kanto. If Sassor attacked, there would be very little that they could do to fend him off.

After a moment of examining the air, Sassor arched his neck and lowered his head to the ground, snout first. He opened his mouth, and began pushing something out of his throat.

Sprenger nearly gagged as a body fell out of Sassor's mouth and hit the snowy ground. He could tell by the black hair and pants that it was a shirtless Soekka, though alive or not, Sprenger couldn't tell.

Soekka unexpectedly flipped over in the snow to look up at Sassor from his back as Sassor raised his head again. Soekka's expression seemed to be just as shocked at what happened as the rest of them were to see it.

"Soekka!" Sprenger blurted excitedly and began running up to him.

Soekka remained sitting on the ground, staring wide-eyed at Sassor, seeming to still be uncomfortable with the idea of being thrown-up.

Sprenger slid to a halt in front of him and offered him a hand up. Soekka took it gratefully. "You did it," Sprenger whispered excitedly.

Soekka smirked humbly at him. He looked up at Sassor, who was staring down from a great height, though not directly, but close. "Please don't do that again," Soekka said. Sassor just flicked his tongue at him.

Sprenger and Soekka turned as Tenni and Kanto walked up to them. Kanto gave Soekka a very small bow, and Tenni copied him.

"Well done, Soekka," Kanto congratulated as warmly as Kanto was capable of. "Though they may not know it, you've made your village proud. You've certainly made me proud." Soekka smiled and gave him a bow of thanks.

Tenni smiled at him. "This goes without saying, but I bet you've made your parents proud too."

Soekka smiled even bigger at that.

"It's not possible," someone growled behind them. Everyone turned to see Juriah standing there. He was alternating giving Soekka and Sassor unreadable looks. "How did you do it without knowing the requirements?"

"Well," Soekka began, but as Juriah began stepping forward, Sassor unexpectedly tensed. Juriah stopped where he was and watched Sassor suspiciously.

Sassor licked the air once more, then shifted his head and stared in Juriah's direction. He began hissing deeply and angrily, his mouth opening slightly.

Soekka looked up. "Sassor, that's-". Sassor unexpectedly struck at Juriah with a loud shrieking hiss. Sprenger saw Juriah step off Sassor's nose as it reached him and go flipping through the air before they were all knocked over by Sassor's body whipping past them after Juriah.

A wave of snow and mud rolled over Sprenger as Sassor swam past. When he pushed himself out of the snow, Sprenger saw Sassor striking madly at Juriah's scent and Juriah hand-springing backwards to avoid one strike after another.

Sprenger frantically looked around for assistance. Everyone was pushing themselves out of the snow and attempting to regain their bearings. Setdo shook snow off of his back and growled angrily.

Soekka ran up next to Sprenger and watched the startling scene unfold as well. "What's Sassor doing?" he asked, shocked and nervous.

He recognizes Juriah, Sprenger realized. "I don't know," Sprenger lied.

Kanto came up next to them. "Everyone stay back until Sassor calms down."

"Juriah will be dead by then," Sprenger argued.

Nobody answered, not seeming to know what to do. Sprenger called for Setdo, who came up to his side. *If Setdo picks up Juriah, he can move fast enough to get him away from Sassor.*

Sprenger looked back over at Juriah, who was dodging one strike after another, each as close as the last. Sassor's attempts were smashing ground, rocks, and trees alike, as he tried to blindly follow Juriah's movements.

Suddenly, Soekka ran towards them, and Kanto barely missed grabbing ahold of him. "I'm his Nymphigori," Soekka called over his shoulder, "he'll listen to me."

"How would *you* know? You've only been a Nymphigori for a few minutes!" Sprenger yelled back to him but Soekka either didn't hear him or ignored him.

Juriah rolled out of the way as Sassor struck past him open-mouthed, yanked his sword from its sheath and stood waiting for Sassor to turn around. Sassor seemed to lose track of him for a moment and began frantically smelling the air and the snow for his scent.

When he caught it, he whipped his head around and shrieked again, but Juriah stood where he was, sword in hand, ready to fight back somehow.

Sassor headed for Juriah, but before he reached him, Soekka jumped on Sassor's massive head. "Stop!" Soekka yelled desperately. Much to Sprenger's surprise, Sassor did so.

The giant snake stopped where he was, then slowly started to lift Soekka stories off the ground as he began coiling up his body underneath himself, then started hissing deeply. Soekka remained spread-eagle on Sassor's head, relying on the Pyslith's gentle movement to not fall to the ground that was now a considerable distance below him.

"No one here is your enemy!" Soekka yelled. "I promise!"

Sassor did not hum at this, but remained silent, seemingly quelled by Soekka for the time being.

He doesn't seem to agree, Sprenger thought nervously as he watched Sassor's cloudy eyes.

-<>-

Tranis could tell Phenex was disappointed that the shirtless boy stopped Sassor before he had killed Juriah. Tranis was disappointed too. He would have enjoyed seeing Juriah of the Hessiets eaten by a Pyslith.

He jumped in the way, Tranis thought, surprised. “That boy has made a bond with Sassor,” he whispered to Phenex. “We’re too late.”

Phenex didn’t respond to him, he just continued to look down on the events taking place beneath them.

The two of them were watching from the ridgeline, crouched behind a boulder and looking down at the clearing below, where they could see everyone. Master Kanto was standing with two of his students: a girl and the spiky-haired boy.

Even more shocking than Sassor was that next to them, was a young Pantrore. Tranis didn’t know that any of them were still alive, but now that he saw one, he wasn’t really surprised. In fact, he would have been more surprised to find out that Juriah had done what he was supposed to do and turned them all over to the council.

Out in the center of the clearing was Sassor, who Tranis could still hear hissing angrily at Juriah. The open glade was covered with evidence of Sassor’s furry. Barely a foot of ground remained untouched by it.

On Sassor’s head was the black-haired boy. *Sortan’s son,* Tranis realized. Tranis never liked Sortan. He was a very unkind man, and respected few others in the scythe world. Tranis had the brief displeasure of assisting him during the wars, and then came to find out that he, too, was in league with Demaedura. The two remained respectful of that fact, but never cared for one another’s company.

Underneath where they were hiding on the ridge was another, rather large, purple Pyslith. It was curled up and watching with black eyes, curiously tasting the air with her tongue. Tranis knew it was a female, for only the males were white, and there was only ever one male.

Slowly, Sassor lowered Sortan's son to the ground, and the boy slid off his head. Master Kanto and the others ran over to them and began talking. Tranis couldn't hear them but he could make out most of what they were saying by watching their lips. Tranis wasn't much of a combat scythe, but he was an excellent spy.

"They're talking about what just happened, and Sortan's son is trying to calm Sassor," Tranis explained to Phenex quietly, still hoping to prove his worth to the Adimortis. He watched for a bit longer. "They're talking about leaving now, and how they can keep Sassor out of sight until they get somewhere, I can't tell where. Kanto wants to leave as soon as possible."

"We have what we need," Phenex said in little more than a grumble as he stood. "We'll head back to the ruins and then we will leave Durado's borders." He turned and began walking away.

"What do you mean we have what we need?" Tranis asked confused. "We're too late. Sassor is under Durado's control again."

Phenex didn't stop, so Tranis went after him. When he was close, Phenex said, "This is better than we originally hoped. Lone Feral Beasts would be extremely difficult to control. Each of them have a list of requirements that must be met and we would need to find someone that meets them. Their Nymphigoris' loyalty, however, can be swayed much easier. Lord Demaedura will easily be able to take control of a Nymphigori that young."

Tranis felt an ironic pity for the young scythe. *That poor boy. He has no idea what demons he has just attracted to himself.*

Chapter 47

Tense Descent

Crunching snow echoed all around them as heavy bodies slithered down the mountain. Stealth was not the group's priority at the moment. They were in a rush and on guard for anyone that may see them returning from the mountains. Before they started their return, Kanto explained to them that they had only accomplished the first dangerous part of the mission. From this point on, secrecy was their mission, and it wouldn't be just their lives on the line should they fail. Though there was less of a worry while they were in the mountains, everyone proceeded with cautionary steps, wondering what would happen if they were to be seen.

The return journey down the mountain was one that Sprenger would not have believed if he hadn't been experiencing it firsthand. He was being escorted by the two species of Feral Beasts that his village once held as allies, and neither was supposed to exist.

Master Kanto was the only one that walked behind Sprenger. In front of him was Tenni, Soekka ahead of her, and Juriah leading the way a fair distance ahead of all of them. To Sprenger's right was Setdo, who stayed close when he could, but frequently veered away from the path to explore the nearby terrain. To Sprenger's left was Sassor, who was too large to even see over.

Sassor kept his head near Soekka's side, who kept a reassuring hand on him whenever possible. The two had not been more than an arm's length from one another since they began their return journey. It became quickly apparent that Sassor was dependent on Soekka to follow any sort of path. Sassor would search for Soekka if Soekka didn't make his presence known for too long, and Soekka was quickly learning to keep his hand on the massive serpent at all times to reassure him that he was near.

Despite the short time, Soekka was already having some trouble controlling and communicating with Sassor. When they returned to the pine tree where they had made camp and left their belongings, they were all suddenly forced out when Sassor tried following Soekka underneath. When Soekka tried pushing him back, Sassor started raising his head, but became trapped under the branches and ended up breaking most of them off and littering the group with woody debris. Sprenger now shared Juriah's worry about bringing such a creature near his village, especially since he and Soekka shared a home that Sassor may try to follow into someday.

Sprenger watched the giant Pyslith's white scales move next to him as they continued down the mountain. Out in the trees, Sprenger could hear the females making their way through the underbrush and occasional snow. They had stayed close to the group, ever since Sassor had emerged from the cave, but never uncomfortably so. They chose to keep their distance and only made sure to keep Sassor in their sights. There were only the five lesser-Pysliths from the hot spring that remained after Juriah cleared out the forest. Much to Sprenger's disgust, when the group began to depart, the females laid their heads on the ground and opened their mouths. The smaller Pysliths eagerly swam into their mouths, and Sprenger had not seen them emerge since they left the cave the day before. Even when they tried to make camp that night, Sprenger had thought they would release them, but all three of the giant Pysliths simply coiled up and waited for morning.

How can they even stay alive in there? Sprenger thought, wondering what it would be like to be carried inside something's mouth like that. He reminded himself that Soekka shared a similar experience, and that he must remember to ask him about it when they got home.

Sprenger looked ahead at Soekka. He now had his wool cloak back on and retrieved another shirt from his pack under the pine (before Sassor insisted on joining him underneath). He had his old air of confidence back and Sprenger could tell that his mind was finally at ease. Though Sprenger could never put it into words, he could always tell when something was off about Soekka, and for the last few weeks there had definitely been something wrong. Now the thing about Soekka that Sprenger didn't realize he missed until it was gone, was back. Sprenger was glad for that.

A new thought crossed Sprenger's mind that gave him an excited smirk. Now that their mission was a success, Soekka was going to be training as a Nymphigori alongside him and Setdo. That idea was an entertaining thought for much of the journey down the mountain. He wouldn't have to be separated from Soekka in order to train with Juriah. Now, they would go together. Even Sprenger knew that the main reason he and Soekka were top of their class was because of each other, and the way they pushed one another to do better. Being trained as Nymphigori together should have the same sort of result in Sprenger's mind.

Then, something else came to mind. He looked at Tenni, who was walking with a calm focus; something that Sprenger doubted many other girls would be able to do when surrounded by such intimidating creatures as Setdo and Sassor. *Tenni's the only one of our squad that's not a Nymphigori. She'll have to train alone with Kanto while we train with*

Juriah. That didn't seem fair to Sprenger, but he didn't see much of an alternative. As Sprenger gave it a bit more thought, he recalled Tenni's apprehensiveness yesterday morning around Juriah. *She probably would have no desire to train under Juriah. Plus,* he reminded himself, *now she'll have time to work on the things she wants to.*

Sprenger reached over and put a hand on Setdo's side, who chuffed softly in response. *Still, I wish Tenni could be a Nymphigori too.* He teased the idea in his mind for a while, admiring the image of the three of them all becoming Nymphigori and imagining what kind of squad that would make them.

Their journey's pace began to quicken as the hillside got steeper and the snow got wetter. In several spots, they had to slide down the path because it was too steep to simply walk without slipping. Sprenger was fine with the snow getting wetter, because it meant they were getting closer to the bottom and to warmer weather. He was already beginning to sweat under his cloak, but didn't want to stop to take it off just yet. He just wanted to go home.

As the snow gradually began to turn into mud, and then the mud into grass, Sprenger finally felt like he was back to somewhere familiar. When they finally reached the bottom of the mountain, Juriah stopped before they exited the treeline. "Everyone take a break while we figure out how we're going to do this," he announced gruffly.

Everyone gratefully found a place to rest and removed their heavy cloaks. They had been hiking down for the entire day, and they only had a few hours before it got dark. They certainly made much faster time going down the mountain than they had ascending it, but it was obvious that they still a long journey ahead of them before they were back to the village.

Tenni and Sprenger sat down in the grass, enjoying the feel of it compared to days of snow. It was a bit damp, but Sprenger didn't care at this point. Soekka sat apart from them, so that Sassor had room to coil up behind him, though it became apparently obvious that nowhere was large enough to accommodate the giant serpent. The white girth of Sassor's coils began to topple some of the trees nearby, ripping the roots from the soil.

After preparing to run to avoid being crushed by a falling tree, the group tensed. Everyone seemed to hold their breath, worried the commotion would draw attention, but luckily, none of the trees fell completely. Once Sassor had stopped moving, the Pyslith was the size of a small building.

Setdo came over and laid behind Sprenger and Tenni, who happily used him as a backrest while Sprenger scratched at his cheek. Sprenger looked over at Soekka, who had climbed onto Sassor's coils to sit by his head and was talking quietly to the snake. His hand gently resting on the tip of Sassor's snout. Sprenger smiled. He was truly glad for Soekka. Sprenger knew what it felt like to feel a new connection to the parents they never knew. It made them feel a bit more complete.

After replacing his cloak in his pack, Master Kanto walked up to Juriah, who was staring cross-armed out over the field that separated them from Durado's forest. "How do you think we could best do this?" Sprenger heard Kanto ask him as he approached.

"It will still take us several hours to move through the forest," Juriah grumbled irritably. "We should wait until dark to take them to the Shattered

Hill, and if we move quickly enough, we may be able to reach it before first light. You will have to go ahead of us to get Jacob to call back all the patrols in the forest before the sun goes down."

"Perhaps we should wait until first light tomorrow," Kanto suggested. "There are more patrols after dark and that will cause a bigger stir if we pull all of them back. We need as few people questioning this as possible." Juriah thought for a moment, then nodded his agreement. Kanto continued, "I will head for the village now. I should reach Durado by midnight. If I hurry, Jacob and I can give out orders that keep all patrols away from your path throughout the day tomorrow. I will ring the alarm bell once to let you know when they're down."

"Fine," Juriah agreed grouchily. "We will camp here tonight."

Kanto looked back at them. "Tenni, you will accompany me back to the village. This is now a mission for Nymphigori. Get ready to leave."

"Yes, Master Kanto," Tenni said before she pushed herself off Setdo and stood. "Ready when you are."

Sprenger stood with her. "See you back at the village," he said with a nervous breath.

Tenni nodded at him. "You too. And be careful." She seemed to not know what else to add, but Sprenger nodded to say that she didn't have to.

There was a bit of movement as Sassor began to uncoil behind them, attempting to follow Soekka as he climbed down to the ground, but Soekka seemed to convince him to stay put. He walked over to where Sprenger and Tenni were standing.

"Thank you for your help, Tenni," Soekka said. "This mission wouldn't have gone so well without you."

She smiled at him. "I'm happy for you, Soekka." She threw her pack over her shoulder. "And I'm excited to see what else our squad will get to do in the future. We are quickly becoming a unique group. Our second real mission after the exams and it's already a high-ranking one. They might as well just call us 'maters' now."

The students chuckled to themselves, but stopped as Kanto approached them. "Let's be off, Tenni." He looked at Soekka and Sprenger. "This mission is not over yet. Keep your focus and remember that it's not too late for this to all go wrong." They both nodded their understanding. "I will expect you at the Rithhold when you've finished." He looked over at where Juriah was standing cross-armed, then looked back at them. "And be very careful," he said apprehensively.

"Yes, Master Kanto," they said together.

With that, Kanto turned and Tenni gave them another small smile and a wave as she followed him. They silently waved back. She and Kanto began their run across the field separating the Ancient Forest from the mountains, and within a few minutes, had disappeared from sight.

Juriah turned around from the where he was surveying the field ahead of them. "Setdo, you leave too," he said sternly. Setdo silently rose from the grass and gave a stretch, exposing his massive claws and fangs as he arched his back.

"Why?" Sprenger protested.

"He wasn't supposed to be here at all," Juriah reminded him, "and he's designed to sneak through the forest undetected. We would be the ones to give him away, not the other way around." Juriah turned and noticed Sprenger's expression. He rolled his eyes. "He'll be fine. Setdo has been sneaking around the patrol scythe his whole life. He'll have better luck about it than we will. If we're spotted, I'm not risking the safety of the Pantrores."

Sprenger turned and reluctantly gave Setdo one last pat on the side. The young Pantrore bounded over logs, back the way they had just come, seeming to have his own route of preference. In moments, he was on the other side of the sloping hills, and the sounds of his movements gradually disappeared as well.

"So now we just wait?" Sprenger asked drearily, not wanting to be away from his warm bed any longer.

"Yep," Juriah said as he looked out over the meadow. "We won't hear the bell until morning so you might as well get comfortable."

"Fun," Sprenger grumbled.

Soekka came up behind Sprenger. "Set up camp then?" He asked.

"I can do that," Sprenger offered. "Why don't you talk to Sassor for a while? There's probably a lot you have to tell him, and I bet if you ask the right questions, he could tell you a few things too."

Soekka smiled at him. "Thanks, Sprenger. For everything. You really are the best brother and friend that a person could have." Sprenger smirked at him. "Plus," Soekka said with reserved excitement, "just imagine how epic our family is going to be in years to come. We're barely even scythe and we're already becoming the stuff of legend."

Sprenger smiled at that, and then Soekka went back over to climb up on Sassor's coils and resume their conversation. Sprenger watched them for a while, then went up and stood next to Juriah.

"Legends can only become so if people know they exist," Juriah said softly, not looking away from the calm meadow between the forests.

"He knows that," Sprenger replied softly. "He's just excited."

"Aren't we all," Juriah grumbled sarcastically.

"Why are you so opposed to this?" Sprenger asked curiously. Juriah just stood there, arms crossed, refusing to answer. The sight reminded Sprenger of a pouting child.

Sprenger turned around when Sassor hummed behind them. Soekka was smiling at the giant eye next to him, while examining the smooth scales on the side of Sassor's head. Sprenger turned back. "I know Soekka's parents didn't die the way he thinks they did." Juriah just looked over at him through the corner of his eye. "The way Sassor reacted to you this morning makes me wonder about some things."

"You are just as shrewd as your mother," Juriah finally said. "But I warn you, there are reasons for things being kept from people."

"Now you sound like Master Kanto after we found out the Old Man had been lying to us."

"He lied because he was personally afraid of the results. There is a lie at work here that was meant to protect others." Juriah turned his head and glared. "And don't ever compare me to Kanto."

Sprenger couldn't help but smirk at that. "I understand," Sprenger said, "about both parts." Juriah turned back to look out again. "I'm not sure I'm ready to stop being mad at the Old Man for keeping so much from us. I don't need to know the truth about this, it's none of my business, I just wanted to be sure you didn't think me to be *that* slow."

Juriah smirked subtly. "You can be thick, but sometimes you catch things that no one else could. And believe me when I say," he looked at Sprenger, "it *is* your business to know. Everything that happens around you is your business to know. It's just not my business to tell."

Whatever that means, Sprenger thought.

The two of them stood there for a while and listened to Soekka's hushed conversation with Sassor while they watched the gentle sway of the grass and trees in the evening breeze.

"Do you think Sassor and Konn will be able to share the Shattered Hill peacefully?" Sprenger asked after a time of silent contemplation.

"I guess we'll find out," Juriah said plainly. "I've been wondering the same thing. We must make sure I have a chance to speak with Konn first and that Soekka speaks with Sassor before they enter the Hill. Those two will recognize one another and we certainly won't be able to separate them if they choose to not be friendly. The Hill is big enough to be shared comfortably, if the two species allow it."

Sprenger groaned again. "When will there be a simple part to this mission? I just want this day to end."

Juriah smirked at that.

Suddenly, Juriah stiffened, and his eyes locked onto something across the meadow. "Look," he whispered quickly. Sprenger looked out into the clearing, and his stomach lurched.

Down the treeline to their right, Phenex had just emerged from the mountains. He was little more than a shadow, due to his distance and black cloak, but Sprenger could see his chain shimmering around his body and the flail's heavy end at his side. Someone else emerged from the treeline behind him, but Sprenger couldn't tell who it was. Both of them took off at a sprint across the clearing.

"Get ready to move," Juriah called back to Soekka. Soekka froze for a moment, as if to confirm

Juriah was talking to him, then stood on Sassor's coil, clearly wondering what was going on.

"We're going after them," Juriah said to Sprenger. Seeming to know Sprenger was about to protest, Juriah added, "This is the first sighting since the attack. We need to know where in the forest they're hiding."

Sprenger threw his head back with a moan. "See, this day just won't end."

Juriah ignored him. "Come," Juriah ushered as he ran out into the clearing. "Leave your belongings and tell Sassor to stay," he called back to Soekka.

Sprenger hesitated, but took off after him, and heard Soekka call for Sassor to stay put but the Pyslith had already begun to follow. Soekka and Sprenger didn't bother to try and stop him as they followed Juriah. They all ran across the open meadow with Sassor slithering right behind them. Off in the trees, Sprenger could hear the female Pysliths crashing through bushes and trees to follow them from wherever they had been resting.

Soekka came up next to Sprenger as they ran. "Look!" he said, pointing up ahead as best as he could in the sprint.

Sprenger could make out the glint of shimmering blades flying from the trees at Phenex and his companion, but neither of them slowed. *Good,* Sprenger thought, *they've been spotted by a patrol.*

A commotion began up ahead as Sprenger saw the silhouettes of two dura-scythe running from Durado's forest to attack Phenex. There was only a brief confrontation with one before Phenex slammed him in the chest with his flail. The other began sparring with him while he no longer held the chain of his flail, but Phenex overpowered him and dropped him to the ground with a heavy kick. Both Phenex and his companion disappeared into the forest, out of sight.

They were long gone by the time Juriah got there, and not long after, Sprenger and Soekka.

Sprenger looked around. One scythe was clearly dead, but Juriah was crouching over the other. "He'll live, he's just unconscious," he said quickly as he stood. "They're in a hurry."

Juriah ran to where Phenex had disappeared into the trees, and Sprenger quickly followed him. In the shadow of the trees, there was one other scythe lying face down on the ground. Sprenger looked away when he realized the scythe's back was smashed in.

"Damn," Juriah said under his breath. "They're in the canopy. Our best bet is to just head the same direction as them." He crouched as if to prepare to run, but then stood again. "Actually," he said, seeming to realize something. He turned and looked at Soekka, who was just beginning to enter the trees after telling Sassor to stay. "Perhaps you will be a useful Nymphigori after all," he said to Soekka, who gave him a curious and suspicious look.

Chapter 48

Traitors in the Shadows

Master Kanto and Tenni quickly made their way through the canopy, sprinting up one branch before hopping to the next, as the last remains of sunlight started to fade through the trees. Kanto was impressed by how well Tenni was keeping pace with him, though he could hear her getting winded. They still had a ways yet to go, but he would slow their pace for her if he had to. Time was critical, but not so much so that he had to exhaust his student unnecessarily.

Kanto noticed movement ahead and slowed, then stopped on a road-sized branch. Tenni landed next to him with a skid, and Kanto almost felt the need to catch her but she recovered on her own. Up ahead was a squad of three patrol scythe standing on another large branch. Though Kanto could not make out any specifics of their features, they each wore the classic tan vest over green shirts of dura-scythe.

"I am Master Kanto," Kanto called up to them, "completing a mission given to me by Scythrith Jacob."

"Understood, Master Kanto," the middle scythe called back, "but there has been an alarm raised. Please stay where you are so that we may speak with you." They proceeded to make their way over to the branch Kanto and Tenni were standing on by hopping from one tree's branch to another's.

An alarm? Kanto thought nervously. *Did someone spot Sassor already?*

The three scythe, two men and a woman, individually landed on the branch Kanto and Tenni had been waiting on. Once they were assembled, a scarred man at the front stepped forward and gave Kanto a bow. "Master Kanto, we have just received word that one of our patrols of the southern treeline did not check in."

That's where the others are, Kanto thought with filling dread.

"Our commander worries that it may be the hidden Adimortis who were responsible," the scythe continued. "We are about to send out squads now."

"No," Kanto said, seizing the opportunity. "Lord Juriah is already in the forest. Send word to all of the patrol bases to pull all patrols back, and as soon as possible."

The squad of patrol scythe shifted uncertainly. "Sir?" The scythe asked confused.

"These are orders from Scythrith Jacob himself," Kanto said, undeterred. "There is something going on at the moment, and that is all you need to know."

The scythe nodded his understanding, knowing that it was not his place to ask further questions. "We will spread out and begin relaying your message then." With another bow, the three scythe took off; one in one direction, and the other two in another direction.

Kanto turned to Tenni. "Now we really need to get to the village. Our luck has left us, and the Adimortis have turned up at the worst time. I need to speak with Lord Scythrith about what to do next."

"What about the others?" Tenni asked, worried. "They don't know about the Adimortis."

"Then there's no better person to be with them than a Hessiet," Kanto assured her. "Now get ready to move and stay close."

"I won't slow you down," Tenni promised him with a confident nod.

-<>-

"What is it?" Sprenger asked quietly.

"It's an old patrol base," Juriah whispered back. "They haven't been used since the last war."

Sprenger, Juriah, and Soekka were crouching low in the brush, staring through the leaves at the collapsed stone base. Behind them, Sassor and the two females could be heard rustling in the debris of the forest floor.

Following Juriah's recommendation, Soekka reluctantly and doubtingly asked Sassor to help them to find the Adimortis. The massive serpent seemed to understand and pulled his considerable girth completely into the forest from the meadow outside the treeline. He began investigating the bodies with his massive slimy black forked tongue, seeming to need to know what other scents were out there. When he lifted his head to investigate the branches, Soekka and Sprenger became worried he would become discombobulated in the branches, as he had under the pinetree in the mountains. Here, amongst the giant trees and their considerable branches, however, Sassor seemed able to navigate much easier. The Pyslith raised his head all the way up into the canopy without difficulty and began to slowly and blindly investigate the branches with his tongue and snout. It took a while for Sassor to follow the trail, and Sprenger wasn't so sure it was working at some points. Sprenger didn't know how long they followed Sassor through the forest, but all daylight was now gone. They became completely dependent on startlight and moonlight through the trees.

Eventually, Sassor stopped at the place they were now, and Juriah was certain as soon as he saw it that this is where the Adimortis been hiding. Their suspicions were confirmed when they got a whiff of burning torch oil inside.

"So what's the plan?" Sprenger whispered nervously.

Juriah quietly made sure his sword was loose in its sheath on his back. "Don't get killed," was his only response.

"That's not a plan," Sprenger whispered back angrily.

Juriah stood from their hiding place in the brush. "I'll go in. You two set up on either side of the entrance and try to stop anyone that comes out." He leaned over and poked Sprenger on the forehead. "But do so carefully. Keep your distance and fall back if you have to." He turned to Soekka. "No Pysliths. You don't know how to control them and I don't need that place collapsing in on me."

"Why don't we just collapse it from the start?" Soekka asked.

"Because we don't know what else may be down there," Juriah explained impatiently. "I'm always looking for new evidence of Demaedura's plans or information about his network, so I need it intact."

"What if all of the Adimortis are down there? Not just Phenex?" Sprenger asked.

"They won't be," Juriah said flatly.

"How do you know?" Sprenger pressed.

"Because I know Demaedura and the Adimortis," Juriah snapped back. "This isn't my first time doing this, Sprenger."

"Okay," Soekka whispered desperately, clearly becoming concerned with the noise they were making in their argument.

After giving Sprenger another irritated look, which Sprenger returned in kind, Juriah scanned the area one last time. "Let's go," he whispered.

The three of them moved closer to the collapsed building, and found a staircase amongst the rubble. Down below, they could hear muffled voices. Sprenger and Soekka silently positioned themselves behind the remaining bits of wall to both sides of the staircase.

Juriah gave them an affirmative nod and quietly began making his way down to the unseen room below.

I really just wish this day would end, Sprenger thought bitterly.

-<>-

"Hurry and pack your things," Phenex ordered. "We need to be clear of the borders by nightfall."

Tranis quickly began stuffing his few belongings in a bag. *It won't matter when we leave if they've discovered those patrol-scythe already,* which Tranis was willing to bet they had. "Where exactly are we going after this?" Tranis asked, trying not to sound suspicious.

"To our nearest base to the east. Lord Demaedura is waiting for us there."

"How do I know he's not just going to kill me when I arrive?"

A hand grabbed Tranis's shirt and spun him around, then grabbed him by the throat. "You're lucky to have lived this long," Phenex growled. "But apparently, Lord Demaedura finds you more valuable alive for the moment."

Tranis pulled at his arm to no avail, but he didn't care anymore. He would rather be killed here and now then have to suffer anymore of Demaedura's haunting.

Suddenly, Tranis fell backwards as Phenex's grip released him. Phenex hobbled over in pain as he was struck repeatedly in the side, then grabbed by the cloak and thrown hard against the stone wall next to them, causing pebbles and dust to fall from the ceiling above. Phenex fell to the ground with a grunt and rattling of his chains.

Tranis whimpered and began pushing himself backwards as he realized who was responsible.

Juriah gave him a deadly look that seemed to demonstrate his lethality in one stare. Tranis flinched away from it, but Juriah turned his attention to Phenex, who quickly stood and began spinning his flail in a small circle at his side.

"That's a pretty scar, Phenex," Juriah taunted.

"An act," Phenex said with a hateful glare, "that is about to be repaid in full." He flung his flail at Juriah who kicked it away and lunged at Phenex with a barrage of assaults. The two became locked in combat that began to encompass the entirety of the small dwelling.

Tranis wasted no time. He ran for the staircase, not looking back. He scrambled up one step after another, until finally the entrance emerged. He desperately ran through it, but was knocked from his feet by someone to his right. He managed, only by reflex, to block the kick to his side but the force still knocked him to the ground. Before he knew what had happened, Tranis rolled to avoid a second foot attempting to slam him into the ground. He quickly got to his feet to see that it was Sortan's son who he had just avoided, and the spiky-haired boy that kicked him coming out of the stairwell.

"I was hoping I would get to see you again," Tranis sneered to the spiky-haired boy. "Because of you, I got caught in my first escape attempt." Tranis had no blade with him, but he readied a fighting stance. They were hardly a formidable-looking pair, and Tranis doubted he needed a weapon to defeat them.

Both boys pulled a blade from their sleeves and stood ready.

"Well," the spiky-haired boy taunted, "I guess you can blame me for the second failed attempt as well."

Tranis smirked to himself. *Your smart remarks will only make this more satisfying in the end for me, you brat.*

Sortan's son lunged for Tranis with his blade, but Tranis spun around him and kicked him in the back, knocking him onto his stomach. Next, Tranis ducked a heavy kick from the spiky-haired boy and knocked his second foot out from under him, he hit the ground with a hard thud and a wince.

Tranis hopped back, making sure to not be between them when they recovered. Tranis was never the best when it came to combat, but these two were inexperienced at fighting another scythe. "You boys fight like cocky students. Perhaps Master Cerri should have kept your egos down while he trained you."

Both boys stood and readied themselves again. They looked agitated, which only inexperienced scythe ever showed. *Let's see how angry I can make you before you start making mistakes.*

The boys ran at him together this time, and Tranis was strained to maneuver through their assaults, but they left him a big enough gap that he managed to do so. He grabbed Sortan's son by his free wrist, twirled him around and threw him on top of the spiky-haired boy, who fell back under the weight.

Tranis smirked again. *They still make mistakes with their teamwork.* Simple experience was winning this fight for him.

The boys scrambled to their feet again, but didn't attack immediately.

"He's an evasive fighter," Sortan's son said. The spiky-haired boy nodded his understanding. Everyone flinched when a large thud echoed from down the stairs, signaling the fight still raging below ground.

Identifying a fighting style is one thing, Tranis thought, *but do you know how to respond to them?*

Sortan's son attacked again, but the spiky-haired boy stayed where he was. Tranis deflected all of the attacks but none had enough force for him to move around. *You do know how to adjust. Impressive.*

Tranis allowed a small punch through, waiting for the second. It came with double the force, and Tranis spun around him and tried striking him back but he seemed to anticipate missing, spun around, and slammed his shoulder into Tranis's stomach.

The two began falling back, but then Tranis gasped in pain as he felt a blade jam into his back. He became crushed between the two boys and felt the blade dig deeper into his body.

The three of them stood there a moment, everyone knowing the fight was over. Tranis could feel his throat filling with blood, and he convulsed as the blade was pulled from his back. Both boys jumped back, and Tranis fell to the ground as they released their hold on him.

-<>-

Sprenger looked down at Tranis as he struggled to take a breath. "Unfortunately, there will be no third escape from the prison," Sprenger said unsympathetically to him. Tranis let out a final, wet breath, and none followed it. "That was for all the people that died during your escape," Sprenger said quietly.

Soekka stood on the other side of Tranis, staring down at him as well. "We got the man that every scythe in Durado has been looking for." He looked up at Sprenger with a smile. "That makes two completed missions today. The best part is that we can even get credit for this one." The boys knocked arms happily.

Sprenger smirked. "Well, we haven't completed the other one yet."

Another crash echoed up the stairwell and Sprenger remembered that Juriah was still down there with Phenex. He looked over at Soekka.

"Should we go down there?" Sprenger asked quickly.

"No, we would be of no help to Juriah. Let's go back to our spots and wait, in case Phenex comes up the stairs."

The boys headed back to the rubble, but then they stopped as clanking chains echoed in the stairwell.

Phenex came toppling backwards out of the stairwell and rolled across the grass in front of them. Both boys quickly flipped backwards to get away from him as he rolled to his feet. Juriah jumped out of the stairs, sword in hand, and waited for Sprenger and Soekka to take cover behind the rubble.

Both boys gladly took the opportunity to get out of the way and hid behind the remains of a toppled stone wall. Sprenger's breath caught in his throat when he noticed Phenex's eyes lock onto him.

-<>-

Phenex recoiled the slack in his chain around his arm. He could feel fresh blood on his head and back. Nothing but flesh wounds, but he rarely endured even those in fights anymore. Juriah was no mere fight, however. He was Lord Demaedura's direct rival, and a Hessiet. Phenex had to keep his focus at all times; there could be no slip-up with this caliber of combat.

Juriah was waiting near the entrance of the base, seeming to allow the two boys with him to take cover before the fight continued. Phenex immediately recognized the boys and stared at the one with spiky hair. *This time I will kill you.*

In the corner of his eye, Phenex could see Tranis laying face down in the dirt. *What a worthless scythe. Couldn't even handle two children.* Now he had to explain to Lord Demaedura why Tranis would no longer be able to translate the journal for him.

Phenex noticed the boys take cover behind a weak standing wall. *Perfect,* Phenex thought. He looked down at his flail's end-piece. Two of the blades were bent from hitting the stone walls below. Fighting in close quarters like that was the last place a chained-weapon should be used. Since it was already battered, Phenex felt little remorse using it as a blunt weapon now.

He started swinging it in small circles, preparing it to be flung. He watched as Juriah tensed in preparation, but he was not Phenex's target. Phenex spun and hurled the flail at the old wall. It crashed into the side, knocking loose several pieces. He could hear the two boys cry out in panic as stones began to fall on them.

Juriah ran at him and began swinging with his sword, but Phenex used his chain to block the blade, and when an opening emerged, Phenex spun again, pulling the chain back around. Juriah was barely able to duck it, but that was not Phenex's only intent. He flung the flail around and, once again, smashed it into the wall, which began toppling down more threateningly. The boys cried out again, realizing the wall was about to crush them.

Juriah attacked again but Phenex kicked him back and began twirling the chain all around him, forcing Juriah to keep his distance. Juriah paused, waiting for an opening that Phenex was determined not to give.

Phenex widened the radius of the chain's spiral, whipping the heavy end near Juriah's middle, and forcing him back farther.

Juriah rolled around the flail's end-piece once again and stood between Phenex and the boys. If Phenex could force Juriah to attempt to save the boys from the falling wall, then he could take the opportunity to retreat. He could see the boys attempting to move farther back into the rubble, but that was the wrong choice. Phenex maintained his spiraling chain and prepared himself to hit the wall one last time and force it to collapse. He aimed for a weak spot near the base that would bring all of it down on them.

Just as Phenex was preparing to strike, one of the boys yelled into the air "Sassor!"

Phenex tensed when he heard the name that he called out. The ground began to shake a bit, and Phenex could hear branches snapping and roots breaking to his left. Phenex rolled back as Sassor's giant head came bursting through the bushes. He shrieked as he came crashing into the clearing, and Phenex was nearly crushed by his body as the Pyslith began to blindly search the area.

The giant beast paused and licked the air, seeming not to know where to go. Phenex could then see two purple Pysliths charging down the path that Sassor had cleared through the roots and brush. On the other side of the giant white snake, Phenex could hear Juriah yelling for him to get out of the way. *Your advantage served as your weakness this time.*

Not wasting his opportunity, Phenex used the giant snake's body to jump up to a branch and swiftly made his way deep into the canopy of the trees.

-<>-

Sprenger watched as Juriah tried to climb over the thrashing Sassor, but there was no room to get past him. Phenex had disappeared behind him, and Sprenger could only hope that he was crushed in Sassor's disorientation.

Soekka ran up next to Juriah and called up to Sassor, who whipped his head around at the sound of his voice. Sassor slowly lowered his head to Soekka, who turned to one of the females that were slithering over Sassor's back. "Get the man in the black cloak!" he yelled up to her. She pulled her head back over Sassor and disappeared on the other side of him but then reappeared again, not seeming to know what to do.

After finding Soekka, Sassor finally calmed enough for Juriah to climb onto him, and there he stood, surveying the clearing. Disappointed, he replaced his sword in its sheath on his back. "He's gone," he growled.

Sprenger gave a sigh of relief, and heard Soekka do the same.

Sprenger perked up as a single gong from a bell echoed through the forest. Kanto and Tenni had apparently made very swift progress to the village. *Little late for that,* Sprenger thought.

Sprenger pushed himself up slowly, and winced as he felt where a few stones had landed on his leg and shoulder. He didn't think anything was broken, but he could feel that the skin was scraped and raw. After a few steps, the pain lightened and Sprenger joined Soekka.

Juriah turned and looked down on them from Sassor's back. "We need to get them to the Shattered Hill quickly."

"Aren't you going after Phenex?" Sprenger asked.

Juriah shook his head. "He's long gone, and I don't know what direction he went in. No, we need to get them where nobody will see them before this whole mission becomes a failure." He hopped down next to them and then started for the trees. "Follow me."

Chapter 49

The End to a Long Day

With a dramatic sigh of exhaustion, Sprenger leaned back onto Setdo's side and closed his eyes. *What a rough day,* he thought tiredly. Sprenger could feel Setdo take deep breaths under his back, and the slow tempo seemed to calm Sprenger's nerves. They had arrived at the Shattered Hill a few minutes ago and Soekka was still waiting until Juriah spoke with Konn before entering.

Once they made the climb into the Hill, Juriah headed over to Konn and had been speaking with him ever since, but Sprenger went over to where Setdo and Satra were laying in the grass and laid with Setdo. The sun was beginning to make its first appearance on the horizon, but the Hill itself was still dark; shadowed by its protective rocky sides.

Compared to the mountains, the night air in the Ancient Forest was warm and comforting to Sprenger. The air was still, with not even a breeze to disrupt it. Only the sounds of birds and squirrels broke the peace of it all. The grass under him was soft and lush. He let his thoughts wander as he listened to Juriah's muffled voice in the background, accompanied by Setdo and Satra's deep breathing. A small nap began to engulf him, though Sprenger wasn't sure for how long.

He was jolted awake by a short roar from Konn that sent Sprenger into a brief panic. He clamored to sit up, but then relaxed against Sedto's side once again when he could not see anything around him that would be considered threatening. He then remembered the roar was the intended signal to let Soekka know he may enter the Hill. Sprenger tried drifting off again, but he knew it was pointless. His heart was still racing.

There were only a few brief moments of peaceful silence, before rocks and boulders began crashing down the sides of the Hill, then landing with dull 'thud's into the grass below. Sprenger sat up and looked up the steep rockface, to see Soekka cautiously making his way down the side. Setdo and Satra both sat up as well, curiously watching the new visitors. Satra's ears flattened backwards and she started to growl deeply when she saw what was coming.

Sassor and the two females were taking their own route down the rockface and were scaling the sides with apparent ease. Their heavy bodies pulled large boulders from the wall as they slithered over them, sending them rolling and crashing to the ground beneath.

Apparently unnerved or startled by the falling rocks, Sedto and Satra got to their feet and ran behind a large plateau of stones, where Konn was laying with Juriah earlier.

As Soekka still jumped from one ledge to the next, the giant Pysliths slowly lowered to the ground across from Sprenger. The three Pysliths settled on the grass before Soekka did, and casually began to coil up and wait. The two females both lowered their heads to the ground and opened their gaping mouths.

Sprenger cringed as three large Pysliths slithered out of one of the female's mouths and two from the other's. They seemed to emerge from under the females' tongues somehow, but Sprenger was too revolted to watch long enough to really understand.

Sprenger had forgotten about the larger Pysliths that were in the cave when they first found Sassor, and shuddered at the thought of spending the entire day in such a grotesque manner.

Soekka finally hopped down onto the grass and looked around the surrounding glade in amazement.

"This is incredible," he whispered. "It looks completely normal from outside."

"Everyone will be safe here," Juriah said as he walked up to them. Konn walked regally behind him towering over everything around him. Even at his full height, the top of Juriah's head barely made it to Konn's white chest.

Sprenger smiled when he saw Soekka go wide-eyed as he took in the sight of Konn for the first time.

"Konn understands what needs to happen here," Juriah continued to explain. "So long as the Pysliths keep their distance, I don't foresee many problems."

"Keeping distance shouldn't be too difficult in this place," Soekka mumbled to himself as he looked around again.

Sprenger couldn't help but notice that Juriah's eyes were glaring hatefully down at Soekka, even as Soekka looked around excitedly. "I guess we'll find out," Juriah said coldly.

-<>-

Tenni sipped the water that Claudia had brought her, and quietly waited by Jacob's desk while he searched for something through the many drawers in the large, wooden desk. After receiving word that Sprenger and Soekka had returned to the village, Master Kanto took off to intercept them, leaving Tenni alone with Scythrith Jacob in his office.

It was relieving news to both of them after an entire night of wondering what was going on to hear that both boys were back. Tenni was going to follow Kanto to greet the boys, but Lord Scythrith asked her to stay behind. She had been waiting for Jacob to find something in his desk since Kanto left, and Tenni began to wonder if it could wait until the next day.

"Ah, that's where you are," Jacob exclaimed as he apparently found what he was looking for. He produced a small, brilliantly polished wooden box and set it on the corner of his desk nearest Tenni. “I would like you to have this.”

Tenni put down her cup, and quizzically reached for the box. She opened it to reveal velvet interior, and gently nestled into the center, a gold coin. The coin was larger than any Tenni had seen before. Its face was indented with Durado’s symbol and the top was hooked to a gold chain with a delicate gold ring. She looked up at Jacob, thankful, but a bit confused.

“Do you know was this is?” he asked softly. She shook her head. “It’s an honor talisman. They are given to those that have demonstrated a trait that far surpasses their expectations. There are several different kinds, but in this case, it is the one for ‘strength’.”

“Lord Scythrith,” Tenni whispered, having a loss for words, “thank you. But I-”

“I’m sure you’re not about to tell me that you don’t deserve it,” Jacob interrupted. His bushy grey eyebrows bounced quizzically at her. “I do not give them out lightly, and I always give them an exceptional amount of thought. You will be hard-pressed to find many scythe with such talismans. You, my dear, are stronger than any scythe I’ve seen for a long while.” Tenni began to blush, knowing full well that she was not worthy of such a compliment. “But I’m not necessarily talking about how hard you can hit,” he clarified, “which I hear is considerable as well.” He smiled gently at her, causing her smirk bashfully. “No, this is strength that far surpasses your arms. This strength you showed in great detail on this mission. It is the strength to stand by your team, to help them, and when needed, to lead them.”

“Lord Scythrith, I didn’t-”

"You put yourself in great danger for your squad and your village" Jacob interrupted again. "You kept a calm and reasonable head through it all. You even pulled Sprenger from Sassor's cave when reason left him, didn't you?"

"Well yah, but-"

"There is darkness coming," Jacob interjected softly. The statement caught Tenni off guard. "Sprenger and Soekka are indeed skilled young men, but they easily lose focus. They listen to those they respect," he reached out his old hand and tapped Tenni in the middle of her chest, "and they respect strength. Those two will be vital to this village's future, and *you* will be vital for them."

Tenni felt a small chill run up her back as Jacob spoke. Then, with a bit of pride, she pulled the necklace out of its case and admired it in her hand. When she flipped it over, she noticed a strange symbol that she had never seen before on the back of the gold coin.

"That is the ancient symbol for 'strength'," Jacob said in answer to her unasked question.

Tenni smiled and gently pulled the chain over her head, pulled her braid out from underneath it and let it hang proudly over her shirt. She held a hand over it and felt it against her chest. She looked up at Jacob gratefully. "Thank you, Lord Scythrith. I will not disappoint you."

He smiled back at her. "Oh, I have no doubt in mind about that."

They both turned their attention to the door as it opened and Kanto walked in. He walked up to Jacob's desk. "They're back," he said, and Jacob gave a small sigh of relief. "I just spoke with Sprenger and Soekka, and they have informed me that the Pysliths are safe in the Shattered Hill, Tranis is dead, and they were not seen by anyone but Phenex."

"What did Juriah have to say about all this?" Jacob asked.

"He was missing," Kanto grumbled. "The boys didn't even see him leave. They said he was with them when they reentered the village but then he just vanished."

Jacob grunted. "Yes, well, he does that."

"There were casualties tonight," Kanto continued in a softer tone. "Two patrol-scythe were killed, and one was injured in an attempt to stop Phenex and Tranis from reentering the forest. Apparently, however, my squad fought with Tranis while Juriah fought with Phenex, and were able to defeat Tranis in the end."

"Remind me to give them the reward that was on his head," Jacob teased.

Tenni smiled at him. She was now seeing why Sprenger admired this man so much. Not because of his rank, but because he had a certain warm kindness and humor in such a stressful lifestyle. Tenni had always admired him too, but always from afar. Interactions with the Scythrith were rare for most people not of rank in Durado.

"Parken has also just informed me that Phenex was seen leaving the boarders," Kanto finished.

Jacob nodded solemnly. "Good. I hope this is the last we see of the Adimortis in our forest."

Kanto nodded his agreement.

Jacob looked over to Tenni with a small smile. "Tenni, my dear, you have had quite the tiresome last few days, and none of this is important. In fact, I even find it all a bit boring myself." He gave her a small wink and she smiled back at him. "I think it's time that you head home and rest for a good, long while. You have earned that in the least."

Tenni gave him a deep bow, that caused her talisman swing wildly from her neck. She then straightened, turned to Kanto, and gave a smaller bow, then headed for the door. She put her hand over her talisman as she walked out of the Rithhold.

-<>-

Jacob waited until the door closed before he spoke. "Are you ready for what will come next?" he asked Kanto, in a much more serious tone.

"Are you?" Kanto rebutted with his typical, expressionless face.

Jacob gave a humored snort. "We will never be entirely certain what the future holds for us, but thus far, our optimism has paid off." He sat back in his tall-backed chair and looked up in silent thought for a moment.

"Do you think Soekka will remain complacent?" Kanto asked skeptically. It was a question that Jacob knew Kanto was nervous to ask. The answer could be a dangerous one for his student.

"That is the golden question at the moment," Jacob answered nervously. "We must hope that the love he has for others and that others have for him, will be enough to quell his family's dark past."

-<>-

Granny Karla pulled both boys into a tight embrace, which they returned eagerly. She was shorter than both boys, but she squeezed her arms around their backs as she buried her head between their chests. "My amazing boys," she whispered to them. "The next great Nymphigori of this village." She hugged them even harder. "I'm so proud of both of you."

The three of them just stood in the center of the kitchen, locked in each other's arms, glad to have their family whole once more.

-<>-

In a well-furnished room, three persons stood in front of an artistically sculpted fireplace, which gave the only flickering light in the room.

Phenex was kneeling and supported himself on one fist. "I'm sorry I failed you, Lord Demaedura." He bowed his head even lower. "There is no excuse for my incompetence."

Demaedura chuckled as he stared into the fire. His black hair curtained the sides of his sharp face, and the firelight exaggerated his amused expression. "Oh, Phenex," he said in a cold, amused voice. "Don't be so hard on yourself. You have given me some very pleasing news."

Brendol stood to the side of the fireplace, half-hiding from sight in the shadows of the room. Being Demaedura's pupil, he was allowed to listen in on whatever he pleased, but only so long as he didn't get in the way. "Who is Sortan?" he asked from his place by the mantle.

Demaedura continued to smirk into the fire. "He was a powerful vassal of mine. He died when you were a small child. More importantly, his son was a small child when he died as well. The situation couldn't be more perfect if I had planned it myself."

"The boy seems to be under Juriah's protection," Phenex growled. "I would have acquired him myself, had the opportunity ever risen."

"I have absolutely no intention of abducting Sortan's son from Durado," Demaedura assured him.

Brendol gave him a confused look, but withheld his question.

"There will be no need for us to steal him," Demaedura elaborated. "Sortan's son will leave Durado of his own free will."

"He doesn't sound very interested in leaving Durado," Brendol scoffed. "Not from what Phenex just told us."

Demaedura chuckled again. "You two don't know Durado like I do. The old fools that control it find comfort in their secrets. They think that hiding truths will keep them safe. What they always forget is that secrets can cause great anger. I know this, because it happened to me. There is a falsehood of power that surrounds secrecy. One that the holders believe will give them an advantage over those that are ignorant." He turned and gave Brendol a wicked smirk. "But their secrets are their ultimate vulnerability."

Made in the USA
Middletown, DE
23 July 2020